MAFIA LEGACY - PERFECTLY IMPERFECT

BEAUTIFUL
Beast

NEVA ALTAJ

Editing by Andie Edwards (Beyond The Proof)
Proofreading by Yvette Rebello
Manuscript critique by Anka Lesko (AML editing)
Italian language consultation by Chiara
Stylistic editing by Anna Corbeaux
Cover design by Deranged Doctor Design
Interior formatting by Stacey (Champagne Book Design)

For all who love The Beauty And The Beast.
I hope you'll enjoy Vasilisa and Rafael.

And to my IG followers: Yes, Roman's POV is included.

Author's Note

Our world is a wondrous place, filled with a multitude of people, cultures, and traditions. No matter what our differences are, there is a common thread that binds us—we're all a part of it. Being a writer allows me an opportunity to broaden my horizons, even if it means not venturing too far away from my desk and laptop.

For the benefit of my wide-spread readers who may not be aware, I've included a few cultural notes that come up through the course of this book and series.

Sicily: location and language

Sicily is one of five autonomous regions of Italy. The local government has administrative powers that allow for the protection of cultural differences and linguistic minorities. However, Sicily is a part of Italy and not an independent country.

The region is the largest and most populous island in the Mediterranean Sea and is located just south of the Italian peninsula. Although Sicily has its own distinct dialect (i.e., Sicilian), and many people are bilingual, the official language is Italian, the same as in mainland Italy.

Thus, the characters in this book speak Italian.

Russian names: patronymic, family, and diminutive

Russian names consist of three parts: first name, middle (patronymic), and surname (family name). A patronymic is derived from a father's name (or another paternal ancestor, in certain cases), with an addition of a suffix. Some readers may be more familiar with a similar cultural practice of using a "son of" reference for family names (e.g., Tomson = "son of Tom").

In Russian patronymic, the ending of the name is changed to indicate the name bearer's gender. For a man, the suffixes of "evich" or "ovich" are used. For a woman, these are "evna" or "ovna." For example, Vasilisa Romanovna Petrova (Vasilisa "daughter of Roman" Petrova).

It should be noted, also, that Russians are prevalent in using short ("intimate") forms of names (e.g., Vasilisa would be shortened to Vasya).

GLOSSARY

Note: When it comes to non-English insults (both Italian and Russian), the literal phrasing is often extremely vulgar but it loses meaning in direct translation. Thus, an equivalent wording is used to depict context.

Italian words and phrases

Vespetta—little wasp (diminutive)

Cumpari—godfather

Signore/Signor—sir. The "e" at the end is always dropped when used in conjunction with a name (e.g., *Signor De Santi*; but, *Yes, signore.*)

Vuole provare del prosciutto?—Would you like to taste the ham?

Che cazzo!—What the fuck?

Stai zitto!—Shut up; be quiet!

Chi è quella?—Who is that (woman)?

Sbrigati, idiota. Ho bisogno di quella vernice.—Hurry up, idiot. I need that paint.

Sei la ragazza di Raffaello?—Are you Rafael's girlfriend?

Pronto—Ready

Cosa è successo?—What happened?

Merda. Venti minuti.—Shit. Twenty minutes.

Buonasera, signorina.—Good evening, miss.

Non toccarla. Lei è mia. Capito?—Do not touch her. She is mine. Understand?

Sì. Ho capito. Mi dispiace molto.—YES. I understand. I'm very sorry.

Potrei ucciderti per questo.—I could kill you for this.

Dice che è urgente.—He says it's urgent.

Ma che fai, stronzo?!—What are you doing, asshole?!

Vaffanculo! Sei cieco? Madonna santa!—Go fuck yourself! Are you blind? Dear Mother of God!

Coglione! Mangia merda e morte, porca puttana!—Moron! Eat shit and die, you pig-whore!

Testa di cazzo.—You dickhead.

Tutto bene?—Everything okay?

La mia principessa russa.—My Russian princess.

Non ti lascerò mai andare.—I will never let you go.

Sei pronto?—Are you ready?

Si. Iniziamo.—Yes. Let's get started.

Vi dichiaro marito e moglie.—I now pronounce you husband and wife.

Farei qualsiasi cosa per te. Perfino lasciarti andare.—I would do anything for you. Even letting you go.

Russian words and phrases

Сволочь—Scum

Придурок—Idiot, moron

Какой ужасный беспорядок.—What a dreadful mess.

Мне он нужен живым, Сергей. Понимаешь?—I need him alive, Sergei. Do you understand?

Trigger Warning

Please be aware that this book contains content some readers may find disturbing, such as mentions of an immediate family member's death, as well as graphic descriptions of violence, torture, and gore.

BEAUTIFUL

Beast

prologue

Rafael

20 years ago
(Rafael, age 19)

"**C**LEAR," I SAY INTO THE PHONE.

A moment later, a man dressed as a maintenance worker exits the exclusive antique and jewelry store at the other end of the long hallway, hurrying toward a door with an emergency exit sign overhead. Even with his baseball hat pulled low, Jemin keeps his head bent and the phone pressed to his ear, trying to hide his face from the multitude of surveillance cameras. The dude is being cautious despite Endri Dushku, the leader of the Albanian Mafia, shelling out a pretty penny to a guy in the mall's security office to fuck up the video feed for ten minutes.

The moment Jemin disappears from view, I enter the staff-only stairway. "I'm coming down."

"No," the voice on the other side orders. "Endri wants a

video of the blast. I set the timer for five minutes, so get your camera ready. I'll be waiting at the garage exit when you're done."

I push up my sleeve to take a look at my wristwatch. It's old, the glass face scratched and the leather strap worn-out. Other than the clothes on my back, it was the only personal item I had with me when my brother and I fled Sicily.

"Fine," I grumble into the phone and cut the line.

It riles me to no end to follow orders from a pretentious asshole like Jemin, but that shit ends today. The deal I've made with the head of the Albanian Mafia expires tonight.

Yesterday, to my utter amazement, Dushku offered me a regular role in the Albanian clan, one that includes all the standard benefits. I was tempted to agree. It would mean security and no shortage of money. But not respect. I would remain nothing more than the Sicilian scum they'd taken in. So, respectfully, I declined the offer.

In the chaotic and violent world of organized crime, very few values are upheld. The sole exception—keeping one's word. And Endri Dushku keeps his promises. Starting tonight, I'm a free man. With the experience and the underground connections I fostered while working for the Albanians, I can easily earn a living and reach my goals. I promised my brother we'd go back home someday. And I, too, keep my promises.

I just have to finish this job.

Cracking the stairwell door, I keep an eye on the second hand as it makes its way around my wristwatch. The faint ticking is the only sound breaking the silence, bouncing off the concrete walls like a damn whisper inside a high-ceiling chapel. The shopping mall doesn't open for another couple of hours, so there's hardly anyone around. Most stores' employees won't be arriving anytime soon, and everyone else tends to congregate in more public areas like the food court. This end of the complex is deserted, the perfect condition for setting up the explosives inside the store filled with old trinkets and shiny delicate crap no one born in this century cares about. The owner of the store is old-school and should have known better than to decline the Albanian clan's "protection." If he hadn't refused to pay, Dushku wouldn't have decided to teach the guy a lesson, starting this week with a bang. The bomb inside the shop will level the fucking thing and destroy the collectibles that are tucked away in a bajillion glass cases.

I'm just setting up my phone to start recording when the happy laughter of a child rings through the mall hallway. My body goes utterly still. There shouldn't be anyone here right now. Least of all kids.

"I don't understand why you had to trouble the poor woman to help us before the place even opened." A female voice drifts toward me. "We could have picked up the dress later."

"I wasn't in the mood to deal with the crowds," a male responds while the pitter-patter of little feet gets closer. "Baby! Come back here!"

"Oh, just let her be." The woman again. "You know she likes those crystal roses inside the antique shop window. There's no one around anyway, and you can still see her from here."

My hand squeezes the edge of the door so hard, the wood cracks. A deafening thump reverberates through my head—my heart beating so fucking loud, it could rival ear-splitting thunder as my brain processes the situation. There isn't enough time to call Jemin and get him to kill the timer. Even if I do, it's doubtful he'll listen to me. He's never given a shit about collateral damage.

Gleeful giggles echo through the space as a little girl, no more than three years old, dashes past the stairwell, straight toward the lit-up display of the antique store. The store that'll be blown to smithereens when that incendiary device goes off.

I don't think—I run.

Adrenaline surges through my veins as I sprint after the child who's almost halfway to the store at this point, squealing with delight. Her arms lift in front of her, reaching toward the glittering crystal flowers showcased under the pod lights of the display window. Ten feet separate us.

Two voices—the parents—are shouting somewhere behind me. They must be flipping out over a stranger chasing after their daughter, but there's no time to explain. Those explosives will go off at any moment.

"Stop!" I roar at the top of my lungs.

The girl halts.

Five feet.

She turns around, her eyes meeting mine. Too late. I'm going to be too late to whisk her out of harm's way.

One foot.

I scoop the girl into my arms just as the loud detonation splits the air.

Pain sears my face and hands as shards of glass pelt my flesh, the sensation so overwhelming that I can't seem to draw air into my lungs. A plume of smoke and dust swirls around me, as if I'm caught in a fierce whirlwind somewhere in the depths of hell. My arms are shaking, but I keep the little girl pressed to my chest, her head tucked under my chin, and my limbs shielding her back.

Please God, let her be okay.

Everything happened so fast that I didn't even get a chance to turn around, never mind get her somewhere safe, but she's so tiny that my body almost completely envelops her. Between the ringing in my head and the blaring of the fire and security alarms, I can't hear her—no terrified wailing, not even a shuddering breath. But I do hear the pounding of running feet and the woman's heartbreaking screams.

A tremor runs down my spine, and my right leg folds under me, my knee hitting the floor. The pain is so intense that drawing enough air into my lungs is getting harder with every breath. I don't have enough strength left to keep myself upright. The only thing I can concentrate on is keeping the girl plastered to my chest. I slide my hand to her cheek and let myself topple sideways to the floor. Immediately, another onslaught of agony stings my face as it hits the glass-covered surface. Jagged fragments pierce the back of my hand that's still cupping the girl's cheek, holding her off the hazardous tile.

It can't have been more than a few seconds since the explosion, but it seems like hours have passed. My vision is getting blurry, everything around me is dissolving into a shapeless haze. Everything except for a pair of wide dark eyes, shining like polished onyx from between the strands of ink-black hair. Blood and smudges mar the girl's cheeks and forehead, but she's not crying. Just clutching my shirt and . . . glaring at me. As if she's annoyed with me for disrupting her playtime. I'd laugh, but I don't have the energy.

The kid's unharmed.

I haven't become a child murderer.

Still just a killer.

Everything around me continues to fade. Is someone screwing around with the lights? The only thing I can see are the girl's onyx eyes.

But then, they too are gone.

CHAPTER

one

20 years later
Present day

BEING KIDNAPPED SUCKS.

Being kidnapped with your bladder full sucks significantly more.

"I need to pee," I mumble.

The jackass across from me looks up from his phone and sends me a sinister smile. It doesn't actually have the impact he aimed for because it instantly transforms into a pained grimace. He presses his meaty palm to his chin, patting the big red bruise spreading across his ugly mug.

"No," he barks and goes back to fidgeting with his device, dismissing me completely. It looks like he's still stewing over me hitting him with my backpack.

The low rumble of the plane's engines competes with the sounds of a football game coming from his phone's speaker. I clasp my hands together to keep them from shaking. Slipping into hysteria would accomplish absolutely nothing, and will likely make my chances of escape even slimmer. I need to stay calm. Or, as calm as possible, considering my current situation.

Easier said than done.

My eyes glide over the swanky interior of the aircraft. On either side of the central aisle, four large recliner seats dominate the space. Toward the front of the cabin, two cushiony sofas face each other. The interior is all pristine beige leather and rich wooden accents. I've been in private planes several times, but this one is another level of extravagance.

As far as conditions for being held against your will go, these could be much worse, but nice surroundings don't abate my growing panic. Jackass number two is sprawled on the sofa on the left-hand side, watching—of all things—a travel infomercial on the big-screen TV mounted to the bulkhead.

My heart continues its staccato beat inside my ribcage, just like it did when these two pricks snatched me off the street and stuffed me into their van. The bastards never told me why they targeted me or where they were taking me. We drove for some time to arrive at a small private airport outside Chicago. The plane was already waiting on the tarmac when we pulled up.

How long have we been flying? An hour? Two? Ten? I'm not sure because they put some acid-smelling rag over my mouth and nose the moment we stepped foot inside this plane. I guess I shouldn't have kneed the infomercial-loving lunkhead in the balls on my way up the airstairs. Can't say he liked it.

I turn back to the scumbag sitting across from me. He's still pretending to be engrossed in the game playing on his phone, but he's been stealing glances at me when he thought I wasn't looking. Fucking creep.

"Listen, if you don't take me to the bathroom, I'll just pee right here." I widen my legs as much as my bound ankles allow. "Not sure the fancy leather will fare well, though."

"Christ!" He leaps from his seat and grabs my arm, pulling me up to stand. "Hank, I'm taking the nutcase to the restroom."

"Keep your eyes on her hands this time or you'll end up sporting another bruise," Hank groans from the sofa, moving his hand to shift his dick as if worried he lost it.

"I can't walk with my legs tied, idiot!" I snap as the man drags me down the narrow aisle between the seats. "And I need you to remove the handcuffs."

"Then hop. And I'm not freeing your hands." He grabs the links between my wrists and pulls.

I cry out in pain. The skin on my wrists is already raw from when he yanked me up the final couple of stairs while we were boarding. That happened after I got up close and personal with his buddy's jewels. My eyes prickle with unshed tears, but I blink rapidly, keeping the waterworks at bay by sheer will. I half shuffle, half hop between the seats before the knucklehead's bruteness has me falling flat on my face. When we reach the back of the plane, he opens the lavatory door and pushes me inside.

"You have five minutes," he growls and slams the door closed.

Like the rest of the jet, the restroom is luxurious. No stainless steel sink and such here; it's all dark-brown wood cabinetry and beige leather upholstery. There is even a small cushioned bench seat in the corner. The elegant-looking vanity and the toilet are on the opposite side. It takes me four hops to reach them.

I take care of my business as fast as my handcuffed hands allow, then look around while trying to calm my nerves. It doesn't really work. There's a sick kind of feeling in my throat, as if I'm going to throw up any second, and the inside of this lavish room seems to be spinning around me. My hands are still shaking, partially from the pain, but mostly from fear. I've experienced a few stressful situations in my life. A shooting, when I was four. Two small fires when our cook accidentally set the kitchen ablaze while trying out French recipes. Even an attempted raid on our home when my father was at war with a rival crime organization

8

some years back. But no kidnappings. Maybe I should have expected this, seeing as my dad is the leader of Chicago Bratva.

When I was grabbed off the street, in broad daylight, I was sure it had something to do with my father. Ransoming the pakhan's daughter can potentially yield someone a lot of money—if the dimwit lives long enough to see it, that is. But now, I don't think it's about making a buck from kidnapping. Considering what I've seen so far, whoever had me abducted has to be seriously loaded. Is this because of some mob feud? Retaliation for something my father did?

Bang!

"Are you done, yet?" an angry voice seethes from the other side of the door.

"I need a few more minutes!" I yell back as I crouch to open the cupboard under the sink. "It's not exactly easy to unbutton jeans while your hands are cuffed."

He barks something in retort, but I don't hear it, too focused on rummaging through the contents of the cupboard. Toilet paper. Towels. Extra soap. And . . . a disposable toothbrush.

"I can work with that," I whisper.

I tear the plastic wrap with my teeth and, somehow, manage to stuff the brush up my sleeve. Then, I continue going through the rest of the supplies.

Sponge. More towels. Condoms. *Really?* Who the hell fucks on a plane? I shake my head and resume. Dental floss. Mm-hmm . . . I rip off an arm's length, wrapping the two ends around my fingers to make it taut, then yank them apart as much as I can, testing out how sturdy it is. My uncle once showed me how to strangle someone using a garrote and—The shitty thread snaps on the second pull. Yeah . . . that won't work. I shift my attention to the lower shelf.

Cleaning supplies, but the bottles are too big to be concealed. Plastic gloves. And . . . a spray deodorant. Men's. Travel size. Perfect.

I grab the container, straighten up, and push the little tube canister into the waistband of my jeans. The door flies open just as I'm adjusting my oversized shirt to cover my hidden stash.

"You done?" the jackass asks. I believe Hank referred to this lug as Vinny earlier.

"Yup." I hit the button to flush the toilet, then wash my hands while the impatient dick glares at me from the doorway. Ass. Hole.

With no other option, I hop out of the bathroom. All the while, the concealed deodorant digs into my hip. I'm not sure what kind of damage I can do with deodorant and a toothbrush, but we'll see. I need to try to escape the moment we land and then find a phone, or I might never get another chance.

My dad has connections all over the US. He'll come for me right away. Or, if we're not close to Chicago, Dad will arrange for someone to pick me up and take me somewhere safe until he can arrive. *And he'll kill these bastards . . .*

Hop.

. . . in a very . . .

Hop.

. . . very . . .

Hop.

. . . painful way.

"We're here," Vinny says an hour or so later. "I'm going to free your legs now, but if you try pulling anything again, you'll regret it."

"Where are we?" I ask meekly, deciding a change in tactics is in order. Maybe if they think I've quit resisting, they'll lower their guard?

The bastard ignores my question. He cuts the zip ties from around my ankles, then grabs my upper arm and jerks me up to stand. "Move."

I tread between the seats and then down the narrow stairs from the plane to the tarmac, with jackass number one behind me and jackass two leading the way. The air is fresh, and the scent of brine carries on the slight breeze. We're close to the coast. Florida maybe? It's much warmer here than in Chicago.

The bastard whose balls I introduced to my knee—Hank—stops at the foot of the stairs, eyeing the dirt road extending away from the runway. I look around, taking in my surroundings. There's not a soul anywhere in sight, and other than one small building off to the side, no other structures. This isn't an actual airport at all. Just an airfield. A paved runway. Grass. And rolling hills. I've never been to Florida, but I don't think it looks like this.

A bird's shrill cry sounds somewhere above me, and I tilt my head up, focusing on the source. It's a seagull. I squint my eyes because the sun is high in the sky. Midday. It can't be midday. I got snatched in the late afternoon.

"Guido is late," Vinny says as he comes to stand by Hank, his meaty grip on my arm unrelenting.

"He'll be here soon." Hank shrugs and reaches into his pocket to pull out a pack of cigarettes.

I push thoughts about the time of day aside and fix my eyes on the lit lighter in Hank's hand. My heart rate skyrockets, adrenaline surging through my veins as I stare at the small flame. This is my chance. But I need my arm to be free.

"Can I have one?" I ask. "Please?"

Hank narrows his eyes at me. "How old are you? Thirteen?"

I suppress the urge to knee him again and smile instead. Similar to my mom, I might be shorter than most women, but I'm sure the asshole can see the swell of boobs under my baggy shirt.

"Twenty-three."

"Yeah, sure," Hank snorts, taking a cigarette out of the pack and offering it to me.

"Do you mind?" I yank my arm away from Vinny's squeezing, sausage-like fingers.

Vinny grunts, but releases me.

I take the offered cigarette and put it between my lips, fighting off a few strands of hair the light wind is tossing in my face. More of the unmistakable sea air invades my nostrils as I slowly move my hands to the waistband of my jeans. Hank flicks his Zippo again and extends it toward me.

My lips widen in a sugary grin. "Thank you."

I lean back and lift the deodorant can in front of me, pressing the nozzle. For a speck of a second, a crisp manly scent wraps around me, but the next instant, the spray reaches the flame and the delicious male fragrance transforms into the stench of burning fabric and charred skin when my makeshift flame-thrower hits its target.

Hank roars and stumbles backward, away from the fiery flow. I never expected to have an opportunity to try out this specific trick Uncle Sergei showed me, but life is full of surprises.

Triumph doesn't last long, however. Pain shoots across the top of my head when Vinny grabs a fistful of my hair. I scream. Tears well in my eyes, and, for the briefest moment, the urge to simply surrender overwhelms me. *No. Not happening.* I slide the toothbrush from my sleeve into my palm. Gripping the bristled end with my handcuffed hands, I swing, aiming at the motherfucker's left eye.

The goon is so massive that my blow merely skims his eyelid, leaving a scrape along his cheekbone. Still, Vinny cries out, and his hold on me slips. The moment I'm free, I turn and flee down the runway toward the dirt road. It's a narrow trail rather than a regular vehicle path, lined with olive trees on either side. Still groggy from whatever shit they spiked me with, and with wobbly legs from being bound for a long-ass time, running is a challenge. I stumble, twice, but the adrenaline surging through my bloodstream keeps me going. This is likely the only chance I'll have to make my escape.

I'm halfway to the dirt track when the deep rumble of an

BEAUTIFUL BEAST

engine echoes off the surrounding hills. A cloud of dust rises among the trees, and a car emerges around the curve. The sleek white sports vehicle, looking completely out of place in these rural surroundings, draws near. For a split second, I hesitate, not knowing if the person in the car is a friend or foe, but I have no other options. I keep running toward it.

I only make it a few steps before all air leaves my lungs as two hands grab me from behind and lift me off my feet.

"You bitch!" Vinny snarls next to my ear.

"Help!" I yell as I kick my legs.

"Fucking stop!"

"Never!" I wriggle left and right, trying to free myself, but his hold doesn't waver.

The white car stops a few feet from us. The driver's door opens, and a blond man in his late twenties steps outside. He's wearing faded blue jeans and a plain white T-shirt.

"Please, help me," I choke out, staring at the newcomer.

He spares me a quick glance, then looks at Vinny. "What is this?"

His voice is raspy and carries a slight accent, indicative of a non-native English speaker.

"The hacker." The growled response comes from just behind me.

What the hell? I was sure I'd been kidnapped because of who my father is, and not because of my little hobby. Maybe these guys don't even know who I am.

Jean guy's eyebrows hit his hairline. His green eyes shift to me, scanning from head to toe, then back up again to stop on my tangled hair.

"Such an interesting turn of events." He meets my stare. "Welcome to Sicily, miss."

CHAPTER
Two

Rafael

Two weeks earlier
De Santi Estate, near Taormina, Sicily

"I'M SO SORRY FOR CALLING THIS EARLY, BOSS," MY IT specialist says on the other end of the line. "But, it happened again."

I rear back, my cock slipping out of my latest hookup. She's sprawled in front of me on the desk, her red hair spilling over the edge. I squeeze the phone at my ear. "What?"

"I don't understand how," Mitch continues in a slightly hysterical tone. "We reinstalled all the firewalls, and I had four guys spend the entire night trying to breach them. Everything seemed solid."

"It wasn't fucking solid if someone got into our system again," I snarl.

"Rafael? What's going on, love?" Constanza pants, looking at me from between her widened legs. Her lips are parted in a flirtatious smile. However, instead of my face, her eyes are fixed on the spot just above my collarbone.

"Get dressed." I turn around and walk across my office to the open balcony doors. "What did they do this time, Mitch?"

"Created a payment order that initiated a wire transfer from our marketing account to a children's church choir in Seattle. But it was only twenty dollars, hardly an inconvenience, yes?"

My hand tightens on the balcony doorframe. "We're the largest personal security company in this part of the world, and someone has been hacking into our systems for months, making us look like morons. You consider *that* a minor inconvenience?"

"Yes . . . I mean, no. Of course not."

My gaze passes over the treetops and the lush greenery of the garden below, all the way to the horizon where the early morning sunlight reflects off the endless expanse of the sea. Further down the coast, my two yachts are anchored in a small marina, swaying on the gentle waves.

When Guido and I fled Sicily twenty five years ago, we had no paperwork to be in the US, so there was no means for me to get a legal job, especially as a minor. Pickpocketing on the streets, I'd barely been able to feed my brother. My only choice was to reach out to the local Albanian clan. They agreed to take me and my brother in. But, they set very clear terms. They'd provide the necessary IDs, a roof over our heads, and food so we wouldn't have to scrounge for scraps, and, in return, I'd have to do their bidding for the next five years, no questions asked. By the time I accepted Dushku's offer, I hadn't eaten in nearly two days. Everything I "earned" went toward rent for the room in the rickety garage that served as our home. Faced with either starvation or accepting a deal from the devil, I picked the latter.

At first, I was given errand jobs—running messages too important to risk sending electronically, dealing coke, or making dead bodies disappear. Then, I got assigned to Jemin, to be his backup. As one of Dushku's enforcers, Jemin was more than happy to take a back seat and have me do all the dirty work for him. Beatings. Torture. And of course, eliminating whoever Dushku deemed expendable, whether they were inside his own organization or someone on the outside who simply stood in his way. I bartered five years of my life and a large part of my soul, to make sure Guido never again went to bed hungry. And then, I spent the next fifteen years building my empire.

It took me two decades to get where I am now. From pitiful scum living on the streets, surviving on crumbs and whatever I could lift from an unsuspecting pocket, to a man whose name demands respect. And inflicts fear. I did it all with my own two hands—clawing and taking—literally stepping over corpses. I might have left my home country as a beggar, but I returned as a ruler. I'm not going to let some goddamned cyberpunk make a fool of me.

"Did you manage to locate the bastard?" I ask.

"No. He's been using VPN and IP address scramblers, pinning his position all over the globe."

"And it's always a different location?"

"Yes. Tokyo. Manila. Chicago. Panama. The Hague. Once, we got a pin in Patagonia. There were nine separate incidents, at different locations every time. Except . . . just a second." The clicking sounds of fingers rapidly working a keyboard come across the line. "The first incursion six months ago and this latest one both show an IP address in the Chicago area. It"—more typing—"appears that these hacks were done from an internet café. But not the same one."

The tapping of heels on the wooden floor resonates behind me. I throw a look over my shoulder to find Constanza standing by the couch. She's wearing the same short red dress I peeled off her an hour ago. One that barely covers her ass and reveals her mile-long legs. Her hair is down, each strand in its place, framing her classically beautiful face. Drop-dead gorgeous. My fucks always are. I'm used to having beautiful women by my side. Money can buy what appearance alone cannot. That's the reality.

"I'm being interviewed on TV Thursday afternoon." Constanza's lips widen into a beaming smile. "There's this amazing black gown I saw at Albini's . . . It would be perfect for the occasion."

I'm sure it would. Albini's is the most expensive clothing boutique in this part of Europe. But before I let her spend thousands of my money on a dress, she'll have to learn to look at my face while we talk. And fuck.

"No. You can get a dress at one of the regular shops. Tell them to put it on my account."

The smile on Constanza's face wavers, but she quickly hides the slip. She closes the distance between us in a few heel-clicking steps and rises on her toes to kiss me. "Thank you, love."

There's a barely detectable flinch as her lips brush mine, and I have to give it to her—she's probably the best actress out of all the women I have screwed. They all try damn hard to hide their disgust. Some manage better than others. As good as she is, though, like the rest of them, Constanza can't stomach looking at my face, even in low light.

I don't mind the fact that the only reason my hookups remain with me for any length of time is for the extravagant trips and lavish gifts I shower them with. Unrivaled luxury—compensation for being subjected to having a beast at their side. It's a fair compromise. Some chicks can tolerate it for longer. Most can't.

A few years back, I picked up a woman at a club. Or rather, she picked me up. A well-known socialite from the mainland, she was in Sicily vacationing with her friends. One of them probably told her who I was. She was flying high on life—or maybe it was something more and I didn't realize it at the time—and was clearly celebrating something that had champagne flowing freely at their table. By the time we made it to a suite at my hotel, she was singing the latest chart-toppers and could barely keep her hands off me. We fucked. Several times. She begged for more. I know how to please a woman in bed. The poor thing even asked me to marry her. But the following morning, when she woke up sober, but definitely hungover, and saw my face, she screamed. Two minutes later, she ran out of the room and straight into a taxi I called for her.

"When are we going to see each other again?" Constanza chirps.

"I'll call you," I say, then gesture toward my suit coat she has draped over her shoulders. "Take off my jacket."

"But it's chilly outside."

"Right now, Constanza. One of my men downstairs can give you theirs."

She pouts a bit but leaves the jacket on the back of the sofa and rushes across the office, closing the big oak door after her. I turn toward the view outside and put my phone back to my ear.

"Listen to me carefully, Mitch. You're going to find that hacker, and you'll do it quickly. I don't give a fuck if you need to station one of our men in every shitty internet café in the Greater Chicago Area. I want the motherfucker found and brought to me."

"But . . . There are hundreds of internet cafés there, boss."

"I don't fucking care!" I snarl into the phone. "Find him. Or I'm going to detach your fucking head from your spine!"

"Yes, boss. Of course. I'll get it done."

I cut the line, then hit my brother's contact icon.

"Raff," Guido yawns through the speaker.

"Do we have anything major happening this week?" I ask as I head toward the door connecting my office to my bedroom.

"Christ, Rafael. It's six in the morning."

"Answer me!"

"As far as I know, no. Most of the available contracts were low-value, so I decided to pass on them. I need to check the postings, but I think I saw a double-hit order added last night. The amount, though, was less than a million."

"Take it," I bark as I step inside the walk-in closet.

"Okay. Who are we sending? The targets are in Germany, and I think Allard's team is already there."

"No." I push the button hidden behind the row of suits and watch the back of the closet slide to the side. A moment later, the ceiling lights flick on, illuminating the interior of the hidden room, and the walls covered in an array of weapons.

"Then who do you want to send?"

"We're not sending any of the teams. I'll be handling this one."

"Why?"

"I had a shitty start to the day, Guido, despite just getting home less than an hour ago. I need a distraction." My eyes skip over the selection of long-range rifles before me. "Any special kill instructions?"

"Mmm . . . Let me see. Nope. No preferences for the method of disposal."

"Perfect. Send me the file and tell the pilot to have the plane ready by seven." I cut the line and take an M40 off the wall.

The last time I personally handled a contract was more than a decade ago, just before I made my return to Sicily. With all the crap I needed to do to take over and then maintain control of the east coast of the island, I had to "retire" my mercenary role. Now, I have eleven teams of hitmen scattered around the world, using the strategically located branches of Delta Security as bases. My brother oversees that part of our clandestine operations these days, while I'm focused on laundering and investing the blood money through the legitimate side of our business.

The business that some son of a bitch has decided to fuck with.

I can't wait to get my hands on that bastard.

Vasilisa

Home of Roman Petrov (the Russian Bratva's pakhan), Chicago

The door of my room flies open.

"Jesus fuck, Dad!" I jump in my chair. "Don't you know how to knock?"

With his eyes narrowed at me and rage etched into his features, the almighty Roman Petrov strolls in. His cane makes a slight tick sound on the hardwood floor as he approaches with quick steps and leans in close to my face.

"You are grounded," he says through his teeth.

"I'm not a child. You can't grou—What are you doing? No! Leave my laptop alone! Dad!"

"NASA?" He puts my laptop under his arm and yanks the power cord out of the wall. "Fucking NASA!?"

Oh, shit. "How did you find out?"

"I cornered Felix and he spilled the beans."

I gape. Felix is Uncle Sergei's friend from way back when Dad's brother was working for the military, but the old goose is more like an adopted family member. There isn't a system he can't crack, and everything I know about cyber sleuthing, I learned from him. He's also over ninety years old, but he would never admit it. For the past decade, he's been telling everyone that he hasn't even hit eighty. I can't believe Grandpa Felix would rat me out!

"I was just fooling around, Dad. I didn't do anything. I swear. I just went in and out."

"Oh? So you just . . . made a little digital visit to the National Aeronautics and Space Administration?"

"Kind of?" I offer him a remorseful smile.

A menacing growl leaves his throat. "I told you, Vasilisa. I told you a thousand times—you can*not* hack into government systems! That's fucking illegal!"

I lift an eyebrow. "You do remember that you're the leader of one of the largest criminal organizations in this part of the world, don't you?"

"Yes. And I don't want my daughter to have anything to do with any unlawful shit."

"Well, if you'd let me help with the family business, I wouldn't have to waste my skills looking for kicks elsewhere," I snap.

"No part of Bratva's business is legitimate, Vasilisa. And I don't want you anywhere near it."

"You won't even let me help Ivan handle customs documents. It took him two nights in the downstairs office to finally get everything sorted out."

"I will not have my daughter forging import manifests for contraband!"

Contraband. I roll my eyes. As if I don't know that Bratva mostly deals in drugs. I'm so sick of being treated like an ignorant kid.

"You take Alexei to meetings with your partners!"

"Your brother is going to take over the Bratva leadership when I step down. He needs to be prepared."

I shake my head. "You're such a hypocrite, Dad."

"The criminal underworld is not a place for a woman, Vasilisa. You're going to finish your studies. Get a regular job. Find a nice guy to date. An accountant, maybe."

I sigh. *Overprotective* doesn't even come close to describing my father. Once, he almost strangled someone I was dating when he saw us kissing in front of the perimeter gate, just because the guy had a shaved head and pierced eyebrow.

"I graduated last Friday, in case you forgot."

"And you're getting your master's degree next."

"I don't want to do my master's, Dad! I want to work. For you."

"Not happening." He points an accusing finger at me. "And this hacking shit ends now, Vasilisa. You're not going to do it again. Promise me!"

"Fine."

"Promise me."

"I promise. I won't hack into government databases of any kind, ever again."

"And?"

I roll my eyes. "Or anywhere else."

"Good." He leans over and drops a kiss on the top of my head. "You know how much I love you, don't you?"

"Yes. I love you, too. Can I have my laptop back now? I need to start applying for that 'regular' job you want me to get."

"Nope."

"Dad, it's not fair—" I sniff the air. "What's that smell?"

My door bangs open again, and the scent of something burning permeates the room.

"Dad!" Yulia, my younger sister rushes inside. "Igor set the new microwave on fire."

"Again?" Dad yells. "I told that idiot that he's retired! Who let him in? I'm going to kill him, along with everyone else working in that kitchen."

He rushes out of my room, and he takes my laptop with him. The bedroom door slams closed, making both me and my sister shriek.

"What was that about?" Yulia asks as she sprawls out on my bed.

"He confiscated my laptop."

"I could see that. He found out about you hacking that company yesterday? What did you do this time?"

"Sent a donation to a church choir." My shoulders sag.

"From the cybercafé near the library, but it looks like Felix told Dad about me poking around NASA's firewalls."

"God, Vasilisa. Why do you keep doing this crap?"

"I don't know. Maybe it's my way of getting back at Dad for not letting me help him with anything." I shift in my seat. "Or because I don't know what to do with my free time now."

"You should go out more. What happened with that guy you were seeing?"

"Oliver?"

"Yeah. The underwear model. He's so hot." Yulia rolls over on the bed, fanning herself.

I tilt my head up, staring at the ceiling, and swivel side to side on my chair. Yes, Oliver is unbelievably handsome. We met in a coffee shop downtown when he sat at the table next to mine. I didn't pay any attention to him at first, too absorbed in the coding exercises Grandpa Felix created for me, but then Oliver moved over to sit beside me and started asking questions about what I was doing.

"I broke up with him last week," I mumble. "He ended up being the same as every other guy who wants to date me."

"You mean, he fell to his knees, begging for permission to adore you?" Yulia giggles. "*Vasilisa the Fair*. Making men trip over their feet since you turned fifteen."

"Not funny. And I hate it when you call me that. It made me despise that fairytale."

"You, my darling sister, might be the only woman on earth who hates being beautiful."

"I don't hate it. But just once, I'd like to have a guy be attracted to me for something more. Not simply because I'm pretty."

"You're more than pretty, Vasya. Even in the dreadful rags you wear."

"There's nothing wrong with my clothes."

"That top is awful. And what the hell do you call that color?

23

Vomit yellow?" She nods toward me. "And don't get me started on the two-sizes-too-large jeans."

"They're comfortable." I shrug.

"Yeah, sure." Yulia puts her hands under her chin and rolls her eyes. "So, what did 'Oliver the Hot' do wrong?"

"He insisted on restarting my phone for me. Apparently, I don't look like a girl who could do that myself. And I quote: '*Why would you trouble yourself with something like that, beautiful? You have me now, and I'll take care of the hard tech stuff for you.*'" I barely keep the snarl out of my voice while trying to imitate the imbecile's tone. "Then, he took my phone out of my hand and did it for me. I earned my undergrad in computer science and graduated summa cum laude, and the asshat actually restarted my phone for me."

"That's so rich." Yulia laughs. "Did he offer to flip the light switches for you, as well? In case you got confused about how they work?"

"Not funny!" I grumble.

"Sorry, but yes. Yes, it is. He just wanted to be your knight in shining armor."

I snort. "We were at the park when it happened. I was still gaping at Oliver fumbling with my phone when a dog got loose off his leash and ran right toward us, barking. My *knight in* shitty *armor* squeaked like a four-year-old girl and hightailed it out of there without even looking over his shoulder to check on me."

"What a bastard! And the dog?"

"He just wanted to play. Licked my hands and face, then ran off." I shake my head and spin a full circle on my gaming chair. "Dad mentioned wanting a normal guy for me. Some accountant, he said. Well, probably when I turn fifty, but . . . I don't think I can make it work with any normal guy, Yulia."

"Why not?"

I arch an eyebrow at my baby sister. "Because a normal guy would piss himself the moment he meets our family. Can you imagine an accountant lounging in our living room and BS-ing with Dad, Alexei, and Uncle Sergei?"

"I think Uncle Sergei is awesome. He wouldn't do anything to your accountant."

"He brought a grenade launcher to dinner last week."

"Well, there's that." She shrugs. "Maybe you should try dating someone from Bratva. Whoever it is, he'll know what he's getting into."

"Yeah, sure. How long do you think the poor guy would live after Dad finds out we're going out?"

"A week?"

"Forty-eight hours, tops. Dad would never let either of us date one of his men. Or anyone from our *social* circle."

I understand our father's need to keep his daughters away from the seedy part of Roman Petrov's world—don't get me started on the patriarchial shit that my *younger* brother never even has to think about—but the thing Dad doesn't fully get is that we're already a part of it. Around-the-clock armed security. Wounded, bleeding men brought into our house to be patched up right on our kitchen island. Constant vigilance against random skirmishes with other criminal organizations. Bodyguards no further than an arm's length away until a potential threat is resolved. Business meetings and even family gatherings often ending with guns drawn. My sister and I were both born into this madness. That's our "normal." Anything else will never feel remotely as such.

"Do you think Dad will make me marry an accountant, as well?" Yulia chirps from the bed.

"Nah. He'll probably find you a dentist. Or a museum curator." I grin, looking at her and picturing a dude with glasses and a bow tie coming to pick her up for their date. "Dad would never let the baby of the family go anywhere near a big bad accountant. Those guys can get involved in frauds."

"Yeah." She chews her thumbnail. "Um . . . I'm going to ask Dad to let me move out before the next semester."

I gape at my sister. "Why?"

"I'm not like you, Vasya. All this commotion, people constantly coming and going, the fucking noise all the time . . . I don't think I can live in this nuthouse anymore."

"I doubt he'd let you."

"Why not? There haven't been any skirmishes with other Families recently. Everybody's just been minding their own business."

"Yes, but . . ." I stare at her. In Russian families, it's common for kids to keep living at home until they finish college and get a job. Especially in families like ours—where extra security is often necessary. "But, it's not that bad here."

The slamming of doors somewhere down the hallway reverberates through the house as if purposely contradicting my statement. Yelling and the sound of running feet mix with the droning of the lawn mower drifting through the open window. Male laughter and good-natured Russian insults clamor for attention in the backyard—Alexei and our cousin Sasha are competing in knife-throwing again. I wonder which one of them will end up getting stitched up in the kitchen today. The stench of smoke seems to be dissipating, but it's still hanging in the air. Mom is going to lose it if it settles into her new drapes. High-pitched female voices are ringing somewhere inside the mansion, spewing Russian curses back and forth. Dad's office is just below my room, and I can hear him roaring at someone over the phone. Probably Uncle Sergei; he's the only one who can make my dad lose his shit in under a minute.

Just another regular day in the Petrov household.

"I stand corrected. Our home is the oasis of peace and tranquility." Yulia laughs from her spot on the bed. "So, are you really going to cease your cyber adventures?"

"Yeah," I mumble and bite my lower lip. I should have sent more moola to that kids' choir while I had the chance.

When I first started hacking my way into random businesses, I quickly found that most of their digital safeguards were a joke. To me, corporate firewalls didn't present any challenge whatsoever. So, I did some digging and picked the top ten private security companies. I've been working solely with their systems ever since, creating back doors into their networks, just like Grandpa Felix showed me. It's not about espionage or financial fraud, simply a question of flexing my computing muscles and breaching the most stringent virtual environments on the planet. I'd get in, then retreat, erasing every trace I'd ever been there. Except for small things. I can't seem to overcome a stupid need to leave behind a tiny clue. A changed code to the service elevator. Reformatted bullet points on the website from basic dots to little stars. Increasing the paychecks of the lowest-paid employees by a dollar. Or, in the case of the big-ass security conglomerate with offices around the globe, manipulating their accounting systems to send small donations to obscure charities and underprivileged places.

Maybe I could hit the "big brawny beast" one last time. A goodbye kiss to my hacking career.

Yes. I'll wait a couple of weeks, just in case. If Dad doesn't return my laptop by then, I'll find another dive internet café and do it from there.

It'll be less than thirty minutes of work, now that I know their system like the back of my hand.

Nothing can go wrong.

Chapter Three

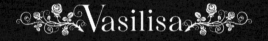

Vasilisa

Present day
Sicily

I STARE AT THE BLOND GUY BEHIND THE WHEEL. HE'S settled back in his seat, an elbow casually draped through the open window while he steers his souped-up ride over roads that see more sheep crossings than vehicle traffic. Meanwhile, dickhead one is flanking me in the back seat, the pissed-off vibes rolling off him in droves, and dickhead number two is obnoxiously gloating after calling shotgun. I can't believe these bastards dragged me to damn Sicily!

How long is the flight to Italy? Mom and Dad probably already know that something's happened and are looking for me. God, I hope they find me soon.

"I need your name," blondie—my kidnappers called him Guido—says.

Yup, they have no idea who I am. I'm not sure if that's good or bad.

"And I need you to let me go," I mumble. "What do you want from me?"

"Me, personally? Nothing. You'll have to discuss the rest with my brother."

"And where is said brother?"

He ignores me for a moment while easing the car to a stop. Then, he pivots toward the back and lifts his phone, snapping a shot of my face before I can even protest.

"He should be home in a few hours," Guido finally responds. His eyes bounce between the two goons with half a brain between them. "Take her to the basement. Give her food and water."

Vinny exits the car, pulling me out after him. I cry out, trying to shrug him off without much luck. Hank grabs my other arm, and both proceed to tow me toward the entrance of the huge sandstone villa. The only thing I manage to catch before I'm hauled inside is that the house is located on a hillside, overlooking the sea.

The interior screams opulence, but it's that understated luxury that's hard to miss. Not gaudy and in-your-face flashy, but homey—comfort etched into every room and amenity we pass. The ceilings are high, crisscrossed with thick wooden beams. The stucco detailing on the walls reminds me of photos from *Architectural Digest* or other interior design magazines. Sunlight streams through the massive French windows that open to the shimmering waters beyond, bathing the pale wood furniture. My steps falter for a moment, and I can't help but draw in a deep breath, taking in the view.

"Move!" Vinny barks, tugging me away from the beautiful sight and to the left of the main doors, toward stairs that must lead to the lower level.

I dig my heels into the floor, trying to resist or at least slow the brute down. Pain shoots through my wrists when he yanks on the handcuffs' chain again, making me cry out as he nearly drags me down the steps to the sturdy-looking wooden door at the bottom.

"Stop whimpering." He opens the door and pushes me inside the spacious but dim, cool room. A slight earthy scent hangs in the air.

I fall to my knees and manage to brace my palms on the frigid tiled floor, barely avoiding hitting my face on the surface.

"And because you were a bitch—no food or water!"

I scramble to my feet and rush toward the door, but it snaps shut just before I reach it. The panic I've been trying to keep at bay pushes its way through my restraint, sweeping through me like a tempest. I grab the knob, finding it locked.

"Let me out!" I bang on the barrier with my fists. "You sleazy motherfuckers! You're going to pay for this! Let me out!" My hands hurt from the continuous blows on solid wood, and even though I know it's in vain, I keep doing it.

I'm not certain how long I keep up my assault on that damn basement door. By the time I relent, the scant light coming from the narrow horizontal windows cut high into the walls has changed to a dusky orange. I press my back to the door and let my body slide down to the floor.

Despite being mostly underground, the temperature is relatively comfortable in the room, but my legs are shaking as if I've been plunged into the dead of winter. My arms, too. I take a deep breath, trying to calm down, but it doesn't work. Soon enough, my whole body is racked by tremors like I'm running a fever. My bravado is gone, and all I want to do is curl into a ball and cry.

What the hell do these people want from me? To punish me for hacking into their damn company? I don't even know which one it is. Why not kill me right away? Why drag me all the way here, across the ocean, just to throw me into some basement? Unless "the brother" wants to kill me himself?

Another shudder passes through me. These are not some

regular businessmen, of that I'm certain. Corporate CEOs don't kidnap people. Only people in my father's world do. And as far as I know, Sicily is run by Cosa Nostra. Bratva has no beef with any of the factions of the Italian Mafia. Maybe I should have told them who I am, who my father is. Now, I may very well end up dead before I ever get the chance to do so.

I look around, searching for something . . . I'm not sure what. Anything. There are a few empty crates in one corner. An old chair in the other, with dark stains on the weathered wood as well as on the floor directly below. I don't want to think about what made those stains. Another chair close by, one that's in slightly better shape.

My focus shifts to the windows. Maybe they're my way out? That hope is dashed as soon as I spot ornate bars on the outside of the glass. Although there are light fixtures on the ceiling, I don't see a switch anywhere. Must be on the other side of the door.

I get up to approach a small sink near the entryway and drink directly from the tap. The two assholes gave me water and some crackers on the plane, but that was hours ago. My stomach picks that moment to twist itself into a cramp. When was my last full meal? Lunch, before they snatched me? I've been feeling lightheaded for the past hour from the lack of food and wearing myself out. All my energy is depleted, and every muscle aches like the last time I was sick with the flu. It feels as if my body is slowly shutting down, and I'm getting drowsy. But, there's no way I'm letting myself faint. I push away from the wall and head across the room.

The only other thing in this space is a massive shelf covering an entire wall. Hundreds of wine bottles are stashed on their sides inside their cubbyholes. I've been locked in a damn cellar. How rustic, and somehow completely befitting the country-style decor I glimpsed upstairs. Approaching the assortment, I pick up one of the bottles. The black label with silver lettering proclaims

31

it to be a thirty-year-old red wine. Must be expensive shit. Such a shame.

My fingers might be trembling as I wrap a corner of my shirt around the neck of the bottle, but my hold on it is strong. I step to the side and slam the premium vintage against the wall. The last remnants of crimson sunlight fall onto the half-broken vessel left in my hand, reflecting magnificently off crystalline edges. My lips quirk at the corners. Uncle Sergei would be proud. Leaning my shoulder on the wall to support my weight, I shuffle to the farthest corner of the room.

I'm pretty certain these scumbags intend to kill me.

But, I'm not going down without a fight.

Rafael

The wrought iron gate slowly opens, revealing a meandering gravel road through the olive trees. I nod at the guard stationed to the right of the barrier, then nudge my SUV along the pale path lit by my headlights, enjoying the subtle crunch of tiny stones beneath the oversized tires. Guido always nags about gravel damaging the vehicles, insisting we should pave the long lane through the estate. Today's youth seems to be inclined to upgrade every single thing, even when there's no actual need for it. I had more than enough asphalt and concrete to last me a lifetime during those fifteen years we lived in the States.

The road gradually widens, transforming into a driveway in front of my house. Two guys from my Chicago division—Vinny and Hank—are standing by the front door, their backs ramrod straight while their eyes follow my car as I park. I wonder how long they've been waiting there, doing good imitations of dumb posts. I would have preferred to send one of my top guys to snatch the damn hacker who's been the source of my annoyance for months, but time and logistics were against me. Since most of our merc ops have focused on Europe in the last few years, the best of my men are scattered across the old continent. Hank and Vinny are on my payroll as bodyguards for the legitimate side—my front company—providing private security. They are capable, but neither is overly bright. I was actually pleasantly surprised that they were able to catch the culprit.

"You have my hacker?" I ask as I get out of the driver's seat.

"Yes." Hank nods. "Safe and sound in the wine cellar."

I take in his charred suit jacket, screaming-red face, and missing eyebrow, then turn to Vinny who's got a bruise on his chin and an angry scrape under his left eye.

"I see he resisted," I say as I reach into my jacket to take out my gun.

Hank clasps his hands behind him, fidgeting. "She."

My hand stills on the gun handle. "What?"

"She resisted. It's . . . it's a woman, boss."

"A woman? Must be a formidable one. Does she breathe fire, as well?" I shake my head and step inside the house, heading toward the stairs leading to the cellar.

The basement door opens with the tiniest screech. Inside, it's chilly and dark, with only slivers of moonlight and the faint ambient glow from the garden coming through the two narrow windows set high on the opposite wall. For a moment, I don't think anyone's here. The space seems empty. I'm about to raise shit over a missing captive when my eyes fall on a petite female figure huddled in the corner. My fire-breathing guest is sitting on the floor with her face pressed to her knees.

I had no idea that my hacker was a woman. If I'd known, I would've had her brought to one of the guest rooms upstairs. There's no reason to deny her comfort while she waits to face me and her eventual demise.

With my fingers hovering over the light switch just outside the room, I stop myself from flicking it on. This woman must be scared. Seeing me would terrify her even more. That would lead to screaming and hysterics, which would transform into crying and pleas for her life. And I'm not in the fucking mood. I just need her to tell me who ordered her to fuck with my business before I quickly and painlessly snap her neck.

Leaving the overhead lighting off, I approach and crouch in front of the girl. With my back to the gaping basement door and the lit-up stairwell beyond, I know my face remains in shadow while the soft glow stretches ahead of me to dimly illuminate the room. My massive frame blocks part of that light, casting its own partial shroud on the tiny heap at my feet.

"Hey." I reach my hand toward her.

The girl's head snaps up, and the light from the hallway falls right onto her face. Her very angry, unearthly, beautiful face. For a moment, all I can do is stare at her, my stunned brain cells struggling to process that she's real. But what strikes me the most is her dark-as-night eyes, glaring at me from beneath impossibly long lashes. I can't name the expression in them, not with my gray matter turning into a useless mass of jelly, but I'm sure I'll be picturing those eyes long after her gaze has shifted.

A faint sense of a déjà vu washes over me, as if a long-forgotten memory is clawing its way to the front of my mind. That furious, exasperated look . . . No, I'm a hundred percent certain I've never met this woman before.

Too stunned by her beauty, I'm a second too late noticing the broken bottle in her hand. She swipes at me, and I rear back, but not fast enough. Pain explodes in my forearm as a jagged edge shreds through the fabric of my shirt and the skin of my right arm.

"*Che cazzo!*" I snap and grab her wrists.

The girl cries out, a pain-filled wail. I look down at her hand-cuffed hands, and rage explodes in my chest. The goddamn stupid cocksuckers didn't even take the handcuffs off her!

I don't have a problem killing anyone who dares to fucking

cross me—be it a man or a woman—but I draw the line at man-handling defenseless females. Not that this one is missing her stinger. If she left her marks on dumb and dumber upstairs, and with my own blood dripping down my arm as evidence, this spitfire is the furthest thing from helpless. I bet she's getting ready to deliver her next strike.

Carefully, I take the chunk of the shattered bottle she's still clutching, then focus on her face again. Her eyelids are half-closed, and her breathing seems shallow.

"Have you eaten?"

"Fuck you," she mumbles, her voice barely audible.

I take her chin between my fingers and tilt her head up. "I asked you a question. Have. You. Eaten?"

It seems to take some effort, but the girl's unfocused eyes slowly lift. "Crackers. When I woke up on the plane," she rasps.

Jesus. That was hours ago and on the back end of a ten-hour flight.

A small whimper leaves her lips, and with her next breath, her head lolls to the side.

Utter stillness.

"Hey." I lightly tap my fingers on her dirt-smeared cheek, but her body just sags against the wall.

Goddamned shit.

Hank and Vinny likely used drugs to knock her out while en route, and, without any food, she's obviously still experiencing the aftereffects. Carefully, I slip my head into the loop created by her handcuffed hands, then slide my palms under her thighs. Rising, I hold the unconscious girl in my arms while she unknowingly clings to me like a cuddling koala.

"Let's get you somewhere more comfortable, vespetta."

I can feel the girl's chest rising and falling as I carry her up the stairs to the ground floor. She weighs almost nothing. Her head rolls left and right on my shoulder, then lists to the side. I quickly raise my hand and cup her cheek, keeping her head in place, with her nose snuggled into the crook of my neck. Her breaths are slow, fanning the skin on the underside of my chin. The warm exhales are so soft, like a flutter of butterfly wings.

"Boss?" Vinny hurries over when I round the corner.

"Uncuff her," I say through gritted teeth. "Gently."

He takes the key from his pocket and rushes around me to work on the cuffs. The girl tenses, and I barely suppress the urge to take out my gun and shoot the idiot in the head right there.

"Hush, it's okay," I whisper into the girl's ear, then look at my men. "Go outside and wait for me by the garage. Both of you. Now."

The woman in my arms doesn't even stir as I climb the stairs to the upper level. If it wasn't for her kitten-like breaths, I'd think she was dead. How could someone so tiny and fragile-looking fight off two grown men, dealing out obvious damage? There can't be more than five feet to her, and I bet she weighs less than a hundred pounds, soaking wet. No doubt they underestimated her. I won't. She might be the size of a nymph, but looks can often be deceiving.

I use my elbow to push open the white door on the right side of the hallway, then bring the girl inside. It's not until I'm facing the big four-poster bed by the window that I realize where I am. My bedroom. I guess the fatigue thoroughly scrambled my brain, because I intended to take her to the guest room across the way. Now that I'm here, though . . . I can't picture her anywhere else.

More high jinks from my tired gray matter is my guess.

No one other than me has ever slept in that bed. Ever. Not even my hookups. I've always fucked either in my office or taken them to a suite at one of my hotels. Having *this* woman *here* is uncanny.

The moment her cheek touches my pillow, she lets out a purr-like sigh and curls into a fetal position. I tilt my head to the side, observing my little hacker. Asleep. In my bed. Tangled strands of jet-black hair partially cover her sweet face, so I reach and push them aside, and then just stare. Like some hypnotized fool.

She's young, in her early twenties most likely. Her slight build, however, makes her appear even younger. The bedside lamp casts soft light on her delicate frame, and it only heightens her perfect features. Even with dirt on her face and messy hair, she's so damn beautiful—almost mythic. I wish I could see her eyes again. They were mesmerizing.

My gaze wanders over her sleeping form, stopping on her wrists. Immediately, rage reignites within me.

Fast, painless death is what I had in mind for her up until the moment she swiped that broken bottle at me in the cellar. Hurt, scared, and barely conscious, but she still fought back. Still lashed out, even when her captors could squash her with one blow.

I thought I'd seen it all during my years as an active member of my assassination crew. Every target tries to fight back. Initially, at least. But then, there's a switch to crying. Or begging. Some offer money to let them go. To let them live. Men, twice the size of this slip-of-a-girl, would piss themselves in fear. Eventually, they all reach that point—that one moment common to them all. The moment they realize there's no way out. That's when the fight leaves them. Their will gives out. The weeping and pleading continue, of course, but they stop fighting back.

But, not her. She tried to kill me, even though she must have known she didn't stand a chance. Her weapon was too inadequate to cause any serious damage. Maybe if she actually managed to hit my carotid artery by some crazy luck. Still, when she met my gaze, just before she swiped that smashed bottle at me, there was so much courage and determination in her pretty yet delirious dark eyes.

I pull the blanket over the girl, then head into my bathroom to get some gauze and antibiotic ointment for her wounds. Her wrists are raw and screaming-red, and there's dried blood where her epidermis broke. I put a hefty amount of the cream on her skin, then secure a thin layer of dressing around her slim carpal joints. This woman may have been a major source of my agitation recently, but for some reason, I can't stand the idea of her enduring even a smidgen of pain.

With one more look at my beautiful and gutsy hacker, I leave the room.

Hank and Vinny are hanging out near Guido's car where it's parked out in front of the garage. I approach and level a heavy look at them both. "Did you enjoy manhandling a woman that's a third of your size?"

"She torched my face, boss," Hank replies, avoiding my gaze. "The fucking bitch is crazy. She must have grabbed a can of deodorant from the jet's bathroom, and then she turned it into a goddamned flamethrower when all I did was offer her the smoke she asked for. Then, she almost stabbed Vinny's eye out with a toothbrush. She's seriously nuts. When we first nabbed her, she hit him with her backpack, swinging it like she was batting at Wrigley Field, for fuck's sake."

"Who put the handcuffs on her? Her wrists are scraped raw."

"Um, I did." Vinny fidgets from foot to foot. "She wouldn't cooperate. It was easier to drag her around with those on."

Drag her. I nod, then reach inside my jacket and pull out my gun. "Do you remember your training and the lesson on manners?"

"Yes," he chokes out, his eyes frantic and focused on the silencer I'm screwing into place. "But . . . you were going to kill her. Why does it matter if—"

He never finishes his bullshit excuse because I press the gun to his forehead and pull the trigger. Blood splashes onto my brother's car, tainting the windows and the sleek body lines of his prized possession. Hank gapes at me from next to his dead buddy, face draining of color as the reality of his worthless future settles in. There's blood and brain matter on his cheek and in his hair.

"Give me your hand," I order.

"Boss, I . . ."

I shove the gun to the bridge of his nose. "Now."

Slowly, he extends his left hand toward me—palm up—his fingers shaking. Before he has a chance to start pleading his case, I've got the barrel butted up to his middle finger and I'm squeezing the trigger. An agonized howl explodes into the night.

"Touch her again, and it'll be your skull next," I bark and head back inside, still fuming. I don't understand why, but I can't get the sight of the girl's wounded wrists out of my mind.

Guido's apartment is on the ground floor, in the east wing of the estate. I find my brother sprawled on his couch, watching TV.

"Had a look at your hacker?" he asks, still focused on his movie. "Did you kill her already?"

I round the couch, grab the front of his shirt, and yank him up. Then, I punch him in the face with my free hand.

"Fuck, Raff!" He presses his hands over his bloody schnoz. "What the hell was that for?"

"Next time you see a woman being mistreated and do nothing, I'll do much more than break your nose."

"I didn't think you'd care. You wanted the hacker dead."

"I didn't know that he, is in fact, a *she*!"

"It never mattered before."

He's right. It never did. Man, woman, a damn unicorn sprouting rainbows and sparkles out of its ass—it never mattered. You mess with my business, I destroy you. So why the fuck am I standing here, after knocking my brother's mug, thinking about the woman in my room upstairs, and wondering if I should head up and toss another blanket over her to ward off the chill?

"If you want, I'll off her," he adds.

"You will not touch her," I growl and hit him again.

Guido stumbles backward, falling onto the couch. "What the fuck is wrong with you?" he mumbles into the cushion he's pressing to his face. "And you're bleeding on my rug. What the hell happened?"

Yes. What the fuck is *wrong with me?* I grab a discarded T-shirt from the back of the recliner, then take a seat and start wrapping the garment around my forearm. "The girl cut me with a broken wine bottle."

Guido blinks at me, confusion written all over his face. "Is she a trained agent or something?"

"I don't think so. She just caught me off guard."

"Rafael De Santi. Caught off guard."

"Yes." I nod as I secure the makeshift bandage on my arm. "Do we know her name? She fainted, so I didn't get the chance to ask."

"No. But I took a picture of her. I'm running it through facial recognition and cross-referencing Illinois DMV records and some local government databases in Chicago. I'll see if we have a match."

Guido rises off the couch and heads toward his desk that's shoved to the side and overflowing with crap. "And it looks like we have a match. She's—oh, shit."

"What is it?"

He glances at me over the screen of his laptop, a slightly frantic look in his eyes. "Vasilisa Romanovna Petrova. She's Roman Petrov's daughter." He swallows, hard. "We kidnapped the Russian Bratva's princess."

"You don't say." I lean back and throw my arm over the back of the recliner. "Small world."

"We have to take her back. Right the fuck now! I'm calling the pilot to get the plane prepped."

Yes, sending her home would be the wisest course of action. It's been close to twenty-four hours since Hank and Vinny grabbed her off the street. Knowing Petrov, he's already gathered his men and is ready to annihilate whoever is responsible for his daughter's disappearance.

My mind drifts to the woman I left sleeping in my bed. "Put down your phone."

"What?"

"Now, Guido."

"Fucking with Bratva is a very bad idea. And I'm not talking about kissing potential future jobs with them goodbye. Even if it was a mistake, Petrov can't be reasoned with if it affects any of his people, never mind family members. She's flying back to Chicago tonight."

"I'm not sending her back. Not yet, anyway."

Guido lowers his cell while he stares at me in disbelief. "Are you out of your fucking mind? What are you going to do with her?"

"I haven't decided, yet."

CHAPTER
four

 Vasilisa

T HE SUN IS ON MY FACE. I CAN FEEL ITS WARMTH. A faint scent of brine is in the air, mixed with a masculine fragrance. Strange buzzing not too far away. Crickets? No, it can't be. There are no crickets in Chicago.

The sound of steps. Retreating.

"Mom?" I mumble into the pillow. "Draw the damn drapes."

More footsteps, but further away now. The unmistakable click of a shutting door.

I squint my eyes open. Then, spring up in bed, madly looking around the unfamiliar room.

The walls are the color of pale-terracotta, adorned with stucco detailing and oil paintings depicting Mediterranean landscapes. An aged white wooden bookshelf, filled with dozens of leather-bound tomes, occupies the space between two sets of opened balcony doors. Long sheer curtains sway with the morning breeze.

I scramble down from the bed and do a quick assessment of myself.

My feet are bare. Someone removed my sneakers and socks, but I'm still dressed in the same outfit as yesterday—gray jeans and an oversized shirt—wrinkled to hell from sleeping in it. And then, there are my wrists. Both are wrapped in gauze, right over my injuries from the handcuffs.

Bewildered, I focus on the two doors on the opposite wall, wondering where they lead. As I head across the room and past the couch that faces the fireplace, the soft plush rug tickles the soles of my feet. That masculine essence in the air is stronger around this spot, but there's another smell here, as well. Coffee. I look down at the low table in front of the couch. A single espresso cup sits atop it. The tiny cup is half-empty, as if whoever was drinking the rich-brown nectar left in a hurry. As heavenly as that aroma is, the male scent lingers. Cypress and orange.

Panic grips me. Someone was here while I slept.

"I see you're up and about. I hope you like your accommodations."

My head snaps up, eyes zeroing in on the blond dude from yesterday. He's in jeans again, and a bright-green T-shirt. Leaning on the doorjamb, he's holding a plate overflowing with food. My mouth waters just looking at it.

Swallowing hard and willing my stomach not to rumble, I take a step back. "Were you here the whole night, creep?"

"Excuse me?"

"You left your coffee."

His gaze slides to the espresso cup, eyebrows furrowing, then casually strolls inside, lowering the plate onto the coffee table right next to the abandoned drink.

"You're free to roam around the house and go outside on the patio, but please don't try to run away. The property is surrounded by an electric fence, and cameras monitor the grounds. The security staff are authorized to shoot if they find you trying to escape. Rafael will come to see you later today to discuss your situation."

"My *situation*?" Eyes flaring, I can't believe he has the gall to make that remark.

"Exactly. It would be to your benefit to behave until my brother returns."

"Your brother? So he's in charge around here? I assume he's the one who ordered me kidnapped?"

"Yes. Yes. And yes, again."

"Then, kindly relay this to your brother." I fist my hands and march across the room until I'm standing right in front of this arrogant pissant. "When my father finds out about this, he's going to chop both of you into tiny little pieces. And then, he'll throw those to our dogs. I'm going to enjoy watching them feast on your flesh while I drink margaritas and relish the sound of your intestines being chewed to bits. After, I'll happily wait until the pooches shit out your digested remains."

Guido's lips widen into a lopsided smile. "Thank you for such a detailed explanation, Miss Petrova. I'll be downstairs if you happen to need anything."

I gape at his back as he leaves the room and shuts the enormous door behind him.

The bastards found out who I am. Or, more importantly, who my dad is. Well, no wonder I got upgraded from the basement to this lavish bedroom. I'm certain the "high-and-mighty Rafael" is currently quaking in his boots, trying to find a way to fix his fuckup. I can't wait to see all these assholes on their knees, begging for their lives—in vain.

I reach out and snatch a pastry off the plate, letting the sweetness of the flaky buttery dough and custard dissolve on my tongue. As I'm chewing, I approach the first of two doors on the left side of the room. It opens to a huge office space. The decor is all dark colors, with more bookshelves along the walls. On the far side, an oversized recliner and an occasional table are set on another thick area rug. But toward the front, a massive desk faces the opened French doors that lead to a balcony.

Hurriedly chewing on the croissant, I rush toward the desk, hoping to find a phone or a laptop, anything really, that would let me contact my family. I come up empty. The blond guy—*what the hell was his name? Guido?*—said I'm free to roam through the house, and I intend to do just that. Just as soon as I go to the bathroom, because my bladder is about to burst. I head back into the bedroom and straight toward the door I've yet to explore.

As I'm drying my hands and planning on returning to the office to search it again, my eyes fall on the enormous bathtub. It's one of those vintage claw-foot tubs, big enough to fit at least three people.

I throw a look at the mirror, eyeing my reflection. Dreadful doesn't even come close to describing my current appearance. My hair is tangled, my shirt and pants are filthy, and I have dirt smeared all over my face.

Lovely.

I'm betting the bossy Rafael probably already called my dad, which means he and Mom are on their way here to come get me. If they see me looking this ragged, God knows what they'll think happened to me. Mom will cry. Dad will lose his ever-loving shit. Likely before I get the chance to tell them I'm fine.

It would be better to clean myself up before the 'rents arrive.

I fill the tub, then take off my clothes and submerge in the warm water, letting the images of my kidnappers writhing in pain on the ground crowd my mind. Although I haven't yet met Rafael, I picture him looking similar to his brother. Blond hair cut close to the scalp, green eyes, an athletic build, but more lean than muscular.

Oh, I can't wait to see them all pay.

I surge back up and search for a shower gel. There's only one option, and a bottle of shampoo next to it. Both with that distinct manly scent. I guess I'm staying in Guido's room, using his toiletries. I squeeze a hefty amount of the body wash onto my palm and continue cleaning myself while the crickets' chirping carries inside through the open window overlooking the garden.

Only after I'm bathed and dried, do I realize that I don't have a change of clothes. Holding the fluffy brown towel tightly around me, I tiptoe out of the bathroom directly to the walk-in closet I spied while snooping. There have to be T-shirts and shorts in there. I can't say I find the idea of wearing Guido's clothes appealing, but it's either that or my soiled outfit.

The door to the walk-in opens soundlessly. Several small pod lights flick on, revealing the huge interior and its contents.

Suits. Dozens of them line the rack on my right. Black. Gunmetal gray. Charcoal. I lightly glide my fingers over the exquisite fabrics. I've always found men in suits hot. Maybe because of the serious air that seems to engulf a man dressed in a fine suit. There's always something commanding about his presence. Potent. Seductive.

A few months back, there was a party at Don Rossi's house, with a specific dress code for the evening. Long elegant gowns for women. And of course, suits for men. My ovaries nearly imploded just from the sight alone. Unfortunately, my excitement was short-lived. At Yulia's insistence, I wore her body-hugging black gown with a high slit on the side. My sister also did my makeup. Every man who approached me ended up either staring at my face or my boobs and mumbled nonsense. A few who managed intelligent words, quickly turned whatever meaningful conversation we were having into something they thought would make me fall into their bed.

An almost identical script, with very few minor variations. *Do you know you're the most beautiful woman in the room?* Or, *You look like an angel who descended from the heavens.* And my absolute favorite: *Marry me. We'll make such beautiful babies.* Really, dude? And my sister wonders why I don't go to parties more often.

There is absolutely no worse feeling than chatting with a guy you're beginning to like and realizing he doesn't actually give a fuck who you are, what your interests are, or even what you're talking about. It makes me feel so . . . hollow. Like I'm nothing more than my looks.

I'm a person, damn it! Not just a shiny trinket to play with.

I have thoughts and feelings, and if any of them bothered to ask, I'm actually capable of getting things done. Things where being a female has no bearing.

Maybe, one day, I'll meet a man who'll like me for who I am on the inside, and won't simply be enamored with my exterior. And who won't hightail it when he meets my dad.

Maybe, he'll be a suit guy.

I let go of the lapel on the light-gray jacket I've been fondling and move over to the shirts. Guido, with his laid-back attitude and washed-out jeans, doesn't strike me as someone who likes to wear suits, but he must, considering the obvious. I have only a vague recollection of last night. The post-adrenaline crash and drowsiness hit me hard, but I remember trying to slash Guido's throat with a . . . broken bottle. Guess that didn't work out for me. Then, I was floating. Probably, being carried up the stairs. And there was a rough palm against my cheek. The blondie had to have brought me to his bedroom. That faint scent I smelled when I woke up, I recall inhaling it while I was draped around his neck. Such a shame that a tool like him has such nice taste in clothes and fragrances. I can only hope he wears one of his bespoke suits when Dad kills him.

White. Black. Gray. His button-down shirts are even nicer. I pick a black one (less chance for my boobs to show through the material since I don't have a bra) and slide it off the hanger. My forehead creases as I hold it out in front of me. What the hell is the size of this thing? It looks gigantic. Glancing at the label, I snort. The number makes absolutely no sense to me. All I can think is it must be the Sicilian way of indicating "tent-size." Guido didn't seem that large to me. I check out a few more shirts,

NEVA ALTAJ

but they're all the same measurement. Maybe blondie lost a lot of weight? No wonder he no longer wears these.

Slipping my arms into the shirt, I peer down at myself. I look just like Mom when she wears one of Dad's button-downs. The hem literally reaches past my knees, and the sleeves are almost double the length of my arms. At least no one will be able to tell I'm not wearing panties. I fold the sleeves over my forearms (half a dozen times), then grab one of the ties from a drawer and wrap it around my waist as a belt.

Next step—find a way to contact my family and determine when they're arriving.

Ten thousand square feet of living space and not a single phone. I've even considered trying to use a browser app on a TV, but I didn't find one in any of the common areas. No other people either, excluding the guards I spied making rounds along the formidable-looking barricade of closely spaced thick metal posts connected by row upon row of smooth cable wiring. That must be the electric fence Guido mentioned, and it seems to encircle the property. I think one of the guards was following me, too, because I felt eyes on me from time to time, but I never saw anyone.

I stumbled upon Guido working on his laptop out on the terrace just off the main living room. When I asked about the "lord of the manor's" plans for gracing me with his presence, he just shrugged. The boss man is probably hiding in some hole, chewing his nails to the quick while pondering what kind of casket to order for his own funeral.

After that, I went down to a small beach that can only be reached using narrow stone steps cut into the side of the bluff. No one tried to stop me. Maybe because it's a dead end, with high cliffs on the three sides and an endless sea on the fourth. Zero escape options. I lounged on the warm sand for almost an

48

hour, then returned to the villa and checked out all the rooms again. One set looked like someone's private living quarters with vastly different décor from the rest of the house—more modern—but some of the doors within were locked. Must be the abode belonging to the "mighty" brother.

Holy shit, there's more life in the catacombs than in this beautiful but devoid place. After hours of exploring, I did bump into a maid while she was wiping down the kitchen counter, and then again when she carried folded towels up the stairs. But both times, as soon as she saw me, she hightailed it to God knows where.

Continuing to drift aimlessly from room to room, I head into the kitchen and open the fridge. Several ready-to-eat packaged entrées are stacked on the shelves. I move mushroom pasta to the side (I tried some of it earlier in the day) and pull out a chicken salad.

I stab a piece of meat, but after a moment, just stick everything back into the fridge. I'm not hungry. I just want to go home, damn it. The round white clock on the wall shows it's almost eleven in the evening. Why am I still here?

There's an opened bottle of red wine on the fridge door. I don't remember seeing it here before. The label is the same as on the bottle I broke in the cellar, and that memory instantly pops into my mind. I pour myself a glass and meander out of the kitchen.

A warm breeze blows my hair as I step out onto the wide terrace overlooking the sea and prop my elbows on the railing. If I weren't a prisoner here, I'd be enjoying the breathtaking view and the sound of the waves crashing on the shore. Out in the distance along the coast, several tiny twinkling lights are aglow. Straining my eyes into the darkness, I lean forward, trying to decipher what they are.

"Fishing boats," a deep male voice rumbles behind me.

I swing around, startled, and the wine splashes everywhere,

including all over my borrowed outfit. With no lamps on the terrace, the only illumination is the ambient light spilling from inside the house through the massive French windows and doors. There's not enough of it, though, to chase away the shadows outside. The figure of a man—a very broad, muscular man—is sitting on the wicker recliner at the patio's far side. His face is hidden by the darkness, but I can see that he's wearing dress pants and a button-down, with a vest over the top. His sleeves are rolled up to his elbows. A length of white bandage is wrapped around his right forearm.

"I got your message." He lifts the wineglass in his hand and takes a sip. "Very eloquent, Miss Petrova. I especially liked the part about defecating dogs."

Goose bumps run down my arms from the rich timbre of his voice. It's hoarse and gruff, but the strong Italian accent makes it sound less gravelly. There isn't a single soft note in it. With his powerfully built body laid back so casually, I feel like I'm facing an indomitable large feline. One who's eyeing his next meal. Me.

"Rafael, I presume?" I swallow as I take him in. He doesn't seem like he's been quaking in his boots, concerned about his life. "When is my dad arriving?"

"I wasn't aware that Pakhan Petrov intended to visit Sicily."

"He's coming to take me home." I retreat a step while panic begins to rise from the pit of my stomach. "You told him I'm here."

"Have I? Why would I do that?"

"Because you know who I am. And because my father is going to kill you if you don't let me go."

He takes another sip of the wine. "Who your father is has no bearing on my plans."

"What . . . plans?" I manage to ask as panic ratchets into terror.

"You will be fixing the mess you created when you intruded into my company's network system, for starters."

"I . . . I have no idea what you're talking about. What system?"

"Please, Miss Petrova, let's not play dumb. I had my brother complete an extensive background check on you. You studied computer science. Graduated with a bachelor's degree earlier this month and have been accepted into an advanced software engineering master's program." An aura of impending doom descends with his every word. "Was it your father who put you up to this? Got you to breach my company's firewalls and create back doors to the network? What was your goal? Find your way to my client list?"

"What?" I choke out. "No. My dad had nothing to do with that."

"So it *was* you, after all."

Shit. I look away. "Yes."

"What was the purpose of your actions?"

"Your IT security is good. It was a challenge to break it. And I was . . . bored."

"You were bored?" His voice is hushed, but there is a dangerous edge to it now. "I have four people working on identifying whatever malware or shit you downloaded into my systems. What you did has left a clusterfuck that they still haven't managed to untangle."

This conversation isn't going the way I expected. I was sure he'd apologize, then stumble over his feet to send me home as soon as possible. This is the furthest thing from that.

With the wind blowing in my face, hurling my hair into my eyes, I take another step back.

"Listen, I'm sorry. I won't do it again, okay? It's just a tiny bit of code. I can fix it the moment I get home. Can you please let me go?"

"One's actions bear consequences, Miss Petrova. That's how

the real world works. Your little game left my company vulnerable to more cyberattacks. So, no, I will not let you go." He lifts his ankle onto the opposite knee and leans back. "I want to offer you a job."

"A job?" It comes out as a shrill while I stare at this lunatic. "You had me kidnapped, drugged, flown to another continent, thrown into a goddamned cellar, and now you expect me to work for you?"

"Yes, I think that sums up the situation rather well. I'm offering three million for your services."

A hysterical laugh escapes me. He's insane! "You can take your millions and shove them up your ass! I demand to be sent home. Right the fuck now."

"I'm afraid that's not an option." Rafael takes out his phone and tosses it to me. "Play the video."

I almost don't catch the thing.

The still image displays high-rise rooftops. The familiar *play* control taunts me from the center of the screen. I press the triangle, starting the video.

Sky. Rooftops. The camera pans, focusing on a man in an all-black tactical outfit, lying close to the building's edge. He's holding a sniper rifle pointed at something on the ground, his eye is trained on the scope.

The view shifts to the left, zooming in on a top-floor window of the building across the street. Another man with a long-range weapon.

I swallow past the knot in my throat, and my grip on the phone tightens.

The camera moves again, to the sidewalk thirty or so stories below. Then, the angle suddenly changes—the same sidewalk, but now the video is being taken from street level. The shot is of a couple, standing with their backs to the lens. The woman has long black hair, and she's clutching the man's forearm in a viselike grip while he holds a phone to his ear. He looks down at the woman and shakes his head, then lowers the phone. They turn around, and rush down the street.

The wineglass slips from my hand and crashes on the stone tiles beneath my bare feet, shards ricocheting everywhere around me.

Mom and Dad.

"You bastard," I whisper. My lips tremble as I stare at the screen.

"Everyone has a price." Rafael's deep voice breaks through my stupor, sounding closer than earlier.

Turning in the direction of that baritone, I come abreast of the broad male chest. I tilt my head up. And up. The light from inside the house has turned Rafael's enormous form into a silhouette, and his face remains hidden by shadows.

"What do you need me to do?" I nearly sob.

His hands take hold of my waist, lifting me. I drop the phone, grabbing at his forearms and kicking my legs.

"Let go of me!"

Rafael ignores my protests, hoisting me higher until our faces are nearly aligned. His breath fans my skin while the woodsy aroma of cypress and citrusy notes of oranges tingle my nostrils. It's the scent I smelled in the upstairs bedroom. *His* bedroom. A small shudder runs down my spine, but this time, it's not from fear. His presence is so profound, I'm finding it hard to draw enough air into my lungs. He seems absolutely unperturbed by the possible consequences of his actions, and I don't think he's faking it. He actually doesn't give a fuck, completely unconcerned about my father's wrath.

"What do you want from me?" I ask again.

He pulls me a little closer. The way he casually holds me, a foot off the ground, is distressing. But in a ridiculously sensual sort of way.

"I want you to overhaul my digital security systems, Miss Petrova."

Rafael

Barely containing my laughter, I watch the expression on Vasilisa's face change from confusion to absolute shock. You'd think I just asked her to kill someone for me.

"You kidnapped me so I could upgrade your firewalls?"

Did I? I'm not exactly sure. When I ordered my men to deliver the fucking hacker, I intended to torture the stupid dick for a bit as punishment for screwing around with my business, and then dispose of him. I never expected a slip-of-a-girl. One who gave my men a beatdown, then tried to slice open my throat. I think that's the first time ever a woman has tried to kill me. And I find it hot as hell.

"Not just the firewalls. I want you to analyze the digital environment used by my company and then rewrite the security protocols for every IT system."

Vasilisa's eyes widen in pure astonishment. With the light at my back reflecting in her dark-as-night irises, those expressive orbs seem aglow. Between her fury and determination, this unpredictable woman has fire in her doe-like eyes. Beautiful doesn't even come close to describing her.

A soft, creamy complexion. Thin, arched eyebrows that frame those mesmerizing onyx eyes. Prominent cheekbones tapering gently to a narrow chin. Small, straight nose. And then, there's her delectable pink mouth, with rosy, kissable lips. The lower one is slightly fuller than the upper, beckoning a man to pull it between his teeth. Every part of her facial features is perfect, so much so that the entire thing defies reality. The sight is simply unearthly, and it's impossible to look away from her.

"That could take days," she blurts out.

Yes, in theory. In reality, however, it will take as long as I want it to take. Vasilisa Petrova might be the most beautiful creature who has ever crossed my path, but for the first time in my life, I'm drawn to a woman because of more than just her looks.

She's bold. Courageous. Feisty. But also kind of grumpy, in such an adorable way.

And I don't intend to let her slip away from me.

I tilt my head and behold the strands of her silky hair that have fallen over her diamond-shaped face. Jet-black, just like the night sky overhead. The tendrils flutter on the breeze, partially obscuring my view of her slightly frantic eyes. I wish I could sweep the wisps behind her dainty ears, but my hands are occupied, wrapped around her slender waist.

"You'll stay as long as it takes. Until you're finished," I say and blow a breath across her face, puffing away the glossy strands.

Vasilisa blinks, then furrows her eyebrows. She still has a hold of my forearms, but her grip has mercifully loosened, and I'm grateful since her nails were digging right into the cut she made last night.

"Why did you do that?" she mumbles.

"I like looking people in the eyes when I speak with them."

Glass crunches under my shoes when I carry my prisoner over the shattered stemware, then slowly lower Vasilisa to the ground next to the guardrail edging the terrace. She tries to step aside, but I plant my palms on the railing at her back, caging her with my arms.

"A word of advice, Miss Petrova. Don't test me. If you try to escape or contact anyone to let them know where you are, I'll give the order to have your family executed. Not just your parents. Your brother and sister will be included in that. But, if you follow the rules, when your work here is complete, you'll be free to go. Are we clear?"

Her body quivers, and I expect weeping to be not far behind. Instead, she juts out her chin and levels me with that stubborn gaze. Bravado, not tears, pours out of her. But as much as she tries to hide her fear, I can see the leashed alarm in her dark glossy depths.

"Why should I believe you? What guarantee is there that you'll let me go after I fix your systems?"

"End goal. It's why I'm trusting you not to run and letting you stay in a nice bedroom instead of keeping you tied up in the cellar for the duration of our deal." I lean forward. "Do you want to go back to the basement?"

Those dark eyes narrow at me in disdain. "I hope you die a very slow and extremely painful death."

"I'll take that as a *no*. Good. Mutual trust is the foundation for all successful endeavors. We'll start tomorrow evening, after I return from work." I let my gaze slide down to her chest, eyeing the cleavage peeking out between the lapels of the man's dress shirt she has on. "Why are you wearing my shirt?"

"What? I thought it was your brother's," she bites out, eyes flashing in exasperation. "If I'd known—You know what . . . never mind. I'll just go find him and ask if he has something I can borrow, if it bothers you that much."

Rage surges inside me. Just a thought of her dressed in anything that belongs to another man, even my brother's, makes my skin crawl. "No. You won't be wearing Guido's shit."

"If I'm being held prisoner here, I need clothes!"

I guess she does. But I quite like how she looks in my shirt. "Feel free to help yourself to anything you want from my closet."

Vasilisa leans back. "Not happening."

She's going to fall off the damn terrace. My hand slides to the small of her back, holding her steady. "Then, you'll walk around naked."

"Fuck you," she says through her teeth. "Get your hand off me."

Reluctantly, I pull away but allow my fingers to graze her

arm in the process. "I look forward to doing business with you, Miss Petrova."

"Well, the feeling is most definitely not mutual." She steps around me and storms inside the house.

I follow her with my eyes as she dashes across the living room and up the stairs, then head back to my lounging spot. My bedroom is just above the terrace, so I have a clear view of the figure that steps onto the upper balcony five minutes later.

The breeze makes her hair float around her face as she leans over the railing, gaze focused on the fishing boats bobbing in the distance, and her bare toes peek out through the guardrail posts. Retrieving my glass of wine from the patio table, I shift further into the shadows, leaning on the stone wall at my back, and keep my eager eyes on my feisty Russian princess.

"What do you mean 'she's staying here'?" Guido gapes at me. "I thought you had our team shoot that video to pressure her not to reveal our identities to Petrov after we send her back."

"That video is insurance. But for another purpose." I lean back on the couch. "I offered her a job."

"You offered a job to a woman you had kidnapped?"

"Yes. I offered her three million dollars for her services. She declined. Her exact words were: 'Take your millions and shove them up your ass.'"

Guido sighs and sits on the recliner across from me. "Fucking Christ. What kind of services?"

"It looks like our network crashed unexpectedly. I want her to fix it."

"Other than the back door she somehow created, there's nothing wrong with our systems."

"There is now. I called Mitch and ordered his guys to scramble our root directories and applications until they barely function. Miss Petrova has been persuaded to remain as our guest until all of the issues are resolved. Since she was not receptive to my money, I was forced to find a currency that she could not reject. Seems she likes her family and is willing to fix our IT systems to deter the threat on their lives."

"So how long is this 'fix' going to take?"

"I instructed Mitch to keep up the sabotage, covertly of course, until I say otherwise." I glance down at my bandaged forearm and smile.

"You like her."

"Yes."

"Jesus fuck, Raff. I know you're accustomed to getting anything you want, women included, but this? Blackmailing this girl to stay here by threatening to kill her parents? There are hundreds of women—beautiful women—who would rush to your side. All you need to do is snap your fingers."

"You mean, wave my credit card."

"Rafael—"

"The subject is closed," I interrupt. "I'm going to pay a visit to Calogero tomorrow. One of his goons has been seen at the Catania Port. Our godfather will keep his butt in Palermo, as we agreed, or he won't enjoy the reminder I'll mete out. I won't allow him to infringe on what's mine."

When I returned to Sicily, Mancuzo—the Cosa Nostra Don at the time—had already lost his hold over most of the eastern part of the island. The territory from Catania to Ragusa was ruled by gangs. It took me two years to rectify that situation and take control of the area. After Calogero stepped into his role within the Family, I agreed to his dominion across western Sicily, but the east coast is under my reign.

"Calogero is bleeding money from using the cruise ships and passenger ferries to transport his product. He needs access to the main cargo shipping lines, and those all run through the Port of Catania. I don't think he'll let it go, Raff."

"Not my problem. I don't want his drugs in my port." I grab my jacket off the back of the sofa and stand up. "I'm going to bed."

"And where will that be, if I may ask? Since, apparently, you gave up your bedroom to our hostage."

"Guest room."

"Why not move her there instead?"

I meet my brother's gaze. "Because the only bed she'll be sleeping in from now on, is mine."

CHAPTER
five

Rafael

THE DECREPIT TAVERNA WHERE CALOGERO TYPICALLY spends his afternoons is located on a dead-end street in the old part of Palermo. Except for the ravages of time and the relentless Mediterranean sun, the place hasn't changed one bit in all the years. The shithole I remember from my youth still looks like a shithole, complete with paint peeling off its outside surfaces.

As I open the rickety door and step inside the gloomy interior, I'm hit with the stench of stale alcohol and the rancid smell of cigar smoke. In addition to that, drifting through the open back door and hanging heavily in the air, is an unmistakable scent of fish from the nearby market. Every seat in this putrid place is vacant. The establishment's only patron is sitting at a small garden table set up on the patio. He's in his early seventies and leaning over a spread-out newspaper, sipping coffee. Behind him, with their backs to the wall but only a few feet away, are two armed men. Their eyes follow me as I cross the empty taverna, heading toward the leader of the Sicilian Mafia.

"What business brings you here, Rafael?" Calogero lifts the coffee cup to his mouth; his eyes never leave the newspaper.

I take a seat across the table and take him in. He might act mighty and all-important in front of his men, but we both know the only reason he's in this leadership position now is because the Family was in complete disarray after I killed the previous don.

"I think you know the answer to that question."

My godfather finally looks up, but his gaze only lingers on my face for the briefest of moments before it flits away. "I have no idea what you're talking about."

I shake my head. Seeing this man wrings hatred in every fiber of my being.

In Italy, a godparent is as close as one can be next to a familial relationship. Some people even consider this bond stronger than true blood ties. When I was a kid, this man was my role model. After my father was killed, Calogero stepped in to fill his shoes. He took my mother, brother, and me under his protection. When Mom and Calogero got together, I never held it against either of them. I believed my godfather was a good man. But the truth is—he was a coward. He might be the don now, but he is still the same old chickenshit who did nothing when his predecessor declared my mother a traitor and executed her.

"Next time I catch one of your men in Catania trying to bribe the port workers, I'll cut out his tongue, and you'll find his dead body dumped at your front door." I slam my hand on the surface of the table, making the coffee cup and the water glass rattle. "Do not fuck with me, *cumpari*. Or you may end up with your throat slit open just like Mancuso."

"You are a disgrace to your blood and to the Family, Rafael," he says through his teeth. His eyes drop to my left arm. "Swearing fealty to our enemies. If you had an ounce of decency, you would have removed their mark long ago."

I lean forward, getting in his face. "It may come as a surprise to you, but some people own their choices."

Calogero's lips pull into a sneer. "You have some nerve. Walking in here as if you own the place, threatening me. One word from me, and you'll never leave this place alive. And a week from now, someone will find your worthless hide washed up on the beach." He tilts his head toward the bodyguards at his back, who immediately reach into their jackets, going for their weapons.

"Really?" I lift my hand, snapping my fingers.

A whooshing sound pierces the air. The two bodyguards hit the ground with a loud thump.

Another bullet hits my uncle's cup on the table, and it explodes into minuscule fragments, coffee splashing his shocked face and soaking the newspaper.

"Words are the only thing you were ever good at." I rise and straighten my jacket. "Keep your men away from my territory. This is my last warning."

I can feel Calogero's eyes on my back as I tread through the bleak taverna and step out onto the street. Men with boxes full of fish or vegetables under their arms hurry down the cobblestone road, either none the wiser about what happened just moments ago or, more likely, not even giving a shit about it. I will never understand why my godfather keeps frequenting this dump. Probably because it was where Don Mancuso conducted his business, and Calogero has always been a man of tradition.

Glancing at the second-story window across the way where another one of my men is holding position, I give him the nod and head toward the next street, to the outdoor market. It's a roundabout route to where I parked my car, but I feel nostalgic.

When I was little, my father often brought me with him when he came to Palermo. As a soldier for Mancuso, he regularly reported to the don, and I spent hours running around the market—playing and often stealing fruit here and there—while

Dad was holed up at that taverna. I would often slip a fig into my pocket when the seller wasn't paying attention. An orange, if my hoodie was baggy enough to hide it. A cluster of white grapes that I then picked and ate while strolling between the stands. It's not that we couldn't afford the delicious treats. Being in charge of overseeing the collection of debts for the don, my father earned well. But I still stole whenever I could. It was a game for me.

I pause at the edge of the market, next to a stand with wicker baskets full of ripe red cherries. My eyes drift over the crowd of locals busying around—picking out produce, laughing. If I wanted to, I could buy this whole place. Every single thing that's on display, along with the people. Too bad it wouldn't bring even a speck of the excitement slipping that one little fig into my pocket elicited.

Turning away from the colorful stall, I put on my sunglasses and head through the market. I can feel everyone's stares, but each contact lasts only a fraction of a moment before their eyes quickly dart elsewhere, and each person in my way zips from my path.

I'm used to their reaction. Even with shades partially obscuring my face, most of the damage is clearly visible.

Some of the things that happened after the blast on my last job for Dushku remain hazy. I recall coming to in an ambulance. Jemin was next to me, his gun pointed at the paramedic. Grabbing me under my arms, he basically dragged me out of the emergency vehicle and stuffed my ass into the back of his car. Then, I must have passed out again. During the drive, I regained consciousness a couple of times. The pain was excruciating. By the time we arrived at the rundown house in the suburbs, I was mostly checked out.

Jemin hollered and had two guys carry me inside a garage and deposit me on a workbench where a 'doctor' spent hours stitching me back together. I lived, despite the less-than-sterile conditions, miraculously avoiding any of my wounds getting infected. The final result, however, was a mess of badly patched muscles and warped skin.

It's no wonder people can't handle looking at me now. Their hushed murmurs mix with the cries of excited vendors. It's a cacophony of contradiction. One I'm well and truly used to.

I pull out my phone and dial Onofredo, the head of security at my house.

"Boss?"

"How many times?" I ask.

"I'm sorry, I don't understand."

"How many times since this morning has our little guest tried to escape?"

"She hasn't."

I halt. "What has she been doing then?"

"Snooping. She went through the desk drawers and cabinets in your office. Even checked under the recliner cushion. Oh, and she found your safe and spent nearly half an hour trying to crack the combination."

I feel the corners of my lips tilt upward. "And then?"

"She's been reorganizing your bookshelves."

"What?"

"Yeah. She pulled off every book, lined them up on the floor, and then started putting them back on the shelves in a different order. Otto checked on her fifteen minutes ago. She was still at it."

"And you're positive she didn't try to slip away?"

"Absolutely."

I furrow my eyebrows. "Alright. Keep me posted."

The crowd continues to part before me like the Red Sea as I meander between the stands. As usual, sellers are yelling, offering their goods, beckoning passersby to approach. A young woman to my left holds a wooden board laden with small pieces of cut cheese and cured meats, inviting customers to taste the samples.

"*Signore?*" she calls after me. "*Vuole provare del prosciutto?*"

I stop and glance over my shoulder. The girl is lifting the platter toward me, a flirtatious grin dancing across her lips. As soon as she eyes my face, though, she tenses. Her smile disappears, and she quickly looks away. Typical.

Continuing my stroll through the market, my mind turns to my beautiful hostage and how cute she looked wearing my shirt. Before I left this morning, I ordered the maid to throw Vasilisa's clothes into the trash. I told myself it was punishment for her nerve to fuck with my life, but in truth, I simply enjoyed the primal possessiveness that overcame me when I saw her in my clothes. I wanted her implicitly marked as mine. I've never felt anything even remotely similar toward another woman before. With over a dozen men guarding the grounds of my property, even though she might not see them—as ordered—it doesn't mean they won't see her. And having my feisty princess dressed in my shirt is a big enough sign that she's off-limits.

As I'm approaching the end of the market, my eyes fall on a stand with an assortment of local fruit. Peaches, *nespole*, and strawberries grace the wicker baskets in front of the seller who's dealing with a customer. Off in the corner, there is a small bowl with a few green figs in it. I didn't think they were yet in season. I hasten my step and adjust my route so I pass right next to the counter. And slip one of the figs into my pocket.

Vasilisa

I place the last book, Émile Zola's *Nana*, on the lowest shelf and take a few steps back, observing my work. This morning, I removed all the books and sorted them by color. It took almost four hours. Most of the afternoon, I spent poking around the villa devoid of another living soul. Then, I came back into Rafael's office and reorganized the books again, in alphabetical order by author's name this time.

Reorganizing things is something I do when I'm stressed. It gives me a sense of control, even if it's over something mundane and meaningless. And currently, nothing in my life feels like it's within my control.

Last night, I barely slept a wink. I spent nearly all of it sitting on the huge bed, wrapped in a blanket and clutching a knife I swiped from the kitchen. Just in case the scumbag got the idea to blackmail me into having sex with him, as well. Only once dawn started breaking did I allow myself to succumb to a couple of hours of restless sleep. I woke up feeling like a wreck, and now I'm even worse off after moving all those tomes around. Twice.

There was no useful information whatsoever in the papers I found on Rafael's desk. I came across something that looked like a lease to a warehouse in the name of the company I hacked—Delta Security—which I assume is his, but the contract was signed by someone else. Printouts of specifications for some sort of surveillance equipment. And a few random receipts for things I couldn't decipher since they were in Italian.

But I did discover a safe that spiked my hopes behind one of the paintings. I couldn't open it, though.

I still know practically nothing about the man who is holding me hostage. Nothing, except his name. And that he likes to read. A lot, based on the volume of books in here. Over nine hundred in total.

It's the most unusual collection. Classic literature. Philosophy. Finance. Chemistry textbooks. Several tomes on human anatomy, with one in particular focused solely on the cardiovascular system. The twelve-volume set of *The History of the Decline and Fall of the Roman Empire*. Even several books on horticulture and botany. Those really made my eyebrows rise.

I'd never have pinned Rafael as a man interested in gardening, but he obviously is, since huge sections within these texts are highlighted, and the hardbacks seem well used.

There are also a few dozen novels. I would love to get lost in a book and alleviate some of my stress through a good story, but most of Rafael's books are in Italian. The only two I stumbled upon that are in English are murder mysteries, and considering my situation . . . Yeah, no thank you.

Mm-hmm . . . Now that I think about it, Rafael hasn't actually threatened me directly. My family, yes. But not me. There were zero mentions of physical harm—no beatings, chopping off of fingers, or threats of death if I didn't do his bidding. Instead, he personally carried me upstairs, treated my wrists, and removed my shoes and socks before tucking me into bed. In his own bedroom, which he seems to have surrendered for my use. All of that after I tried to slice open his throat. I cringe, remembering his bandaged arm. I wounded him in self-defense, but I still feel bad for hurting him.

Rolling up the sleeves that have unwound once again, I pick up the empty plate from the lunch the maid brought me and head out of Rafael's office.

Just like earlier, the house appears completely abandoned. No creatures stir as I pass by beautifully decorated rooms. It's eerie as fuck, yet I can't help but stop every once in a while to admire the rustic elegance of the decor. Even as someone with zero knowledge of interior design, I can clearly see that every piece of furniture and every accent was chosen to complement the mansion's understated grace.

Every room has enormous French doors or windows that open wide and let in the warmth and intoxicating scents of the Mediterranean, making it feel like the house itself is a part of the natural landscape. Still, it's an odd sensation to be inside such a gigantic space, entirely alone. Each time the wooden floorboards creak under my bare feet, I startle.

The vast kitchen greets me with haunting silence. There's no sign of the maid who delivered my meal. The girl seemed utterly terrified as she tiptoed into the office and found me cross-legged on the floor, surrounded by stacks of thick hardcovers. She gaped at me for a few moments before leaving the plate on the pile of books and hurrying out as fast as her feet would carry her.

Maybe she thought I was crazy. Can't blame her if she did. I doubt it's normal behavior for a hostage to sort her captor's books instead of trying to find a way to escape. But running is not an option for me. I'm certain Rafael was serious when he threatened to kill my family if I tried to get away. I could hear it—crystal-clear—in the tone of his voice.

He also said no one will bother me here, which has proved true so far. With that, I'm daring to believe that he'll let me go after I fix the mess I've made. I'm still not certain how that actually happened, but whatever. I just want to get on with it and get it done as fast as possible so I can go home.

And I would do that if only "his tyrannical ass" would appear already. It's ten in the evening! *Goddammit.*

I'm stuffing cold grilled zucchini into my mouth at the kitchen island when the sound of a car door being shut brings me out of my reverie. I rush toward the window that overlooks the driveway and lean over the sill, catching a glimpse of a huge male shape stepping inside the house.

He is finally back. Rafael. The almighty tsar of this outlandish prison.

Anger and irritation swirl inside my chest as I hurry across the kitchen toward the entrance hall. That son of a bitch spewed his malice, threatened to hurt my family if I don't do his bidding, but then left me to worry the entire day, rotting in paradise.

When I reach the entry hall, Rafael has already ascended to the second-floor landing.

"Nice of you to finally show up!" I call after him.

He stops and slowly turns to face me. Even though he's shrouded by shadows since the upper floor's lights are off, I know he's looking right at me. I know it instinctively—like a prey that can sense a predator's deathly focus, realizing too late that some fates are impossible to escape.

"Eager to start fixing your handiwork?" His low, throaty voice fills the space between us.

"Extremely."

"Go get my laptop from Guido. I'll be waiting for you in my office."

I watch his retreating form as he disappears around the corner, then curse and head toward the east wing, to what I've discovered is his brother's apartment.

"This is a mess," I mumble, staring at the laptop screen. Getting rid of the code I changed took less than ten minutes, but the catastrophe of missing strings and wrong commands I'm looking at can't be the result of that. "It didn't look like this the last time I visited your network."

"Visited? Nice euphemism for breaking the law by hacking into an unauthorized system, Miss Petrova. My company isn't a gallery exhibit."

I look beyond the screen, my eyes focusing on his imposing frame leaning back in the recliner on the far side of the room. Other than the small desk lamp beside me, every light in the office is off. The faint glow that does reach him allows me to see that he's in a three-piece suit again, but little of anything else.

"Says the guy who kidnaps women off the street," I comment, then go back to inspecting the code.

Rafael was already lounging on that chair when I came in carrying the laptop. In his gruff voice, he told me to take a seat at the desk and get started. Since then, he's remained nothing more than a dark shape. Silent, for the most part.

Is he brooding?

Planning my demise? Watching me?

What is he hiding?

"Do you have rabies, Rafael?"

"I don't believe so. Why do you ask?"

"You sure?" I glance at him again. "No fever, muscle spasms, hallucinations?" I briefly pause to give him time to respond, but he remains mute. "Because you seem to be experiencing sensitivity to light. Should I be concerned that you might pounce? Try to bite me?"

A deep laugh thunders from the shadows, rich and velvety, filling the space. My fingers hover above the keyboard as that sound swaddles me, like a thick, warm blanket.

"If I start experiencing those symptoms, I'll let you know."

Ugh. Not only does he wear suits and smell amazing, but he can also take a joke at his expense. It's as if the universe got a hold of my "perfect man" checklist and started ticking off all the boxes. Too bad Rafael is a kidnapping, blackmailing bastard.

Still, I'm curious to know what he looks like.

"I'll do what I can from here, but I'll need to check your main server at some point. Is it in the house?"

"It's at my corporate building, in Taormina."

"I'll need access to it." My eyes dart to him over the laptop's edge. "And I'll need clothes. Your cleaning staff seem to have taken away my things. I want them back."

"Yet, you appear to be handling that situation rather well. That's my favorite shirt, by the way." How he says it, with a hint of amusement in his tone, makes me wonder if there isn't some hidden meaning behind his words.

"Is this some twisted payback? Weird psychological torture to make me feel more powerless or something?"

"Maybe. Or maybe I just enjoy the sight of you in my clothes, Miss Petrova."

I swallow, brushing off the silly excitement that swells within me from the husky, deep timbre of his voice. Like a lover seducing his partner into bed, each syllable strokes my skin, promising naughty carnal things.

"I will not go around wearing your tent-size shirts. Also, I need underwear, mister."

"That can be arranged," Rafael says and leans forward, placing his forearms on his knees. Suddenly, it's twenty degrees hotter in here. I can feel his eyes on me, searing me from the darkness.

Taking a deep breath, I push up the sleeves of the borrowed shirt that keep slipping down my arms. Pulling up the diagnostic software, I set it to run a scan of the system, then grab a pencil from the desk drawer and start chewing on it.

"Why did you reorganize my bookshelves?"

"It's therapeutic," I mumble around the good old HB2 in my mouth while warnings pop up on the screen. The invoicing application in the accounting directory is flagged as non-responsive. The data storage system has a warning about updates not being installed. Even the maintenance system shows errors.

"This is not possible," I murmur, gaping at the list that keeps growing. "My code was only designed to create a back door, not to fuck up the rest of the network."

"Maybe someone else stumbled upon your 'back door' and decided to sabotage my company. My competition, most likely."

I throw him a look. "You seem awfully calm about that fact."

"Why shouldn't I be? You're going to fix everything."

The pencil cracks between my teeth, so I take it out and refocus on the laptop screen. The scan is still running. My eyes wander to the single green fig lying on the desk by the pen holder. It was there when I came into the room, looking scrumptious as hell, tempting me to take a bite. I reach out and pick up the fruit. The moment my teeth break the smooth leathery skin, sweetness fills my mouth, and I moan.

"You like it?"

I glance at my kidnapper. "Yes. I've only tried figs once before, and those weren't even half this tasty."

"You know what they say—stolen fruit always tastes sweeter."

"You stole it?" I ask, munching on the bell-shaped delicacy. "Why? You're obviously loaded."

"Old habits die hard."

I arch an eyebrow, waiting for him to elaborate. He doesn't. I shrug and get back to watching the diagnostic program run its course. Minutes pass. An hour. Rafael remains in his spot, observing me in silence.

It's disturbing.

Unnerving beyond all measure.

I like it.

But feeling his steadfast stare is making me fidgety. The urge to glance at him magnifies with every passing second, and it's getting harder to fight the pull.

Squirming in my seat, I grab the small pad of yellow sticky notes and start doodling on it with the ruined pencil. No one would ever accuse me of inheriting my mom's artistic talent—Yulia is the lucky recipient of that—but I need something to focus on. Something that will keep my eyes from wandering to the massive shadow at the far end of the room.

I try drawing a bird, but I keep getting distracted by Rafael's mere presence. Even as I succeed in not glancing his way once, my poor creation ends up looking like a horse.

In this deafening silence, while the scanning process steadily progresses, I swear that I can feel my captor's eyes boring holes into my head. Crumpling the note, I throw it away and start another sketch. I draw the shape of a man sitting on a chair. Okay, it's a stick figure, wearing pants, but the idea is the same. I add a jacket and a vest underneath, which ends up looking like an apron. Then, a big wide mouth full of sharp teeth. To finish, I draw a speech bubble.

Fix your mess, Miss Petrova!

A smile pulls at my lips as I tear the sticky note from the pad and attach it to the top right corner of the laptop screen. It's really bad, actually. Yulia spent hours trying to teach me how to draw. Somehow she's always managed to transform weird cylinder shapes into people's faces, but I've never quite got the concept.

When I glance up, Rafael is still laid back in his recliner, arms crossed over his chest. I didn't notice him removing his suit jacket, but it's now lying on the armrest. The combination of the white shirt and dark vest he's wearing makes his chest look even wider.

A single ding signals the end of the diagnostic scan, and the results window displays sixty-seven detected errors. More than half are flagged as critical.

"Good. The analytics are done. I'll start with the accounting program first thing in the morning." I close the laptop with a loud clap and bend to unplug the power cord.

"The laptop stays here. We'll continue tomorrow evening. Same time."

"And what am I supposed to do the whole day until then?"

"You're free to do whatever you wish, as long as you keep our agreement in mind. Good night, Miss Petrova."

Gritting my teeth, I rise and march straight to the door that leads from the office to the bedroom where I've been sleeping. And I make sure to slam it closed in my wake.

I head to the en suite bathroom to take a shower and brush my teeth, then put on another of Rafael's fancy shirts, using it as a nightgown.

I'm somewhat comforted that Rafael doesn't seem to want anything from me other than fixing his damn computer system.

Aside from those few comments about my clothes, he hasn't said or done anything that tells me he's interested in me.

It's strange. I'm so used to guys trying to get me into their bed within minutes of meeting me. Rafael's apparent indifference has left me feeling slightly confused.

Maybe I'm simply not his type?

Good!

Right?

I fall asleep with a kaleidoscope of images occupying my mind. Lines of code. The big blue expanse of the sea and the sun reflecting off the glistening waters. And the concealed face of a man watching me from a darkened corner.

CHAPTER
six

S TILL A BIT UNNERVED BY THE BAFFLING HOURS OF PUSH-and-pull with Rafael in his office last night, I emerge from the bedroom, ready to head downstairs for breakfast. But greeting me on the other side of the door is a big white bag with intricate golden handles. An elaborate gold logo gleams on the front panel—*Albini's*—printed in a traditional script. Crouching, I carefully untie the gold ribbon bow that's holding the sides of the tote together.

Inside, nearly a dozen elegant little boxes, and among them, a velvety-looking white card with the same golden logo on the front. Taking it out, I scan the neat masculine handwriting.

You can keep using my wardrobe for the rest of your attire.

R.

I lift one of the boxes, peeking under the lid. A beautiful black lace lingerie set is nestled inside. I'm certain the rest of the boxes will contain more of the same.

"The nerve of that man," I growl, but I'm unable to stop

the corners of my mouth from curving upward ever so slightly. I take the bag inside and leave the contents on top of the bedcovers, my mind tripping over the images of the delicate lace in Rafael's hands.

A tremor runs through me. I can almost feel the roughness of those hands as they glide across my heated skin, pulling the exquisite black thong and sending that scrap of lace to join the matching bra somewhere over his shoulder.

Diverting my thoughts from a path best not traveled, I head downstairs, ready to confront the scoundrel.

In the kitchen, I find Guido leaning on the counter and holding up a bowl of cereal, his eyes fixed on the phone lying beside him on the wooden top.

No sign of Rafael.

"I hope there is something other than bird food to eat for breakfast in this house," I say as I pass him on my way to the fridge.

"Doubt it."

"Where's your brother?"

"At work. Why?"

"I need to call my family."

Guido raises an eyebrow at me.

"Based on the system scan I ran yesterday, I'll be staying here for at least a week. Probably more. I need to let them know I'm alive and well."

"I'll check with Rafael, but don't get your hopes up. He won't allow it."

Guido picks up his phone, his thumb working to hit a listed contact—his brother's, I assume—and then holds it up to his ear. His tone changes from easy-going to irritated, rapidly filling with anger as he argues in Italian. When he passes me the phone, his face is a mask of fury.

"Miss Petrova," Rafael grumbles from the other end. "I'm listening, but do make it quick. I'm in a meeting."

"I want to call my family."

"Yes, Guido told me." A strange gurgling sound comes through the line, blended with muffled groaning. "That wasn't a part of our deal."

"They need to know that I'm okay. My parents are probably going out of their minds without a word from me in three days. Please, I'm just going to—"

A shrill howl explodes in my ear, and I quickly pull the phone away. I gape while the screams continue, loud and clear despite the speakerphone being off, until they slowly transform into whimpers.

"Did I interrupt you beating the crap out of someone?" I ask, cautiously returning the phone to the side of my head.

"*Stai zitto!*" Rafael snarls at whoever is on the other end. "Maybe. Did you like your present, vespetta?"

"You're asking me that now?" My eyebrow lifts in astonishment. "If I say no, will you let me call home?"

Another scream erupts from wherever my kidnapper happens to be at the moment, but it's more subdued this time. "Nope."

"Then, I absolutely loved it," I say.

"I'm glad to hear that. You can call your family. No details on where you are, or how you got here, or you know what will happen. *Capito?*"

"Yes."

"Good. Put Guido on."

Based on Guido's sour expression when I pass him the phone, he's not happy with Rafael's decision. They argue for nearly another minute before Rafael's brother hands the device back to me.

"Twenty seconds," he barks. "And you make the call right there."

I stare at the screen, pondering whether I should call Mom or Dad. Dad would undoubtedly lose his shit and start yelling, demanding to know where I am. I won't be able to say a word until he's done. My twenty seconds will be lost. Mom it is, then.

My fingers shake as I punch in the numbers, and when the

line finally connects, I almost break down and start crying. I lose a precious five seconds trying to pull myself together before I can utter a word.

"Hey, Mom."

"Vasya?" my mom's groggy voice comes through the line. "Oh my God! Where are you, baby?! We've been going crazy—"

"I'm fine, Mom. Listen, I can't talk long. I just wanted you to know I'm okay and that I'm coming home in a couple of weeks."

"What? Tell me where you are! Right now!"

"I'll call again in a few days, okay? Love you."

I barely finish before Guido snatches the phone out of my hand and cuts the line. "Time's up. Can't risk them tracing the call."

His tone contains a trace of smugness, as if taking that phone from me is the most gratifying thing he has done in a long time. My teeth squeak from the forceful way I clench them. It's either that or letting the tears welling in the corners of my eyes burst free.

But I won't give this little prick the satisfaction of seeing me cry.

Turning on my heel, I march to the wall cabinet on the opposite side of the kitchen, grabbing a chair from the dining table along the way. The damn thing has to be solid wood because it weighs a ton. By the time I reach my intended destination, my arms hurt from hefting the bulky object. I set the chair next to the cabinetry, climb it, then start pulling glassware off the top shelf and setting it on the counter.

"What are you doing?" Guido asks behind me.

I ignore him, focusing solely on my task of reorganizing. It's the only way I'll be able to distract myself from worrying about my family.

Blindly, I empty the cupboards of cups and glasses that have all been haphazardly placed on one shelf, and the stemware that was mixed in with tumblers and other cocktail glasses.

"*Какой ужасный беспорядок,*" I mumble as I move on to

the middle shelf. They even have cake stands wedged in the same place!

"I asked, what the fuck are you doing?" Guido snarls next to me and slams the cabinet door closed, barely missing my fingers.

Eyes fixed on his hand keeping the door shut, I take a deep breath, then face the dickhead. The look he levels me with is loaded with narrowly restrained contempt and malice.

"Do you have a problem with me, Guido?"

"Yes, I do."

"And what problem might that be?" My voice may sound strong, but truthfully, I'm barely holding myself together. I have no qualms about confronting men with an overabundance of testosterone and asshole personalities under normal circumstances, but this fucked-up situation is proving a bit too much. "The last I checked, I'm not here because I want to be."

Guido's nostrils flare. He leans toward me, getting in my face. "If you get my brother killed, I'll fucking murder you."

Two treacherous tears escape, sliding down my cheeks. Returning his resolute gaze, I make myself smile. "Feel free to try."

He bangs his fist on the cupboard and storms out of the kitchen. Only after he's gone, do I lower myself to the counter, sitting down between the rows of glasses and cups, and wipe my cheeks.

Jesus Christ, what did I get myself into?

And why in the hell does the idea of my dad offing Rafael not sound as tempting as it did before?

Rafael

Magnificent.

There is no better word to describe the woman sitting cross-legged at my desk, mumbling to herself while her fingers fly over the keys as she fixes the mess my IT team purposefully created. Mitch assured me that it would take days just to sort out the financial system, considering how thoroughly they corrupted the software.

It took her a couple of evenings and less than a dozen hours.

Tonight, she's working on the file management system, untangling the permissions to the subfolders of our data repository. Apparently, this should keep her busy for a week. Mitch's guys better have done their jobs properly and scrambled it up real good, otherwise, heads will roll.

"Did that pencil do something to offend you?" I ask, eyeing the thing in question.

Vasilisa lays down the pencil she's been chewing for the past hour and sends me an irritated look. "Nope. It's just an unwitting victim."

"Of what?"

"My thought process. The extent of the clusterfuck I'm trying to resolve here is colossal. It's frustrating. Who set up your NAS?"

"I have no idea what NAS is or who set it up. IT is like hieroglyphs to me."

"Oh?" Her eyebrows arch quizzically. "A man willing to confess that he doesn't possess absolute knowledge on a particular subject? That's a first."

"I'm a rather simple being, vespetta. Give me a goal, and I'll reach it, brutally obliterating all obstacles in my way. I don't have the finesse for solving such cerebral problems, I'm afraid. But I have you and your brilliant mind at my disposal to deal with that now."

Vasilisa stares at me with wide eyes and her lips slightly parted, looking utterly bewildered. Even in the dim light, I can see color creeping into her cheeks. I'll need to work on delivering my compliments, obviously.

"Um ... right." She quickly looks away. "NAS is a data storage device. It should automatically back up twice a day, but instead, the files are being wiped out."

"Mitch would be the person who could clue you in on whatever you need to know about that."

"I'd like to have a word with Mitch, then."

"Okay." Taking out my phone, I extend it toward her. "Here."

Vasilisa's head snaps up. "I didn't mean right now. Christ! It's almost midnight."

"Mitch is paid to be available twenty-four seven. He won't mind." I nod toward the cell. "Call him and ask what you need. Now."

Her eyebrows lift, then she slowly rises and approaches, her steps cautious and guarded. She appears worried that I might pounce on her. And maybe she's right to be, because the temptation to do just that is a barely leashed torrent coursing through me.

She stops a couple of steps in front of me and looks down at my extended hand.

"And you can't just let the man sleep and have him called tomorrow?" she drawls, eyeing the phone. "You're one shitty employer."

"No, I'm not. Every single man who works for me is amply compensated for their service."

"So, are they just that? Employees, nothing more?"

"Extremely well-paid employees." I press the call button with my thumb. "Ask away."

Vasilisa looks up, her eyes meeting mine. Neither of us can actually clearly see the other's face in the darkness, but I can *feel* her gaze boring into mine as she tries to penetrate beyond the surrounding gloom.

"Boss?" Mitch's voice breaks the silence.

Slowly, Vasilisa's fingers wrap around the phone on my palm. The instant her skin comes in contact with mine, I close my hand on hers, holding her in place. She tenses immediately but doesn't try to break herself free.

"I hope your wrists have healed," I say as I brush my thumb over her knuckles. "I'm sorry you suffered that."

"They have," she whispers. "And I hope your forearm is on the mend. But I won't say that I'm sorry."

A smile pulls at my lips.

"Boss?" Mitch insists again. "Can you hear me?"

I let go of Vasilisa's hand. Her fingers feather over my palm as she lifts the phone and puts it to her ear.

"Hi, it's your boss's pet hacker speaking," she quips.

Her eyes are still locked on mine even though she can't really see them. I'm sure of that the same way I know her fingers brushed my palm on purpose.

"I need some information on the NAS server you set up."

My gaze follows Vasilisa as she returns to the desk and remains locked on her for the next hour while she listens to whatever Mitch tells her and simultaneously types away on the laptop. None of the mumbo jumbo she mentions makes any sense to me, but I still soak up every single word. She has the most alluring voice—a little husky but honeyed in a sweet way that, listening to it, makes me imagine how she would sound while pinned under me.

It's not a daydream, but a promise to myself. I will claim Vasilisa Petrova as mine. In every way possible.

I take a sip of my wine and continue watching her as she once again draws the pencil between her teeth, holding the phone wedged between her chin and shoulder. These evenings have somehow become the highlight of my day. I could gladly spend hours simply observing her doing her work, or talking with her to try to figure out what it is about her that has me so enthralled.

Yes, her beauty is beyond compare, and looking at her feels like viewing the most sublime work of art, but her appearance is not the sole reason for my obsession. I'm completely captivated by her tenacity and determination to do whatever it takes to keep her family safe. She hasn't tried to run even once, according to my security team's reports on her movements. Neither did she try to slip any information to her family when she used Guido's phone to speak with her mother the other day. The strength of this girl's will is astonishing.

So is her daringness to snark back at me. People don't *ever* do that. All too afraid of my wrath.

Fear is good. Necessary. It makes it so much easier to get them to dance to my tune. However, I don't want my vespetta to be scared of me, which is why I've taken such great lengths to hide my face from her. I want her defiance. Her banter. And more of her ridiculous-looking doodles.

My lips quirk as I remember the sticky note I found on the laptop after one of our evenings. It took me a few moments to realize that the strange-shaped creature with an apron was a rendition of me. The speech bubble drawn next to it is what eventually clued me in.

"Okay, I'll try that." Vasilisa lowers the phone to the desk and pushes away some of the dark strands falling over her eyes before resuming her work.

Tonight, she used another tie of mine to gather her hair at the top of her head. She tried to corral the mass, but a big part of it escaped during the evening and is now falling in tangled strands around her lovely face. My fingers itch to touch the soft tendrils, and I have to keep reminding myself why I can't go to her and do exactly that.

"I see you decided to expand your garments," I say, eyeing the jacket from my suit that she put on over one of my dress shirts. The getup looks ridiculous on her—swallowing her small frame. It does look like she's wearing a tent.

"I was cold," she mumbles without looking up.

Every muscle in my body goes rigid. "Cold?"

"Yes. Your jacket works, but I would appreciate something actually in my size. Your hospitality leaves a lot to be desired, Rafael."

"What else do you need?" I growl. She was cold. Because of me!

Vasilisa's eyes rise from the laptop screen, focusing on my spot in the corner. I immediately lean deeper into the shadows.

"Letting me go home isn't an option, I assume?"

"No."

"T-shirts. Leggings. A hoodie. Socks. Pajamas. And a hairbrush. Oh, and some real breakfast foods. I hate cereal."

"Is that all?"

"And women's deodorant, please. I don't want to keep going around smelling like you."

My cock instantly turns to granite at the mere idea of her carrying my scent. "Fine."

She props her fist under her chin and tilts her head. "Why won't you let me see your face?"

"I have my reasons."

"Is it so I won't be able to identify you later? Are you concerned I'll tell my dad what actually happened, and he'll chase you down?"

"Maybe."

"Wise. You should be very afraid of the pakhan's fury."

"I'm quite terrified, Miss Petrova." I take a long sip of my wine. "I'm sure Roman has gotten even more surly than he was the last time we met."

Vasilisa eyes me with an open-mouthed stare, then rapidly blinks twice with those long black lashes. "You know my dad?"

"We collaborated on a couple of occasions." I lean further back and watch her face. She's even prettier when she's confused. "There aren't many people who need the services my business offers, or who can afford them. And I personally know most who do."

"But . . . but you run a private security firm. I checked your company's website. The basic offered package costs a few thousand a month, hardly an astronomical amount."

"I wasn't referring to my front business, Miss Petrova."

"Then, what were you referring to?"

"That's between Roman and me," I tell her. "It's rather late. Maybe we should continue this tomorrow."

"Dude! That's it? You just dropped this bomb, and now you're sending me off to bed without further explanation?"

I'm greatly tempted to tell her the truth. She can't be so naive that she doesn't know what her dear old daddy does. But knowing Petrov, he's likely tried to shield her from the worst of it. Would she be surprised to learn that over the past decade and a half my teams have eliminated multiple targets for her father? That one of those hits I executed myself?

"Children's respect and trust in their parents should never be compromised, vespetta. I don't want to taint your opinion of your father."

"Oh, you're such a gentleman, with utterly high moral standards." She points her chewed-up pencil at me. "I know exactly who my dad is and what he does for a living. What kind of services did you provide to him?"

"The same ones I offer to all my clients. A swift and final resolution of very delicate matters, handled with the utmost discretion, of course."

"Which means?"

"It means, I kill people."

Two dark eyes turn into glaring slits. "My dad doesn't outsource."

For a few moments, I can only stare at her. "He doesn't . . . outsource?"

"Correct. When he needs someone gone, my uncle handles the issue."

I cock my head, observing my little hacker in a new light. "And you're okay with that?"

"Of course I'm not okay with that. It's just . . . That's how it's always been. How his world works. And by relation, mine, too. I'd rather my dad grow organic tomatoes for a living, but that's not him. He might be a villain to most people, but to me, he's just my dad."

Interesting.

Most women within the criminal society feign ignorance of how their fathers, husbands, or brothers make a living. Even though they have no qualms about spending the blood money, they still profess innocence to the outside world.

"Do you work for your father? I'm sure Petrov finds your skills very useful."

"No," she mumbles.

"Why not?"

Vasilisa looks away, disappointment and hurt etched into her doll-like features. "Roman Petrov would never allow his delicate flower of a daughter to dip a toe in anything related to Bratva."

"Just like the intricate, fragile-looking lily of the valley, perhaps?" I comment. The look she gives me is pure menace. "Which, if used properly, can lead to cardiac arrest and fatality."

Vasilisa frowns in confusion.

Yes, I definitely need greater finesse when delivering compliments to women. This woman.

"And you know that . . . from personal experience?" she asks.

"I prefer *Aconitum* in business matters. It works faster. Some contracts have very short turnaround times."

Rosy lips pressed tightly together, Vasilisa looks down at the laptop screen. I can practically see the wheels turning in her brain.

"What's your last name?" she asks without looking at me.

Well, well . . . She connected the dots at last. "It's De Santi."

"Rafael De Santi," she rasps. "The Sicilian."

I smile. "At your service, Miss Petrova."

Vasilisa nods and squirms in her chair nervously. Her shoulders are slumped, making her look even smaller in my suit jacket. The sleeves have unraveled and fallen nearly half a foot past her hands.

She looks so lost all of a sudden, and that pang of guilt hits me again.

"I'm not going to hurt you."

"Yeah," she murmurs. "It's late. I think we should call it a night."

"Of course. Sweet dreams, vespetta."

Keeping her eyes glued to the floor, Vasilisa slides off the chair and heads toward the door connecting the office with my bedroom. She's trying to appear nonchalant, but it's obvious she's running away.

When she reaches the door, however, she halts. "What does it mean? That word. Is it an insult?"

I watch her, so beautiful and regal even in that enormous jacket that seems to have swallowed her whole. She truly looks like a princess.

"It means little wasp," I say.

"Oh." She throws a quick glance over her shoulder in my direction, then disappears across the threshold.

I wait until the door shuts behind her before I approach the desk and lift the yellow pad of sticky notes. There's a doodle on the top piece. A dreadfully done stickman holding the handle of a protest sign in his hand.

World's shittiest employer.

I can't suppress my laugh.

Peeling away the note, I take out my wallet and slide the new doodle next to the earlier sketch she made.

CHAPTER
seven

Vasilisa

RICKETS AGAIN. THEIR SONG DRIFTS THROUGH THE open window, filling the room with a melody I found comforting in previous days, but now, it feels ominous somehow.

I fasten the final button on an enormous white dress shirt and glance at my ghostly reflection in the bathroom mirror. My lack of sleep is evident in the shadows under my eyes. I still haven't been able to wrap my mind around the fact that the man keeping me captive is actually *The* notorious Sicilian.

Bratva is not huge on gossip. Not like Cosa Nostra—those guys are the personification of the fucking rumor mill—but still, word gets around fast, and whether you want to or not, you hear things. Everyone in our circles knows about Rafael De Santi, a.k.a. The Sicilian.

There are several options for eliminating someone in our world. However, if you need it to be done professionally and fast, and if you have a couple of million to spare, you hire The Sicilian's team. They're the only ones with a twenty-four-hour turnaround guarantee, regardless of the location or the target. And no wonder. His front company has branches all over the world. What better strategy than to have his men in position and with relative ease of access because they've already infiltrated the security of the most prominent members of high society—bodyguards for his potential future marks? Ingenious.

I look behind me, my eyes wandering around the bedroom I've been staying in. My gaze glides over the two men's dress shirts thrown on the back of the couch, then to the right, taking in the charcoal suit jacket folded on the seat of the recliner. It has a ketchup stain on one of the lapels. My doing.

Considering where I ended up, I should have realized this sooner. But, it didn't even cross my mind that my Rafael is actually Rafael De Santi. From what I heard of The Sicilian, he should've just killed me, regardless of who my father is. Not let me sleep in his bedroom. Or wear his clothes . . . Maybe he does see the "clothes thing" as some weird mind game? A punishment or something? He almost admitted as much. Right?

As I step out of the room, there's another "delivery" waiting for me in front of my door. Several large white bags sporting the same gold logo as before. I grab the satin handles and carry the load to the couch that faces the fireplace, then start opening them one by one.

A beautiful white cardigan with oversized mother-of-pearl buttons is in the first bag, neatly folded and wrapped with a gold ribbon tied into a bow. I try it on and glide my palms over the soft material. I have a lot of nice things at home, but I don't think I've ever touched something so downy. This must be cashmere or something similar. Hardly anyone ever gets me the correct size when they buy me clothes, and typically everything is at least one or two sizes too big. But this . . . this is a perfect fit.

The next bag has a pack of socks (one hundred percent organic cotton, based on the label), as well as fluffy fur-topped open-toe slippers. I try them on, and my eyebrows hit my hairline. I guess being a hitman requires an unprecedented ability to make precise visual assessments, because the pretty slippers are also the perfect size.

At the bottom of the same bag, I find a black silk nightgown with a plunging neckline. I bite my lower lip as I take out the sexy nightie. The fabric seems to glide like water over my hands. Did Rafael order someone to purchase this for me, or did he do it himself? Something tells me he picked this one out on his own. Was he imagining how I would look in it? And all those lacy panties and bras? Maybe I should put the silky thing on tonight before heading to resume my work in his office, just to see if he'd still be so indifferent.

Whoa. What?

I immediately force that outrageous thought out of my mind and stuff the nightgown back into the bag. No, I am not getting excited by the mere idea of the most dangerous man in this part of the world fantasizing about me wearing this revealing little thing.

The last bag has a hairbrush, a few other toiletries, and two cans of deodorant. A very familiar-looking deodorant. I take them out. The aerosol cans are the same exact product and scent as I found in the bathroom. I snort and look at the bottom of the bag. There's a rectangular red velvet box with a pearly-looking white card attached to it.

> *I apologize for being such a shitty host.*
> *The color should go well with my shirts.*
>
> R.

I take out the velvety box and open the lid. It makes a tiny creak. Inside, a gorgeous gold necklace is nestled on a satin cushion. A multitude of pale-gray diamonds line the entire length of it. With my mouth hanging open, I carefully lift the necklace from its cradle, noticing how the sunlight bursts off the gleaming gems. If these are the real deal, this must have cost a fortune.

Gray diamonds are incredibly rare and hard to obtain. My mom has a ring with one. Dad had to tell her the stone was fake because she wouldn't actually wear it otherwise.

This pretty thing must be the most beautiful and extravagant piece of jewelry I've ever held in my hands. Too bad I don't accept presents in lieu of apologies. So I put the gorgeous necklace back into its box, set it aside, and head downstairs.

The mansion is vacant, as usual, with only the smell of crisp sea air filling the space. But as I cross the entry hall, a new, sweet aroma drifts in from the terrace and invades my nostrils.

Decadent fresh pastries.

I step outside and can only stare.

The patio table has been relocated to the middle of the terrace and is covered in a white tablecloth. Its surface is overflowing with platters featuring a selection of tasty-looking baked goods. Croissants. Tarts with a multitude of colorful fillings. Then, there are three-tiered stands laden with all kinds of fruit and berries. And jugs of freshly squeezed juice of several varieties.

There's enough food here to feed an army.

In the middle of the table, leaning against the strawberry custard is a yellow sticky note.

My heart rate ratchets up as I bring it closer, gaping at a drawing. It's hardly a lifelike masterpiece and is done in plain blue pen ink, but I'm certain it's me, reclined in the office chair, pencil clenched in the frowny-looking mouth. Rought lines around the face probably represent the stray strands of hair, while the rest is depicted as a glob on top of the head. There's another bold curve with a wider tip that I'm guessing is supposed to be a man's tie, twisted around the mass of tresses.

My eyes flit over all the details once more, then I look at a note scribed in strong male handwriting under the sketch.

I want some real food for breakfast.

A small giggle escapes me while warmth surges inside my chest.

Rafael De Santi. The man whose name alone makes people tremble in fear, left me a doodle on a sticky note. I slip the paper into my pocket and look around the terrace, but there isn't anyone else here. Sighing, I pull up a seat at the table and pick up a slice of tart from the closest platter. For the briefest moment, I hoped Rafael would be joining me for this feast.

My hand stills on a juice jug. I'm attracted to him. Attracted to a man who threatened to kill my family. Who is keeping me a prisoner. And I have no idea what he even looks like.

Peachy.

After I'm done with breakfast, I carry my plate and glass to the kitchen. The jumpy maid is there, putting the groceries away into the fridge, and the moment she notices me, she shrieks.

"Sorry. Didn't mean to startle you," I mumble, nodding at the plate in my hands. "I just brought this back."

The girl blinks in confusion, then rushes toward me and basically snatches the plate and glass from my hands and loads them into the dishwasher.

"Um . . . I could have done that. Okay, I'll go bring the—"

The maid dashes past me right out of the kitchen. I glance at her retreating back, seeing her scurry onto the terrace, where she starts collecting the breakfast leftovers.

Ooookay. I have no idea what I did, but the woman seems to be terrified of me for some reason. Deciding not to stress her further, I leave the kitchen through the side door that leads to the garden.

As I'm strolling along the driveway, raised voices carry toward me on a slight gust of wind from the direction of the estate entrance. One is male, sounding exasperated but determined. And the other is female, obviously distressed and shouting in a high-pitched tone. With my hands clasped behind my back, I continue down the gravel path, toward the source of the commotion. Poking my nose in other people's business is not something I usually do, but my curiosity has been piqued. It's a rare break from the monotony of a lifeless mansion.

The first thing I notice when I approach is a shiny red convertible parked on the other side of the gate. A woman, wearing a tight white dress, is standing next to the car and yelling at the guard while pointing her finger at the house. The man seems to be trying to calm her down, without success. The only thing I grasp from their conversation is Rafael's name. Suddenly, the woman's head snaps in my direction, and her long hair—nearly an identical shade to the car—flicks through the air in the process. Her eyes travel down my body, from the top of my head where Rafael's tie is keeping my bun secure, to the pale-gray shirt of his that I'm wearing.

"*Chi è quella?*" the redhead sneers through her teeth. It's more than clear she is not happy to see me here.

The guard rushes to her side and practically manhandles her into the driver's seat. Glaring at me the entire time, the woman spits out a slew of unpleasantries. Her irate words and hand gestures leave me with no doubt about that, despite the barrier of language. Then, she reverses the car and disappears into a cloud of dust.

I pivot and head back toward the house, while an unexpected pang of disappointment pierces my chest.

Rafael has a girlfriend.

The warm, salty breeze whips the loose strands of my hair into my eyes. I adjust the soft white cardigan around me and reach for the wine glass I've set between the succulents on my left. My gaze is drawn to the distant shimmer of yellow lights scattered across the dark expanse of the Mediterranean. The fishing boats.

I waited over an hour for Rafael in his office tonight. When

I arrived at the agreed-upon time, he wasn't there, and eventually, I concluded that he wasn't coming and trotted downstairs. I roamed the empty rooms, but as always, it felt strange being alone in such a vast yet magnificent space. Even Guido was nowhere to be found. After a while, I returned to the kitchen and grabbed a bottle of red wine and a glass, then came out to the garden.

This is a beautiful site, with a myriad of succulents and wildflowers thriving in crevices and graveled beds built around rocks and boulders along a natural slope. An olive tree with its widely spreading branches casts a shadow onto the massive flat stone I'm sitting on, just steps away from the thick trunk of the evergreen. I found this spot this morning during my exploration of the grounds, and the view from here is even more majestic at night.

The crunch of gravel somewhere behind me startles me, and I almost spill the wine all over my new cardigan.

"I was afraid you managed to slip away, Miss Petrova."

My body relaxes. It's just my kidnapper-slash-host-slash world's deadliest assassin. The fact that this realization brings me comfort is highly concerning.

"Between the cliffs, the electric fence, and your Uzi-carrying security, my options for escape are rather limited." I lift the bottle to pour more wine. But it's empty. Crap. "You weren't in the office when I came by."

"I had some things that needed to be taken care of."

I look over my shoulder and find Rafael leaning on the olive tree, swallowed by the shadows.

Always in the dark.

"Your girlfriend dropped by earlier today."

"Hardly a *girlfriend*, but an ex nevertheless. She's not handling the breakup that well," he says. "Apparently, she's still mourning."

"You broke her heart?"

"Worse. I canceled the credit card I gave her."

I chuckle, then turn back to watching the sea. The sound of his steps over the stones is faint but drawing near. Clothes rustle as he takes a seat behind me. He stretches his long legs on each side of me, and even though we're not touching, I can feel his heat as his huge frame surrounds me, and his presence seems to envelop my body and soul.

"I left your extravagant gift on your desk."

"Didn't you like it?" his deep voice, just next to my ear, whispers. My heartbeat picks up.

"It's lovely. But gifts do not replace an apology in my eyes."

"Why not?"

"Well, this might come as a surprise to you, Rafael, but you can't buy people."

"It worked well for me in the past."

"That's really sad," I mumble into my nearly empty glass. "You don't have to hide from me anymore, by the way. I know who you are, so there's no need."

"I know." His warm breath feathers my earlobe. "How do you like my house?"

"It's both beautiful and scary."

"How so?"

"There's no one around, except that one maid who runs away the moment she sees me. Why does she do that?"

"She probably doesn't know what to make of you. I rarely bring women to my home."

"Not even victims of kidnapping?"

"No." His breath fans my cheek. "What's wrong with my house?"

"Nothing's wrong with it. It's just so damn quiet all the time. I'm not used to it."

"And what are you used to, Miss Petrova?"

"Noise. Maids running around, arguing with each other. People always coming in and out, and doors banging open and shut. At home, there was always someone yelling. Like, our housekeeper screaming at someone because they tracked mud onto her pristine floors. Or Dad roaring at the gardener to turn off the lawn mower because he's trying to work with my brother. Our cook, Igor, wailing from the kitchen because Valentina put too much salt into the pot. My sister's high-pitched shouts from her room when she finds that I took her favorite T-shirt and returned it stained. The quiet here gives me the creeps." I finish my wine and set the glass between my legs on the rock. "Why don't you have staff?"

He's silent a moment too long, and I think he may not answer.

"I have staff," he finally says. "I just sent them away because I didn't want you to be uncomfortable with so many unfamiliar people around."

I burst out laughing. "Oh, how considerate of you. Especially after having me snatched off the street, stuffed into a van with my hands tied and mouth gagged, and then flown to another continent. None of that was an issue. Yet, you sent the maids away so I wouldn't feel uncomfortable?"

"Kind of."

I tilt my head to the side, my peripheral vision aligning with his mouth. At least that's what I figure. With the moon behind us and low in the sky, he's hardly more than a murky outline. "What do you want from me?"

"I told you. Fix my systems, and you're free to go."

"And that's it?"

"And that's it, Miss Petrova."

I nod and look back at the fishing boats on the dark horizon. "Then give me the laptop so I can work faster."

"I'm afraid I can't do that."

"You really are a jerk." I sigh. "When will you let me call my family again?"

I feel him shift and hear the rustle of fabric, and then he

extends his arm around me. His phone lies in the palm of his hand, the screen lit up with my father's name.

"Won't my father know it's you?"

"This is my private number. Very few people have it, and the pakhan is not one of them. It's untraceable anyway." He hits the dial icon, and I gingerly lift the phone to my ear.

"What?" My dad's growl comes through the line the moment the call connects.

"Hey, Dad," I choke out. "It's me."

"Vasya! Jesus fucking Christ, baby! We've been going nuts. Where the fuck are you?"

"Everything's fine, don't worry."

"Don't worry? You've been missing for days! Are you with one of those punk friends of yours again? Because if you are—"

"I needed a break, Dad," I mumble.

"You needed a fucking break? Because I took away your laptop? This is the fourth time I've rallied the whole of Bratva to search for you, goddamned terrified that something awful happened! I thought you grew out of your teenage tantrums. I want you home. Right now!"

"I'll be back soon. Kiss Mom, Yulia, and Alexei for me."

"Don't you dare hang up on me! Vasilisa!"

"Love you," I whisper and cut the call, my vision blurring as I scan the vast darkness before me.

The fishing boats are gone, and the waters are smooth as glass, reflecting the distant moonlight. The quiet is tangible all of a sudden. No other sound than my breath.

And Rafael's, so close behind me.

"That was interesting." Rafael's voice breaks the tranquil stillness.

"Eavesdropping on people's private conversations is impolite."

"Eavesdropping is defined as secretly listening without the

other party's knowledge. I'm pretty sure that your father's shouts could be heard all the way in Catania."

"Semantics," I grumble.

"What did he mean by 'this is the fourth time' that Bratva has been searching for you?"

"I have a record of periodically running away from home for a handful of days. The last time I did it, I was seventeen."

"Your way of trying to draw attention to yourself?"

"I wasn't trying to get attention." I sigh. "My father is an overprotective, controlling, and utterly paranoid man who loves his children more than anything in this world. The way he shows that love, however, can be a bit too much to process. Sometimes, it makes me feel as if I'm suffocating. When I was younger, I didn't know how to deal with it. So a few times, I slipped away and spent a couple of days with one of my friends to decompress."

"Did it help?"

"Somewhat. It's not as if I could confide in anyone. You know, I have no idea why I told *you* all of this."

"Because you're drunk."

"Maybe." I pick up a small pebble from the ground and throw it toward the sea. It doesn't reach it, of course, just rolls down the rocky hill, coming to rest buried somewhere in the grass. "Don't hurt my family. Please."

"Keep your part of our deal, and I won't."

"They didn't do anything to you. Why should they bear the consequences of my deeds?"

"Because when you're engaged in a high-stakes game, vespetta, you're never alone on that playing field."

Another sigh leaves my lips. "Will you let me call them again?"

"Yes. If I'm not here, you can ask Guido."

"I would rather avoid all contact with your brother unless there isn't another choice."

We aren't even touching, yet I instantly feel the moment Rafael stills behind me. "What did he do?" The words sound strained.

"Nothing. He just made it perfectly clear that he doesn't want me here." I slowly scramble to my feet, needing to distance myself from this man. His closeness is so much more pleasing than it should be. "We have that in common since I don't want to be here, either."

The ground seems to be moving under my feet, making me stumble as I take a step forward. A thick male arm wraps around my middle, crushing me to a hard-muscled chest.

"Let go," I mumble, while everything around me seems to be spinning.

"And watch you take a nosedive?" His cheek brushes my temple as he speaks next to my ear. "I don't think so."

"I won't—"

A yelp escapes me when Rafael slides his other hand under my knees and lifts me into his arms. Since the moment he sat behind me, my heart has been beating double-time, but now, it feels like it's going to explode. My awareness of him is so consuming that my mind blanks on everything else. I don't even try arguing. We're so close that I can feel his breath on my lips. At this distance, I can make out a little more of his face—the short stubble along his chin and the prominent eyebrows over his shaded eyes—but his overall features remain hidden, veiled by the night.

The scent of cypress and oranges tingles my nostrils as Rafael carries me up the uneven stone steps that lead to the mansion. Olive trees line the trail on either side, creating a natural canopy and a tunnel-like atmosphere over the winding path. Once in a while, moonlight breaks through the overhead branches and casts sharp angular shadows that dance across his face. With mere inches between us, I can feel every movement of his powerful frame. The vibrations send an electric current zipping through all of my cells directly to my spine.

And lower.

It shouldn't feel this good, being snuggled into him like this. But it does. Maybe it's the wine. I don't feel that drunk, but I don't see any other explanation for why I enjoy being held by him so much.

"If I say I'm sorry for being a shitty host, will you accept my gift?"

I raise an eyebrow. "I'll certainly consider it. But you'd need to actually say it."

A deep, thunderous roar fills the darkness as he laughs.

"I'm sorry for my insolence," he says, amusement still lingering in his tone. "And for the treatment you received from my men. Hank has been sent back to Chicago, so he won't bother you again." These words carry none of the mirth of the earlier statement.

"Alone? What about his sidekick, Vinny?"

"Vinny . . . has been dismissed."

"You fired him?"

"Mm-hmm. I guess you could say that." He bends as we pass under one of the lower branches, and his cheek brushes my forehead. "I'll have someone drive you to Taormina tomorrow so you can buy whatever clothes you need." His cologne tingles my nostrils, but not in that irritating way that makes me want to sneeze. Oh no. It beckons me, urging me to get closer and take another sniff.

"Can't you take me?" I blurt out.

Rafael halts. I can feel his chest rise and fall.

"I can," he says, his voice sounding clipped as he resumes his stride. "But if you change your mind, I'll have Otto drive you."

"Why would I change my mind?"

He does not answer.

We emerge from the rock garden and approach the mansion

across the immaculate lawn. There are no more trees around us, just fresh-smelling grass and fragrant flower beds, bathed in the soft light of the moon. Those lines on Rafael's face which I thought were dancing shadows? They stay in place, despite the lack of branches above our heads.

Rafael

Pebbles crunch under my feet, the tiny sounds fracture the silence around us, as I carry Vasilisa. I feel her eyes on my face as I ascend the terrace steps. The light above the French doors that lead inside the living room is on. The same for the interior of the house. No more shadows to hide within.

My gaze is fixed on the path before me, and I keep moving with measured strides. Will she scream or simply faint in my arms? Somehow I doubt my little hacker is a screamer, so I ready myself for her body going limp. I take that final step and halt directly under the light fixture.

Waiting.

A moment passes.

I take a deep breath.

Look down.

For a second, I'm taken aback by how beautiful she is up close. Two dark eyes focus on me through long silky lashes, skimming over my features just as mine did with hers. A couple of heartbeats is usually the longest it takes before people look away after seeing me. But Vasilisa takes her time, examining every jagged line of the mess that is my face. She doesn't even bat an eye. Maybe she's in shock.

Finally, her gaze meets mine.

"I could have sworn you were blond, Rafael."

I narrow my eyes at her. "That's it?"

"What?"

"Your reaction. You're not going to scream?"

"Oh, it takes a lot more effort for a guy to make me scream."

My cock is instantly hard. "Good to know."

I resume carrying her through the house, up the stairs—all with the most epic hard-on I've had in ages. When I reach my bedroom, I stop outside and gently lower her to the floor.

"Otto will be waiting for you at ten to take you over to Taormina to shop tomorrow. Get anything you want, don't look at the prices."

"Can I get my T-shirt and jeans back for the occasion? I'm sure the salespeople will throw me out if I walk in wearing your shirt and nothing else."

I lean slightly forward. "Don't worry about that."

"If you say so." She tilts her head to the side, simply looking at me for a couple of moments, then adds. "And I haven't changed my mind."

In less than a second, she disappears into the room.

I stare at the door for a few heartbeats, then turn on my heel and head downstairs, directly to the east wing. When I step inside Guido's apartment, he's just leaving his bathroom, toweling his hair.

"We had a situation in Marseille," he says, walking toward his closet. "I tried calling you, but you weren't answering your phone."

I grab the back of his neck and plaster him face-first to the closet door. "What did you say to her?"

"I guess I don't have to ask who 'her' is?" he mumbles into the wooden surface.

"Answer me!"

"She's going to get you killed! I don't get this crazy obsession you've developed for this girl, but when Petrov finds out, he'll fry you!"

"What I do with my life is none of your fucking business!"

I tighten my grip on his neck and lean to whisper in his ear. "If you ever upset her again, you won't like the consequences."

"Christ, Raff." Guido shakes his head. "Please, let me arrange for someone to take her back home before she realizes who you are. Because we're doomed if she does."

I release him. "Too late for that."

"*Ohhhhh*, fuck." Guido throws the towel on the couch and turns toward the dry bar.

My brother rarely drinks booze and only keeps a few alcoholic options for when Mitch comes over. The two of them go way back to our time in the US, with Mitch following us back to Sicily when we made the move. Guido is not one to share the details of his love life, so I only know the status of his on-again-off-again relationship with his boyfriend based on the presence of those bottles. Little bro hides the liquor when he and Mitch break up. I guess this means they're back together now.

Guido drops on his recliner a minute later, with three fingers of whiskey in the tumbler in his hand. "What will happen when you let her go, and she tattles to her father?"

"We'll cross that bridge when we come to it," I tell him. "I need you to get me some house staff."

"House staff?"

"Yes. As soon as tomorrow morning. Five additional maids. Two gardeners. Does Rigobaldo's wife still cook at that restaurant in Messina?"

"I think so, yes. Why—"

"Make them fire her. I want her here. She'll cook for us."

Guido throws back his drink, getting into a coughing fit as soon as he swallows. "You hate having people in the house, Raff. I've been trying to convince you to hire a second maid forever. Now, all of a sudden, you want me to magically get you eight people to work here overnight?"

"Make it twelve, and make sure they can understand English. And I want them to make noise. Order them to argue."

"What?"

"You heard me. At least four times a day, I want to hear them yelling. Or singing. Or grumbling about something. I don't give a shit about what, but make sure they're loud."

"I swear, you've lost your fucking mind. Will you at least tell me why?"

"No. Just do as I said. If Vasilisa asks, they've all been working here for years." I turn to leave but stop at the threshold and toss over my shoulder, "Make sure they slam the doors open and shut. Often."

CHAPTER eight

C LANG.

  I squint my eyes open, then quickly shut them again. My head is killing me. It feels as if someone is drilling holes through my temples.

Clang. Clang.

"Sbrigati, idiota. Ho bisogno di quella vernice."

More ruckus. People talking loudly in Italian.

What's going on?

I drag myself out of bed and walk onto the balcony to look over the railing. Two men in white overalls are propping up a huge door against one of the massive stone pillars on the terrace below. The third one is approaching them with a bucket of paint in one hand and a small brush in another. Further to the left, amid the flower beds, another man is trimming the branches of a shrub and singing while he works.

Behind me, the sound of running feet echoes through the hallway outside my room, followed by female voices. Several of them. What the hell is happening? I scrunch my nose and walk to the door. Cracking it open, I peek outside. There's a maid plugging a vacuum cleaner into an outlet on the landing, saying something I don't understand to another girl with a stack of folded towels in her hands. I stare at them in amazement until the woman with the vacuum notices me.

"Hi there." I wave at her.

For a split second, she simply gapes at me, then looks at the towel girl and barks a few quick Italian words. The other girl yells something back, throws the towels at the first one, and dashes down the stairs.

Ooookay.

I shrug and close the door. Turning around, I'm ready to hit the bathroom when my eyes fall on the red velvet box lying on the coffee table. The lid is open, revealing the beautiful necklace Rafael left as a gift for me. He must have brought it in here while I was sleeping. Next to the jewelry case is a tasty-looking fig. Is this one stolen, also?

I approach the coffee table and sit down on the sofa, right in front of the box. The sunlight streaming through the windows falls directly on the gray gems, making them sparkle like tiny brilliant flames. Accepting necessities like clothes and toiletries from Rafael is one thing. But this? Absolutely not.

How can I accept a gift from a man who keeps me prisoner? It would definitely send the wrong message.

Hesitantly, I reach out and stroke the string of diamonds with the tip of my finger, incapable of suppressing the small smile tugging at my lips. The color certainly does go well with his shirts. How would Rafael react if I actually wore the necklace? Its Y drop is rather long, so the prominent gemstone would probably reach the valley between my breasts. The mere notion of having Rafael's eyes on my cleavage stirs up the butterflies in my stomach.

I bite my lower lip, then take the magnificent necklace and put it around my neck. Just as I thought, the diamonds at the bottom of the Y-shaped linear strand end up nestled between my girls. Closing my eyes, I slide my fingertips across the pretty stones, imagining it's Rafael's hand. His scent fills my senses, and I realize the faintest traces of it are in my hair, likely because he carried me last night. Or maybe it's just his shampoo.

Whatever the reason, I like it.

Usually, I'm concerned with making sure men's hands remain off me. It's the other way around with Rafael. Every time he's been close, my skin tingled with the need to feel his touch, but most of those times, he's kept his distance. Because of his apparent indifference to me, I initially thought he wasn't attracted to me in the least. Now, however, I'm pretty sure I was wrong about that. It's not indifference, but rather caution. I bet he thinks I'd be scared of him.

I will never forget the expression in his eyes when he stepped under the light last night, allowing me to see him for the first time. So hard. Feral, even. I'm certain he expected me to scream in terror after viewing his face. But scars don't scare me. Where I come from, most of the men carry some kind of battle wounds, both on the outside and where no one can see.

Mikhail—my father's interrogator—doesn't only have a heavily scarred face, but is also missing an eye, as far as I know. I still find him hot as hell. Even with an eye patch.

Then, there's my uncle Sergei, who still has his psychotic episodes from time to time because of his PTSD. If his wife isn't around when it happens, bystanders often end up hurt or worse.

Every single person who gets dragged into the criminal world must deal with the aftermath. It's the reality, and we all live it. Still, I wonder . . . What happened to Rafael's face?

It doesn't make him any less attractive, though. If the circumstances were different, I wouldn't mind going out with him. If I'm being honest with myself, I quite enjoy the time we spend together. Especially the bickering. I'm drawn to the aura of menace he seems to be wrapped in. Captivated by it like a moth beguiled by a flame. And now I crave his touch. The caress of a man who keeps me captive. Who holds the power of life and death in the palm of his hand, and won't hesitate to use it against my family. Me wanting him is beyond twisted.

I quickly unclasp the necklace and put it back in its box. Then, picking up the fig from the table, I head into Rafael's office to return the gift, all the while munching on the fruit with pleasure.

Thirty minutes later, I emerge from the bathroom, clad in a dove-gray dress shirt that reaches below my knees and a black necktie that serves as my belt. My freshly washed and brushed hair is braided down my back, and secured at the end with a length of dental floss. Faux-fur slippers are the finishing touch on my elegant attire. I'm ready for my shopping trip.

This day can go one of two ways. One, I get back to the mansion with some suitable clothes. Or two, I end up seated in a padded room across from a guy in a white coat, answering questions like: *Do you hear voices?*

Descending the wide stairway to the ground floor, I notice several more maids rushing around, cleaning the already rather clean surfaces. Two workers whom I saw on the terrace earlier are removing one of the windows to the left of the front door. Through the gap, I spot a gardener, not the same one as before, kneeling by the flowerbed next to the driveway, pulling out weeds.

The notes of an Italian song reach me as I approach the kitchen. I stop at the threshold and glance inside. A tall dark-haired woman in a simple black dress is working dough on the island, while music plays from the tiny old-school radio on the windowsill. The smell of freshly baked bread tingles my nostrils, making me salivate just from the scent.

"Um . . . Good morning," I say.

The woman looks up from her work and scans me from the end of my braid, that I pulled over my shoulder, to the tips of my toes peeking out beneath the fluff of my slippers. The expression on her face runs the gamut from surprise to absolute confusion.

"*Sei la ragazza di Raffaello?*" she asks, her eyes wide.

"I'm not sure where Rafael is. Sorry."

"Me, Irma." She points one flour-covered finger at herself, then at me. "You. Rafael's girl?"

"Um . . . definitely not. Rafael's prisoner would be a better term." I point at myself. "Vasilisa."

The woman tilts her head to the side, giving me another once-over, her eyes stopping on the tie I used as a belt.

"Rafael's girl." She nods. "Good match."

"I'm not his—" I try to clarify but Irma has already turned her back to me and is taking something out of the oven.

Leaning over the kitchen island, I'm floored by the large pan of what looks like a thick-crust pizza in her hands. And, my God, it's not even burned.

"I see you're up." Guido's voice comes from behind me. He sounds almost friendly.

I reach for the plate with a big slice of pizza that Irma passes to me and turn around. "I see your staff are back."

"Yeah," he mumbles, then meets my gaze. "I'm sorry for going off on you the other day. When it comes to my brother, I tend to get overly protective."

"Rafael doesn't strike me as someone who needs anyone's protection."

"Only when it comes to protecting him from himself," Guido says, eyeing my tie-belt. "Finish the job you need to do here. As fast as you can."

"Well, that's the plan."

"Plans change." He looks up, meeting my gaze. "I hope this one doesn't, or, I'm afraid, we'll end up waist-deep in dead bodies."

I narrow my eyes at him. "What are you talking about?"

"Be careful. When my brother claims something as his,

there's no force on this earth that would make him let it go. Finish the job. Then, go home, Miss Petrova."

I watch Guido's back as he busies himself with the coffee machine, wondering what the hell he meant by his cryptic words. The clock on the wall shows a minute past ten. Stuffing the rest of my breakfast into my mouth, I leave the kitchen and rush across the entry hall where a couple of maids are mopping the floor.

A badass gunmetal gray Maserati SUV is parked outside the front doors, its black-tinted windows reflecting the morning sun. Leaning on the side of the vehicle, with his arms crossed over his chest, is my jailer himself. He's wearing black dress pants and a vest, with a gray shirt underneath, all immaculately tailored to fit his large frame. The sleeves of his button-down are rolled to his elbows, revealing heavily inked forearms that are corded with muscles. His dark hair is slicked back, and only now do I notice that he has a small metallic hoop in his left ear.

"Good morning," I murmur while feeling a blush creep up my cheeks. God, I can't believe I actually voiced that thing about men making me scream last night.

Rafael cocks his head to the side, observing me. The sun is shining directly onto his face, allowing me to see every single imperfection. It's plain as day that he must have been incredibly handsome before suffering whatever it was that happened to him. A car accident maybe? He still is, though. Gorgeous. Despite the scars. And then, there's that dangerous vibe he has going for him that's seriously alluring. It's as if the very air around him is charged with unrestrained energy, warning me to stay away, but at the same time, beckoning me closer.

"I wondered where that tie was."

My hands go to my waist, adjusting my "belt."

"Second drawer on the left, with the rest of them. Um . . . I reorganized your walk-in."

"I noticed. It took me ten minutes to find what I needed this morning. You sleep like a log, by the way."

"You can't just venture inside my bedroom," I grumble, approaching the car.

"*Your* bedroom?"

"Fine. I'll move my stuff to some other room."

"No, you won't," he says, opening the passenger door.

I take the hand he offers me and step up into the SUV. "Why not?"

"My house, my rules."

The door latches shut with a hollow thud.

Rafael's steps are unhurried as he rounds the front of the massive vehicle and takes a seat behind the wheel. He reaches for the aviator sunglasses on the dashboard and puts them on.

"I hope breakfast today was to your liking."

"Yup. Homemade pizza is every prisoner's wet dream."

"Good. If you want something in particular to eat, just tell Irma and she'll prepare it."

"You mean, I can choose?" I shift, leaning my back on the side window and drawing my legs up and under me on the seat cushion, mere inches from the gearshift. Despite my racing heart, I'm hoping the position makes it seem like I'm not a ball of twisted nerves. It also allows me a direct view of his profile.

"That's how personal chefs usually work. You tell them what you want. They make it happen."

"Maybe in your household." I shrug. "At home, we usually have to pick from a selection of marginally burned, charred, and completely inedible. Our cook is actually a heavy machinery mechanic with zero finesse when it comes to kitchen appliances."

"You can fire him."

"Fire him? Igor taught me to tie my shoelaces and let me and Yulia braid satin ribbons into his beard when we were kids. He's practically a family member."

Rafael turns onto a wider road that meanders between

the hill on the left and an olive orchard on the right. When he shifts the gear stick, his knuckles lightly brush my knee, sending a shockwave of tingles through my whole body. My mind instantly wanders to last night, to him carrying me from the garden. I might have been drunk, but I remember every detail of how it felt to be held by him. The low thrumming in every fiber of my being, from the top of my head to the ends of my toes. The awareness of each point of contact between our bodies. The feeling of wanting to be nowhere else but in his arms.

Why am I so attracted to this man? I shouldn't be, all things considered. I should despise him, or, at least, be wary of his games.

Maybe it's because he's never been patronizing toward me. He actually listens to what I say and doesn't just nod like a dummy while ogling me, hoping that pretending to listen will make it easier to drag me into his bed. Or maybe it's because, with him, I don't need to pretend to be something I'm not.

My entire life I've been surrounded by hard, dangerous men. They're who I'm used to, and I can't see myself making a connection with some nice, unassuming guy. I've tried. I've truly tried. None of the guys I ever dated made me feel an ounce of the thrill I do simply sitting in the same car as enigmatic Rafael De Santi.

"Can't you find some other role for him, then?" he asks.

"Who?" I blink in confusion. What were we talking about?

"Your cook-mechanic."

"Oh, yeah. Um . . . Igor really likes to cook. And bake, unfortunately," I mumble. "It's always Igor and my mom who make birthday cakes. You don't want to know how those end up."

"Why?"

"Because Igor is the one giving instructions. And my mom prepares the thing."

"What's wrong with that?"

"Igor doesn't speak English. And my mom knows exactly ten words in Russian."

"What a peculiar family." He glances my way, his mouth arched in a teasing smirk which does funny things to my lady parts.

When he focuses back on the road, I steal a look at his left hand gripping the top of the wheel. Usually, I don't like it when men wear jewelry—it makes them seem overstated somehow. Rafael has three rings—white gold, or maybe platinum. Two on his forefinger and one on his thumb. There are also several chain-link bracelets around his wrist. They shouldn't look good paired with his stylish attire, but just like that hoop in his ear, they actually work for him.

The back of that hand, just like his face, is heavily scarred. I glance down at his right hand resting on the gearshift. More rings. Another bracelet, open-cuff this time, on this wrist. And even worse scarring than on his left hand. Maybe it wasn't a car accident. Did he get these marks on one of his "jobs"? A failed assassination attempt that saw him captured and . . . tortured?

"What about your family?" I look up and over, focusing on the landscape beyond the windshield. "Do they know what you do for a living?"

"Our father was killed when Guido was just a baby. And since our mother died, it's just been Guido and me. Been that way for about twenty-five years now."

I furrow my forehead. I thought his brother was in his late twenties. "How old is Guido?"

"Twenty-nine. He's ten years younger than me. I've raised him since he was four."

"But, that would mean you were fourteen at the time."

"Correct."

No, that's not possible. At fourteen, he was basically still a child himself. I stare at Rafael, wondering for a fleeting moment if he's simply fucking with me. But I don't think he is.

113

"How?" I choke out.

"Determination and tenacity, with a hefty load of stubbornness in the mix, can achieve many things. I promised Guido that I wouldn't let us be separated." He glances over at me. "And I always keep my word." His voice sounds rougher. "You should remember that. That way, if at some point you happen to get an idea of running away—please, don't."

I raise my eyebrows. "Please?"

"Yes." He turns to face me. "Because I *will* execute your family if you do."

I break our locked stare and turn back to watching the landscape out the window. I don't care how he got those scars. I don't give a rat's ass about anything to do with Rafael De Santi. Just like Guido said, I'll do the job, then go home.

And I'll never see this heartless man again.

I take Rafael's extended hand and get out of the SUV (the seat is rather high, otherwise I wouldn't have done it). Several feet in front of me, a man in a suit is holding open the door to a boutique. The whole building is baroque-style architecture, with elaborate floral motifs and smooth stucco framing the doorway as well as the windows on the upper floors. The ground floor has a lot of rough stone and is segmented into sections separated by thick white stone columns. Right above the entrance is an unobtrusive plaque displaying the same gold logo as on the shopping bags Rafael left outside my room.

"This doesn't look like a place that sells jeans and hoodies," I comment.

"I'm sure we'll find some," Rafael says and, placing his hand on the small of my back, ushers me forward.

"*Signor De Santi!*" A man in his early sixties, wearing a suit and dark wire-framed glasses, rushes toward us as soon as we walk in. "*Benvenuti!*"

"English," Rafael says next to me, then nods toward a couple by a display of handbags at the back. "Get them out."

"Of course." The man bows ever so slightly to Rafael and turns toward the security guy standing by the door, speaking to him in Italian. After a brief exchange, the security person nods and walks up to the couple. Almost without a word, he practically drags them outside and locks the door.

"That was exceptionally rude," I whisper.

Rafael leans down, bringing his lips right next to the shell of my ear to whisper back, "I don't give a fuck."

I tilt my head to the side, my nose bumping with his. "I thought Italians were nice people."

"Not all." His green eyes bore into mine as if searing right through me.

"Yeah, some like to kidnap helpless women."

"Exactly." He straightens to face the older dude with the glasses. "This is Baccio Albini, the owner. He'll make sure you find everything you need."

"Absolutely. And the girls will help with sizing, pairing recommendations, or whatever else is required." The proprietor motions to three women in tailored gray dresses standing in front of the antique glossy-white checkout counter. They look almost regal as they pose with their hands clasped demurely before them, but they can't hide the expression in their eyes. Each one is staring at me as if I'm some kind of three-headed alien. I guess they don't get many customers wearing nothing but a man's shirt that's ten sizes too big.

"Um . . . Thank you. " I offer a smile to the older man, then head toward the rack of blouses.

Fifteen minutes later, I step inside a luxurious space that apparently serves as a dressing room. In the middle, a white chaise lounge and two matching armchairs that look like they came straight from the Victorian era have been arranged around a plush round area rug, creating an elegant sitting nook. Toward each end of the room, there's a dais with a standing three-paneled wall mirror in a gilded frame that faces the seating area. The two platforms are each surrounded by an overhead track with a set of satin drapes that could be drawn to offer privacy to whoever is making use of the 360-degree view.

"Are you sure you don't want to try anything else, miss?" the sales assistant holding the clothes I've picked out asks.

"I'm sure." I smile and take the pile consisting of two pairs of jeans, four blouses, and a pair of flats from her. "Thank you."

The other two saleswomen are hovering behind her with looks on their faces that teeter between confused and appalled. Mr. Albini, however, appears as if he might get sick at any moment.

"Is our selection not to your liking?" he chokes out, beads of sweat glistening along his hairline. "I can assure you, every piece here is of exceptional quality. We pride ourselves on offering the finest apparel in the whole of Sicily. Please, let me show you our designer dresses. Only the finest mulberry silk and Alençon lace from France."

"Your merchandise is beautiful, but I don't need anything else at the moment."

"But . . . but Mr. De Santi mentioned you need everything. Twenty-plus pairs of pants. Tops to match. Shoes that complement each combination. Dresses. A few cardigans, perhaps." His tone escalates from overly concerned to outright panicky. "How can I go out there and tell him that aside from these select things, you were not able to find anything you liked?"

"Really, I don't need anything else but these."

"Please, miss . . ." Albini pleads, twisting his fingers in front of him. "Mr. De Santi will be very displeased with me. Can I show you our selection of evening gowns, at least?"

I shake my head and walk out of the room, patting the old man's arm as I pass him. "I'll be right back."

The outer area of the boutique is huge, filled with white wooden shelving and racks that match the antique front counter displaying the best of the haute couture. Off to the side is an elegant sitting area with a big leather couch. I assume this is where husbands, boyfriends, or lovers typically wait while their better halves shop. It appears that kidnappers are welcome here, too, since that's where I find Rafael. He's leaning against the cushions with his arms spread across the back of the sofa and one ankle braced on the opposite knee.

"Is something wrong, vespetta?"

My eyes turn into narrow slits. Damn him. Why couldn't he have picked a cliché moniker like "beautiful" or "angel"? I hate those. "Mr. Albini is in there nearly peeing his pants because, evidently, I failed to pick up all the items on your shopping list. He's so terrified, I'm worried he's going to have a heart attack."

"He's just afraid I'll kill him if he doesn't get you what you need."

I roll my eyes.

"I want you to be comfortable during your stay here, Miss Petrova. If my intent is derailed because of Albini's inability to provide acceptable service, I'm going to punish him. Therefore"—he nods in the general direction of the clothing racks—"you better resume choosing things you like. Something other than shapeless jeans and baggy tops, if at all possible."

"I like jeans and baggy tops."

"Why?"

"Because . . . I . . . I just like them," I say and look away.

I detest shapeless jeans and baggy tops.

Pretty dresses. Tight tops in bright colors. Skinny jeans paired with silk blouses and sky-high heels. That's what I love to wear. It makes me happy. The heels especially because I feel less like Thumbelina from the fairytale Mom liked to read to me when I was a kid. Too bad that's exactly what makes people see me as an empty-headed bimbo every time I doll up.

"You don't want Albini to end up in the emergency room on such a lovely day, do you?"

"Fine." I cock my hip and point a finger at him. "But just so you know—buying me a shitload of expensive clothes won't make me like you any better."

A small smile tugs on Rafael's lips as he props his chin on his palm and watches me with amusement dancing in his eyes. "You have no idea how astonishing I find that little fact."

Ugh. I pivot and storm off toward the rack with blouses while Raphael's deep laugh chases me. As I'm browsing the nearest selections, out of the corner of my eye, I notice Mr. Albini and the three sales ladies peeking around the slightly opened dressing room door, their heads stacked in a row like tilted face emojis.

Rafael

It looks like my little hacker is trying to get back at me for making her buy more clothes . . . by picking up everything at the store that's available in her size.

I fold my hands behind my head and take in the sea of white bags spanning the floor around the front counter. There must be at least fifty. She's made Albini one happy camper, that's for sure. I don't recall ever seeing him as excited as he is at this moment while ringing in the twenty-third pair of heels.

"I think that's the last one, Signor De Santi," he says as one of the saleswomen places the box in a bag.

"Not yet." I rise from the couch and walk up to Vasilisa, who looks like a deflated balloon amid the whiteout of her purchases. When she started piling items on the counter over two hours ago, she was looking very smug. She threw me a look that said *You asked for it*, beaming a rascally smile at me. I bet she expected me to stop her. When I did nothing to curtail her efforts, she kept bringing more and more things to the front, and her face slowly shifted from that mischievous grin to an exasperated countenance. Now she just looks tired. No wonder, after nearly three hours of trying on clothes and shoes.

"I don't think they have anything else in my size," she grumbles.

"You forgot a dress."

"I don't need one."

My eyes sweep the store, halting at the display of elegant gowns. The centerpiece is a floor-length gold dress. The square neckline exposes the shoulders and instantly brings to mind timeless beauty and elegance. The sheer tight-fitting bodice and long sleeves are embroidered lace, featuring an intricate floral design, but the pleated skirt is all flowy solid-colored silk. And, along the front on the right side, a full-length slit that reaches the upper thigh. The dress is sophisticated and decadent at the same time. It would look beautiful on any woman. On this one in particular—it would look sexy as fuck.

So would a pair of black stilettos with a wide ankle strap adorned with a gold clasp. The shoes are sitting on the small nearby stand, but I can already see them on the shapely legs of my unwilling houseguest.

"Albini," I say and nod toward the gown. "Shoes, as well."

"That won't fit," Vasilisa mumbles following my gaze.

"Albini will make sure it's adjusted. Go try it on."

Vasilisa's dainty teeth sink into her lower lip, brutalizing that soft pillowy flesh as she regards the store attendants removing the gown from the display. With her eyes twinkling and filled with wonder, she exudes pure innocence and ravenous yearning, similar to a child longing for their favorite candy while knowing they can't have it before finishing their lunch.

"Okay," she whispers and trails behind Albini as he carries the gown toward the dressing room.

I wait a few of minutes, then follow. The owner has stationed himself at the door, hands clasped in front of him.

"It's the most exquisite garment we have, Signor De Santi. Every stitch is made by hand, sewn with a golden thread. I'm sure the lady will—"

I turn the knob and step inside the fitting room, closing the door in Albini's face. The drapes on the far side are drawn, but there's a narrow gap between the panels. As I approach, I catch a glimpse of Vasilisa. Those sexy black stilettos are on her feet, and she's got the skirt of her dress pulled up a bit and seems to be twirling in place.

"Um . . . I think I'll need help with the buttons."

I cast a look at the saleswoman who was just about to offer her assistance. "Out," I whisper.

She tenses, then rushes out of the room, taking the other two attendants with her.

"Well, it's not as bad as I figured. Only half a foot too long," Vasilisa continues from behind the curtain.

Seizing the two sides of the heavy drapery, I slide them apart, revealing Vasilisa as she holds up the skirt and examines the hem.

"But these buttons at the back are hard to"—she looks up, her eyes widening upon seeing me in her space—"reach."

"Turn around."

For a few moments, Vasilisa remains unmoving, her onyx-colored eyes staring into mine before she slowly pivots. Our gazes clash again in the mirror, and I hold her eyes captive while finding the first button at the small of her back. It's tiny and round, and it takes me two tries to fasten it.

Is it because of my big fingers?

Or is it simply her, messing with my concentration?

I move my hands up to the next button, lightly brushing

the silky skin along her spine with my fingertips. She trembles at my touch.

Is it in fear?

Button number three, done.

Another shiver.

Or is it from the uneasiness of having someone like me touch her? Does she find me repulsive?

I gently stroke along her skin, languidly this time, and enjoy the prolonged contact.

Vasilisa's breathing becomes rapid. Maybe the dress isn't enough. It's just a piece of cloth, hardly suitable compensation for her consideration of my advances. More jewelry, perhaps? She hasn't worn the necklace I bought her. Maybe it's too heavy for every day? A bracelet, then. I'll drop by my jeweler and see what he has in his latest collection.

There's only one button left, the final one between her shoulder blades. I place my thumb at the base of her neck and slide it down, over the peaks and valleys of her spine, marveling at the feel of her soft skin. Then, I fasten the last button and just watch my Russian princess in the mirror.

The delicate floral lace wraps her upper body like a second skin, the pattern accentuating her little waist and elegant arms. The flowy silk skirt falls around her gorgeous legs, hiding them from my view, except for her right foot, which peeks out from between the folds.

She looks ethereal. Like she came from another world.

I take a step closer, so my front touches her back, and bend until my chin rests on top of her head.

"Tell me, Miss Petrova, how many hearts of men have been stomped by your tiny feet so far?"

Those dark eyes narrow in the mirror. "None."

"I don't believe you."

"To be able to crush someone's heart, it must be given to

you first, Rafael. But, male pride on the other hand . . . Yeah, there have certainly been a few victims who saw theirs trampled."

"That, I do not doubt." I reach out and lightly stroke the dip of her neck. Her bare neck. "Where is the necklace I bought you?"

"In the box. Back in your office."

"Why?"

"You can't expect me to accept presents from you Rafael."

"You didn't seem to have a problem buying out half of the boutique. Why would one more little trinket matter?"

"That was me getting back at you for agitating Albini, and you know it. But I won't wear jewelry bought by a man who's keeping me as a prisoner. Do you shower all your hostages with gold and diamonds?"

"In my experience, people will choose to dismiss or ignore many things if the offsetting gift is expensive enough."

"Well, sorry to be the one to break it to you, but money can't buy everything."

Her words slash through my chest like a knife. Is she alluding to me holding her against her will or to my looks? I'm guessing, the latter. The gown idea was stupid. Anybody can buy a dress. I need to give her something more astonishing. More exquisite. Something that will help her see beyond my fucked-up face. But what if there's nothing that will get her to do that? Would she ever be able to?

Gritting my teeth, I take a step back. My hand falls away from Vasilisa's neck, but my fingers keep tingling from that too-brief contact. Irritation and fury roil in my chest as I give her one final look in the mirror.

"Time to get going," I say in a clipped tone and leave the dressing room.

CHAPTER
nine

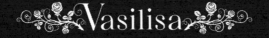

"THIS CAN'T BE RIGHT," I MUMBLE, STARING AT THE laptop screen.

"A problem, *vespetta*?" The deep voice comes from the corner of the office where Rafael is sitting.

A pleasant shiver runs down my spine, as it does every time he calls me that in that particular tone. Husky. Seductive. Intimate. Like smooth velvet gliding over my body, teasing my skin. My naked skin.

I grind my teeth, pushing away the mental images of me in Rafael's arms while he traces his finger down my spine, just as he'd done a week ago at Albini's. It was a mere few light touches, hardly noticeable, but I still can't get them out of my mind.

"I fixed the data storage repository the day before yesterday, but it looks like someone managed to fuck up the software again," I say, refusing to allow myself to look anywhere but at the screen.

It's hard enough to keep my focus with him just in the room, constantly feeling his attention on me. Although I've gotten used to men looking at me and learned to disregard their ogles years ago, Rafael's stares are very hard to ignore. He doesn't glare at me with lust-imbued eyes that seem to strip away my clothes, making me feel cheap and somehow dirty, as if there's nothing more to me than shapely flesh. Instead, it feels like Rafael is trying to peel away my outer layers, eager to reveal what lies beneath.

"That's unfortunate. You'll have to fix it again."

"I can't believe that a glorified decoy of a company can sprout so many issues."

"It may serve as a front for my clandestine enterprise, but the profits from it nearly match its shadow sister."

"So, not all personnel of Delta Security are actual hitmen?" From what I saw while working on the systems, there are over a hundred employees in his private security company.

"Of course not. One four-man team per branch only."

"They always go in teams? What if there's only a single target?"

"Are you planning on becoming my competitor, Miss Petrova?"

"Nope. Just curious." I shrug. "You don't have to tell me."

But I truly want to know. I want to know so much more about him. The random tidbits I've picked up are not enough. Not that I expect him to tell me confidential things about his business.

"Most hit contracts are for a single target," Rafael says, surprising me. "But that doesn't mean they're easy. We're talking about very public, high-ranking individuals who have tight personal protection and often reside in heavily guarded locations. If they end up on my agenda, it often means that my business rivals have chosen to pass on the job, and not for the lack of lucrative value. As such, even though it may take only one operative to execute the target, to ensure his infiltration and subsequent extraction proceed smoothly, he needs support.

Two team members provide surveillance. Another serves as a backup in case things go awry."

"Do the jobs often go wrong?"

"Sometimes." His tone changes, voice drops and comes out sounding almost savage. "I lost an entire team once."

"What happened?"

"One very important detail got missed." He grabs the wineglass off the table and, with brisk steps, crosses the room, stepping out on the balcony. "I didn't realize that the woman we were hired to assassinate was the girlfriend of a rival hitman. The bastard executed all four of my men before they even got the chance to reach their target. Fucking Mazur."

He launches the glass at the balcony banister. The stemware shatters, the sound of the breakage echoing through the air.

"You killed the guy who slaughtered your men, I assume."

"No." Rafael leans back on the railing, crossing his arms over his chest.

Slight shivers run down my spine from the intensity of his darkened gaze.

He doesn't say anything else, just watches me from a distance, as if waiting to see if I'll ask for an explanation. I want to. The interest this man ignites within me is beyond compare. Every time I think that I *get him*, he does something to contradict my conclusions.

"Why not?" I ask, a bit cautiously. "Why not retaliate for the killing of your men?"

"There are rules in every trade. In mine, one does not accept a hit contract against a fellow hitman or his family, no matter what the offered price is."

"I didn't expect there'd be an established etiquette in a business that deals in death."

"There is." His jaw hardens. "I broke the rule. And my men paid with their lives for my mistake."

A sudden urge to go to him and offer some kind of comfort overwhelms me. Even with the shadows that obscure most of his features, anger and self-blame are clearly written on his face. That doesn't track with him seeing his men only as hired work-force. Doesn't fit the picture of the shitty employer he hasn't denied being. There's more to Rafael De Santi than he wants to let on.

I glance at the sticky note I found stuck to the corner of the laptop screen. It's a drawing of a scene from this morning—of me, while I was having breakfast on the terrace. Alone. I believed he had already gone to work at that point.

The proof of that erroneous thought is in my hand. I smile at his attempt to capture little details, especially by using nothing more than a simple ballpoint pen. No one but me would ever be able to tell that the half-smudged blobs on the ends of the "doodle-me's" fingers are the marmalade stains from when I was stuffing a croissant into my mouth.

There are four more sketches just like this one, hidden in the drawer of my nightstand. Every time I stumble upon one, I need to fight not to give in to giggles like a schoolgirl. I wonder, what does he do with the doodles I leave for him? Probably throws my crude drawings in the trash.

Rafael's phone rings.

"*Pronto*," he barks.

I'm still staring at the sticky note when my desk chair is suddenly yanked back, the casters smoothly rolling over the floor. "What—"

"How the fuck did that happen?" Rafael leans over the laptop with the phone pressed to his ear.

With him this close, I can hear the muffled speech of a man on the other side of the line, but his English is heavily accented, which makes it hard to grasp what the guy is talking about. Rafael grabs the wireless mouse with his free hand and just nods to whatever the man is saying while minimizing the multitude of windows on the screen.

"Wait a second, Hans." He lowers the phone to the desk and looks at me.

"You want the chair?" I ask.

"Yes."

I nod and start untangling my legs from beneath my ass as I rise, but Rafael wraps his arm around my waist and lifts me.

"Chill, man!" I protest. "I was getting up."

"I may need you. You're staying." He drops onto the chair and sets me on his lap.

I stare at Rafael's profile as he rolls the chair closer to the desk and picks up the phone again while keeping his other arm tightly wrapped around my middle. He hits the video call option and leans the phone against the desktop pen holder. A video feed of a man wearing a black balaclava, so only his eyes are visible, fills the screen. His location appears to be a swanky room, with luxurious furniture and paintings in the background.

"Continue," Rafael tells the guy as he once again reaches for the mouse.

"The target pushed a hidden control of some kind, just before Allard executed him, and that sealed both of them inside the panic room."

"You can't get to Allard from the outside?"

"Negative. The door is reinforced steel, and we don't have anything to break through it. There's no other way in. We tried overriding the system from the main control board inside the house, but the panic room is an isolated network. Its circuits are not integrated with the primary house security."

On the screen, two windows pop open side by side. The first shows a guy dressed in tactical gear, complete with several weapons strapped to his chest, lounging in an antique-looking chair with a tumbler of amber liquid in his hand. I'm guessing he's the one stuck inside the panic room. The other video feed shows Mitch, Rafael's head IT guy whom I finally met in person at the Delta Security headquarters while doing a firmware update on the main server yesterday. He's sitting up in bed, wearing a familiar-looking bright-green T-shirt. I'm pretty sure it's Guido's.

"What about overriding it from the inside? Allard?"

"Not possible." The guy with the drink says. "The locking mechanism requires a thirteen-digit code to open the door. Only a single try is allowed, otherwise, an alarm is sent directly to their guard force."

Rafael squeezes the bridge of his nose. "Mitch?"

"I'm inside the security company's system, trying to find the access code for the door, but all their client data is encrypted. The decryption tools I've tried so far have failed."

"Keep trying. How much time do we have?"

Mitch takes a look at his wristwatch. "A little over an hour. We need to get Allard out before the staff arrive at seven. Punctuality is like a goddamn religion in Japan."

The pressure from the arm around my waist heightens. Rafael tilts his head, pinning me with his gaze. "How long would it take you to break a thirteen-digit code?"

"About four hours," I say.

"Fuck."

"It's been an honor working for you, boss." The man—Allard—takes a sip of his beverage and then sets it on the nearby table. "Tell the guys to retreat," he says and cocks his gun.

"Allard!" Rafael snarls and hits the top of the desk with his fist so hard that I jump on his lap. "Holster your fucking gun!"

"We all know how Yakuzas handle those who kill one of their own. They take torture to another level. We can't risk them finding me alive."

I bite my lower lip, my gaze bouncing between Rafael and

the trapped man on the video screen. No run-of-the-mill employee would be ready to kill himself to protect his employer. No matter what Rafael has told me, his men obviously care about him. And he for them.

"Is there a computer anywhere in the house?" I ask.

Three pairs of eyes snap to me immediately through the screens. I didn't realize that the camera on our end of the conversation had been broadcasting, as well.

"Why?" Rafael's voice rumbles next to my ear.

I turn to face him and bump his nose with mine. "Everything nowadays requires login credentials. Food delivery apps. Streaming services. Even the goddamned app to run a robot vac. No one can keep all that crap in their head."

"I'm fairly certain the *kumichō* of the Yakuza organization doesn't bother with vacuum cleaners, vespetta."

"*Sooooo* not the point here." I'd roll my eyes but the situation sounds precarious. "What I mean is, everyone has a secret file on their PC where they keep a list of their passwords and codes. Don't you?"

"Yes."

"There you go." I look directly at the camera and direct my question to the guy wearing the balaclava. "Did you see a laptop or a desktop computer anywhere?"

"One. In the study," he responds in heavily accented English. He sounds German. I assumed that the men working for Rafael would all be Italian, but based on the fact this conversation is happening in English, and the array of accents on the line, it appears that The Sicilian's crew has been gathered from across the globe.

"Good. I'll access it from here. Go there and get me the IP address."

"What if it's locked?"

"People are lazy," I say. "Personal computer passwords are typically less than eight characters long. Connect your phone to the laptop and run the program. I'll have Rafael send you the link. It should take no longer than ten minutes to break in."

The balaclava guy nods and, in the next breath, he's sprinting through the house.

As it happens, the owner of the swanky panic room must have been one of the laziest humans. His laptop password was only six digits, nothing more. My forwarded code breaker cracks it nearly instantly, allowing me to connect Rafael's laptop with the dead guy's in under a minute.

Finding the file we need, however, takes nearly a full hour. Generally, people tend to use the same word as their password in multiple applications. They vary it slightly with special characters, but the root remains unchanged. I first run a scan for the same keyword as the laptop login, then set up filters to search all files for documents that contain multiple repeated strings of letters. With narrowed-down options, I look through each flagged result manually, hoping that the next one I open will be the list of passwords. The fact that I'm simultaneously using the translator app in order to read each document, just to figure out if it's what I'm after or a recipe for homemade miso soup, makes the whole thing more difficult. My eyes sting and my head is killing me from the constant strain by the time I finally find what I'm looking for.

"There." I point at the number combination in the middle of the document, one that is right under the login credentials for a porn streaming site. "The panic room access code."

A slight shiver runs down my spine when Rafael takes my chin and tilts my head to face him. His eyes bore into mine and, for a moment, I forget how to breathe.

"If you're wrong, you've just signed my man's death sentence." His voice is low and slightly menacing, but the look in his eyes holds no threat. Just awe. "Are you sure?"

"I'm sure," I say, exhaling the pent-up breath.

Rafael nods and releases my chin, then turns and dictates

the code to Allard. Bewildered, I stare at Rafael's harsh profile. No further questions. He doesn't ask me to confirm one more time. Does not demand an explanation of why I'm confident that my conclusion is correct, or has Mitch double-check it. He is simply ready to risk his man's life on my word alone. He's trusting me and my skills by doing so. Believes in me.

A sense of satisfaction and pride swells within me, invading every single cell of my being. All those times I've aced tests in college can't compare to this feeling.

I look back to the screen where Allard is now facing the control panel at the door, his camera zoomed on the tiny narrow screen above the keypad. I suck air into my lungs and hold it, watching him input the numbers. When he enters the last digit, there's a barely audible click, but it echoes like thunder through the line.

It worked.

Rafael reaches out to his phone and turns it off, then closes the lid of the laptop. In that instant, sitting on his lap completely still, I become hyperaware of every point of contact between our bodies and every sensation that each connection evokes. His thick, heavily muscled arm wrapped around my waist. The warmth that seeps from his chest as he presses it to my aching back. The faint tingling of my cheek where his stubble brushes my skin.

"I never would have thought of that." Deep, smoky voice right next to my ear. "Have you found a list of my passwords, as well?"

"Yes," I utter. "You really need something more creative than *desanti1234* for your online banking app."

A sultry rumble of a laugh vibrates through me. "Have you been tempted to send another donation to a church choir, perhaps?"

I can't suppress the grin pulling at my lips. "Very much."

Rafael lightly brushes my chin with his thumb. "Thank you for helping save my friend's life."

"A friend?" I raise an eyebrow. "And here I thought your employees are just that—employees. Would he have really killed himself to avoid being captured?"

"Undoubtedly. When I first met Allard, he was rotting away in a cell of a Chinese prison, convicted of political espionage on behalf of France. His less-than-gracious hosts had been 'working' him for weeks, and he kept insisting on his innocence and that he came to China as a student in a foreign exchange program. I busted him out of that hellhole."

"So you saved an innocent man. That's noble. But what were you doing in a Chinese prison?"

"Following through on the hit contract for the French government—eliminating their most praised, yet recently compromised asset." A wicked smile pulls on Rafael's lips. "Zacharie Allard."

I snort. "So, not innocent after all?"

"Nope."

"You dropped the job, then?"

"I called my contact in the French government and told them I had the kid. I also relayed to them that their man hadn't broken his cover. They still insisted I proceed with neutralizing him anyway." Rafael's jaw hardens. "Allard withstood days of intense physical and mental torture, all without spilling a single secret. And his superiors still decided to reward his loyalty with a death sentence. So, yes, I dropped the contract."

"And recruited Allard to work for you."

"Of course. I offered him triple the pay he was getting from his treacherous agency. It was one of the best deals I've ever made."

"Don't you think that, maybe, you saving his life had something to do with him agreeing to work for you? Not the money."

"Money is the ultimate force that makes the world go round. People may not like that truth, but it doesn't make it less real." His finger is on my lips now, tracing the shape of the lower one.

"You're wrong," I mutter, captivated by his eyes peering into mine.

"I didn't peg you for naive, vespetta. But you're young and still have much to learn."

Rafael's phone starts to ring again. The touch on my lips disappears as he picks up the device off the desk and presses it to his ear.

"*Guido? Cosa è successo?*"

As soon as Guido starts talking on the other end of the line, Rafael leaps out of the chair. With me still seated on his lap, and him maintaining a viselike hold around my waist, I end up dangling half a foot above the floor, my back plastered to his chest.

"Rafael!" I tug on his forearm. "Do you mind?"

The hold around my middle loosens just a tiny bit. Just enough to let me slowly slide down his body, allowing me to feel the brush of every inch of that rock-hard front against me.

"*Merda. Venti minuti,*" he barks into the phone.

The hand still on my hip disappears and, the next moment, Rafael is heading across the room, toward the door that leads to the bedroom. He's still speaking in rapid Italian, and even though I don't have the faintest idea what he's saying, the clipped tone of his voice makes it clear that something is wrong. In a few long strides, he cuts the call and steps inside "my" room.

I dash after him, my heels clicking on the hardwood floor. With no hoodies or baggy pants available at Albini's, my new wardrobe consists of skinny jeans, shorts, and pretty blouses. I did get some canvas sneakers, but they're still boxed and pushed under the bed because I've been wearing heels most of the time.

I can't remember the last time I dressed so prettily and didn't feel bad as a result. There's no difference in Rafael's behavior toward me, either—he treats me exactly the same as he did while I walked around in his tent-size shirts. It's such a fucking relief. Yet, at the same time, I've been feeling slightly frustrated. Today, I put on a blouse with a particularly low neckline, and he hasn't glanced at my breasts even once. Not that I want him to.

Well, maybe a little.

Ugh.

This man confuses all my senses, and I don't even know what I want anymore.

I catch up with Rafael as he's stepping into the walk-in closet. Momentarily confused about his intentions, I almost miss as he presses his thumb to the small wall-mounted screen behind the row of his suits. A barely audible click sounds and the back wall of the closet begins to slide to the side. The next instant, Rafael disappears into a previously hidden room.

Trying to be as silent as I can, I tiptoe through the gap where Rafael pushed the suit jackets apart and find myself in a room that's about half the size of the walk-in closet. A counter runs along the entirety of the opposite wall, the space below it is filled with dozens of drawers. Above, nearly all the way to the ceiling, are cubbies, shelves, and brackets, but it's not clothes they hold. It's weapons. Knives. Dozens of various caliber handguns. Long-range rifles. In one of the corners, utility crates are stacked nearly waist-high, and more weapons are slotted into gun racks mounted on both sides of the room.

The last time I saw so many weapons in one place, was when Uncle Sergei showed me his armory (well, one of them, at least). I made the mistake of telling Dad and ended up grounded for a week. Uncle Sergei sported a busted lip for days afterward. If Dad ever finds out that my uncle taught me how to use most of the weapons in that armory (the other one contains explosives and assault weapons, and Uncle Sergei has never allowed me to see those, unfortunately), he would totally go apeshit.

Rafael opens one of the top drawers below the counter and takes out a few small boxes, setting them on the countertop in front of him. Ammunition. He removes his black suit jacket and throws it onto the counter, too, revealing the dark-gray dress shirt he has on underneath. Reaching into another drawer, he selects a shoulder harness and puts it on, adjusting the straps. After grabbing two handguns off the shelf before him, he checks their ammo, then slots the pistols and the extra magazines into their holsters.

"Rafael? What's going on?"

"This is turning out to be an eventful evening. I have to go resolve a misunderstanding at the port." He approaches the side wall and takes down one of the mounted rifles, then pulls out a box with ammunition from another nearby drawer.

"You usually solve misunderstandings with a Remington?" I choke out as panic builds in my chest.

Rafael's head snaps up, his gaze collides with mine while a corner of his lips quirks upward. "Is that worry I hear in your voice, Miss Petrova?"

My body goes rigid. "Nope. I think you mistook it for excitement."

A strange look settles on his face, and with his eyes never leaving mine, Rafael takes a step toward me. I take one back. He keeps advancing, I keep retreating. Until I'm in the walk-in closet again, and my back is pressed against the rack of his shirts. Rafael stops in front of me and leans over until our faces align.

"I've never met a woman who can identify a particular

make of tactical rifle," he says, astonishment glowing in his eyes.

I draw in a breath, and my olfactory receptors swell with his scent. Fresh. Seductive. My gaze lowers to his lips. Two thick scars bisect the lower one, making it misshapen, before continuing down his chin. How would it feel to have those lips on mine? What would they taste like? I raise a hand, pressing my palm to his chest. Hopefully, that will be enough to stop me from leaning in further and trying to find out for myself.

Rafael reaches out and brushes his knuckles down my cheek. "You can keep the laptop to finish what you started, but the activity on that device is monitored. If you get inspired to contact someone online or share things you know you shouldn't, please remember that one word from me, and your family will lose their lives in minutes."

And just like that, my worry for him transforms into rage.

I push him away and I scurry out of the walk-in and back to the office to get the fucking laptop. I can't wait to be done with this crap so I can return home. I thought this "job" would last only a few days, but I've been here almost three weeks.

We both enter the bedroom at the same time. I'm heading toward the bed with the laptop under my arm, while Rafael makes a beeline from the walk-in to the door. As we pass each other, our hands brush ever so slightly.

The touch lasts less than a heartbeat, but it feels like the back of my hand is singed. I climb into the huge bed and, folding my legs under my ass, open the laptop in front of me.

"Sleep well, vespetta." His husky voice comes from the entryway.

I don't bother looking up from the screen, simply raise my hand and flip him the bird. A thunderous laugh fills the space between us before the door shuts in his wake.

An hour later, I can still hear the roaring in my head.

Rafael

I step out of the car. "Who started it?"

"Rizzuto," Aurelio, my main man at the Catania Port, says. "One of the cranes has been out of commission since Friday, causing delays. Rizzuto tried to bribe the freight forwarder to get bumped to the top of the import customs queue and then through the inspections and out the gate. He went ballistic when they wouldn't do it. Port security got involved, and there was a confrontation. Rizzuto holed up in the admin offices, taking the terminal operators hostage, and is threatening to start shooting unless his cargo is processed and released tonight."

I look up at the third floor of the building that serves as the port control tower. Rizzuto is one of the biggest alcohol smugglers in Sicily. He brings in high-end French and Spanish wines and pays hefty bribes to have port and customs officials rubber-stamp the necessary clearances. I don't give a fuck what he's peddling as long as he keeps up his part of our deal and drops half a million into my bank account annually for letting him use the Catania harbor. Delays are not uncommon, as Rizzuto is well aware of. And he doesn't have a history of being unreasonable.

"Has anyone checked his containers?" I ask.

"No. They're still at the stacks."

"Let's have a look at them."

Even at such a late hour, the port is buzzing with life. Shouted orders fill the air as the cargo is loaded and unloaded from the vessels by gantry cranes. Forklifts and terminal tractors move around the storage yard, stacking the containers that then undergo final inspections before being released for dispatch and loaded onto the distribution trucks. I don't like all that commotion, so only come here when it's absolutely necessary. Assassinating people is so much easier than working with them.

"Open the first one," I tell the dockworker standing by the three green containers in the temporary storage area.

The man hurries to unlock the heavy-duty swing doors and then moves out of the way. I take the crowbar from Aurelio and step inside.

Wooden crates bearing the logo of a well-known French winery in Bordeaux are neatly stacked one on top of the other, filling nearly the entire steel container. A faint woody odor permeates the air. I jam the chisel end of the crowbar between the two boards of the closest crate and push. The planks break and splinter. White powder spills from the plastic package that got torn up by the busted edge of the destroyed box frame and drips to the floor next to my shoe. I catch a dribble of the fine particles with my fingers and bring them to my mouth. Cocaine.

Spitting out the bitter traces, I throw the crowbar aside. "Find a suitable place and incinerate the whole load. I want it done by morning, Aurelio."

"Sure, boss."

I nod and head back out, while fury rages inside me. There's only one person on the island who can get his hands on coke this pure.

Guido is lounging by his sports car, chatting with one of the forklift drivers, but when he sees me returning to the control tower, he heads toward me. "Aurelio messaged me. What's going on?"

"Calogero tried to smuggle his drugs in Rizzuto's cargo." I grab the rifle out of the back of my SUV and slam the door shut.

"Fuck. You sure it's his?"

"Yes." I cock the rifle and head to the tower's main entrance. "Go help Aurelio organize the torching of that shit," I tell my brother over my shoulder.

The bottom level of the building is a vast warehouse, used to store machinery and cargo that's been held up at port for various reasons. The floors above are filled with administrative offices. My footfalls make hollow sounds as I climb the metal stairs to the top level where the control room and port operator center are located.

"Has he calmed down?" I ask the man standing guard at the door.

"A little. He still won't let anyone leave the room, but he stopped waving his gun after we told him you're here."

I nod and step inside the control room.

Rizzuto is sitting in one of the chairs facing the wall of windows with a view of the container terminal, his gun is casually draped across his thighs. Four operators are gathered in the opposite corner, their eyes frantic.

"Rafael!" Rizzuto smiles. "I'm so glad you could make it. Hopefully, we can resolve this misunderstanding quickly so I can have my cargo processed and on its way as planned."

His eyes fall to the rifle in my hand, and that smile gets wiped off his face immediately. "Umm . . . I'm sorry if I overreacted, but I'm on a really tight schedule."

I pull a chair toward me, positioning it across from Rizzuto, and take a seat. "Why the haste?"

"I have a new buyer. Not a very patient fellow that one." He tries to hide his nervousness behind his casual posture, but I see the beads of sweat along his temple.

"Mm-hmm. Tell me, how much did Calogero pay you to smuggle his cocaine through my port?"

Rizzuto's face pales.

"It's mine," he chokes out while his hold on the gun tightens. "You know I wouldn't dare bringing Cosa Nostra's drugs here. I swear on my mother's grave, Rafael. I—"

I press the barrel of my rifle to his forehead and pull the trigger. The top of Rizzuto's head explodes in a mess of bone, blood, and brain matter, with some of the carnage propelled through the shattered glass. Lowering the rifle, I rise and leave the room, passing the group of hysterical workers on my way out.

Outside the building, I find Guido by his car again, staring at the blood and chunks of flesh scattered across his windshield.

"The fuck, Rafael!" he grunts. "Will you stop littering my car with people's remains? That's disgusting!"

"Sorry. I forgot you parked just below." I throw the blood-ied rifle in the back my vehicle. "Make sure everyone keeps their mouths shut about what happened here tonight. Let's see what Calogero does when he realizes his drugs never left the port."

"He'll probably send his men to investigate."

"If he does, you know what needs to be done." I slide behind the wheel and step on the gas.

When I get home, I take a shower in the guest room, then slip inside my bedroom. My little hacker is curled up in my bed—asleep—still wearing the same outfit she was in when I left. The top two buttons of the pale-peach silk blouse are undone, revealing a glimpse of the white lace bra underneath. My eyes slide down her legs, clad in white skinny jeans, to the ivory stiletto sandals strapped to her delicate feet. She obviously dozed off while working, since my laptop is lying open next to her in bed.

I lean over and carefully unbuckle her shoes. As I'm doing so, my eyes fall on the lit-up laptop screen. It displays the website of my front company. The URL and the corporate name are correct, but instead of the dark-navy header and silver text, the feature image is of two cartoon frogs wearing pink hats. And the little green croakers are winking. Meanwhile, our customers' reviews on the slider, have been changed to a cursive font with hearts dotting every lowercase "i" on the page.

Setting the heeled sandals by the bed, I move the laptop

to the nightstand and pull up the duvet to Vasilisa's chin. My little trickster. I reach into my pocket and take out the jewelry box I picked up on my way home, then place it by the laptop. The store owner nearly had a stroke when he found me on his doorstep at four in the morning. The blood all over my jacket and shirt didn't help. It took him several attempts to spit out the words that the bracelet I ordered would arrive tomorrow. I had to pacify my irritation by buying a pair of ruby earrings instead.

They aren't exquisite enough. Hardly the exceptional pieces I need, since the stones are nothing but a common cut. But they were the most expensive thing he had in the store. If it comes to it, I'm prepared to buy every exclusive piece of jewelry in Sicily for Vasilisa, in hopes that she may be open to accepting my advances. Maybe she'll even consider going out to dinner with me.

After lightly brushing the tips of my fingers across Vasilisa's cheek, I head to the recliner by the fireplace. It has a direct view of my sleeping tormentor, so I get comfortable in what has become my coveted nightly spot. It's too late to get my own shut-eye anyway, and watching my sweet prisoner is much more enjoyable than a couple of hours of rest.

CHAPTER
Ten

Vasilisa

"T HIS IS AMAZING," I MUMBLE WHILE SHOVELING A mixture of scrambled eggs, bell peppers, and some sort of green stuff into my mouth. "Seriously, Irma, you should open your own place instead of working for Rafael. Nobody in this house eats here except me anyway, so it's a total waste of your talent. Truly, you should just quit."

Irma throws a look at Guido, who's sipping his coffee on the other side of the dining table, and he translates for her. When he's done, she just blinks at him in confusion, then throws me a smile and busies herself putting the dishes into the dishwasher.

Male voices drift through the open window—the handy-men are still here. They've finished painting all the doors and windows, and have now switched to graveling the driveway. For whatever reason, they're removing the existing cover—which seemed more than decent to me as is and didn't look like it needed replacing—and spreading new crushed rock.

In the kitchen, the two maids appear to be busy. One is rewashing the pots—by hand—after she wiped (for a second time this week) the inside of the cupboards, while the other is tenderizing meat on the island countertop. Guido's forehead creases, and he jerks slightly, with every loud strike of the meat mallet. It's really funny to watch.

I have no problem with household noise. Compared to home, this is almost like being at a library. Still, it's much better than it was before Rafael ordered the household staff to return.

"Why am I the only one who eats in this house?" I ask Guido between bites. It's weird, and somehow sad, having all my meals alone. "You normally take your bowl of bird food somewhere else, and I've never seen your brother eat anything here at all. Does he even need sustenance, or does he just hunt his prey in the neighborhood and drink their blood?"

"Guido is an introvert who likes to eat his meals in his apartment." The velvety voice rumbles behind me. "And I usually eat at work."

My eyes track Rafael as he goes to the coffee machine and pours himself a cup. He's in a brown three-piece suit today, paired with a black dress shirt. The top two buttons are undone. No tie. Brown and black together don't sound like a good fashion combination. For him, however, it definitely works. But he looks really tired, and unfortunately, still drop-dead gorgeous, despite the dark circles under his eyes.

"Is there anything else you'd like to know about my habits?" he continues. "Or were you simply interested in inviting me to have lunch with you, Miss Petrova?"

"Having lunch in your company would be the low point of my day," I say and grab a glass of milk. "You look like crap, by the way."

Absolute silence descends on the room. The maid who's been putting the pots back into the cupboards is staring at me open-mouthed. The other one is doing the same, her mallet frozen in midair as if she were struck motionless by lightning. Irma was preoccupied stirring something on the stove, but now she's just got the spoon in a death grip, and her wide eyes are fused to the nearby wall. Guido's gaze, on the other hand, darts from me to Rafael and back.

"No better way to start a day than by getting compliments," Rafael says and takes a sip of his coffee.

"Did you resolve the *misunderstanding* last night?" I ask.

"Yes. It just took a little longer than expected." He approaches the table with an unhurried stride and unceremoniously takes a seat beside me. "Love what you did with our website."

I choke on my milk.

"That was her?" Guido snaps from across the table.

"Do we have another hacker with a grudge against me who also has unbridled access to our systems?"

"Mitch has been trying to fix the issue for the past two hours, but there's some malicious code implanted into our server-side scripts and any change he makes won't stick."

Rafael cocks his head, observing me over the rim of his coffee cup. "She'll fix it."

"She will?" I raise my eyebrow.

"Yes. And she'll go to dinner with me as punishment for her misbehavior."

"Dinners weren't a part of our agreement."

"Neither was further fucking with my business. And, I wasn't asking, vespetta. It's a perfect opportunity to wear your new earrings."

"Yeah, too bad I left all of them at home." I reach for a slice of cherry tart, feeling Rafael's eyes punching holes into my head the entire time. Feigning innocence, I take a bite and meet his gaze. "Oh, you mean the ones you left on my nightstand mere hours after reminding me that you're holding the lives of people I love in your hand?"

"Yes."

"They are in your desk drawer. The second one from the top."

Rafael's hand shoots out, seizing my chin between his fingers. The silence in the room becomes so absolute that a feather could drop, and the boom would echo off the walls. With eyes narrowed, Rafael leans forward, drawing level with my face.

"I'll come get you at six," he says through his teeth, then releases me and storms out of the kitchen.

I look back at my tart while fuming internally at my own reaction. My problem? I'm actually excited about going to dinner with him. *Goddammit.*

"We should have gotten that dress from Albini's," Rafael says as he pulls into the parking lot of an upscale restaurant with a terrace perched on the edge of a hillside, overlooking the sea.

"It's an evening gown meant for wearing to galas or other such suitable events. Not to dinner at a local eatery hot spot."

"Then, I guess we'd have to find a suitable event," Rafael says as he reverses and parks.

I'm actually tempted to say we should. That dress was the most beautiful one I've ever seen. But, the last time I chanced going out in something similar, I regretted it right away.

On that occasion, I attended a charity fundraiser with a guy I was sort of seeing at the time. He was the son of a Chicago politician, several years older than me, and I thought he would be more mature than my previous dates. I asked about the work his father was doing, but the guy completely ignored my questions, too focused on my cleavage. He also kept insinuating that his apartment was only a block away. The entire fucking evening.

Is a normal, meaningful conversation too much to expect from a date? It must be, because when I mentioned that I agreed to go out so I could get to know him a little better, he looked at me all confused and asked: *Why would you dress like that if you don't want to be fucked?* I stopped dressing up at that point. Stopped going out, too. It simply wasn't worth it.

Agreeing to try on that gorgeous gown at Albini's was a moment of weakness. I missed wearing pretty things, and that dress was beyond stunning and impossible to resist. When Rafael barged into the dressing room, I momentarily worried what his reaction to seeing me in it would be.

He didn't even bat an eye.

My gaze flits toward Rafael as he turns off the ignition. He must be the first man who hasn't tried persuading me into his bed within an hour of meeting me. Going by the looks he's been giving me, I'm fairly certain he finds me . . . intriguing? Probably in the same way a lab worker is fascinated with a new strain of bacteria, though. He might enjoy observing it, but isn't actually tempted to kiss the thing.

It bothers me a bit. His apparent immunity to me. And the fact that it does, bothers me quite a lot. I'm so fucking confused about everything. Why am I so drawn to Rafael? Why does my heart skip a beat every time he comes near? Is it just some kind of wacky curiosity? I'm not certain that it is.

Tonight, I picked a revealing, open-backed sparkly silver halter top that ties around the neck. Along with it, I've put on super-tight black pants and metallic gray six-inch heels. I was one hundred percent sure Rafael's jaw would drop when I stepped through the mansion's front entrance to where he was waiting by the car. The only thing he said? *You may get chilly in that top, vespetta.* And then, he opened the passenger door for me.

Is he even attracted to me?

Sometimes I think he is, but other times, like tonight, I think he's just amused by me.

I watch Rafael as he exits the vehicle, his three-piece graphite suit fitting his large frame just as it should—tailored specifically for him. He checks all my boxes. Tall. Dark-haired. Heavily muscled. Stylish. Doesn't turn into a dickheaded teenage boy when he happens to be in my company. I don't care that his face is so scarred that it's basically misshapen. Rafael is the hottest man I've ever laid eyes on.

He's also a mean asshole who kidnapped me and threatened my family. That gets him instantly disqualified from my list.

But I want him to kiss me anyway.

The valet opens my door, offering me his hand. "*Buonasera, signorina—*"

Strong fingers wrap around the man's wrist, cutting off the rest of the guy's sentence.

"*Non toccarla,*" Rafael says through his teeth, glaring at the young man who looks like he's a second away from pissing himself. "*Lei è mia. Capito?*"

"*Sì. Ho capito, Signor De Santi. Mi dispiace molto,*" the man chokes out and quickly steps away.

"What happened?" I ask as I take Rafael's extended hand.

"He wanted to repark my car," he says, helping me out. "I thanked him and said no."

"That didn't sound like a *thank you* to me. And he is the valet. It's his job to park cars. Why wouldn't you let him?"

Our gazes collide. We're standing face to face now. Okay, more like face to chest. Even with sky-high heels on, I have to crane my neck quite a bit to be able to meet Rafael's eyes.

He dips his head, and one of the strands of his slicked-back hair falls forward, tickling my forehead. With my hand still in his, he gently strokes my knuckles with his thumb.

"I don't allow other people to touch what's mine, Vasilisa."

A shiver runs down my spine from the way he pronounces my name, with a hint of an Italian lilt. It feels like the softest caress.

"It's just a car," I whisper.

His eyes crease at the corners, and then he moves his

hand to the small of my back, urging me toward the restaurant entrance.

There are around twenty tables inside, and half that many on the cliffside terrace. Grapevines have climbed and twisted around the pillars and along the banister edging the vista and up across the white overhead arbor, creating a beautiful canopy that must shelter the outdoor tables from the midday heat. Right now, though, as we cross the veranda, bits of the nighttime sky and brilliant stars play peekaboo through the gaps in the greenery.

Whimsical is the only way I can describe the sight around me, and I feel as if I've entered another dimension. One that promises romance and an enchanted evening.

If only it were true.

But the ambience in this restaurant is breathtaking. When we pass through the interior, I notice a girl in a pretty, long dress playing the harp in the corner, close to the bar. The subtle tones of the strings mix with the quiet chatter from the people seated nearby.

The hostess leads us to the one unoccupied table at the far side of the terrace, and by the time we reach our destination, the voices of other patrons gradually die down, only the distinctive melody from the harp remains. Every person—both inside and dining alfresco—seems to be intently focused on their meal, their eyes glued to the plates set before them.

"Looks like you're quite popular around here," I comment as I take a seat on the chair Rafael has slid out for me. "Are they expecting you to pull out your Remington and off them all before the appetizers arrive?" I look around the place, where people are slowly resuming their hushed conversations.

"I was born here. This is a locals-only restaurant, and everyone in Taormina knows me," he says. "When I returned to Sicily and took control of the east coast, the people living here became mine. They are under my protection."

"Their faces don't give off that 'oh, I feel so protected' vibe. Scared shitless would be a much more accurate description."

"That's because they know what I did in order to take over."

"Let me guess. You 'retired' your predecessor? I didn't think that's how Cosa Nostra worked."

Rafael sits across from me and leans back in his seat. "I'm not a member of Cosa Nostra. And I did 'retire' my predecessor and every one of his followers who didn't flee to Palermo when I moved back home."

"Well, no wonder the atmosphere here feels weird."

A waiter brings a bottle of wine, presenting it to Rafael, who nods his approval without even glancing at the label. His eyes are solely focused on me.

"You don't seem bothered by uncomfortable social situations."

"Please." I snort. "After spending over twenty years with a family like mine, anyone could handle whatever the universe decides to throw up. Especially during social gatherings."

"Care to elaborate?"

I pick up the glass of wine the waiter has poured for me and take a long sip. This is not how I thought this evening would go. I don't know what I actually expected, but it certainly wasn't this pleasant feeling due to just being in Rafael De Santi's company.

"Well, a few months ago, my dad threw a surprise party for my mom's birthday. There were around forty people at the table, and we were in the middle of a toast when my uncle barged in, fully armed and covered in blood."

"That must have been uncomfortable."

"Not really." I shrug. "The problem was, he left bloody stains on Mom's favorite carpet, so my dad started yelling and then shot him."

"Roman killed him?"

"Of course not. Uncle Sergei arrived straight from work and was wearing Kevlar, so he just sprawled on the floor and stayed there until he caught his breath. Some of the guests got a little nervous, though."

"Remarkable. " He leans forward and props his elbow on the armrest, dropping his chin onto his palm. "I still find it hard to believe that Roman accepted your 'I needed a break' excuse for going missing."

"As I said, it's not the first time I've disappeared. And I wouldn't go so far as to say he 'accepted' it, considering the amount of yelling he does every time I call. Maybe I should have told him that I was caught hacking NASA and was recruited to work for the government instead of getting put behind bars."

"You hacked NASA?"

"Once or twice." I lift my glass to hide my grin and empty its contents. "I could have complained how the supervisor I was assigned is one mean bastard."

A deep laugh rumbles out of him. Dear God, even his chuckles are sexy. I'm so absorbed in watching him that it takes me a couple of moments to register the absolute silence that once again descends around us. It's just like this morning in the kitchen. Everyone has stopped what they were doing, even the waiter who just finished refilling my glass, and is staring at Rafael's back.

"I'm sure you're giving him hell." He leans across the table and takes my chin between his fingers, stroking my skin with his thumb while his eyes bore into mine. "Can you hack into any system?"

Our faces are barely inches apart, but I find myself leaning further into his touch.

"Depends on the system," I whisper. "And its security, of course. But in theory, yes."

His thumb drifts to stroke my lower lip, and my breathing ratchets up. The swarm of butterflies nestled in my stomach from the moment I slipped into his car, takes flight. I can feel their fluttering wings as the excitement overwhelms me. Rafael draws nearer, his eyes gleaming. Is he going to kiss me? My lips part in expectation of that first contact.

"Would you hack a certain freight company for me, vespetta?"

My excitement plummets. "What?"

"I'd like you to change the shipping details of a certain container. It's supposed to be delivered to Genoa next week. I would prefer for it to end up somewhere else. Maybe Shanghai."

His thumb still stroking my lips is epically fucking with my brain. I can feel his touch all the way to my core, and it's evoking images of much more than kissing. So, while I'm ready to combust on the spot, he wants to discuss some goddamned shipping details?

I reach for my glass and take a large sip of the robust wine. The server approaches, filling it up again. Good.

"Nope. Why would I do anything for you outside of our agreement?"

"Because I asked you to."

"And do you always get what you want?"

"Usually, yes. Even if it means trashing your baggy clothes to force you to accept your beauty."

I suck in a breath, then grab the wineglass and empty it again, my eyes cast downward. "You've never called me beautiful before."

"Because you've probably heard that phrase spoken a million times by countless shallow men. Because you *must* know that you're beautiful and that men can't help but notice and sing your praises. And I'm willing to bet that you hate hearing it." He places his finger under my chin, lifting my gaze to meet his. "It doesn't work, you know. You can wrap yourself in a fucking tablecloth, and men will still fall to their knees before you, Vasilisa. There's nothing wrong with that."

Yes, there is.

151

When I was little, it didn't matter if you were pretty or not—children just wanted to play.

I'd be lying if I said I didn't enjoy the attention I started getting when I got older, especially in high school. Boys were always approaching me, saying how pretty I was, asking me out all the time. All the guys wanted to be with me. And the girls wanted to be me. I enjoyed it a helluva lot. God, I was so vain then. Or simply too young. But, little by little, things started to change. More accurately, actually, *I* started to change. And I remember the exact day that was the tipping point.

Our tenth-grade music and theater teacher announced that I'd been cast as the lead in the school play. I was so happy and proud of myself because of how hard I worked to get the role—learning the whole script by heart and spending hours practicing in front of the mirror. I even skipped my sister's birthday party so I could rehearse a bit more before my audition the following day. But after the announcement, I heard other students whispering: *Oh, everyone knows she just got the role because she's pretty.* Everybody kept saying it, and by the time the classes let out, even I believed it. The next morning, I told my teacher that I quit. Then, I went home and cried.

After that, similar things happened quite often. It wasn't my paper on world hunger that got me chosen to speak during a school event, but rather because *she would look good on the poster.* And I didn't graduate high school with a 4.0 GPA because I had taken extra online courses, it was because *she got extra credits for flashing her tits at the dean.*

"You know, I got the highest grade in my cryptography class last semester. The best result in the past decade," I say.

"I'm not surprised."

"Everyone said it was because 'the professor wanted to bang me.' Not because I worked my butt off studying."

"Why do you care what anyone thinks?"

I look up and meet Rafael's gaze. The space between my

temples feels strangely light and airy. I should probably cut back on the wine. Especially since my tongue has gotten loose. Why is it so easy to talk to him?

"People are not islands, Rafael. We don't exist alone, detached from everything. You can't just ignore others' opinions."

"I don't agree."

The lantern hanging among the grape leaves above our table swings in the soft breeze, casting an intermittent glow over his harsh features and making the lines on his face even more pronounced in the interplay of light and shadows. His thumb resumes its gentle caress on my chin, sending pulses of pleasure along my skin. My fingers itch to do the same to him.

"Oh? And yet, you spent days hiding from me. Why?"

"People have very strong reactions when they see my face for the first time. Women especially. I didn't want you to be afraid of me."

"There are many things that scare me, Rafael. Your face isn't one of them."

"Tell me what they are, and I'll vanquish each one."

"Heights. Water creatures. Malls."

"Shopping malls?"

"Yes. I can't handle them." I hold his gaze. "But my worst fear . . . is of my loved ones getting hurt. Will you please pull your henchmen whose crosshairs are aimed at my family?"

The muscle in Rafael's jaw ticks. He doesn't reply.

"Please," I whisper. "I promise I'll keep to our deal and stay until my job is done."

It doesn't feel so unbearable anymore. Staying here. With him. If I were brutally honest with myself, I'd admit that my heart constricts as if it's being squeezed by a viselike grip whenever I think about leaving. I quite enjoy our everyday bickering. I like spending time with him. I like . . . him. My God, why couldn't we have met under different circumstances? I have no doubts that I would have totally fallen for Rafael then. But maybe, regardless of our situation, I already have? No. Absolutely not. It's simply the wine talking.

Rafael takes a deep breath, his nostrils flaring as his eyes sear into mine, then leans back in his chair and pulls out his phone. My heart thumps so fast it could break through my ribs as he dials someone and puts the phone up to his ear.

"Guido, recall the team on the Petrovs . . . Yes, now."

"Thank you," I say when he hangs up.

Rafael's hand shoots out, grabbing the back of my neck. His gaze locks with mine, his green eyes glistening with menace. "Break your word, and you know what'll happen. Do you understand?"

"I won't break it."

"Good. Let's order." He gestures at the waiter offhandedly.

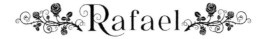

Rafael

The diners at the other tables keep throwing covert glances in our direction throughout our meal. They don't think they're being obvious, but I catch every single look.

By morning, everyone living in the area will know that I had dinner with an unknown woman. Taormina is a small town, and here, I'm the primary subject of gossip.

There are two popular topics of speculation. The first—what happened that caused me to look like this. Theories are endless, from a car crash in the US to being tortured by Mancuso before I made my escape as a kid. The second revolves around my love life. Guido told me that every time I'm seen with a new hookup, there are bets on whether she'll be the one who'll capture my alleged heart.

I don't have a problem with prying eyes trying to catch glimpses of us. But I do have an issue with men ogling my woman.

Like the guy sitting at the table to our right. He's been salivating over my Russian princess for the past few minutes. It started with an occasional subtle peek as soon as we walked in, but his stares have been getting bolder. Making sure Vasilisa is still engrossed in choosing her dessert, I take the paring knife from the rustic citrus board that had accompanied our platter of a whole roast chicken. It's small but extremely sharp.

"What are these?" Vasilisa asks, looking over the selection of sweets the waiter brought out.

"Cannoli," I say, testing the tip of the knife with my thumb. "They have a creamy sweet ricotta cheese filling, as well as other variations with vanilla, chocolate, and pistachio."

Pinching the blade with my fingertips, I assess the distance, then flick my wrist and send the knife sailing in a slight arc. The tip lodges in the wooden tabletop, right between the fucktard's dinner plate and his hand holding a fork. The man tenses, gaping at me. I motion with two fingers to my eyes, then point to the knife protruding inches from his flesh, silently letting him know that it's the only spot he's allowed to look at. The guy quickly nods, his eyes snapping down to the table surface.

"Why did you do that?" Vasilisa asks, her gaze zeroed in on the knife. I hoped she wouldn't notice.

"There was a cockroach. Nasty little buggers." I take one of the cannoli from the serving tray and lift it to her mouth. "Delectable traditional filling. Try it."

Vasilisa blinks, her eyes bouncing between mine and the pastry, then slowly leans forward and takes a small bite of the offering. Powdered sugar and some of the cream end up on her rosy lips, broadcasting flashes of her sinful mouth wrapped around my cock straight to my brain.

I've been probing the entire evening—small touches here and there to garner her reaction to me. She hasn't recoiled once. I'm tempted to conclude that those ruby earrings did make a difference, even though she returned the gift. Still, even with the incentive, her behavior is unlike anything I've come to expect from a woman. Vasilisa's eyes remain locked on mine as I brush the remnants from her lips with my thumb and keep stroking the plumped flesh even after the confection is gone.

Time stops as my finger traces her mouth, until my phone vibrates on the table with an incoming message, breaking the spell.

"Um . . . thank you," she mumbles and straightens quickly.

"Anytime." Amused by the look of confusion on her face, I smirk and pick up my phone. The text is from Guido, letting me know that several of Calogero's men were seen in Catania earlier tonight. "I'm afraid we have to leave."

"Yeah, um . . . sure," she stammers through her words. "I left a diagnostic program running on the server I fixed yesterday. It should be done by the time we get back, so I can resume working."

"As much as I'd like to spend the evening watching you work, it'll have to wait till tomorrow. I have to go to Catania as soon as I drop you off." I rise and remove my suit jacket, holding it out in front of me.

Vasilisa glances at the jacket I'm offering, then back up at me, arching her eyebrow. "I'm fine, thank you."

"There are goose bumps all over your arms," I growl. "Put it on or I'm going to force you into it. Now, please."

Grumbling something in Russian, she turns around and slides her arms through the sleeves. When she faces me again, my eyes sweep over her, marveling at the sight of my little trickster in my suit jacket. I'm extremely territorial when it comes to my personal things, clothes especially. Allowing anyone to wear something of mine is too intimate. And I don't do intimate. But seeing Vasilisa dwarfed by my huge jacket has the same effect on me as seeing her wearing my shirts. It makes me instantly hard as granite.

Every man who sets eyes on her now will know that she's mine. The thought makes my cock swell even more, aching painfully behind the zipper of my pants. Maybe I should throw away all the clothes I bought her and have her walk around in nothing but my shirts again?

"You know, this deal of ours would be concluded much faster if you let me keep the laptop and work throughout the day," she says while trying to fold the sleeve and squinting her eyes.

"Exactly." I gently move Vasilisa's hand away and begin rolling up the sleeve for her. "How much did you have to drink?"

"Just two glasses. Maybe three." She tries to pull her arm free, stumbling backward in the process. My hand shoots out instantly, wrapping around her waist to keep her steady.

I pull her flush with my chest as I glance at the wine left on the table. The bottle is nearly empty, and I only drank half a glass. I guess she resorted to getting wasted to endure looking at my deformed face for a couple of hours. She's not the first. One of my past hookups always got drunk before meeting up with me.

I move my hand off Vasilisa's waist and take a step back. "Let's go."

She barely manages two full steps without swaying. Fuck. I wrap my arm around her again and slide the other one under her knees, lifting and cradling her to my chest. With her face only inches from mine, I can't help but expect her to scream or wince. But, just like that night in the rock garden, she only bats her long lashes at me. Her unfocused gaze meets mine, and I recall that she was drunk then, also. Maybe that's the reason for her lack of reaction.

"You can close your eyes if it'll make it easier," I say.

The corners of her lips tilt up, an impish smile lights up her dark depths. She wraps her arm around my neck and leans closer, touching the tip of her nose to mine. "Sorry to burst your bubble, Rafael, but you're not *that* tall. My fear of heights doesn't kick in until I'm twenty feet off the ground."

I take a deep breath, fighting the urge to seize that bratty mouth with mine. I want her. I want her more than I've ever wanted anyone before. And I don't hold back when I want something.

"One million," I say, staring into her dark eyes.

Vasilisa's brow furrows. "One million?"

"The amount you'll get for this kiss," I growl and slam my mouth to hers.

Vasilisa

I can't think. I can only feel.

The taste of him. The warmth, spreading through my chest.

The most alluring flame singeing me from the inside out.

Rafael's mouth attacks mine with such ferocity that I can't even draw a breath, but who the hell needs air? I wrap my arms around his neck, squeezing with all my might as I kiss him back like it's the end of the fucking world.

It just might be. Mine anyway. But I'm ready to burn in the fire he sparked.

The incessant ringing of a phone finally penetrates my daze. I hadn't realized how quiet everything was around us until now. Rafael's phone keeps going off in his pocket, but he ignores it completely, continuing to ravage me with his mouth.

The smell of him, the same scent that is now mine, is making me crazy. I tug his lower lip with my teeth, suck on it. A low growl leaves his throat, and then he bites me. Nips on my tingling lips. My fingers tunnel through his hair, pulling, messing it up. He always keeps it slicked perfectly back. Vehemently controls everything about him. Not anymore.

It's glorious.

It's wild.

He's unrestrained.

"Signor De Santi." An unknown male voice breaks through the trance that surrounds me.

Rafael's lips go still, then slowly release mine, letting me draw the first breath in what feels like hours. Despite my grip on his strands, he tilts his head and glares at the waiter. The man, standing mere feet away, flinches and seems to shrink in stature, but holds up a phone to Rafael.

"*Potrei ucciderti per questo,*" Rafael barks at the little dude who looks like he'd rather be anywhere else but here.

"*È Guido, Signor De Santi,*" the poor guy stutters. "*Dice che è urgente.*"

"I'm sorry, vespetta. I have to take this," Rafael says as he gently lowers me to the ground, then snatches the phone from the offering hand and starts yelling at the caller.

During his menacing tirade—I can tell by the tone of his voice—that lasts for at least two minutes, Rafael keeps his free arm wrapped around my waist, basically crushing me to his front. I put my palms on his chest, feeling the vibrations deep within him, while trying to gather my senses.

Rafael De Santi kissed me.

And I kissed him back.

My God, I've lost my fucking mind.

With one last bark, Rafael throws the phone onto the table, and his hand slides to the small of my back. Giving the waiter another glaring look, he quickly ushers me toward the exit.

I don't say a word as Rafael helps me inside the car, completely shaken by that kiss. By my reaction to it, really. I'm both excited and appalled. My heart still hasn't stopped its mile-a-minute race by the time he gets behind the wheel.

"So . . . trouble in hitmen paradise?" I ask as casually as I can muster. Maybe we can pretend that earth-shattering kiss never happened.

Rafael cocks an eyebrow at me, then starts the car. "No. It's something . . . let's say it's personal."

"Will that personal matter require a Remington, as well?"

"Maybe. Calogero Fazzini's men rarely learn their lesson without it."

My eyes snap to him. "The don of Sicilian Mafia?"

"Yes." He nods. "And also, my godfather."

I blink in confusion. "But you said you're not a member of Cosa Nostra."

"I was never initiated into the Family. When I was fourteen, I fled to the States with Guido."

"Why?"

"Because my mother broke the omertà."

I suck in a breath. Omertà is Cosa Nostra's code of silence. The basic principle is that one must keep their lips sealed, especially when dealing with legal authorities or outsiders. It's an extreme form of loyalty—a code of honor and conduct—that places importance on solidarity against government involvement, even if upholding its tenets includes one's mortal enemy or a personal vendetta. Within the Mafia, breaking the omertà is punishable by death.

"Cosa Nostra killed your mother?"

"The previous don, Mancuso, did it himself."

A shudder runs down my spine. "Why did you come back to Sicily?"

"So I could kill Mancuso." A small smirk pulls at his lips. "My godfather took over the Family less than forty-eight hours after I slit Mancuso's throat. We struck a deal then, Calogero and I. He rules the west coast, and I control the east. But it seems he's trying to break that agreement now." Rafael stops at a red light and turns to face me. "And I always make sure people fulfill their promises to me, Vasilisa. Do keep that in mind."

I nod and shift my gaze to the ribbon of road in front of us. The temperature in the car seems to have dropped, or maybe it's just the feeling of dread brought on by Rafael's warning. I wrap his jacket tighter around myself and spend the rest of the journey staring at the dark landscape visible beyond the windshield.

CHAPTER
eleven

25 years ago (Rafael, age 14)
Taormina, Sicily

"THE BODY OF A MAN THAT WASHED UP NEAR PALERMO has been identified . . ."

I put the dinner leftovers into the fridge and glance into the living room. My brother is perched in the middle of the sofa, eyes glued on the TV screen and the anchor who is relaying the news. "Turn that off, Guido."

"They found a dead man!" my brother exclaims with wide eyes.

"Now!" I bark. "Go brush your teeth, then straight to bed."

"No. I wanna see. Mamma, please."

Our mother looks up from the dishes she's been washing and points her sudsy finger at Guido. "Listen to your brother. Upstairs. Quickly."

My baby brother mumbles a pretty nasty curse word and, throwing the remote on the sofa, dashes across the room.

"Watch your mouth." I lightly slap the back of his head as he passes me by. "Next time, I'll wash your mouth out with soap."

"You say it all the time!" he throws over his shoulder, then runs down the hallway to our bedroom.

Our house is becoming too small for the three of us. Mom really wants Guido to have his own space, a proper bed—not the pull-put sleeper chair he currently uses. She also figures I deserve some privacy and tried giving up her own room to me. Right. Like I'd ever let my mom sleep on the living room couch. We just have to hang on for a bit longer, and then we might be able to move. Once I'm sixteen, I can finally be initiated into Cosa Nostra. For now, the small jobs they have me do from time to time bring in a little to help pay our bills, but when I'm an official member, that's when the serious money will start to roll in.

I shake my head and reach for the remote when a crash sounds behind me. Spinning around, my attention lands on my mother. She's standing utterly frozen in the middle of the kitchen, eyes wide and brows pulled up into a worried furrow. Pieces of a shattered plate cover the floor at her feet.

"Mom?"

"Turn up the volume," my mother chokes out, her stare is panic-stricken and fixed on the TV screen.

"Are you okay? What—"

The shards of porcelain fling and ping off various edges as she rushes toward me, kicking the broken pieces of a plate up with her feet, and snatches the remote out of my hand.

"... *detective was heading up the task force responsible for a successful operation that saw half a ton of cocaine seized by the police at the Port of Catania last week. His disappearance was reported two days ago . . .*"

The news anchor continues to speak, and, with every passing second, my mother's face grows paler. She has her hands pressed to her mouth, and her whole body has started to shake. I don't understand why the death of some cop would unsettle her so much. It's not that uncommon. Once in a while, one turns up dead, especially if they dared to mess with the mob.

"Mom?" I take hold of her shoulders. The last time I saw her so distraught was when Mancuso's men came over with the news of my father being killed. "What's wrong?"

She grabs my arms so hard, her nails dig into my skin. The impact of her alarmed gaze nearly sends me reeling. "We have to flee, Rafael. Right now."

"Flee? Why would—"

"I know that man," she stammers. "The detective whose body was found. I . . . I've been passing him some intel."

An ice-cold shudder runs down my spine. "What?"

"He approached me a while ago, offering protection if I help him bring down the local Cosa Nostra."

"Protection?" I roar. "We are *under* protection, Mom! That same Cosa Nostra you ratted out was keeping us safe! I'm supposed to be initiated into the Family in just over a year! What were you thinking?!"

"That!" She shrieks and shoves my chest with her hands. "I won't watch either of my sons be lowered into the ground in a casket. Calogero promised me he would keep you and Guido out."

"The don would never agree to that, Mom. We all know that I'm expected to join their ranks in Dad's place."

A pained groan leaves her lips. "And I know that Calogero already had you run a few errands for the Family, even though he knew that it's not what I want for your future. He swore he loved me and promised to make sure Mancuso agreed to let you off the hook. And I believed him. I've tried to save my sons from their father's fate, realizing too late that I spent years warming the bed of a lying snake."

I stare at my mother in shock. "I thought you loved him."

"I did!" she whispers while tears flow down her cheeks. "Up until the moment he told me that there's nothing he can do to keep you from Mancuso's clutches. So I took matters into my own hands. And I failed. Dear God, they will kill us all."

"Mom." I take her shaking hands into my own. "What did you tell the police?"

"Everything. I told them everything I knew. Including about that drug shipment. But the police were not supposed to raid the port. I was told they would continue their surveillance because they didn't yet have enough evidence against Mancuso himself. That detective assured me the three of us would be whisked away before anything that could give away my involvement happened. He said he needed to keep me safe as a potential key witness for the prosecution."

My stomach drops to the floor, dread consumes me. Inside my head, alarms begin to blare. Half of the local police force is on the Cosa Nostra payroll. One of Mancuso's lackeys must've found out that the detective has been talking to someone inside, and they took him out. Dumping dead bodies into the sea is the Family's standard MO.

"We'll fix this," I rasp. "They don't know it was you. We will—"

I cut off at the sound of a vehicle pulling up in front of the house. My head snaps toward the window overlooking the front yard. Not one, but two black cars pull into our driveway. The first is a regular-looking sedan, just like the one Calogero drives. But the second vehicle is a sleek limo with tinted windows. The don's car.

"They know." Barely audible words leave my mother's lips.

Turning away from me, she rushes to the kitchen cupboard and hysterically starts pulling out the cleaning supplies.

"Go get Guido," she says. "You can climb out of the window. God knows you've done it enough times."

I grab the gun from where I keep it hidden on the top shelf among the jars of spices. "I'm not going anywhere."

Mom approaches me, her eyes are filled with unwavering

resolve as she pushes a plastic bag into my free hand. "Money. There's also a note with the contact number for a man in Messina who will arrange for the two of you to get to America."

The sound of approaching feet. Several of them. Coming up to our front door.

"Mom . . ." The words get stuck in my throat.

"My actions will be seen as the ultimate betrayal, Rafael. They will not let me live. And they will kill you and Guido, too, if you remain here. You know that as well as I do." She gently untangles my fingers from around the handle of the gun, taking the weapon away. "If you love me, you will go grab your brother and run."

My mind is spinning, trying to find a way out. There isn't any. Breaking the omertà means a death sentence for the entire family. Children who are too young and know nothing of Cosa Nostra's dealings may be spared. But Mancuso is not a benevolent man. He will want to make an example of us all. I'm already dead, that's a certainty. Guido is only four, but I have no doubt the don will choose to kill my brother, as well.

I grab my mother's hand. "You're coming, too."

"They will come after us. But if I . . . stay . . . it might be enough. And that may mean they won't chase you."

No! How can I run and just leave my mother to her death?

The shrill ring of the doorbell reverberates throughout the house, thundering inside my skull like a blasted block of TNT. "I can't."

"Think about your brother, Rafael." Mom pulls my face down and drops a kiss on my forehead. "Please. Don't break your mother's heart."

I swallow, hard. My throat is barely working.

Wrapping my fingers around the plastic bag, I squeeze it with all my might.

"That's my boy." She nods. "Go. And never return here."

Despair clashes with rage inside my chest, tearing me to

pieces. My mother's hand falls from my own. I take a step back, then run down the hall. Just before I dash inside the bedroom, I stop for a mere second to look at my mom one final time. She's paused by the front door, her head held high, reaching for the handle.

"I'm coming back," I whisper as I shut the bedroom door behind me. "I'm coming back and I'll kill them all."

I repeat that promise over and over while I cradle my sleeping brother to my chest. He mumbles something about his car toys while I push open the window pane. With him in my arms, I slip through the gap and run toward the line of trees lining the back of the property.

And I keep repeating my promise like a mantra, standing hidden behind an evergreen shrub, my eyes trained on our living room window.

Watching the don of the Sicilian Cosa Nostra press the barrel of his gun to my mother's head and then pull the trigger.

Chapter Twelve

Vasilisa

WHEN WE REACH THE MANSION, THERE ARE FOUR black vehicles parked in the driveway. A man with a semiautomatic weapon stands by the front door.

"Wait here," Rafael says as he turns off the ignition and exits the car. There are no traces of that laughing man I had dinner with less than an hour ago.

Walking up, he exchanges a few sentences with the newcomer, then returns and opens my car door.

"I'll take you to your room," he says, his face set in hard lines. "It would be best if you remain there for the rest of the night."

"Okay."

Rafael nods, then slips his arms under my legs, lifting me out of the seat. I open my mouth to protest, but then my eyes fall on the big dark spot staining the gravel at Rafael's feet. Looks like a spill of engine oil on the driveway. The man with the rifle holds the front door open so Rafael can carry me inside. I expect him to put me down any second until I notice more stains on the floor of the entry hall. Now, however, I can see they're not black as I thought, but rather dark crimson.

Blood.

I tighten my hold on Rafael's neck, staring over his shoulder as he climbs the stairs. The trail of blood curves along a path from the entrance to the doorway leading to the wine cellar, where it disappears out of sight. I'm not a stranger to blood. My father's men often need to be stitched back together at our house, usually in the kitchen. But I've never witnessed so much of this vital bodily fluid in one place.

"What happened down there?" I whisper as Rafael carries me inside the bedroom.

"Nothing yet. They're waiting for me to start."

Moonlight streams into the darkened room through the open balcony door, bathing the interior in a bluish glow. It's tranquil, the distant crash of waves upon the shore and the rhythm of our breaths the only sounds. The gleam of the heavens reflects in Rafael's eyes. They're the only thing I can clearly see with his face partially obscured by darkness.

But even in the scarce light, the mess of thick uneven scars across his features can't be missed. One line in particular stands out. Nearly three inches long and running from his chin, across his lips, and veering slightly at the side of his nose, creating a split in the stubble-covered lower part of his face. There is another, almost as prominent, starting just over his ear and crossing his left cheek to his mouth. It pulls the corner of his lips downward, giving him a permanent scowling look.

Rafael looks as if someone tried to patch him up, but did a piss-poor job of it. Aside from the main raised tissue, there are small cross scars that remind me of railroad tracks. It's as if additional scarring formed around the areas where the sutures were applied, and now his skin has the mishmash, bumpy appearance of a button-tufted cushion. Being this close to him, I can understand why people find him scary. I don't, though. But the way he makes me feel? That terrifies the shit out of me.

I place the tip of my finger on the edge of his lips, just where another ridge of raised flesh begins, and track the jagged line toward his cheekbone. Rafael doesn't move, just stands there in silence, allowing me to explore the rest of the scars marring his face.

"Are these from a car accident?" I whisper.

"You're the first one who's dared to openly ask," he says. "No. Just an op that went wrong."

"When?"

"About twenty years ago."

I glide my fingertip back to his lips, tracing the shape of the lower one. Such a hard, sinister mouth.

"Please take care," I say as I watch light chase shadows across Rafael's face.

"I always do." His deep voice rumbles through the darkness, and in the next moment, he seizes my lips with his.

The kiss is another earthquake. A catastrophic seismic event that shakes me to the foundations of my soul, destroying everything in its path. Logic and reason evaporate, wiped out by his touch. The worry about letting myself get close to someone whom I should resent flies out of the second-story window. The fear that I'm falling for a man who is my captor disintegrates. Its fragments are swept away into the sea. I can't think of anything other than craving more of Rafael. Clutching his neck, I respond to every kiss. Every bite. Nothing else matters.

Rafael pulls my lower lip between his teeth, giving it one last nibble, then slowly lowers me to the floor.

"Keep the door shut, so the screams don't wake you," he whispers next to my ear.

In the next breath, he's gone.

The closed door only helps so much. Muffled screams still reach me through the balcony. The cellar windows must have been left open. I pull my soft cardigan tighter around me and resume biting my thumbnail.

Torture as a way of obtaining information or delivering a punishment is not uncommon in the criminal world. I've never witnessed it, but I don't have to be there to know that's what's happening on the underground level at the moment. Does Rafael mete out the agony himself, or does he have someone else do it for him while he watches? Even knowing his reputation, I find it hard to imagine him doing it. The man who leaves me drawings on sticky notes wouldn't be slaughtering people in his home, right? Maybe the stories I've heard about the feared Sicilian are exaggerated. Or is he just as people paint him—a ruthless, cold-blooded killer?

I crack the bedroom door open and take a peek outside. There's no one around. Tiptoeing down the hallway, I try my best to keep my steps light so the floorboards won't squeak, giving me away. The faint echo of whimpers and subdued screams seems to seep through the walls.

Halfway down the stairs, one of the wooden treads creaks under my bare foot. I startle, looking around, afraid someone may have heard it. But the entry hall is deserted.

Except for the vintage sconces on the walls, all lights are off, making the space feel ominous. The blood trail on the floor is gone, except for a few crimson spots here and there. Avoiding the remnants, I quickly cross the hall and turn left toward the stairway leading to the wine cellar.

I halt before the thick cellar door and stare at the knob. This is a mistake. I have zero interest in witnessing a torture session.

But my fingers are itching to turn that handle. Push open the door. To see *him*. The real him.

The urge to get a glimpse of that other side of him is coursing through me. The side he's never shown me. I want to know everything about Rafael. *Need*. I need to know the whole truth about the man who has invaded my thoughts from the moment I met him. Maybe seeing him at his beastliest will snuff out this silly attraction of mine. Maybe seeing blood on his hands will make me recoil from his touch next time, not revel in it. Maybe, just maybe, this ridiculous pull I feel toward him will finally break.

The screams coming from beyond the barrier have waned. I wrap my hand around the knob. It's ice-cold under my fingers, freezing my skin. Holding my breath, I crack the door open.

A lone beam of light shines down from the antique wrought iron chandelier, illuminating a figure reclining on a rickety wooden chair in the middle of the otherwise dark room. His back is turned toward the door, but I know it's Rafael. There's no one else here. Except for . . . the bodies.

Five men, their clothes torn and bloody, are lying on the floor throughout the room. The stench of blood and bodily fluids is intermixed with the smell of smoke, making me gag.

"I didn't expect to see you here, vespetta." Rafael's voice breaks the silence. He still has his back to me.

"How did you know it was me?" I choke out.

"You're the only one who would dare intrude on my meeting."

He takes a lengthy drag on his cigarette, then tosses it at the face of a dead man, where it lands with a disturbing muted sizzle. Then, in a blink-of-an-eye fluid motion, he slams his hand against the front leg of the chair, leaving a knife lodged in the wood. Right next to a glass jar filled with bloody lumps of . . . something. Something that looks like . . . severed human tongues.

Rafael slowly rises from the chair and turns to face me. The front of his shirt and sleeves are saturated with so much blood the fabric clings to his body.

"I didn't know you smoked," I mumble, still gaping at the crimson stains on his button-down. It's the only thing that pops into my stunned mind to say.

"A nasty old habit I still indulge in from time to time." He covers the distance between us in a few long strides and stops right in front of me. "Why are you here?"

"I . . . I'm not sure." I swallow and meet his gaze. "Aren't you going to yell at me for coming down?"

"Why would I?"

"Because . . . I don't know. You didn't want me to see this? If I would have walked in on my father doing anything like this, he would have tanned my hide."

"Shielding someone you care about from harm is one thing." He braces his hand on the doorframe and bends until our faces are at the same level. There are blood stains on his left cheek, as well. "Shielding them from reality is a completely different thing. Because, in our world, it could lead to death."

I nod, my eyes wandering to one of the corpses. "Who are they?"

"Cosa Nostra. They came to Catania to find out what happened to the drugs they tried to smuggle through my port."

"Did you have to kill them?"

"What would Bratva do if they found members of a rival organization dealing on their turf?"

Exactly the same thing. My eyes find Rafael's again. "Is any of that blood yours?"

"Would it bother you if it was?"

"Maybe." My voice is barely a whisper, as if I find that realization hard to process.

The corner of Rafael's lips curls upward. Slowly, his bloody

172

fingers pinch my chin, tilting my head up. "None of it is mine, Vasilisa."

His mouth seizes mine in an instant. There is no softness in his kiss. Just ferocious claiming. I manage to gulp a breath as I grab a handful of his shirt for support and kiss him back. I shouldn't. I know I shouldn't, but I can't fight his spellbinding pull. I bite his lower lip, sucking it into my mouth. He growls, and his tongue invades me, too.

The fabric under my touch is wet and sticky, but I can't make myself care. My mind is drifting, unable to process anything but the taste of him. His scent. His heat. The only skin-to-skin contact is our lips, but my entire body is buzzing like a live wire. No other man has ever made me feel like this.

When he finally releases my mouth, the air moves through my lungs in short, fast bursts. As if my respiratory organs suddenly remembered how to work. I stare into Rafael's hard green eyes. They glow with unhidden desire while he towers over me, so big and sinister-looking, with smears of blood and dead bodies as a backdrop. As if he's the dark ruler of hell.

"Your pretty lips taste like the pure essence of sin." He brushes his thumb over my mouth. "I wonder if your pussy will be just as scrumptious when I devour it."

A tremor runs down my spine, vehement from the tone of his voice, shaking me all the way to my core. It doesn't sound like a question, but a promise. One I would gladly see him fulfill.

Turning around, I dash up the stairs. Running away from Rafael De Santi and the treacherous feelings he stokes within me.

CHAPTER
Thirteen

Vasilisa

"SIGNOR DE SANTI ASKED ME TO PASS YOU A MESSAGE, miss," one of the maids says from the terrace threshold. "He's waiting for you in his car. You're to bring the laptop with you."

"You can tell Signor De Santi to kindly go fuck himself," I toss over my shoulder and look back at the horizon.

Jerkwad. It's been hours since I found Rafael's latest "present," and I still haven't been able to calm down.

I barely slept last night, too shaken by Rafael's kisses and the messed-up feelings they evoked. Thrill and enjoyment, right along with contempt for myself because I liked the experience. I don't go around letting random men kiss me senseless. Especially not men who keep me captive! I tossed and turned for hours, trying to eradicate the mental images of Rafael doing much more to me than merely kissing.

And then, when I woke up, even more confused than I was the night before, I found another velvet box.

I didn't even need to see the gift to know that he'd been

in the bedroom while I was sleeping. I could detect the traces of him drifting in the air. It's not that his scent is strong, but it seems my nostrils are attuned to it, capable of noticing even the faintest whiffs.

A beautiful rope chain bracelet was lying in the box, the three braided strands of gold and embedded diamonds gleamed in the morning light. Next to the jewelry box was a lavish crystal vase overflowing with several stems of white orchids. Underneath was a check with my name on it, in the amount of three million dollars. One for each kiss we shared. I don't remember the last time I felt so miserable and used, like some kind of whore. I kissed that jackass because I like him. Like him way more than I'm willing to admit. And he left me a god-damned check!

"Did you get my message, Vasilisa?"

An inappropriate but pleasant shiver rushes through me just from the timbre of his voice. I grit my teeth and keep my eyes focused on a distant spot before me. "Yup. I sent one back, but the maid was probably too afraid to relay it to you."

Heavy footfalls sound behind me, getting closer. I can feel each thump reverberating in my chest while every nerve impulse hums inside my body. Rafael comes to a stop right in front of me, blocking my view of the deep blue sea.

"And you saw the present I left you?" he asks.

I squint my eyes at him, taking in his huge form looming over me. He's wearing khaki dress pants and a white shirt with the sleeves rolled up to his elbows, revealing the black ink covering his forearms. The first few buttons on the shirt are undone, and I can see fragments of another tattoo on his chest.

"I did," I say as calmly as I can. "I tore up the check and flushed the pieces down the toilet."

"The flowers, as well?"

"Nope. Those are in the trashcan in the kitchen. Didn't want

to clog up the sewer lines. Too big. And you can find the bracelet in your tie drawer."

Rafael cocks his head to the side, staring at me intently.
Dark aviator sunglasses hide his eyes, making it difficult to decipher his exact expression, but I don't miss the way his jaw
hardens.

"I have the details for that container I need you to reroute.
Modify the freight shipping forms so it ends up in the Port of
Shanghai."

"The container was not a part of our deal. Feel free to play
with your fricking steel box yourself."

"You work for me. That means you'll do whatever I need."
He removes his sunglasses and pins me with his gaze. "We're
operating from another location today. You have five minutes
to get the laptop and haul your ass to the car."

"And what if I don't?"

"I don't think you want to play that game with me." He puts
his glasses back on and strides away. "Five minutes."

I squeeze my hands into fists with all my might and wait
until the sound of his footsteps fades, then head upstairs to get
the damn computer.

As I run out of the mansion five minutes later, Rafael is
standing by the SUV, holding the passenger door ajar, as if he
never had a doubt that I was coming. I guess, if you hold the
power of life or death at your fingertips, and the lives of someone's family hang in the balance, you'd expect that someone to
dance to your tune. Damn him.

I throw the laptop onto the back seat, then press my temple to the passenger-side window, creating as much distance
between us as possible.

The tension inside the vehicle could be cut with a knife. We
drive in utter silence for a better part of an hour, winding our
way on mostly deserted narrow roads flanked by olive groves
and vast farm fields. Slowly, a few country homes pop up among

the ever-present hills and valleys of the beautiful rural landscape. Rafael turns onto a lane that runs along the coast, descending into a quaint village. I slide down my window, gawking at little old houses squeezed right next to each other. The balconies facing the street are laden with a multitude of colorful flowers, some cascading over the railings and nearly to the ground below. The scent in the air is alluring. Near the doorways of a lot of houses, elderly women—sometimes alone, sometimes in groups—sit on either rickety chairs or ancient-looking recliners. Enjoying life? Or keeping their eyes on their surroundings?

We're driving through the crossroads when Rafael hits the brakes so suddenly that the seatbelt almost rearranges my insides. I'm still coming to my senses while Rafael pushes his head through the open window and starts yelling. He's so loud that I need to press my hands over my ears to prevent me from going deaf. It doesn't help much.

"*Ma che fai, stronzo?!*" Rafael roars, waving his hand at the pickup truck that's stopped in the middle of the intersection, blocking our way. "*Vaffanculo! Sei cieco? Madonna santa!*"

The driver of the other vehicle has also stuck his head out and is yelling back, while the man beside me keeps serving up what I'm sure are profanities. My gaze slides back to Rafael, taking him in with awe. He looks nothing like the cold-blooded killer I witnessed last night. Now, he's acting just like a regular guy. Well . . . a very angry regular guy, one aggravated by a traffic fuckup. It's . . . beyond cute. And sexy as hell.

"*Coglione! Mangia merda e morte, porca puttana!*" he snarls as he hits the wheel with his palm, then steps on the gas and surges through the intersection, barely missing the truck.

"*Testa di cazzo,*" he mumbles shaking his head, then looks at me. "*Tutto bene?*"

I gape at him, then burst out laughing. "I have no idea what you said in the last five minutes, but it sounded painful."

A small smile pulls at his lips.

"Well, I told that idiot to go fuck himself in a very painful way. Sent him to hell because his brain is in his testicles. Called him an asshole and a dickhead, and invited the pig-whore to eat shit and die. Then, I asked if you were okay." He stretches his hand and brushes my chin with his thumb. "*Are* you okay, vespetta?"

"Yeah," I breathe.

Rafael steers the car to the left and stops outside an old one-story house. A massive shrub, or maybe a small tree, with vibrant purple flowers creeps up the walls of the structure, its vines twisting together to create a natural canopy over the front door. In its shade, curled into a ball on a doormat, sleeps a large calico cat. A woman with a long gray braid, who looks to be in her eighties, is knitting on the nearby bench. The moment she notices us, she abandons her work and eyes Rafael while he exits the SUV and tosses his sunglasses onto the dashboard.

"I'll be right back," he says and shuts the door.

The gentle breeze ruffles the hair around his face, tossing a few dark strands across his eyes as he approaches the house with long, confident strides. His shirt accentuates his broad back, the fabric straining across his biceps and shoulders.

Rafael brings to mind an image of a vengeful Roman god, but one who traveled through time to the present. The idea is bolstered by the gun he tucked into the waistband at his back. The scene from last night—him covered in blood—forms before my eyes, and my heart rate surges in alarm.

Is he going to kill the poor old woman?

I grab the door handle and fling it open. I don't give a fuck what beef he might have with her, I will not sit back and watch as he kills someone's grandma.

I'm out of the SUV and ready to run over there to stop him when Rafael crouches before the woman. She doesn't seem to be alarmed by his presence at all. A small smile lights up her face as she leans forward and starts whispering in his ear.

It lasts for nearly five minutes. The woman speaks, and Rafael listens, nodding every now and then. Once she finishes, Rafael straightens and turns to leave. The woman suddenly grabs his hand. I stare, speechless, as she drops a kiss on his knuckles.

When she lets go of Rafael's hand, her gaze meets mine. Eyebrows furrowed, she watches me silently for a second or two, then says something and gestures to the left. Rafael shakes his head. More serious-sounding words follow in rapid Italian, leaving her lips as she points to the flower pot by the front door. A sprawling plant with bright-red flowers. Sighing, Rafael looks toward the heavens, then approaches the planter and picks a single bloom from the lot.

My heart thumps heavily in my chest as he closes the distance between us and lifts the flower toward me.

"It's a geranium. Thought of almost as a weed around here," he says. "I know it will get flushed down the toilet, but she insisted."

"And why would you assume that?"

"Well, that was the fate of the orchids. Why would a weed fare any better?"

I take the flower from his hand. "Think about it a bit, and the answer will come to you."

Lifting the flower to my nose, I inhale the mild sweet aroma and get back in my seat.

"So, is she your family?" I ask when Rafael gets behind the wheel.

"An associate would be more accurate. If you want to know what's happening around here, nothing beats the grandma surveillance network."

"Hmm, it looked like more than that to me. Do all your associates kiss your hand?"

"It's a sign of respect. And appreciation for the help I provided."

"What kind of help?"

"There's no shortage of corruption throughout Sicily. With enough money, one can get away with many things," he says. "A few years ago, a business mogul arrived with an intent to level the village and transform the area into a vineyard. He tried to buy the properties and the surrounding land, bribing the local officials left and right to obtain the necessary licenses and permits."

"But nothing came of it?"

"Of course not. Since I separated the bastard from his head." He starts the vehicle and glances at the purple vine climbing the old wall that's covered in peeling paint. "Dead bodies make an amazing plant fertilizer."

With my mouth hanging open, I follow Rafael's gaze to the blooming bush, then look over at the grandma, who's gone back to her knitting with a serene smile on her face. "You buried a body next to her front door? Does the poor woman know that?"

"Of course. She even picked the spot."

The engine roars to life, and pebbles crunch under the massive tires as Rafael reverses, startling the cat sleeping on the doormat. The furball leaps from its napping spot directly onto the blooming bush. Frantically, it climbs the thick vine and squeezes between the branches just above the door.

"Stop!" I reach out, laying my hand over Rafael's on the steering wheel. "You scared the cat. It went up the tombstone shrub."

The rumble of the vehicle dies. I turn my head and our gazes collide, making me forget about the chubby calico. Rafael's eyes are searing mine, holding them captive, and I find myself leaning toward him. I can feel the scar ridges on his hand under my palm, crisscrossing his skin like some bizarre art deco trellis pattern.

"Tombstone shrub?" Rafael's gaze shifts down, falling on my mouth, and I belatedly realize I may have drawn his attention by worrying my bottom lip between my teeth.

Is he thinking about the kisses we shared last night? The ones he "paid" me for?

Good God, even after that fiasco, I still want to kiss him again. So bad.

"Um, yeah." I quickly release his hand and look back at the cat. "Do you think it will come down on its own?"

"Yes."

"It doesn't look that way to me." The cat looks terrified, testing the branch before it with one paw, but quickly retreating. "Can you help it down?"

"It will jump down the moment we leave, Vasilisa."

My heartbeat skyrockets like it always does when he calls me by my name. I take a deep breath and look at him. "Please?"

Rafael lifts his hand and lightly brushes my cheek with his scarred knuckles. The air gets caught in my lungs.

"*La mia principessa russa,*" he whispers.

Another stroke along my chin before he exits the car and heads toward the house where the distraught cat is still crammed between branches heavy with purple blooms.

Mesmerized, I watch as Rafael jostles the bush limbs and flowers, trying to get his hands on the scaredy cat. The calico might have looked like it was eager to get down, but it's taking Rafael more than five minutes to grab it because the little thing keeps twisting around the offshoots and foliage. When he finally gets a hold and starts pulling the mewling fluffball out from between the tangled vines, the cat scrambles out of Rafael's hands and leaps back onto the bush. Then, using one of the thicker branches, it expertly dashes to the ground and runs away.

Laughter bubbles inside me, and by the time Rafael gets into the driver's seat, I'm laughing so hard that tears stream down my cheeks.

"I guess you were right." I snort, then fall into another fit of giggles. "Sneaky little thing."

"Of course I was right." There's a small smirk on his lips when he starts the SUV.

Rafael reaches for his sunglasses on the dashboard, and

while he's putting them on, I notice faint red markings on the back of his hand. The surrounding skin is turning fire-engine-red.

"Oh my God, the little rascal scratched you!"

"It wasn't the cat. That's a bougainvillea bush." He meets my gaze. "Its thorns are toxic."

I stare at him—this dangerous, unscrupulous man, who only minutes ago disclosed that he buried a dead body under that same bush. And then, without protest, he went to "rescue" the cat because I asked him to, all while knowing he'd get hurt in the process.

Warmth swells inside my chest, melting away one of the many layers of protection I've been trying to build around my heart. One of my remaining safeguards from Rafael De Santi.

"What are we doing here?" I ask as we walk down the wooden dock.

On the far end of it, two white yachts lightly sway on the gentle waves. The first one is a huge monstrosity with two levels above the main deck and looks more like an outlandish hotel than a sea vessel, while the other one is significantly smaller but still big enough to dwarf a lot of speedboats I've seen zipping around Lake Michigan in Chicago. A guy wearing white shorts and a striped T-shirt is unwinding ropes from the metal hooks bolted to the dock.

"We'll be working from my yacht today."

I come to a sudden stop. "Why?"

"I thought you would enjoy spending a day outside the house." Rafael places his palm on the small of my back, ushering me forward. "And those workers are getting on my nerves with all the racket they're making."

"You mean the guys who've been varnishing the

bookshelves for the second time this week? Well, I don't mind them. Maybe we should go back."

Rafael halts and puts his hand under my chin, tilting my head up. "What's wrong?"

"Nothing."

"Vasilisa. What's wrong?"

I throw a glance at the boat behind him. Yulia and I have been talking about taking a cruise one summer, but I've never gathered the courage to actually go.

"What if it sinks?" I blurt out.

"Why would it sink?"

"It's a boat. They sink all the time."

"Contrary to what you see in the movies, sinking a water vessel of this size is rather difficult. Unless the yacht hits rocks or collides with another seacraft, there's no way that's going to happen." He bends so our faces are almost level. "Don't worry. You'll be safe."

"And what about water creatures? Like sharks!"

"Well, we'll be on board. Several feet above the waterline." His lips pull into a tiny grin. "And in the event we get into a *Sharknado* scenario, and deadly fish start raining down from the sky, I have a few large caliber weapons stashed below deck."

My eyes turn to slits as I glare at him. "That movie was beyond stupid."

"I don't agree. The original *Sharknado* is an all-time classic." Rafael brushes my chin with his thumb, then steps away.

I trail in his wake to the narrow boarding ramp that's connected to the smaller yacht, eyeing the thing with suspicion. Rafael steps onto it first, then turns around, extending his hand to me. Slowly, I place my palm into his. His fingers wrap around mine, his huge hand completely swallowing my own. With his sleeves rolled up and the midday sun shining down, I can see that it's not only his hands that bear a plethora of varied uneven scars. There are many on his forearms as well. A particularly long one starts at the inside of his wrist, splits the realistic-looking image of a toothy green snake coiled around two black crossed daggers, then continues all the way up to his elbow.

"Watch your step."

I look up and meet his gaze. "Don't let go."

Something dangerous flashes in his eyes as he tightens his hold on my hand. "Never."

The wind blows my hair into my face as I go over the bill of lading for the shipping container Rafael wants me to reroute. It took me almost an hour to get into the freight company system and find the exact cargo ship onto which the container in question was loaded. It shouldn't have taken me more than twenty minutes, but I kept stealing glances at Rafael as he stood at the yacht's helm, navigating.

I initially set up my "workstation" on the main deck, inside what looked like a cozy, luxury living room, but I felt queasy after ten minutes and climbed up to the upper deck, planting myself on the curved brown leather sunbed behind the driver's seat. Or . . . at least, that's the excuse for settling here that I choose to believe. Seasickness sounds much more acceptable than coming up to this lounge just so I can be closer to the man I can't seem to ignore.

"Why are we sending this poor container on a trip around the world?" I ask as I continue modifying the records.

Rafael glances at me over his shoulder, then looks back toward the horizon. "Because Calogero's drug shipment is inside."

"Well, he won't be happy when he finds it in Shanghai."

We've come to a stop, and Rafael shuts down the engines. Amid the sound of waves lapping against the yacht's hull, the telltale clang of the lowering anchor comes from the nose part of the boat.

"I'm counting on it."

I'm sure he could have gotten one of his tech guys to do this for him, but the fact he asked me instead, makes me giddy with excitement. There aren't many options for women within Bratva. It's not like I can go around beating up people who owe us money or provide protection for drug shipments. One of the reasons I chose computer science as a major is that I wanted to help my family in some capacity with my IT know-how.

Grampa Felix is too old to keep up with everything that gets thrown at him and the lightning speed with which the technology is evolving, and I hoped Dad would allow me to take over the cyber tasks. Instead, he almost had a heart attack when I shared my idea with him. After nearly an hour-long tirade about how I would never poke a finger into the Bratva business, Dad promised that he would find me a "nice, safe job" in some financial institution. Someplace where I can meet a "nice, safe accountant" whom I could date.

I hit *Enter*, saving the changes I've made, and take a peek at Rafael. He's leaning with his back on the helm console, hands in his pockets, watching me. The wind has made a mess out of his hair, and several strands of his dark tresses have fallen across his forehead, making him look less harsh somehow. I can't believe that a man who hunted me down, had me kidnapped, and then flown halfway around the world so he could wreck me himself for daring to invade his domain, values my skills more than my own father.

"What did your sister say?"

"She asked why I was calling at six in the morning." I completely forgot about the time difference when I phoned her earlier. "Then, she said Dad sent out a Mafia version of an APB about me."

"Oh? How does that work?"

"I guess he called every criminal syndicate in the country and threatened to annihilate whichever one is holding me hostage. Or anyone who has info on my whereabouts but hasn't shared it."

"So he still believes you're somewhere in the continental US?"

"Yes. I'm usually more careful when I check in with Dad, always keeping the time difference in mind."

"Interesting." Rafael smirks. "Someone might figure that you're actually enjoying your stay in Sicily."

I blink, then quickly look away when the realization hits me—*I am* enjoying it here. Being with him.

"Don't be ridiculous," I mumble, pretending to work again. "Can you call Mitch and ask if the new login credentials for the client database are working on his side?"

"No."

My head snaps up. "Why not?"

"Because we should go for a swim first."

I suck in a breath. Images of Rafael without his clothes on flood my mind, setting off a tingling sensation in my core. Wrong. So so wrong. I can't be falling for a man who left me a check as payment for the kisses we shared. Who won't allow me to return home.

Clearing my goddamned mind is useless. Those thoughts invade me again, even more intense and erotic. The two of us, naked, as he covers my body with his. Rough palms stroking my skin while his piercing green eyes singe right through me. Killer's eyes. I'm turned on and ready to combust in spite of him being a cold-blooded murderer. Or maybe . . . maybe it's those sinister vibes he gives off that make him more alluring.

"Um . . . I'm going to skip it. There's some stuff I need to wrap up." I quickly look back at the laptop.

"Suit yourself."

His hand brushes my arm as he walks by me, heading to the main deck. I keep my eyes glued to the screen, but eventually, my curiosity gets the better of me. Tempted by a force stronger than my willpower, I throw a look over my shoulder to the swim platform at the rear of the boat. But I don't see him. Rising a bit out of my seat, I spot Rafael at the frontmost point of the yacht, unbuttoning his shirt. All the air rushes out of my lungs as I watch him remove the garment, revealing his perfectly defined broad back.

His pants are next.

I'm still lightheaded, taken aback by how beautiful he is, when he hooks his fingers into the waistband of his underwear. *Oh my God, he wouldn't!* The briefs slide down, giving me the briefest glance at his amazing hard ass before he dives overboard. His body soars in a straight line for a split second, and a heartbeat later, a splash in the water sounds below.

My palms are pressed to my burning cheeks. I can't believe he did that. And he'll be naked when he climbs back onto the yacht, meaning I'll be able to see everything I missed in that lightning-fast glimpse. All six and a half feet of buck naked, wet, magnificent male body.

How am I going to feign indifference to that?

I scramble off the sunbed, intending to hide somewhere on the main deck until Rafael is once more clothed, but the overwhelming urge to see him gets to me again. Maybe I could just have a quick look without him noticing?

Crouching low to the deck, I sneak to the front of the helm station and peek over the side, trying to see beyond the bow of the boat. The deep blue waters are still, except for the gentle ripples on the surface. Zero bare-assed assassins anywhere in sight. I run to the back of the flybridge, but it's the same. Just the calm vastness of the Mediterranean.

"Rafael?" I call.

Nothing.

Where the fuck is he? How long can a person stay underwater? It's been at least two minutes. I scramble back to the open cockpit and descend the metal ladder to the rear of the boat and then the steps to the waterline.

"Rafael!" I yell from the swim platform, scanning the depths in vain. "This is not funny!"

Did he drown? What if something has eaten him? Fuck. Fuck. *Fuck!* I shove down my shorts and fling off my top, remaining only in a matching set of a white lace bra and panties. My heart is pounding in my chest, and worry for Rafael is pressing me down, but I can't make myself step off that platform into the sea. Ever since I watched *Jaws*, I have a deep-rooted fear of sharks. I can swim well enough, but only in swimming pools.

"*Rafael!*" I scream this time, drawing out his name. There's no answer.

A hysterical whimper leaves my lips as I lower myself to the edge of the decking and dip my feet into the water. If a sea monster ate Rafael, it must be a super huge one to be able to swallow him whole. If it comes after me, I'll probably barely register when it opens its mouth. Quick, painless death.

"Fuck you, Rafael," I huff and slide off the platform into the terrifying depths just as a large water-distorted shape surges from below.

I scream and shut my eyes. Water splashes all around me as I flail my arms, trying to get away, and my back collides with the swim ladder extended below the surface. Something big and thick wraps around my waist. I scream again, kicking my legs to hit—

"*Ma che cazzo!* Vasilisa!"

I freeze. Open one eye. Then the other one. Rafael is in the water in front of me, his right arm wrapped around my waist, while he grips the ladder behind me with his left hand.

"I thought you were the fucking Kraken," I blurt out while fighting to draw in a calming breath.

He cocks his head, the motion dislodging a few drops of water from his hair directly onto my breasts. "The Kraken?"

"Yes!"

His lips are pressed tightly together and his eyebrows furrowed. I think I might have angered him. A deep rumbling sound comes from his chest, and, in the next moment, he bursts out laughing.

"It's not funny!" I wrap my arms around his neck, holding on to him for dear life. "I thought you drowned, you jerk! Do you have any idea how terrified I am of swimming in the sea? I almost had a heart attack while considering how to outswim the sharks and octopuses and whales and . . . and . . . giant turtles so I could get to you!"

Rafael's eyes suddenly darken. He's not laughing anymore. His hold on my middle tightens, crushing me to his chest. I go very *very* still, hyperaware of his body basically plastered to me. His gaze captures mine and holds it with the same ferocity as his arm clutches my body. And his stone-hard cock presses right at my core.

"There is only one monster lurking in these waters now, my fiery lily of the valley." He bows his head, placing a kiss on my shoulder. "But I think you know that he won't ever do you any harm."

A thrilling shiver runs down my spine, followed by another when he kisses my neck. My chin. The corner of my mouth. I feel like I'm a conduit for high-voltage power, but there's no outlet for all that raw energy. I'm snared in his electric field, and every time his lips touch my skin, a total system meltdown happens. Finally, his mouth seizes mine. Biting. Taking. Claiming. I kiss him back, even though I know that I shouldn't. Shouldn't let this happen. But whatever cognitive ability I possessed, got fried. Short-circuited. Burned to a crisp.

I tighten my hold on him, plastering myself tighter to his chest, while he ravages my lips. This is wrong. I know it is, but I can't seem to care. All sense of reality is getting lost amid the myriad of emotions swirling inside me. Excitement. Elation. Happiness. It's so damn good to be held in his arms, with his body enveloping mine. His naked body. I can feel his hard cock brushing against my core, the lacy fabric of my panties the only barrier. I want more, and my whole being is buzzing with that need. More of this manipulative, complicated man who's been plaguing my thoughts since the second we met.

I pull his lower lip between my teeth and bite it. Hard. "I can't believe you left me a check for our kiss, you jackass."

"And I can't believe you flushed my millions down the drain." He bites me back. "I'm going to fuck you now, Vasilisa. I'm going to fuck your pussy into oblivion, the same way you've been fucking with my goddamned mind for weeks, turning it into a useless mush. Can you even imagine the willpower I had to have to resist taking you into my arms and making you mine, to not simply say: *Screw it all, I want her*?"

"Yes," I pant. Knowing how much I've been fighting to maintain my own self-control, I have a pretty good idea. My fantasies have been taking over my mind night and day—what it would be like to forget who he is . . . what he's done . . . and to just let go? I guess I'm going to find out because my brain checked out the moment our lips touched. Primal desire and need are now in command. I can't fight myself anymore. "Please fuck me into oblivion."

His grip around my waist tightens like a vise. He lets go of my lip that's been trapped between his teeth and growls into my mouth.

"Hold tight."

I don't question his order, just do as he said. My hands slide into his hair, anchoring my grip around his neck. Instantly, his arm around my waistline shifts, his palm glides over to push my panties down. As if triumphant in overcoming that barrier, the seawater swells against my pussy while the delicate lace slides down my legs and disappears into the deep.

Rafael strokes my ass with his palm, then moves lower, between my ass cheeks, straight to my core. Deft fingers brush my folds. And with his movements, the warm waters of the Mediterranean delicately splash my opening, even flooding inside. Rafael attacks my lips with the same rhythm as his fingers caress my sensitive flesh. It's pure insanity.

My whole body feels like it's scorching on the inside, heat rising through the water. Scalding. Steaming. The very air around us feels thick like fog. Wrapping my legs around his waist, I press my pussy to the tip of his cock, and close my eyes.

Rafael's lips go still on mine. "Look at me."

I blink my eyes open, once again fighting for breath. Rafael's face is set in hard lines, jaw clenching, making the scars on his face more distinct.

"Don't fucking dare close your eyes." A low, dangerous-sounding growl escapes his throat as he slides the head of his cock inside me.

"Okay," I whisper.

"Good."

He pushes in a bit deeper. He's too big. I can't breathe. A shaky whimper leaves me. I cling to him with all my strength, my eyes piercing his.

"I don't do slow, vespetta. But for you, I'll try."

Another inch. Having him inside me feels intrinsic. Intense. I've never had sex in the water, and the sensation is incomparable to anything I've experienced before. Or maybe it's just him. His finger is still stroking my flesh, that spot between my core and the nerve-rich center of my ass, applying constant pressure. That touch alone nearly pushes me over the brink. And his dick isn't even halfway in me.

Somehow, he's still gripping the ladder with his left hand. Without breaking our eye contact, I grab his trunk-like biceps and tighten my legs around his waist. Taking more of him inside. My entire body trembles as he slowly fills me up. More. And more. Both of us panting. With just the sun overhead and the tranquil sea around us, we're in our own wild world.

If it was anyone else floating in these waters with me, I'd long ago have been in a full-blown panic, cast to the coldest depths. But, it seems my mind completely believes that Rafael De Santi truly is the biggest threat in this blue vastness. And all I can feel is him. Just when I think I can't take any more, my walls stretch further. My body adjusts to his size.

When he seems to finally be completely within me, I can barely draw a full breath. The teeniest movement from him will probably make me shatter. But Rafael holds utterly still.

"Tell me . . . Did you really jump in the water because you thought something happened to me?"

Air leaves my lungs in shallow bursts as I search his green orbs. His left iris is a shade lighter than the right one. I never noticed that before.

"Did you?" he insists and, unbelievably, pushes deeper.

I almost come.

Sliding my palm up his neck, I grip the dark wet strands and squeeze. Rafael's cock twitches inside me. His body is so taut, every muscle straining. My God, he is beautiful like this.

"Yes." I tilt chin, nipping his lower lip. "How would I have gotten back to the mansion if you drowned?"

Another growl leaves his mouth, rough and feral. He retreats, then slams into me with such force that my mind totally blanks. His mouth captures mine again. Biting. Taking. My core trembles with a sensation of pleasure bordering on pain while he pounds me with fast, deep thrusts. His hand grips my ass, holding me steady, while wrecking me in the most visceral way. There isn't a drop left of his previous self-control, as if my blatant lie has unleashed the beast.

"Mine," he growls, biting my lower lip. "From the moment you swung that broken bottle at me, I knew you'd be mine."

"I'm not yours," I choke out, fighting for breath while kissing him back.

He trails his lips along my chin, then buries his face in the crook of my neck. "You smell like me." His teeth graze the sensitive skin below my ear. "Taste like a mouthwatering dessert, custom-created to satiate every craving impulse of my DNA alone. Your flavor drives me crazy."

Rafael slides out, then impales me with his cock again.

"Your sweet pussy trembles so beautifully with my dick inside you, asking for more. Do you want more, Vasilisa?"

"Yes . . ."

A deep, powerful thrust of his hips makes the water around us ripple. My trembling hands slip off his wet, rock-hard shoulders from the vibrations of that impact. I hook my arm around his neck and meet his feral stare. *You are mine,* it says. Just as his words did. Just like the telling warmth in my belly that's threatening to consume me wholly. Just like my treacherous heart that's yearning to reply, *I'm yours.* Like this is where I've always meant to be.

Dear God, I'm in love with him. I don't know how or when it happened, but I've had these feelings for quite some time. Was it the sticky notes that did me in? Or those stolen figs he keeps leaving for me? No, I don't think it was any single act. It's the way he makes me feel every day—like I have finally found myself.

Rafael is pounding relentlessly into me again. A scream builds in my chest, wanting to be let out. I grit my teeth as hard as I can to keep it from escaping. Too afraid to confess the ecstasy I feel, even with mere lust-filled vocals. Wave after wave of pleasure surges over me, pushing me over the crest. I shakingly cling to Rafael, our gazes locked together, as I come right there, in the arms of my captor, surrounded by the glittering expanse of the warm glistening sea.

"That's it, vespetta. I told you you're mine." With one final plunge, Rafael buries himself to the hilt and explodes inside me.

I close my eyes, relishing the feel of him. But also feeling guilty for enjoying the most intense pleasure I've ever experienced.

"Look. At. Me." Brassy, growled words.

I shake my head. My God, what have I done?

"Now, Vasilisa."

This man. A ruthless brute. One who threatened to kill my family. My parents. My baby brother and sister. There isn't a doubt in my mind that he could do it, too, and more than likely, without blinking an eye. I know it. Just as I know that no other man will ever make me feel the same. The way he does. Like I'm surfing the gentlest currents, and at the same time, falling into the deepest abyss.

I can't look at him.

I'm not ready to face the reality. To accept the irrevocable truth—that I am in love with Rafael De Santi.

A stream of fast-spoken Italian erupts from him. By the tone of his voice, curses, I'm sure. Water sloshes around me as Rafael climbs the ladder, carrying me onboard held up by only one of his arms.

"There are towels in the bathroom," he grunts, putting me down onto something soft.

When I open my eyes, I find myself sitting on the sofa inside the salon on the main deck. Rafael stands before me, his chest rising and falling with labored breaths as he glares at me.

Without another word, he turns around and steps outside. A moment later, I hear his footfalls as he climbs the ladder to the flybridge, and shortly after, the yacht engines come to life.

Rafael

The leather rim of the yacht's steering wheel creaks from the force of my grip. For the past twenty minutes, I've barely kept a leash on my temper, barely prevented myself from storming down to the main deck—where Vasilisa has been hiding this whole time—and demanding an explanation.

The list of things I need her to explain is rather long. Starting with why the fuck did she act like a scared little guppy just moments after she so beautifully shattered in my arms. I didn't expect cuddles, but I did fucking want her to look at me. She had no problem looking at my face before. Did having sex with me disgust her? Because of how I look? I wouldn't be surprised if a beauty like her has only ever had pretty boys as lovers.

Red haze covers my eyes at the idea of other men who have been close enough to her to touch her. Who *have* touched her. I grit my teeth and squeeze the wheel harder. I'll rip apart any man who's ever put his hands on her in the past and any fucker who might think he has a chance to do it in the future. Vasilisa Petrova is mine. *Mine!* And I'll do whatever it takes to make sure she wants to stay with me.

I'm steering the yacht back to the marina when I catch movement out of the corner of my eye. A speedboat, anchored by the sea stack at the entrance to a cove, just up the coast from here. The Mediterranean might be in the public domain, but everyone in this part of Sicily knows that these waters are mine. So it's either stupid tourists or my godfather's men. No one else would be crazy enough to wander here.

I pilot the yacht to the dock and head to the starboard side to throw the marina boy the rope.

"Don't tie it," I bark. "I'm heading out again right away."

The faint tapping of small bare feet sounds behind me. I turn around and find Vasilisa standing with the laptop bag in her hands, staring at the deck.

"I called Guido. He's coming to drive you to the house."

She looks up, her eyes finally meeting mine. "What about you?"

I don't reply. Wrapping my arm around her waist, I pick her up and, holding her to my side, leap onto the dock.

"Put some after-sun lotion on your face when you get back. You've got a bit of a sunburn." I lower her to the ground and jump back on board the yacht.

The marina boy tosses the rope to me. I coil it neatly and, without bothering to look back at Vasilisa, climb up to the flybridge and start the boat, taking it out in reverse. I last about thirty seconds before I kill the engines and turn my eyes toward the marina.

Vasilisa is still on the dock, her hair fluttering in the wind. I can't see her eyes from this distance, but she is looking in my direction. Standing several feet away, the marina boy is staring at her. I snap. Grabbing the phone from my pocket, I dial the salivating little shit.

"Signor De Santi?"

"Keep staring at my woman one second longer," I snarl, "and I'll turn back to gouge your eyes from your stupid head!"

"Of course, Signor De Santi," he wheezes.

I cut the call and cross my arms over my chest, watching my little hacker. She enjoyed being fucked by me. There was no mistaking the sweet little sounds—the moans and whimpers—she made, or how her body trembled under my touch. The way she clung to me while I pumped into her. How beautifully she unraveled in my embrace. The problem developed only once we were done. After she realized she let the monster take her.

Well, I can't change the way I look, but I will find a way to make her see past my appearance.

She flushed my check down the toilet. Threw my flowers away. She even refused the jewelry I bought for her. Maybe it wasn't opulent enough? I should have known better and gotten her something more expensive. A mistake I won't repeat. No matter how good-looking, no man can compete with my power and will. And none can provide for her the way I can. I need to make her understand that.

Her attention gets snagged by an approaching vehicle. Guido parks his sports car next to the path that leads to the dock. I keep my eyes on Vasilisa as she throws one last look in my direction, then walks up to Guido and his ride. Only after she's safely inside my brother's pride and joy do I turn on the engines and steer the yacht back toward the cove where I saw that suspicious boat.

Vasilisa

No stars tonight. Just a tiny sliver of moonlight that had punched its way through the clouds, not even enough to illuminate the garden below the balcony. I can barely make out the shapes of a few olive trees in the distance and the oleander shrub next to the antique water pump at the edge of the lawn. Everything else is murky, just like my feelings. I tighten my hold on the massive bath towel wrapped around me while I run my hairbrush through my still-wet hair and sigh.

What am I going to do when Rafael comes home? He still isn't back from whatever caused him to storm out on his yacht this afternoon, and I've been on pins and needles for hours. Can I pretend that nothing happened between us? I don't think I can. Every time I close my eyes, I'm back in that water again, reliving every second of it. Reproaching myself for enjoying it too much. For wanting *him*.

"You'll catch a cold, Vasilisa."

I tense.

Steps. Slow and determined, coming closer. Warmth at my back as Rafael halts just behind me. Fabric rustling, and then he puts his suit jacket over my shoulders.

"Did you put something on that sunburn?"

"Yes," I whisper, staring at the grounds below. "Where did you go on your boat earlier?"

"I thought I spotted trespassers. But it was just dumb tourists." His hands come to rest on the balcony railing, one on either

197

side of me. "After, I had to drop by Messina to resolve a fuckup with a local drug gang."

"I didn't know you dealt in drugs."

"I don't. That's what Cosa Nostra does within their part of Sicily. Here, on the east coast, there are a few small groups that deal drugs, and as long as they follow my rules, I let them be."

"And if they don't?"

He lets go of the railing, and his hands encircle my waist. I hold my breath, entirely tuned in to his touch as his palm glides lower, under the edge of the towel and between my legs.

"If they don't, I personally execute the whole gang. Just like I had to do tonight."

And there it is—one of the main reasons why I am so madly pulled toward him. No sugarcoating. No pretense. Even while keeping me here against my will, he's treating me as an equal. I'm well aware of how the metaphorical scales stand between us—he is stronger, meaner, and holds the lives of my loved ones in his scarred hand. And yet, I've never felt domineered by him. He's never made me feel inferior in any way.

"We need to talk," I choke out while he slides his finger between my folds.

"About?" his rough voice taunts next to my ear. Then, he pushes his finger inside me.

"About today." I grab the railing for support and widen my legs. "About this."

A kiss lands on the side of my neck. "I'm all ears."

He pulls his finger out only to push it back inside, deeper. His other hand slips to the inside of my thigh and drifts higher. Tremors shoot down my spine, all the way to my core, the moment his thumb finds my clit. My breathing picks up. Panting, I clutch the towel to my breasts and lean against his chest.

"What did you want to discuss, vespetta?" he prompts, upping his pace.

Yeah, what did I want to discuss? That what happened today

on the yacht can never happen again, while I moan in pleasure with his finger buried inside me?

"Nothing," I choke out as my wetness soaks his hand. "I don't want to talk about this. Or earlier today. I just want . . ." A small whimper escapes me. What in the hell do I want?

He curls his finger and presses against a spot that makes me see stars. "You just want me to fuck you?"

A supernova goes off in my body, obliterating every cloud in the sky.

"Yes."

I slide my hand from Vasilisa's trembling pussy and bring it to my mouth.

"Alright," I say, licking her sweet juice from my finger. Then, I scoop her into my arms and carry her to the bed. The wall-mounted reading lamp over the headboard is lit, its glow bathes Vasilisa's milky skin. "You can turn off the light if you want." Grabbing the sides of my dress shirt, I tug them apart, sending a multitude of buttons clattering to the floor.

Vasilisa just gapes at me, her eyes glued to my fingers as I slowly unzip my pants. My cock is so fucking hard that even walking was difficult. No woman has ever had me so worked up that I actually had to control myself and fight not to explode before I was even in her. She wants me to fuck her without discussing the subject? Fine. We can start with that.

The moment my clothes are off, I climb on the bed and cover her body with mine. She is so fucking small. I brace my weight on my forearms, fearing I'll squash her beneath me. Her snarky personality is so overwhelming that I often forget how tiny she really is. And with so much pent-up aggression inside me at the moment, I don't think I can hold back and go slow like I did earlier today.

I capture her lips with mine in an angry kiss, then shift to the small dip between her collarbones. My palms glide down her ribs as I kiss her breasts. Her stomach. The spot just below her navel. The towel comes loose and tangles under her, giving me unrestricted access to her body, which quivers under my touch as I move lower, to her pussy. It's still wet. She opens her legs wider, and I bury my face in her delicious center.

Mewling little moans leave Vasilisa's lips as I lick her pretty pink slit, keeping my movements slow at first, then gradually upping the rhythm, focused on every sound she makes. I'm going to learn every single secret of her body. Explore every inch of her skin. Every sensual spot. I'm going to learn to play her like the most delicate instrument, make her crave my touch and no one else's. As I slide my tongue inside her, she arches her back so hard that, for a moment, I fear she'll hurt herself.

"Easy." I move my palm along her spine, feeling her body vibrate like a violin string in my hand. "Just a little bit more."

Two more licks, ever so languid this time, before I close my lips around her clit and suck it into my mouth.

Vasilisa's low, delirious sounds fill the room, transforming into reverent screams when I take a nip of her sweet bud. Her fingers squeeze my hair as her body begins to shake uncontrollably. She's ready. With one last lick of her soaked pussy, I move up her body, trailing kisses along her soft skin. Marking every inch of it as mine.

I wasn't her first, and she might not yet realize this, but I will be her last. The alternative is not an option.

"Have you ever had a man worship you, Vasilisa?" I bend my head until our foreheads touch and slide the tip of my cock between her folds. "Not just your beautiful face and your gorgeous body, but every single thing that makes you—*you*?"

Her pretty eyes widen. Her lips part, but no words come out.

"Do you know how much it turns me on, to watch you bite that damn pencil every night while you fix the mess inside my company's systems? Seeing how your genius mind works is a damn aphrodisiac, vespetta. Every time after we finished a 'work session,' I had to rush to the bathroom to jerk off, all to prevent my dick from exploding."

The air leaves her lips in quick, sharp puffs. I slam my mouth to hers, mixing our breaths together, and push with my hips just enough to get my cock halfway inside. She pulls my hair and opens herself for me even more. My restraint is hanging on by the tiniest thread, so when she tilts her pelvis up in invitation, it snaps completely. I thrust into her, burying myself in her silky warmth.

"Your pussy was made for me." Nibbling her glistening skin, I move my lips along her jawline. "Do you like how my cock fills you to the brim?"

"Yes." A throaty moan next to my ear.

"Good. Because it's the only cock you'll ever have inside you from this point on." I retreat, then slide into her again. "You're staying in Sicily, Vasilisa. Forever."

"No, I'm not."

I seize her chin with my fingers and pin her with my stare. Her face is flushed and her lips quiver, but the look in her eyes is fierce and determined.

"You gave me your word," she continues. "When I'm done fixing your systems, I'm free to go."

I lose my ever-loving shit.

Grabbing the back of her neck, I plunge into her. My sanity is gone. My sense of reality—nonexistent. I ravage her kiss-swollen lips as I pound into her like a madman. The only things I can fathom are Vasilisa's panting, the feeling of her legs clutching my waist, and the smell of her shampoo. My shampoo. I'm never letting her use any other. She is mine.

My eyes are glued to her face, absorbing every single detail about her. The way her lips part when she draws in a breath each time I thrust inside her. The strands of her hair, plastered to her flushed face. The fluttering of her long black lashes as she rides the pleasure I give her. There isn't a more beautiful sight on this earth.

The bed creaks and protests under our weight. Vasilisa's ragged breaths turn into ardent cries as she nears the edge. I can feel her walls clenching around me, but I force myself to hold back. It's the most magnificent torture. As her climax approaches, I change my pace and continue to move inside her with deliberate slowness, prolonging the delicious tension between us. Finally, her body starts to shake again, and a loud scream escapes her lips as she reaches the peak of ecstasy. I let her enjoy that bliss for just a moment, then thrust hard, balls-deep into her tight little cunt, triggering yet another orgasm before she eases off her last.

A burst of white fills my vision, and I'm overcome with spasms as my cum paints Vasilisa's insides. My lungs are struggling to draw in enough oxygen, and heat settles in my chest. I've never felt this way. Did too much of my blood get redirected to my cock?

Or maybe, that's how it feels to make love to someone you're in love with.

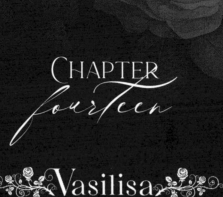

CHAPTER
fourteen

Vasilisa

I WAKE UP TO THE SOUND OF CRASHING WAVES COMPETING with arguing voices drifting from somewhere downstairs. And faint traces of a familiar scent. I blink my eyes open, my gaze landing on the red velvet box lying on the nightstand.

It's been a week since Rafael took me out on his yacht. Seven days since I plunged into uncharted waters. Instead of surfacing to find myself close to a solid shore, I'm more adrift than I've ever been.

We still have our "work" evenings in Rafael's office. I continue trying to fix the bizarre issues in his company's systems that keep popping up no matter what I do to sort them out. Rafael keeps lurking in his dark corner, sipping his wine until he declares that we're done for the night.

But there's a major difference to this "new" normal. When I head to the bedroom, Rafael follows.

And we fuck.

In near complete silence. Aside from our moans and grunts, and constant panting. We just have sex.

Lots and lots of mind-blowing, unhinged sex.

He leaves me so spent that I can't manage to wake up before noon the following day. When I finally rise, Rafael is already gone, and the only proof that we spent the night together is my sore pussy and the whiffs of cypress and orange in the air.

And every day, there's a new velvet box on the nightstand beside my bed.

The first gift was a beautiful gold necklace with a teardrop diamond pendant. I was tempted . . . so goddamn tempted to blast the thing into the sea. I managed to restrain myself. Instead, I threw the box at Rafael's head that evening before taking my seat at the desk. He didn't even comment on it. Just caught the necklace and put it away in his pocket.

The next morning—a new velvet box. Slightly larger, containing a matching set of sapphire earrings and a bracelet. I left it by his wine glass before making my way through the office door. Our sex was angry, but we didn't say a word.

Day three—another necklace. Rose gold this time, with a huge round diamond solitaire. A gorgeous, classical look. I shoved it into his hand for good measure. He took it without complaint. Pants pocket, and it was out of sight.

A wristwatch on day four. Solid gold and covered in diamonds. On day five, a "full house" designer set—earrings, necklace, bracelet, and even a brooch, all in a diamond-covered jewelry case. On day six, a fucking tiara!

Every night, I returned his gift without a thank you. And each time, Rafael just put it away. Not a word. Not an indignant sound. Just a set of instructions on my next task.

And then, sex.

Epic. Raw. Sex.

Which neither of us talks about.

I push the covers away and sit up in bed. What will it be today? Another watch? Another necklace? One that's half my weight in gold and precious gems?

Sighing, I lift the lid on the gift box.

And stare at the contents, unable to breathe.

A delicate white gold chain—a rather simple design—with a small pendant in the shape of a lily of the valley. Polished stems suspend the brilliant-cut diamonds on the flower drops, and marquise gemstones line the leaves.

Gingerly, I stroke the glistening shape with the tip of my finger, while warmth spreads through my chest. This looks delicate and expensive, but nowhere near the other extravagant gifts.

It's the only one that speaks directly to *me*. It's the only one that acknowledges *us*. Not his wealth.

As I take the chain out of the box, a yellow sticky note falls from the underside of the satiny cushion. It flutters to the floor and lands face down. Bending, I collect the note, turning it around to see what it is.

A drawing of me. Naked. My hair loose around my face. Around my neck, the lily of the valley necklace.

I stare at the note in my hand, then look at the necklace in the other. After eyeing that elegant pendant for a long, long time, I unclasp the chain and put it around my neck.

The clatter and clang of the cutlery echo through the otherwise silent kitchen. I ignore the looks of concern the maids are throwing in my direction and pull out another drawer to add its contents to the growing pile of utensils already on the counter.

I'll need at least half an hour to sort everything. Maybe even an hour, if I go slow. After I'm done, I'll have to find something else to occupy my time or I'll fucking flip trying to deal with a tangle of emotions that have me all tied up.

I'm wrapped in a thick fog of uncertainty where only blurry, distorted shapes are visible. The guilt is suffocating. I feel like a hypocrite for sleeping with my kidnapper and loving every second of it. For enjoying each moment I spend with him and missing him when he's not here. I'm just so fucking confused by everything. His feelings. My own. Am I truly in love with Rafael, or is it just Stockholm syndrome? Would I feel the same if he wasn't forcing me to stay? Hell if I know. I can't trust my heart, can't make any sense of my thoughts, can't be positive about my emotions until I get out of this haze. Rafael is the shroud that consumes me.

And him? Does he have true feelings for me, or is it simply a twisted need to possess an elusive prey that would not blindly succumb to the gilded cage he offered? All that fucking jewelry . . . I have no intention of spelling it out for him, letting him know that I don't need his fancy trinkets. He's a smart man, and if he truly cares for me, he should realize it on his own—I don't want his expensive gifts. I want freedom. And I want him to never again wave the threat to my family as some goddamn flag in front of my face.

I look down, eyes zeroing in on the lily of the valley pendant around my neck. Maybe he's coming to his senses at last.

"Miss?" One of the maids touches my shoulder. "Otto is here. He has a package for you."

I look up from the line of forks I'm making, sorting them by size. "What kind of package?"

"It's from the boss," Otto says as he approaches the kitchen island and sets a large rectangular box on the counter. The *Albini's* gold logo is prominently displayed on the top.

I open the lid and shift the white tissue paper, revealing an abundance of golden silk and lace.

The dress I'd tried on when Rafael took me shopping.

"Boss said he'll come to get you around eight," Otto adds.

"Get me?"

"For cocktails."

I raise an eyebrow. "And if I'm not interested in having cocktails with him?"

206

"He mentioned you may feel this way. And instructed me to tell you that, if you decline, he won't be allowing you to make any more phone calls."

Biting the side of my cheek, I slam the lid shut and push the box away. I've got forks to sort instead of dealing with this nonsense.

Coming to his senses, my ass.

How is it possible to like the man and yet want to strangle him at the same time?

Rafael

"Fuck," I groan as I take off my button-down to inspect the cut. Shallow but rather long, it's a diagonal gash across the ribs on the left side of my torso. Still bleeding. In need of cleaning and a good dressing. Seeking the first aid kit, I open the medicine cabinet above the sink.

A street fight. I can't believe that I got into a fucking street fight because of a woman. It was just a random group of stupid drunk punks throwing bottles at the wall of an alley. I could have just passed them, but no. I stopped the car and then got into a meaningless fistfight with four young idiots just so I could ease some of my frustration.

The reason for my frustration? A tiny little Russian princess who has been pretending that there's nothing going on between us. I went along with her request not to discuss what is happening in my bedroom because I thought that fucking her would be enough. It's not. I don't want her to simply be my nightly fuck. I want our banter. The teasing. Those awful doodles. I want all that and more. But she is still insisting on fixing my IT systems as fast as possible. So she can leave.

When I'm done wiping up the blood and disinfecting the

cut, I use a couple of Steri-Strips to bind the skin together and slap a dressing over it. Finished playing nurse to myself, I head to the closet in the corner of the guest room. Most of my clothes are in the walk-in of my bedroom, but a few garments have been left hanging here, as well.

I choose a gunmetal gray shirt and black jacket, then leave the room and walk down the hallway to Vasilisa's door.

Knock. Knock.

A minute passes.

I knock again, but nothing happens.

"Vasilisa." I bang my palm on the wooden surface. A sharp pain shoots up my side from the impact.

Silence reigns for a few more moments, but then, the clicking of heels draws closer. The door swings open.

I lose my breath.

And stare.

Fuck me.

"Don't worry, your dog is ready, Mr. De Santi."

My brain has checked out, because I just continue to stare like a motherfucker.

Vasilisa puts her hands on her hips and lifts her chin at me. "So, are we going or not?"

"Yes," I say.

One fucking syllable. That's the only thing the mush that is my gray matter manages to come up with. I'm too dumbstruck by the sight before me. It doesn't matter what Vasilisa wears, her beauty is unearthly. But seeing her now—I can't fucking breathe.

My eyes journey up her slender leg that's peeking out from between the folds of the gold silk, over her tiny waist and the intricate lace that hugs her breasts and arms, and finally, come to a halt on her face. She doesn't have any makeup on other than on her eyes. Using an eyeliner and black eyeshadow, she created a smoky look that makes her onyx depths appear larger and more expressive. Her raven hair is gathered into a low bun at her nape, but she left a few strands loose, naturally framing her face. The overall effect is simply striking.

"You're not my dog," I manage to utter somehow.

"Oh? So I can say *no* to going out for the damned cocktails you've ordered me to be ready for, and there won't be any consequences?"

I grit my teeth. "You can say no."

"Amazing. *No!*" she barks and slams the door in my face.

I squeeze my hands into fists, trying to calm the fuck down, then knock on the door again. It opens a moment later.

Vasilisa stands at the threshold, her arms crossed over her chest. Her eyes are aglow with unhidden fury.

"Would you like to come with me to somewhat of a party tonight? Not an order this time, vespetta. Just an invite."

"So you'll be okay with it if I decline?"

"You can refuse, and I'll turn around and leave. I won't force you. But I would very much like you to accompany me." I reach out and stroke her stubborn chin with the tip of my finger. It's been a long time since I had to work to convince a woman to go out with me. "Please?"

Vasilisa studies me, her eyes wide as she bites her lower lip. Not for the first time, I get lost in her dark magnetic stare for a heartbeat, pulled toward her by an unexplainable force. I move my finger along her jaw, then down her neck, and stop at the dip between her collarbones. "You didn't like the necklace?"

"I did."

"But you're not wearing it," I lament, caressing the smooth skin below her delicate bones where I imagined the necklace would rest. "Why?"

"This ploy with all the fucking jewelry, Rafael . . . It makes me feel cheap. You know? Like you're paying me for sex."

My body goes still. I never wanted her to feel that way. I just . . . wanted to make her like me. To make her want to stay.

"That wasn't my intention. And I apologize if it came across that way." I look up, meeting those dark pearlescent eyes. "But I would really like to see that necklace on you."

"And why is *this* one so goddamned important? You didn't have issues with me returning the other things to you."

"Unlike my previous gifts, I had no reason for buying it other than wanting you to wear it."

"What other reason could there possibly be?"

"To make you like me."

"Expensive trinkets will never make me like the man who threatens to kill my family if I won't dance to his tune."

"That's unfortunate." I snake my hands through the slit of her skirt and grab her butt cheeks, pulling her flush against me. "You like my cock well enough, though." Lifting her, I carry her into the room and deposit her sweet peach of an ass on the antique dresser. This girl. She fucking slays me. I lean forward, letting our noses touch. "Don't you, Vasilisa?"

"You have a high opinion of yourself. It's amazing." She sneers through her teeth, then . . . mewls as I slide my hands under her panties.

I press my thumb to her clit, rubbing it in slow, tight circles. For a few breaths, I just soak up her soft moans, then hook my fingers on the flimsy string.

"Should I remind you of how your body trembles while I eat your pussy? Or how you beg me for more every night? Lift your gorgeous ass, baby." She might be glaring at me with disdain, but she does as I ask. I slide the lacy thong down her legs and undo the button on my pants. "Or, maybe, I should help you recall your elated screams as I fuck you senseless?"

"Just normal physical reactions. Nothing more."

"I've missed you talking back to me. It turns me on so fucking much." I grab her hips and bury myself halfway inside her.

Vasilisa gasps and wraps her hands around the back of my neck, tunneling her fingers into my hair. Soft, quiet breaths leave her slightly parted lips as I rock my pelvis, urging my cock deeper. My cut side is screaming in pain, every forward motion tearing at the binding. It would have been easier if I drove into her tight little pussy in one go, but I'm afraid I'd hurt her.

I have fucking nightmares that I'll crush her while we sleep. She's so delicate. Yet, so damn fierce at the same time. They say that the deadliest substances come in the smallest packages. It's true. My lily of the valley is my personal brand of poison, and there's no antidote for it. Not for me. She's coursing through my veins, and nothing on this earth will ever purge her.

I slide inside her another inch. A loud whimper leaves Vasilisa's lips. She pants, adjusting to my size, her walls squeezing my cock so tightly that I nearly blow my load. Moving my hand to her pussy, I start massaging her clit again. I *need* her right there with me.

Vasilisa stares into my eyes, hers so devastatingly beautiful in their darkness. I don't understand why I'm so bewitched by them. Is it the raw desire I can clearly see within those depths? There's no pretense. She's not fucking faking it. She doesn't shut her eyes, blocking out the view. Doesn't try to forget the beast of a man who's bringing her pleasure. It's not the money or expensive gifts that make her unravel at my touch. Just the ecstasy she finds in my arms. Me. Just me. I've gotten so used to paying for everything I want, that I've forgotten how it feels to hold something freely given.

But she still wants to leave.

I cup her jawline with my hand, tilting her face to meet mine. "Now, you're going to be a good girl and take a deep breath."

"Why?" she pants.

"So I can give you another 'normal physical reaction,' Vasilisa. Deep breath. Now."

She threads her fingers through my hair and inhales. I thrust inside her to the hilt. Her eyes roll back as she trembles, her body shaking in my embrace. Hushed whimpers escape her as

I retreat, but then they turn into fervent moans when I drive into her again.

My side burns while I pound into her soaked pussy, faster and faster. As she comes, Vasilisa's moans transform into rapt screams, reverberating off the bedroom walls. I marvel at every note, every ragged breath, every whimpered whisper. I swallow all her sighs. Pry every shuddering quiver from her body. Imprint it all on my memory.

My beautiful Russian princess.

I keep my eyes locked on hers as I explode into her welcoming heat, spilling my seed but keeping my secrets.

"*Non ti lascerò mai andare, Vasilisa.*"

A string quartet is performing on a small stage set up to the left of the main entrance. Instead of a classical piece, however, they are mid-rendition of a popular movie score. Draped in black cloths, high-top tables are scattered throughout the main lobby, with tealights inside tiny fishbowls making up the centerpieces. The guests are the who's who of locals and frequent visitors alike. Dressed to the nines, they mingle and hover near the tables, their never-empty cocktail glasses catching the glow of the candles.

Dozens of eyes follow us as we move further into the space. Nothing uncommon about that. My reputation always precedes me, and my face never fails to garner curious looks. But tonight, all stares seem to be reserved for the woman walking by my side.

I should have expected it. Human beings are naturally drawn to wondrous things. And she is so exceptionally gorgeous that, once tempted eyes are set upon her, they struggle to look away. The primitive parts of our brain just can't seem to process that something so stunningly beautiful could possibly be real. That makes the stares inevitable.

Still, I can't handle this shit. I'm acutely aware of every

single man looking at Vasilisa, and my fingers itch to pull out my gun and start shooting the motherfuckers. Every. Each. One. Right between the eyes.

"A lot of people here," Vasilisa comments beside me. "You're not concerned that someone may recognize me and send word to Bratva?"

"Not particularly. People around here know not to stick their noses in my business, unless, of course, they're willing to face the consequences."

"I have a distinctive feeling that the said consequences wouldn't include working on your firewalls."

"It would be hard to do such a task without their hands"—I look down at my little hacker—"or heads."

"Rafael!" a male voice booms over the people's chatter.

I tighten my hold on Vasilisa's waist and glance at the source. Nazario Biaggi, the son of Calogero's underboss, is squeezing himself through a wall of guests, heading in our direction. We went to school together, and before I left Sicily, we were best friends. Nazario was never initiated into the Family, picking a construction career over Mafia life. It's the only reason he's allowed to set foot in my territory.

"I'm glad to see you tonight," he says with a smarmy smile as he approaches. "Especially in such lovely company."

Nazario's gaze rivets on Vasilisa, his eyes eating her up. Rage and jealousy, like molten fucking rock boiling just under the surface, explode inside my chest while I watch him extend his hand toward her.

"Touch her, and I'll snap your neck," I say in Italian, then pull Vasilisa closer to me and switch to English. "This is Nazario Biaggi. One of my business associates."

Nazario's eyes flare in surprise, but he quickly hides it and pulls out one of his flirtatious grins. "Always a pleasure meeting one of Rafael's . . . candied delights. Does the lady have a name?"

Blood colors my vision as I try to control an overwhelming

impulse to punch him in the face for daring to smile at my woman. Nazario has always been a flirt, but I've never given a fuck when he ogled my hookups before or when he flashed his grin at them. He might be loaded, a construction industry mogul, but his wealth doesn't even come close to mine. I could buy everything he owns in the blink of an eye. No woman would ever leave me for him. Except *her*. Because, apparently, my money doesn't interest her in the least.

"I'm happy to meet you, Mr. Biaggi," Vasilisa chirps, her sugarcoated tone slashing me right through the heart.

She likes him. Of course she does. Women always fall head over heels for Nazario, and they would even if he didn't have a dime to his name. The pencil-dick is that good-looking, I suppose. Envy grips me in its claws, shredding my insides into pieces.

"The lady's name is Gummy Bear, but I'm the sour kind," Vasilisa continues with a smile. "And I'd very much appreciate it if you'd stop staring at my boobs."

My head snaps up. "You were ogling my woman's cleavage?" I growl, switching back to Italian.

"No, not at all." Nazario takes a step back and clears his throat. "My father wanted me to pass along a message. About a week ago, several Cosa Nostra men were found dead in Palermo, their tongues were missing. Dad was concerned that you may have had something to do with that."

"Oh? Did he share his concerns with the don?"

"Yes. Calogero assured him that a gang from Trapani killed them." He cocks his head, eyeing me with suspicion. "So, it wasn't your handiwork after all?"

"I would only ever kill my godfather's men if he broke the terms of our agreement. But the don would never go against his word, would he?"

"Of course not." He nods and his voice drops lower. "But

should anything of that nature ever happen, my father would like to be the first to know."

"Well, let the underboss know I'll keep it in mind." I tighten my hold on Vasilisa's waist and motion toward the bar. "Let's go get a drink."

"Gummy Bear?" Rafael asks as we walk up to the bar.

"Seemed like a suitable name for an eye candy." I shrug. "What was that discussion about? It sounded pretty serious."

"Nazario subtly informed me that my godfather seems to be losing the support of some Cosa Nostra members."

"Are they going to oust him from power?"

"If he fucks up, yes." He passes me the beverage handed to him by the bartender.

"Never a shortage of drama in the Cosa Nostra world." I take a sip of my drink. "Grape juice? Really?"

"I've noticed that alcohol doesn't agree with you." He places his hand on the small of my back and ushers us back toward the mingling crowd.

This cocktail party is being hosted in the lobby of an antique building. The grand foyer features a domed ceiling, decorated with intricate hand-painted scenes depicting lush gardens of paradise. The elaborate details are everywhere—walls, columns, inlaid colored marble.

My eyes glide over the tiled floor with its incredible floral mosaic, then across the ornate floor-to-ceiling windows, and settle on the stucco decor and humongous old-looking paintings.

"I don't think I've ever been inside such a beautiful building," I whisper.

"It was the summer mansion of a seventeenth-century

nobleman who got rich through the silk trade," Rafael says. "He lost it in a game of cards, and the property changed hands quite a few times over the next four hundred years. When it went up for sale two years ago, it was basically a ruin. The complete restoration took nearly a year and a half."

"I can't believe they've kept everything the same. Even the wall paintings?"

"Those are called frescos. And yes, they've been restored, as well."

My eyes slide back to him. "You know the new owner?"

"Quite well, actually. An unscrupulous motherfucker that one. But he has a weakness for cultural relics"—Rafael reaches out and brushes my cheek with his knuckles—"heritage . . . and . . . a feisty little hacker who keeps rejecting his gifts."

The musicians switch to a slower melody, a highly emotional piece with a violin in the lead. Everyone is having a great time, but I'm only partially aware of the people moving around us. I'm completely tuned in on Rafael, ensnared in the twin green beams that seem to blaze right through me.

"Should I take that as a compliment? Being called a weakness doesn't sound like much of one," I whisper.

"It depends on your view of such things." His hand moves along my chin. "Let's say someone opens fire right now. There's a high probability of that happening, considering the number of enemies I have. If I were alone, I'd simply go for my gun and neutralize the threat. If I had to give chase, I'd do it. There wouldn't be anything here that would distract me from accomplishing that objective.

"But, since you've accompanied me here tonight, I would handle that scenario differently. Your safety comes first. The elimination of the attackers is paramount, but only to ensure your well-being. Going after them, if it means leaving you behind, is less important. Meaning, Vasilisa, you are my highest priority, but also undeniable liability."

"So why did you bring me, if I'm such a liability?" I choke out.

Rafael's eyes crease at the corners as a small smile tugs his lips. He bends forward and wraps his arm around my waist, slowly lifting me flush against him. I grab his shoulders for support, alarmed by the fact that he's bearing my whole weight with only one arm. But Rafael doesn't seem to be bothered by it at all. His eyes never waver from mine while he raises the tumbler in his other hand and casually takes a sip.

"Because, believe it or not," he says as he puts the now empty glass on the table beside him, "I enjoy your company way too much. And I've missed our chats."

I suck in a breath, unable to look away from his eyes. Our faces are so close that his warm breath brushes my skin. My lips. "You would risk getting shot, all so you could talk to me someplace I can't simply ignore you?"

"Any day," Rafael growls before his mouth descends on mine.

The taste of him invades me. Fire spreads through my veins, the most consuming flame searing me from the inside. God, I've missed him, too.

I tried distancing myself from thoughts of him, hoping that doing mundane tasks would somehow help lessen the dangerous, messed-up feelings I'd been developing for Rafael. Over the past week, I've reorganized his walk-in twelve times, simply because touching his things brought me comfort. Aside from sex, we haven't touched at all. No kisses outside the bedroom. I've tried to tell myself that this pull I feel toward him is nothing more than a sexual attraction. It's not.

And this kiss proves it. As I kiss him back, the sensation overrules everything else. Common sense. Self-preservation. Suffocating guilt. Nothing matters, except him.

When his lips leave mine, our eyes remain locked, and suddenly, I can't seem to get enough air.

"Is kissing in public considered impolite in Sicily?" I ask as he lowers me back to the ground. An unexpected hush has descended upon the room. No one is talking. They are all just gaping at us. "Why is everyone staring?"

"They've been staring since the moment you stepped into the room. It was curiosity and surprise at first. Now, I'm pretty sure they're simply terrified of you."

I don't get the chance to ask what the hell he means about people being afraid of me because my eyes catch on the dark crimson stain spreading across Rafael's shirt.

"Rafael . . ." I take the side of his jacket and move it away. A big area on his left side is soaked in blood. "Dear God. What happened?"

"A minor slip-up in my assessment. I wrongly concluded this won't need stitches." He rights his jacket and buttons it as if there's no issue at all. "Guido will take care of me when we get back." His tone remains calm, but there's something else swirling in his green depths now. "There should be a singer coming up soon to give a little performance, and the servers will be bringing out the cassata cake. I think you'll like it."

"We're not waiting for a damn cake while you're bleeding all over the place!" I whisper-yell.

"It's a Sicilian specialty. You have to try it."

I stare at him in shock. "You need a doctor."

"Guido can handle it. Wouldn't be the first time."

"I meant for your head, придурок!"

Rafael's lips tilt into a devious smirk. "Is that a Russian pet name, vespetta?"

"It means 'moron'!" I sneer through my teeth, grab his arm, and pull him toward the exit.

Shocked faces stare at us while people part to let us pass. Rafael doesn't seem bothered by the fact that I'm basically dragging him through the hotel lobby. There's actually a slight smirk flashing across his features.

"I guess this means we're not staying for cake?" he asks as we step outside.

"You guessed right."

"Mm-hmm. I think you might like me after all, Vasilisa, just a tiny bit. Skipping dessert for my sake? I feel rather special."

Ugh. This man. I watch him closely, throwing frequent looks at him as we traverse the parking lot to Rafael's SUV, looking for signs of distress. He seems fine. Is that normal? How much blood has he already lost?

Once we reach the wicked-looking Maserati, I tug on the lapel of his suit jacket. "Bend over, please. I need to check your pupils."

Rafael braces a hand on the car roof and leans forward until his face hovers right in front of mine. I cup his jawline with my palms and tilt his head slightly to the side, toward the lamplight. My God, his eyes are so beautiful. There's a glint to them that reminds me of the sea glass I found at the shore. Opalescent. And brazenly focused on me. And when he looks at me as he is now, I get the impression that he wants to swallow me whole. Every time, it makes me weak in the knees.

"Why are you checking my pupils, Vasilisa?" he asks, his voice rumbly.

"I'm not sure. Doctors do it in the movies all the time." I move a stray strand of hair off his forehead.

"A pupil test is done to check for brain injury. It has nothing to do with bleeding."

"Well, I'm checking them regardless. Stay still."

His eyes appear normal to me. But his skin feels warm. I touch his temple with my fingertips, then his cheek with the back of my hand. Fuck, I can't figure it out. Lifting on my tiptoes, I press my lips to his forehead.

Rafael goes stiff as a board, his every muscle rigid with tension.

"What are you doing?" he asks. The tone of his voice is strange. I can tell he's uneasy, but I haven't a clue why.

"Checking for fever." I reposition my lips to his temple. Then back to his forehead. Nope, his temperature seems fine. For now. I brush my knuckles down his cheekbone. "We should hurry. You need to take antibiotics."

Rafael cocks his head to the side and dips lower, his eyes boring into mine. "I already took some. But if it'll make you less worried, I'll take them again."

"I don't think that's how meds work," I choke out, mesmerized by the dangerous glint in his eyes.

"And I didn't expect you to fret about my well-being."

"Of course I'm worried! We're practically in the middle of nowhere. It's at least a half-hour ride back to the estate. How are you going to drive in your condition?"

"What condition?"

"The you're-bleeding-all-over-the-place condition!" I shout while tears gather in the corners of my eyes.

"My blood vessels aren't doing the driving, vespetta."

A frustrated whimper leaves my lips. I wipe my tears with the back of my hand, then grab his arm, shaking him.

"How can you be so fucking unruffled? You're hurt! What if you go into shock? Or bleed out? I don't know first aid, Rafael! And what if I need to get you to the ER, and you're unresponsive? I don't even know your blood type! Or if you have any allergies to drugs. What if—"

Rafael's mouth crushes mine. As usual, when he kisses me, I completely forget everything but him.

"You can drive," he mumbles into my lips. "Or we can just get in the car, and you can ride my cock. Make sure my blood is redirected elsewhere."

I bite his lower lip. Hard. Then, force myself to break the kiss. "Keys."

Rafael's eyes narrow into smirky slits while he takes the keys out of his pocket and drops them on my extended palm. I hoist myself into the driver's seat, reaching for the wheel. But it and the pedals might as well be in a different time zone.

"Umm . . . Where is—" I start to ask, but I'm already sliding forward.

"Here," Rafael says while holding the switch on the outward edge of the seat base. "I don't have any extra cushions," he continues while pressing another control to raise the seat, "but I'll make sure there's one in the vehicle from now on."

"Cushions?"

"Yes." He rounds the car and gets in on the passenger side. "It'll be easier for you to see over the wheel with additional padding."

I shake my head. Did The Sicilian just tease me?

"Do you have GPS?" I ask as I start the engine. "I can't find my way over those damn winding dirt roads."

"I like the winding dirt roads. One of the main reasons I love the Taormina area is because there aren't many highways around here."

"What's wrong with nice solid highways?"

"They fuck up the landscape."

I steal a look at him with the corner of my eye. "How are you feeling?"

"Strange."

Alarms instantly go off in my head. "What's wrong?"

"I've never let anyone drive my car before."

"Why not?"

"As I told you already, I don't like having my things touched. That includes my vehicles. My clothes." He turns on the GPS, then meets my gaze. "My bed."

Biting my lower lip, I quickly look back at the road in front of us. I've been wearing Rafael's clothes since I got here. In fact, he went to great lengths to make me wear nothing *but* his clothes for days after my arrival. And I've been sleeping in his bed all this time.

"Why?" I ask.

"Because, long ago, I lost everything I owned and had nothing left that was mine. Every single thing I have now, I fought through blood and sweat to possess, but I gave up a large chunk of my soul doing it." The easy cadence of his words changes, and his tone shifts, taking on an edge. "I don't share things I had to barter my soul for, Vasilisa."

"But you shared them with me."

"I did." Crow's-feet radiate from the corners of his playful eyes. "Because you're mine, too."

That's such a chauvinistic line. But instead of raising my hackles, his possessiveness sends a pleasant warmth throughout my chest. His words leave me melting. God help me. I'm moments away from curling up at his side and purring like a happy little kitten.

"I'm not yours," I mumble and turn onto the main road. "Blood loss is making you delusional."

"Then, you will be." Rafael opens the glove box and takes out a pack of cigarettes.

"What the fuck is wrong with you?" I gape at him.

"What?"

"Smoking can lead to a higher chance of you bleeding out and also affect the healing of the wound, that's what." I rip the pack out of his hand and throw it through the open window.

"You do realize that if I die, you'll be free to return home, don't you ?" He sets his warm palm on my thigh, right over the flesh made bare by the slit in my dress. "You know, I can vividly envision your beautiful promise of where the dogs will chew me up and shit out my remains. It's probably the most intriguing death threat I've ever received."

My fingers tighten on the wheel, and I keep my eyes firmly glued to the stretch of road beyond the windshield. He's right.

With him out of the picture, I'd be able to go free. The possibility never actually crossed my mind. Actually, the mere notion of something bad happening to him triggers a falling sensation in the pit of my stomach.

I step harder on the gas pedal.

His hand slides to my inner thigh, then drifts up. "Mmm . . . I had no idea there are such advantages to being the passenger."

The tips of his fingers lightly graze over my panty-covered pussy.

"Rafael." I suck in a shuddering breath. "I'm driving."

"And you're doing a great job." With another gentle stroke, the force of his fingers intensifies. "How do you like the SUV?"

A tremor races down my spine, and I nearly swerve off the road, coming too close to the roadside barrier. "It feels like driving a tank. I prefer lower-riding cars."

"Okay. I'll order a sports convertible for you."

"I don't want you to buy me a car! Please, remove your hand."

"No. I don't think I will."

His touch is getting bolder, the pressure firmer. Despite the flimsy lace keeping the skin-to-skin contact at bay, his deft fingers stroke inside my folds. The abrasiveness of the fabric on my sensitized skin only heightens my reaction. The navigation screen shows we're less than five minutes from the estate. But there's no way I'll stay lucid that long if he continues his ministrations.

"I'm going to stop the car," I pant.

"And let me bleed to death? I am feeling quite lightheaded all of a sudden." With a swift move, he shoves the crotch of the panties to the side and slides his finger inside me. "You're soaked, Vasilisa."

I choke on my breath, almost losing control of the damn vehicle again. His thumb circles my clit, the sweet torment making me whimper. My nails sink into the leather of the wheel as I squeeze it harder. Zaps of electric current run through my nerve pathways as Rafael keeps up his persistent teasing of my tender flesh. A slow stroke in and out, followed by another more vigorous one. And then, he changes the angle of his wrist and pushes his finger deeper.

"We're going to crash." My inner muscles spasm. I'm going to go mad if he doesn't stop what he's doing. Or maybe if he does.

The property comes into view at the end of the road. I pull the remnants of my sanity and composure together, focusing all my concentration on the iron fixture as it slides too slowly out of the way. We're going to hit the stupid thing. I lay on the horn like the lunatic I apparently am at the moment.

The Maserati careens through the gap, missing by mere inches both the structure and the shocked security guard holding the gate open. My core weeps with the sweetest agony while Rafael continues his relentless strokes, pulling his finger almost completely out, only to thrust it further inside.

By the time we reach the house, I'm so out of my mind that I'm barely aware of hitting the brakes. The jolting stop propels my body forward, impaling me onto Rafael's finger. White stars explode in front of my eyes as I come all over his hand.

Air escapes my lungs in wheezing puffs. All I can do is maintain a death grip on the steering wheel as Rafael finally releases my pussy and starts unbuttoning his pants.

"Your driving skills are exceptional, vespetta," he says and unclasps both of our seat belts. "Let's see how you do with riding."

Huge hands grab my waist, and, in the blink of an eye, I find myself straddling him, with a rock-hard cock teasing my entrance.

"You're crazy," I choke out as I sink down, taking him inside. "If you bleed out, it'll be all your fault."

Lust-filled eyes squint with mirth as Rafael plunges into

me from below. "You're going to be the death of me, Vasilisa. One way or another."

I keep ahold of Rafael's neck as I ride him, angling my hips so that I can take more of him in. My core is quivering, already I'm on the brink of coming again. His left hand cups my face while he teases my pussy with the other, applying pressure with his thumb on the spot where my folds meet. It's driving me mad, loony. The sounds of my panting fill the SUV as I let myself get lost in Rafael's eyes. Insanity. This is sweet insanity from which I never want to recover.

Rafael's chest rises and falls as his breathing picks up, becoming more ragged. Seeing him coming undone is an erotic elation in itself, but when he pulls me forward, smashing his mouth to mine in a wild, possessing kiss, I lose myself completely. Orgasmic bliss consumes me, burning away the last specks of the walls I erected around my heart in a futile attempt to keep Rafael De Santi from claiming it.

CHAPTER
fifteen

Vasilisa

"WHY ARE YOU DOING THIS, VASYA, BABY?" My mother's voice sounds sad and worried through the line. "It's been almost two months. Please come home, and we'll sort out whatever it is that's the problem. We miss you so much."

I close my eyes and lean back on Rafael's naked chest. We tried working on his data repository twice this afternoon but ended up in bed both times. "I miss you guys, too, Mom. I'll be home soon."

"You say that every time and—No! Roman! Give me back the phone!"

"Vasilisa." My father's low, rumbling growl practically explodes through the speaker. "The instant I find out where you are, I'll be dragging you back home and locking you up in your room. Forever!"

"Sure, Dad." I sigh. "Can you put Yulia on the phone, please."

He grumbles something in Russian and, a few moments later, my sister chirps. "Hey, Vasya. How are you?"

"I'm fine. How—"

"Dad has Felix tracing your calls," she whispers urgently. "He's been doing it for weeks, but he can't pinpoint your location. I heard Gramps tell Dad that he'll be switching to another tracking software and—"

I immediately cut the line. How long did we talk? Rafael said his phone can't be tracked, but still . . . Panic grips my chest, and suddenly it's hard to breathe.

"Vespetta?" Rafael drops a kiss on my bare shoulder. "Is something wrong?"

Did they pin my location? Bile rises up my throat. My father could be out the door and on his way to Sicily right at this moment.

I turn around so I'm straddling Rafael's chest. My eyes find and lock onto his gaze as the storm brewing inside me becomes a hurricane. This is exactly what I wanted, isn't it? For my dad to find me and bring me home. But, the thing is, I don't want that anymore.

I don't want to go home.

But I also can't remain with the man who won't let me choose between staying and leaving.

"Vasilisa?" Rafael threads his hands through my hair, pulling me down for a kiss. "Will you tell me what's going on in that pretty head of yours?"

"My father is tracing the calls," I mumble into his lips.

"Of course he is. But he won't be able to discover where you are. No one will."

"And you won't let me leave until I'm done fixing your system?"

He takes my bottom lip between his teeth and nips it. "That's right."

I cup his face with my palms and pull away, breaking the kiss. "Then stop instructing your men to sabotage the work you had me dragged here to do."

Rafael's eyes flare dangerously. He couldn't have seriously believed that I wouldn't figure out what he's been doing. The system "disruptions" that keep popping up can't be the result of an external source. I realized this two weeks ago but I went along with the farce because I didn't want to leave. Didn't want to leave *him*.

"I want you to stay," he growls as he shifts his hand to my pussy, teasing me with his finger.

I gasp. Everything is still tender, but his touch feels so damn good. As he starts stroking my clit with his thumb, I feel myself getting instantly wet. Biting my lower lip, I widen my legs to give him more access.

"You want me to stay," I whisper, holding his gaze, "or, *do* you want me to want to stay? Those are two very different things."

Rafael's other hand slides to the back of my neck, gathering a fistful of my hair while he pushes another finger inside my quivering core.

"No one can offer you what I can, Vasilisa." The grip on my hair tightens slightly. "Name whatever you want, and I'll give it to you. Money. Jewels. A yacht, if you want it. I have two, but I can buy you a new one. If you don't like Sicily, just pick a spot, and I'll get you a house there. It'll be in your name." He pinches my clit, making me cry out. "Any damn thing you desire, I'll deliver."

"So, anything, except the freedom to decide whether I want to stay with you?"

"You will want to stay with me," he growls as he moves his hands under my ass. "I'll make sure of it."

With those words, he pulls me forward until my hips hover just above his face. His warm breath feathers over my wet folds before his tongue slides between them. A shiver shoots up my spine, causing me to arch my back and moan with pleasure. With his fingers digging into and massaging my rounded cheeks,

Rafael slowly licks up the length of my slit. I hold onto the headboard like a lifeline as he continues to feast on my pussy. The sounds of crickets and distant voices outside fade into the background as I lose myself to the sensation of his hot mouth on my most intimate parts. Nothing else exists except for Rafael. Nothing else, at this point, matters.

His skilled tongue delves expertly, exploring every curve and crevice, ravaging me with masterful precision and powerful waves of pleasure that I never want to end. The room becomes a hazy blur, and my body melts into divine oblivion. My every gasp, every sigh blends in harmony with muffled groans and languid *mmm*s, accompanied by the sound of his lips and the gentle swivel of his tongue.

The graze of his teeth on my throbbing bundle of nerves sends a jolt through every cell of my body. The headboard rattles from my furious grip while I struggle to breathe as he seals his mouth to my clit and sucks it in. My body shakes from the sheer intensity of the pleasure he's giving me, and a loud shout rips out of me as I climax, exploding into a million tiny particles.

Air leaves my lungs in short, shaky bursts as I try to pull myself together. Rafael licks my pussy one more time, then kisses my inner thigh, and gently lowers me to sit back on his chest.

"I'll worship every part of your body like this, Vasilisa. Every day. Every night," he says as he slides his hands up my ribcage and over my breasts to wrap them around my neck. With his thumbs at my chin, he strokes my lips. "You're going to become so addicted to my touch, that just the thought of being away from me will manifest as physical pain."

I pant as I search his eyes, finding steely determination reflecting at me from the green flinty rocks. He's wrong, though. I'm already addicted. And just like every addict, I want more.

Just one more. That has become my mantra. *Just one more day with him, and then I'll put a stop to this crazy train. Just one more night in his arms, and then I'll find a way to leave. Just one more bone-melting kiss . . . Just one more soul-searing touch . . . Just one more moment in heaven.*

And slowly, each of those "ones" became a two. Then, three. Then, ten. Then, a yearning for forever.

But the time has come, and this counting game has reached a point where it can't continue anymore.

"I'm going to take a shower, and then I'll resume my work."

"We both know there's no need for you to work for me anymore," he barks.

"Of course there is. I'll finish the configuration changes today, and then I expect you to arrange for me to go home. I will not be kept a prisoner here any longer."

"I don't see you in chains, Vasilisa."

"Because the shackles you've chained me with are not tangible."

Rafael's eyes darken, upheaval swirls in their depths. He grabs my chin, pulling me closer to his hard-lined face.

"I'm in love with you, Vasilisa."

My heart stops beating. For a fleeting moment, every molecule in my body is completely still while I process the words I've been longing to hear. But there's no joy in hearing his declaration. That feeling of soaring through the clouds is missing entirely because I can't believe that what he said is true. He might have a strange way of showing it, but I do think he feels something for me. I'm just afraid it isn't love.

Love is the purest of emotions. It's not selfishness. Not ownership. What he feels is an obsession over someone who didn't easily fall into his hands. It will pass, be replaced with something new. And in the end, it won't even matter. Nothing will change for me. Except for the presence of a crippling fear. Did I fall in love with a man who's not capable of loving me back? A man who will do anything to keep me with him. Anything, except let me go.

"I can't do this anymore, Rafael." I press my shaky palms to his cheeks and lean down to caress my lips over his. "We had a deal. If you don't keep your side of the bargain, I will withhold mine, and find a way to leave."

Rafael

Dread explodes inside me. Panic surges in my chest, spreading throughout my body. I don't know what I should do to make her want to stay. I would never hurt her parents or siblings, but the threat to their lives is the only leverage I have. What if she does manage to find a way to flee? I wrap my arms around her middle and roll us until I'm on top.

"I swear I'll kill them," I growl, watching her eyes widen in alarm. "If you dare to run from me, Vasilisa, I'm going to destroy your family and I'll make you watch."

A shadow passes over her face, transforming her shocked expression into anguish.

"Move," she hisses.

"No."

"Get your hands off me!" She wraps her fingers around my throat, squeezing. "Or I'm going to choke you to death."

Instantly, my cock resembles a steel rod. It always turns me on when she goes feral. "I love you! Can't you understand that?!"

"And yet, you keep hurting me every day by making me choose between you and my family."

I grit my teeth so hard that it makes my fucked-up facial muscles ache. "You're staying. And if you're going to hate me, so be it."

Vasilisa pushes on my pecs with her palms. I let her wriggle out from under me and follow her with my eyes as she gets off the bed. Wiping her eyes with the back of her hand, she walks to the bathroom but stops at the threshold.

"You don't love me, Rafael. You don't even know the meaning of the word." Her voice is barely a whisper, but every sound particle pierces my chest like a blazing blade. "The only thing you know is how to buy things. And when your money has no power—you just take."

A soft click resonates as she steps into the bathroom. I sit motionless in the bed with the scent of our lovemaking in the air, enveloping me in its embrace while all I can do is stare at the closed door. Hushed sniffling seeps in from the other side. I made the woman I love cry. That realization crushes me like a ten-ton block of concrete. Despair settles in my gut as I cross the room and press my forehead to the wooden surface.

I'd never do it. Would never harm her family, even if she somehow did find a way to run away, breaking our deal. Her love for them must be boundless if she was willing to spend all this time with a monster like me to ensure their safety. What would it be like to have her *love me* like that? For her to *want* to be with me? Not because it would keep her family safe. Not because I can make her melt from pleasure with my touch. I want her to stay because of *me*. I want her to love me because of who I am. Not for what I can give her. And what have I done? Coerced her, and tried to buy her love.

My lily of the valley is right.

I need to let her go. Return her to where she belongs.

Back to all those handsome, perfect men who are a part of her world.

Collecting my scattered clothes from the floor, I leave the bedroom. Down the hall, one of the maids is dusting a sconce and humming a melody under her breath. When she sees me approaching, a strangled shriek leaves her lips. Her cheeks blush bright red, and she tries hard to look anywhere but at my naked body.

I continue along the corridor, eliciting a few more startled cries from other staff who see me trudge past in my newfound stupor.

"Raff?" Guido's voice comes from the stairway. "What in hell—"

"Not now." I step inside the guest room, heading to the bathroom.

"I gather the moment might not be the best, but this is urgent."

"I said, not now!" I slam the bathroom door shut.

Adjusting the water to scorching hot, I step inside the shower and press my palms on the tiled wall.

"I just found out that Calogero bought several properties southwest of Messina," Guido's muffled voice comes through the door.

I take a deep breath and close my eyes. Scalding water beats down on my head and back, but it doesn't strip away the rage and misery festering inside me.

"Raff?" Loud banging on the door. "Did you hear what I said?"

"Yes."

I tilt my head up, letting the spray hit my face. Fucking Calogero. I can't bring myself to give a shit about what that motherfucker is doing. Not now. He can go buy every goddamned inch of land in Sicily, for all I care.

"And? What are we going to do about it?"

Turning off the tap, I step out of the shower stall and grab the edge of the sink. Handling the Calogero issue is long overdue, but I wasn't willing to risk an open confrontation with Vasilisa in my home. I guess I don't have to worry about that anymore since she's leaving. Unless . . . unless she decides to come back.

The mirror over the sink is completely fogged up, blurring my reflection. I wipe the condensation off with my palm and stare at the monstrous visage looking back at me. Yeah, as if a beauty like Vasilisa would ever choose to spend her life with a beast like me.

Throwing all my strength behind it, I hit the mirror with my fist. It shatters into jagged pieces. Blood gushes from my split knuckles, crimson dripping to the reflective fragments, seeping into the cracks and edges of the remnants below. It reminds me of me, that fucking broken mirror. A multitude of messed-up shards, just like my currently splintered soul. And all that red—the tears of my bleeding heart.

I snatch the towel off the hanger and open the bathroom door.

"Gather twenty men," I say as I wrap the towel around my waist. "I want everyone armed and ready to go in thirty minutes."

"Go where?"

"To burn every damn building that bastard bought."

"Now? In the middle of the day? Why not wait till nightfall?"

"Because if I don't wreck something right the fuck now, I'll kill the first asshole who crosses my path!" I snarl. "Is that enough of a reason for you?"

"Quite a solid one. I'll go gather our men."

I light a cigarette, then nod at Otto who's directing men with jerricans of gasoline. "Keep away from the trees, I don't want them damaged."

"Sure, boss." He returns the nod and heads toward the top of a hill where the one-story modern villa is surrounded by a much older but well-tended orchard, its trees heavy with fruit.

"I think you should reconsider," Guido says next to me. "Burning Calogero's properties on our turf is one thing, but this is a completely different matter."

"I know." I take a long drag of a cigarette and eye the luxurious mansion. It's my godfather's favorite getaway. He likes to bring his business partners here so they can enjoy the beautiful scenery of the western part of Sicily while having drinks on the spacious, shaded terrace.

It's also where he took his vows when he became the don. Earlier today, when I torched the two warehouses he bought outside Messina, that was a simple statement. But this? This is a declaration of war.

"There's no turning back after this, Rafael. You know that, right?"

"Yes."

"And what are we going to do with his men?"

I look at the four men kneeling by the greenhouse, their hands tied behind their backs. The bastards managed to shoot one of my guys while we stormed the place. I reach into my jacket, pull out my gun, and aim at the first dickhead in the line. The sound of my 9mm splits the air.

The other three men look at the body splayed before them, then start fidgeting, trying to get to their feet. I send two more bullets flying. One hits its target in the head, the other, in the neck. The last of Calogero's men was able to stagger to his feet, but now he's just standing there, staring at his dead buddies.

I holster my gun and set off across the lawn. With my peripheral vision, I spot Otto in front of the main house, motioning to my men to get outside. He's holding a Molotov cocktail in his hand. I stop in front of Calogero's surviving goon and pin him with my gaze. "Turn around."

The man swallows and follows the order. His bound hands are shaking behind his back.

"You're going to deliver a message to your don." I cut the zip tie at his wrists.

For a few heartbeats, he remains rooted to the spot with his back to me, then, he chances a glance over his shoulder. "What's the message?"

"Everybody clear!" Otto's voice thunders from the driveway, followed by the sound of shattering glass.

Orange flames quickly engulf the interior of the house, climbing the walls to the outside and licking up the terrace posts. Dark smoke rises into the sky, spooking a flock of birds in the orchard. En masse, they take flight, their frantic cries mixing with the sound of crackling wood.

"That's the message." I nod toward the burning building, then turn around and head toward my SUV where Guido is leaning against the grill, watching the raging fire.

"Now what?" he asks when I approach.

"Recall every team from our European bases. We'll need the manpower."

"Already did. They'll be here in the morning."

"Good. Have them deployed at all the likely places where Calogero may hit us back. He'll need a few days to regroup before he makes his move, so we have a brief window of time to prepare." I get behind the wheel and pull out my phone. "And up the security on the house. I have to drop by Catania, and it'll be a few hours before I get home."

"Let me guess. Another visit to that jeweler?"

"Maybe."

"You just started the damn war, but instead of helping me coordinate our men and make plans, you're heading off to shop for trinkets for your Russian princess?"

"Exactly." I hit the gas.

All the lights except for two sconces on the landing are off, shrouding the hallway in darkness as I walk toward my bedroom. I stop in front of the door and listen, but I can't hear anything. Without making a sound, I turn the handle and slip inside.

The reading lamp over the headboard is lit, illuminating the bed. The neatly made and empty bed. Vasilisa is on the couch by the fireplace. Asleep.

I leave the golden bag on the nightstand and crouch beside my sleeping beauty, taking in Vasilisa's face. Her eyes are a little puffy, and there are a few crumpled tissues on the floor. She's been crying. A knot forms in my stomach. Reaching out, I brush my knuckles along her soft cheek, then slide my arms under her, and carry her to the bed.

Once I have her tucked in, I head to the walk-in closet and start gathering Vasilisa's clothes. She will be mad as a wasp at me in the morning, but it doesn't matter. I want to see her wearing nothing but my shirt again.

It'll probably be the very last time.

CHAPTER
sixteen

H E WAS HERE LAST NIGHT. I KNOW IT THE INSTANT I open my eyes and find myself in bed instead of on the couch.

I couldn't make myself go to sleep in the same bed where he gave me the most magnificent pleasure, only to crush me with his threats afterward. The other side of the bed is empty, but when I flip around and bury my nose into the pillow, his smell is all over it. The impulse to hug that pillow to my chest is strong, but at the same time, I want to tear the damn thing to pieces.

"I'm locking the door tonight," I mumble into feathery softness, then spring out of bed and maniacally start pulling off the sheets and pillowcases. Once everything that bears his scent is removed, I head into the bathroom to have a shower. A foot over the threshold, I come to a jarring stop. The neatly lined up products—shampoo, shower gel, deodorant—mock me from the shelf beside the tub. All of them are his. Whether I want it or not, I'm going to be covered in his scent.

Well, not happening.

I grab the bar soap from the dish next to the sink on the vanity and get into the tub. It's the only cleanser that doesn't contribute to his manly scent, so I end up washing my entire body, hair included, with it.

Twenty minutes later, when I emerge from the en suite smelling like baby powder and with my hair in a frizzy mess (washing it with hand soap was not a good idea), I notice the exquisite-looking golden paper bag set on the coffee table. With slow steps, I approach the couch and take a seat, staring at the offering, feeling defeated. He bought me a present. Again.

I pull the bag toward me and take out two velvet boxes. The larger one holds a white gold tennis bracelet adorned with dozens of diamonds so flawlessly clear that they reflect the light like tiny little mirrors. A small diamond-encrusted charm hangs from the dazzling alternating cluster of gemstones on the stunning band. The shape is of the lily of the valley. I look down at my chest where the identical pendant rests over my cleavage. It's the only gift from Rafael that I kept and wear.

My eyes sting. I press my fingers to the bridge of my nose and take a deep breath before opening the second box. It contains a set of matching earrings. This is not a random purchase, but a thoughtful token a man would give to a woman he loves. I struggle to swallow over the lump that's lodged in my throat. How could he? You don't threaten to kill the family of someone you love. And you don't keep your loved one captive.

Carefully, I put the jewelry back into the bag, wipe the tears from my eyes, and head to the walk-in closet. The overhead lights turn on when I slide the door aside, illuminating the rows of empty shelves on the left wall where my clothes have been. I do a three-sixty, looking around in confusion. Rafael's suits, shirts, and everything else are still there. But other than my underwear and socks, and the fluffy white cardigan, everything else of mine is gone!

"That jackass," I snap and reach for his dress shirt. But then, I change my mind.

He wants to play dirty?

Game on.

"What a lovely morning," I chirp as I step inside the kitchen, heading straight to the stove where Irma is cooking scrambled eggs. "Can I have some of that goat cheese on the side, as well?"

"Yes . . . of course," she mumbles, her eyes as wide as saucers as she takes in my outfit.

"Thanks." I smile and sit down across from Guido at the counter-height breakfast table. His eyebrows are in his hairline while he stares at me and does a great imitation of a fish struggling to breathe.

"Are we implementing a new dress code around here?" he asks.

"Not as far as I know." I take the coffee carafe and pour myself a cup. "Why do you ask?"

"Yesterday, I stumbled on Rafael storming through the house in his birthday suit. He traumatized all the female staff. And now . . . you." He motions with his cup in my direction.

"Your brother confiscated my clothes. Again." I shrug and take a long sip. "I had to work with what I had available. It's not like I'm naked."

"I beg to differ." He shakes his head. "I'll tell Irma to pull down the blinds."

"Why?"

"Because the gardeners are gawking at you and salivating. They may end up cutting off their fingers instead of rose bush branches."

"I prefer natural light."

Guido sets his coffee on the table and stands up. "I'm out. Don't want to be around when Rafael sees you and loses his shit."

"And why would Rafael lose his shit?" A deep voice comes from somewhere behind me.

"Fuck," Guido mumbles.

I grab a knife and start spreading butter on the bagel I picked up from the platter on the table.

"Good morning, Rafael," I say like I don't have a care in the world and slowly swivel around on my chair.

He stands in the kitchen doorway, absolutely motionless, for an excruciatingly drawn-out moment. The only part of him that isn't stone-still are his eyes. They are scanning my body, pausing on the see-through lacy bra that hides basically nothing, then continuing down my exposed stomach to the small triangle of the matching white thong. I did put on my fluffy cardigan, but I chose to leave it fully unbuttoned.

"Everybody. Out," Rafael says in a hushed tone as his eyes move back up to my breasts. "RIGHT. THE FUCK. NOW!" he roars with his next breath.

"But, I haven't finished my breakfast, yet." I blink at him innocently.

His face is a mask of sheer rage as he crosses the distance and stops right in front of me.

"Guido," he growls through his teeth, but his furious stare is focused on me. "If there is a single man left in this house in the next ten seconds, I'm going to gut him on the spot. That includes you. GET THE FUCK OUT!"

I take a bite of my bagel and watch Irma and Guido dash past Rafael. They hastily close the kitchen side door following their exit, but it doesn't suppress the frantic shouts and sounds of commotion elsewhere inside the house.

Rafael leans forward and grips the table on either side of me, caging me with his massive body and arms. He looks so pissed that I wouldn't be surprised to see fire flaring from his nostrils at any second. "What. The fuck. Are you doing?"

"This was all that was left on my side of the closet. And I won't wear your clothes again."

"You will." He gets in my face. "Even if I have to carry you upstairs and forcibly put one of my shirts on you."

I bring up my hand and press the tip of the knife under his chin. "Feel free to try. And see what happens."

Inhaling deeply and with obvious effort, Rafael narrows his eyes at me, then grabs the back of my neck and slams his mouth to mine. I barely have enough time to drop the knife, and it clatters to the hardwood floor with a resounding clang.

"I could have cut you, you idiot," I mutter into his lips as I return the kiss with equal vigor.

"Wouldn't be the first time."

I wind my arms around his neck, pulling him tighter against me, and hook my feet behind his back. His hardness presses right into my core, and wetness soaks my thin underwear. My God, I'm so angry at this man, but I still vehemently crave him inside me. He might be a ruthless jerk, but I'm utterly crazy about him.

I draw his lower lip between my teeth, biting it. He bites me back. His right hand flexes on my nape while his left glides up along my inner thigh to the lace covering my pussy.

"You're fucking soaked, Vasilisa," Rafael growls, pushing the lace to the side and dragging his finger through my folds.

Tremors rack my body from the raw need I hear in his tone.

"I'm going to lick every last drop of your sweet nectar." He grabs me under my ass and deposits me on top of the table. "Right the fuck now."

I'm shaking as I lean back to lie on the cool surface where the plates and cups are still scattered. I reach for the edge, but my hand catches on something, and the unlucky item smashes on the floor. Rafael lifts my right foot and presses his lips on the inside of my ankle, then slowly trails kisses up my leg. When his mouth reaches my pussy, he presses his face to it and inhales.

"Fucking heaven," he rumbles as he breathes in my scent one more time.

Wrapping his fingers around my ankle, he sets my foot on his shoulder, then shifts his attention to the other leg.

Ankle.

Inner thigh.

Pussy.

He covers every inch of my skin in slow, hard kisses before he hooks my foot over his shoulder. With a low guttural grunt, he tears my thong in half, and the delicate lace falls away.

I'm already half-gone when he buries his face between my legs. My lips part as I strain for more air, trembling with every stroke of his tongue.

Languid. Methodical. He *is* intent on licking every last drop. My core is quivering with the need for more. I grab his hair, pulling his head into me as I crest the swelling wave of pleasure. His lips close around my clit, sucking it into his mouth. I scream. My release is imminent, I can feel it, but Rafael's touch is suddenly gone.

"More!" I mewl.

"I'll give you more, vespetta." A barely-there caress with warm fingers at the entrance to my throbbing core. "But only if you promise to put on my shirt afterward."

I open my eyes to find Rafael standing between my legs as he continues to tease my pussy, a self-satisfied smirk on his face.

"No," I pant.

"You're sure?" He raises his hand to his mouth and licks my glistening juices off his fingers while staring brazenly into my eyes.

My core clenches with a desperate ache for him, but I keep my mouth shut.

"I don't think it would take more than ten seconds to make

you come at this point." As if to cement that statement, he places his thumb over my clit, applying the slightest pressure.

I arch my back and shudder in response.

"See?" He slides just the tip of his finger inside me, making me whimper.

The smile on his face turns devilish. With deliberately slow movements, he unzips his pants and releases his huge cock.

"Come here," he says as he slides his hands under my ass and pulls me toward him.

I wrap my arms around his neck and glare into his eyes. They are locked on mine like magnets while he takes a step to the left and leans my back on the fridge. The head of his cock brushes against my weeping pussy, ratcheting up my frustration even more. I'm losing my sanity because of this man.

He slides his cock into my channel, no further than an inch, and stops. "So, do we have a deal?"

"Damn you," I moan. "Yes, I'll wear your fucking shirt."

His cock plunges inside me with such force that I choke on my breath and fall apart into infinite tiny pieces.

Steam saturates the air as it rises from the enormous bathtub, fogging the bathroom mirror and the window. I close my eyes and lean my chin on my knees while Rafael strokes my back, drawing random patterns along my spine.

"You have breadcrumbs in your hair."

"Hmm, must be because you chose to lay me out on the table like a breakfast spread while you fucked my pussy with your mouth."

"I don't remember you complaining at the time." He takes one of my tangled tresses between his fingers. "Why does your hair smell like baby powder?"

"It's the soap. I didn't want to smell like you."

His arms wrap around my middle, pulling me to his chest. The next moment, he leans back, fully submerging us both.

I spit the water from my mouth after he allows us to surface and mumble, "I guess, this means you're not a fan of my new fragrance."

"You're correct."

Behind me, there's the distinct sound of a bottle being uncapped, and then his hands are in my hair, massaging my scalp, as the scent of his shampoo envelops me.

"This doesn't change a thing between us, Rafael," I whisper.

"I know."

He turns on the shower wand and begins rinsing my hair. I tilt my head and close my eyes while he rakes his fingers through my strands, his ministrations incredibly gentle. Cherishing. Tender. The ache in my chest is unbearable. I can't let this man have my heart. Even though I want to. I want to so damn much. But I'm afraid he'll crush that fragile muscle so terribly that there will be nothing left of it in the end.

"You win, vespetta."

"Win what?"

A kiss lands on my shoulder blade. "You're going home."

Air gets stuck in my throat. Slowly, I turn around and meet his gaze. "You'll take me to Chicago?"

"Yes." He cocks his head to the side. "I thought you'd be ecstatic."

"I am. It's just . . ." I stare at him in confusion. "Last night, you threatened to wipe out my family. Is this another one of your games?"

"No. You'll be home within forty-eight hours."

I laugh and leap on him, splashing water all around the bathroom.

"We need to come up with some story for my dad," I say into his lips between kisses. "I don't think he'd be thrilled that I was kidnapped."

"I'm sure he won't be."

"We'll think of something. I can't wait for you to meet my sister. Yulia is the only normal person in our family." I kiss his chin. "God, I hope Sergei won't be there when we arrive. I don't want to shock you right away."

"Very few things can shock me, Vasilisa. And I've already met your uncle."

I lean back. "What? When?"

"We're in the same line of business, so our paths have crossed more than once. He really is something else."

"He is." I grin. "Most people don't get Uncle Sergei, but the truth is—he's just a big golden retriever."

"A military-trained, trigger-happy, seriously deranged golden retriever."

"I guess that sums him up rather well." I glide my palm down Rafael's chest and wrap my fingers around his cock. It's rock-hard. I arch an eyebrow. "Again? We just had sex. Twice."

"You're lying over me, naked. What do you expect?" He takes my waist and slides me down onto his rigid length.

Being in the water makes the sensation of him sliding into me surreal. Just like the first time we made love.

"I wish we had time to go out on your boat again. To that Kraken spot," I pant as I ride him.

The corners of Rafael's lips tilt upward, but the smile doesn't reach his eyes. They seem . . . sad, for some reason. "Aren't you still worried about the water creatures?"

I wrap my arms around his neck and slam my mouth to his. "Well, yeah. But, you'd save me, wouldn't you?"

"Always. From anything," Rafael rasps as he drives into me from below. "Myself included."

I don't get a chance to ask him what he means by that because, suddenly, he's slamming into me as if something's possessed him. Usually, his initial strokes are slow and gentle until I adjust to his size, but not now. I like it.

He surges deeper with every thrust, filling me up completely, making me gasp for my next breath. His muscles are hard under my palms, taut with strain. He's so much larger than me that it makes me feel protected, even without a threat of any kind nearby.

Even though I don't need his protection.

Strange how I've never felt threatened by him. Not even in the beginning.

I cling to Rafael's neck as he pumps into me, staring into his sultry eyes.

"Today, you'll be wearing nothing but my shirt," he grunts as he keeps pounding into me relentlessly, bringing me closer to the edge each time he hits my G-spot.

Despite the bathtub being huge, I don't think it was meant to be used like this. It wobbles left and right from our frenzied pace, water spilling over the rim and flooding the tiles.

"Do you understand, Vasilisa?"

"Yes!"

Air escapes me in short, shaky huffs while my pussy spasms around his cock. My mind is all mushy. Gone. Nonexistent. Another powerful slam, and I'm destroyed. Throwing my head back, I scream my pleasure, just as Rafael's roar thunders through the room, and we both sink into rapture.

"Gray or black?" I lift two hangers in front of me.

"Gray." Rafael nods toward the shirt in my left hand. It's the one I wore when he took me shopping at Albini's. His favorite.

"Am I allowed to wear underwear underneath? You said shirt only."

"You can go without. I banished all men to beyond the house walls." He opens the nightstand drawer and starts taking out the velvet jewelry boxes. A minute later, he approaches, holding the necklace of gray diamonds and gold. "Will you wear this for me today?"

I smirk and turn toward the mirror.

Rafael comes up behind me and pushes my hair away. "How did you get this?" he asks as he sets the necklace around my neck.

"What?"

"This small scar here." His finger brushes the skin below my shoulder blade.

It takes me a few moments to realize what he's talking about. "I don't actually remember. I only know what Mom told me."

"What happened?"

"I was at a mall with her and Dad. Mom was going to buy a dress for some event. Apparently, I slipped away from them and ran toward the jewelry store because I liked looking at the crystal roses and other sparkly things in the window display."

Rafael's finger stills on my back.

"There was some kind of explosion. Inside the store," I continue. "Some guy grabbed me just before it happened. He saved my life."

"How old were you?" Rafael asks as he resumes stroking my skin. His voice sounds strange. Strained somehow.

"I was three. And we never found out what happened to the man who saved me. Dad said he tried to find him when things settled down but had no luck. The guy was taken to a different hospital than where we ended up, and after, he just vanished. The only thing Dad knew about the man was that he was Albanian."

"Oh?" Rafael presses his lips just over the mark, then continues stroking my scar.

"Yeah, he had an Albanian tattoo. Dad recognized it." I turn around to face him. Rafael's hair is wet, and some of his inky-dark strands have fallen forward. I reach up to sweep them back, but my fingers gravitate to his face, tracing the hard contours of his features. "I wish I knew who he was, you know," I say in a whispered breath.

Rafael's eyes crease slightly at the corners. "Why?"

"I owe him my life. Where I come from, it's the ultimate debt." I smile. "You of all people should understand the importance of debts, Rafael."

He leans in and brushes his knuckles along my chin.

"It was just kismet. Right time. Right place. Your Albanian guy probably forgot all about it a long time ago. You're not indebted to him." His fingers seize my chin, tilting my head up for a kiss. "Were you hurt anywhere else?"

"Nope. Just that one cut. Everybody said it was a miracle."

"Good." He nods and pulls me closer. "How about I work on generating another 'normal physical reaction' out of you now?"

Rafael

"It's two in the fucking morning," Guido grumbles as he takes a seat on the deck chair next to mine. "I thought you were upstairs."

"Can't sleep." My eyes are fixed on the dark horizon while I take a sip of my wine.

"Well, you should try, because we might not get the chance in the upcoming days. I got word that Calogero is covertly mobilizing his men." Leaning forward, he braces his elbows on his knees and lets out a heavy sigh. "I hoped it wouldn't come to this."

"We knew Calogero would retaliate after we destroyed his investments. He will try to hit us without the rest of the Family finding out. Ten men, fifteen tops, who will keep their mouths shut."

"Are you going to kill him?"

"Yes."

"Other Cosa Nostra members will execute you, Rafael. You can't kill a fucking don and get away with it!"

"I'm pretty sure I've done that already."

"That was different! No one other than Calogero knew you were the one who executed Mancuso."

"Loyalty and respect are the key pillars of the Cosa Nostra creed, Guido. If a member goes against his word, he loses face, and with it, the respect he holds. But if it's the don who breaks his word, it affects the whole Family. The damage to their reputation is absolute. I contacted old man Biaggi earlier and expressed my deep concern for how the Family may view their leader after finding out he broke his word to me. We came to the conclusion that it would be beneficial for all—me and the Sicilian Cosa Nostra—to keep that shame from reaching the light of day."

"What does that mean?"

"It means that if I decide to alleviate their don of his existence, the Family will look the other way. So, you see, any problem can be resolved, if you know which buttons to push."

"He's our godfather, Rafael."

"And that's the only reason I let him live this long," I snap and drain the rest of my wine. "But he used up all of his credit."

"Rafael—"

"I called him. A month or so after we got to the States. I called our dear cumpari and I begged him to take you under his protection." I meet Guido's shocked stare. "He refused."

"Why did you do that?"

"Because I was afraid you'd fucking starve if you stayed with me."

"I didn't know it was that bad."

"It was. But I managed to find a way to get us out of it."

"By swearing fealty to the Albanian clan. You did it because of me."

I set the glass on the tabletop and look at the pair of crossed daggers with a snake coiled around the blades inked on the inside of my left forearm. More images surround the tat, so it's not as prominent as it once was. Still, someone who's walked the darker paths in life will know what it represents.

"Why haven't you removed it?" Guido asks, glancing at the Albanian gang mark on my arm.

"It's in the past now," I say, scrutinizing the inked design. I could've had it covered up, but I'm not ashamed of anything I did so I could feed my brother.

I lean back on the chair and fix my gaze on the distant fishing boats scattered across the sea. "I'm going to call Roman Petrov and tell him I have his daughter with me."

"What?!" Guido leaps out of his chair. "Are you out of your goddamned mind?"

"Nope. I'm sending Vasilisa back to the States."

"Why? Don't get me wrong, I was against this crazy idea of yours from the start, but—"

"I'm in love with her, Guido."

He gapes at me. "And you're letting her go? That makes no sense."

"You know . . . when I was a kid, I loved playing behind Mom's house, trying to catch butterflies. There was a southern white admiral that was always fluttering around the roses. I tried to capture it for days, absolutely fixated on that poor thing because I wanted to have it for myself. I spent hours next to a thorny flower bush, doing whatever I could to trap the creature, but it always slipped away. Until one day, I finally caught it. I put it into a marmalade jar and set it in my room, by the bed."

"A determined son of a bitch, even then." Guido snorts.

"It died the next day. Maybe I squeezed it too much when I caught it, or it just couldn't live in a fucking jar. When I went behind the house to look for another, there weren't any. I never saw another admiral back there again." I tilt my head to the sky and close my eyes. "Vasilisa reminds me of that butterfly. I can't force her to stay with me. I thought I could, but it wouldn't be right. She's going back to Chicago tomorrow evening."

"Tomorrow?"

"With Calogero planning retaliation as we speak, I can't risk putting her life in danger. I almost got her killed once. There won't be a second time."

"What the hell are you talking about?"

"Do you believe in destiny, Guido?"

"Destiny? Like shit that was meant to happen?" He raises an eyebrow. "Of course I don't. It's just mumbo jumbo for superstitious idiots."

"Maybe. Maybe not. Remember my last job for the Albanians?"

"As if I could ever forget. They told me you probably wouldn't make it. That butcher they took you to barely managed to stitch you together. I hope that kid survived, because you nearly died playing the hero."

"She survived." I nod. "She's currently sleeping upstairs in my bed."

My brother's face pales. He slumps on his deck chair, staring at me in shock. "That's . . . not possible."

"Yeah. Fate has a weird sense of humor."

"Does Vasilisa know?"

"No."

"You should tell her. You saved her life. Almost died because of her. Use any means at your disposal to keep her. Even Petrov wouldn't object to your relationship. You know how seriously the Russians take a life debt."

"And have her tied to me because of some sense of obligation?"

"Why would it matter? You love her. And you want her to be with you."

"I thought you didn't like my little hacker."

Guido looks away. "The way you've been acting since she arrived here . . . Having her wear your clothes, getting the staff, leaving damn love notes for her all over the house—"

"Drawings," I point out. "Not love notes."

"Please. I don't recall seeing you hold a fucking pen in the last decade. And you've had your assistant booking 'dates' with your hookups for longer than that."

I smile. "Maybe they are love notes, after all."

"And that!" He points his finger at me. "That dopey-ass grin. You've been going around wearing one for weeks. Our men have been scared shitless, thinking God knows what."

"Why?"

"Because you have exactly two facial expressions, Rafael— agitated and furious. You never smile."

"People change."

"Yes." He sighs and looks toward the horizon. "It was always just you and me against the world. I was pissed at her because I was afraid she'd get you killed. I still am. Petrov is going to go bal- listic if you tell him you've been holding his daughter hostage."

"Most likely. I'm sure he'll be sending someone to put a bullet between my eyes the moment he finds out. I just hope it isn't Belov."

"Yeah. Vasilisa would never forgive you for killing her pre- cious lunatic of an uncle."

"I know."

"Don't let her go, Rafael. Make her stay. Offer her some- thing in return."

"Unfortunately, some things can only be attained for free." I stand up and look at my brother. "I'm letting her go because she needs to make her own choice. Maybe she'll decide to come back to me. Maybe not. But even if she doesn't return, she'll al- ways be mine and no one else's. I'll make sure of it."

CHAPTER
seventeen

Vasilisa

"I JUST *LOOOOOVE* HOW IT MAKES THE LIME TASTE LESS sour," I slur before I lick the salt off my hand and knock back the shot of tequila, then lift the citrus slice to my mouth and suck.

The glow of the tealight at the center of the table reflects in Rafael's eyes while he stares into mine, making it seem like his irises are on fire. He lifts his tumbler of whiskey and takes a small sip. He's still working on his first drink, while I've downed at least four already. Or maybe it was five?

Rafael said the plane to Chicago is scheduled to depart in a few hours, so I'm not sure why he insisted we come out to this club tonight. But I'm not complaining. The music is awesome, and the drinks are even awesomer. I've been so damn nervous the entire day, racking my brain for potential stories we could tell my dad about my absence. The tequila allowed me to come up with options that I hadn't considered before, and it's making me think we can definitely pull this off.

It's also making me wish all these people around us weren't

here. I lean in and take a deep whiff of Rafael's scent. God, he's so yummy.

"You should try it with an orange," he says, beckoning a waiter over with his hand. "It brings out a slightly different flavor."

"You know . . . if I didn't know better, I'd think you're trying to get me drunk." I grin, then grab a fistful of his shirt over his chest because the room started spinning. Can clubs spin?

"And why would I do that, vespetta?" Rafael's arm wraps around my back, pulling me closer.

He dips his head and looks right into my eyes while speaking in Italian with the server who approached us. Feeling more steady on my feet, I let go of Rafael's shirt but plant my palms squarely on his chest. I still need that contact to ground me. The heat of his body seeps through the soft fabric of his graphite gray button-down, and it strikes me that he isn't wearing his usual vest and suit jacket over it. With the top two buttons of his shirt undone and no tie, this is the most casually dressed I've ever seen him in public.

"I have no idea. But I think you are." A snort escapes me. "Are you plotting to have me do a dark deed for you again and need me intoxicated to make it happen?"

"Maybe."

"I would, you know. Even sober, I would. I'd send all the fucking containers from every damn tanker in the world to China if you asked me to. It would create an international shipping disaster, but I'd do it. For you."

Rafael just keeps watching me. Why are his eyes sad again? Is he worried about what my father might do to him when we get to Chicago? He shouldn't be. I won't tell Dad the truth. We'll tell him that Rafael and I met by chance. And after I admit to Dad that I'm in love, he'll understand.

The waiter returns and sets a new shot of tequila topped with an orange slice on our table. Staring fixedly into Rafael's eyes, I grab the shot glass and throw back the throat-burning liquid.

"You forgot the orange," he says, lifting the slice of citrus to my mouth.

My lips close on the orange piece and suck the tangy juices off the rind. "You were right. It does taste better."

Rafael's eyes flare. The fruit vanishes from my mouth, replaced with his hard lips and tongue. They take. Brand. Consume me.

Rising onto my toes, I bury my hands in his hair, pulling on the dark strands. A mix of flavors explodes across my taste buds. Salt. Him. His whiskey. Him. Orange. Him. Him. Him.

I feel a slight squeeze on my waist as he lifts me and deposits me on the barstool, all without breaking our kiss. His rough palm glides along the inner side of my thigh, bound for higher places. I hook my leg behind his. My head feels fuzzy, like I'm floating, but I'm not sure if it's from the alcohol running rampant through my veins or because Rafael's fingers are sliding under my panties.

"You're mine, Vasilisa," he growls into my mouth. "You will always be mine, no matter what you decide."

Decide? Decide what? The ability to form a coherent thought flees as his fingers push inside me, doing those devilish tricks of his that make me forget the outside world exists at all. His thumb moves over my clit in slow steady circles, while two of his fingers caress my spasming walls. In and out. Gentle. Maddeningly gentle pressure.

My body trembles, the tremors intensifying with every stroke, pushing me closer to oblivion. His other hand softly cups my chin, squeezing lightly once in a while as he demolishes my lips. The myriad of sensations is overwhelming. I moan while losing myself in bliss.

More. I sink my nails into the skin of his nape. I need more. And he seems to know it. Rafael presses his thumb on my clit and curls his fingers upward inside my channel. And I . . . explode. Coming all over his masterful hand.

"I'll miss this, vespetta." The husky voice next to my ear sounds distant somehow.

Everything seems to be spinning around me. I wrap my arms around Rafael's neck, letting my body sag onto his. A beautiful weightless feeling surrounds me as he picks me up and carries me. Where we're going, I don't know. I don't care. As long as I'm with him. But the lights hurt my eyes, so I bury my face in the crook of his neck. Music and voices growing distant.

"*Sei pronto?*" Guido's voice. I didn't know he was here.

"*Si. Iniziamo,*" Rafael replies, then dips his head until his mouth grazes my ear. "I have to sign some documents while we're here. It won't take long."

"Okay," I mumble.

Footfalls on the wooden floor echo around us as Rafael heads to the door at the end of the narrow hallway. Guido holds it open, allowing us to pass through. The room we step into smells of old paper and cigarettes. Several men are already inside, standing around with expressions on their faces that I can't quite read. In the middle of the room is a desk, and an older man in a brown suit is sitting behind it, a massive thick red book open in front of him.

With me still in his arms, Rafael sits down on one of the empty chairs before the desk, making sure I'm comfortably situated on his lap. The room grows quiet, and then the old fellow across from us starts speaking. His soft voice and the melodic Italian words soothe me into that tranquil void where reality and dreamland mesh, leaving me feeling like I'm soaring upon warm currents of air.

Jesus fuck, I should have stopped after that second shot of tequila. I'm going to pass out in the middle of Rafael's meeting. What if I drool? The man keeps speaking, but now he seems to be drifting far, far away. I'm so out of it that, for a moment, I thought he said my name. That doesn't make sense, though.

I don't know him. I snuggle closer to Rafael, nuzzling his neck and inhaling his scent.

"Vespetta." Rafael's breath fans my ear. "I need you to say *yes*."

"Yes," I mumble.

My eyelids feel so heavy. The speaking continues. Then, there's shuffling and rustling as people approach the desk. They seem to be signing something. It must be a very important contract since there are so many of them here. Rafael's hold on me tightens as he takes the pen from Guido and leans forward, scribbling something into the thick red book.

"I need your signature here." Rafael places the pen in my hand, but it slips from my fingers and clatters to the floor.

"You want me to sign?" I open my eyes to a blurry room. "Why?"

"To confirm that you were present at the signing of the contract. It's tradition." He hands me the pen again and pulls the book closer. "Just here."

"You have weird traditions." I giggle and, setting the ballpoint on the line at the bottom of the page where Rafael is pointing his finger, sign my name. "Will I get a cut of whatever deal you just made?"

"Yes." His lips are on mine now. Tasting. Claiming.

I let myself be enraptured by his mouth while my consciousness slips away. The last thing I hear is the old man's more vigorous Italian words. He's probably chastising us for kissing in the middle of a business meeting.

"*Vi dichiaro marito e moglie.*"

Rafael

Bright lights flank the runway. My plane is ready for takeoff, waiting for its passengers to arrive. Guido stops the car a few feet from the jet and turns off the ignition.

"Raff. We're here."

I sweep the hair that's fallen over Vasilisa's face away, lightly caressing her soft cheek with my knuckles in the process. She looks so young when she sleeps. "I am aware."

"When will you be coming back?"

"I'm not going with her, Guido."

"But, I thought . . . Why?"

"I told her that I love her, but she didn't believe me. She said I don't know what loving someone truly means. And she was right. I tried to make her stay with me by buying her presents. And issuing threats. I'm letting her go, so she can decide for herself." I open the car door and step out with Vasilisa safely cradled in my arms. "Take your bag from the trunk and hurry."

"My bag?"

"With a change of clothes. You're getting onto that plane to make sure my wife arrives safely at her family's home."

"I'm not going anywhere. Calogero will retaliate in the next twenty-four hours. You need me."

"I know. And I'll handle him. Alone."

"The fuck you will! He has more than ten men on his personal security team!"

"Shut. Your. Mouth. Because if you wake Vasilisa, I'll strangle you," I sneer through my teeth. "The deal I made with Biaggi includes a no-witness guarantee. I'm going to take down Calogero myself."

"Raff—"

"This discussion is over."

Standing at the foot of the airstairs, the flight attendant clutches the sides of her blazer to her chest as she watches me approach. I climb the steps, Guido following close behind me.

Inside the cabin, I carefully lower my precious cargo onto the beige leather sofa. Vasilisa stirs, her eyes cracking a little.

"Are we home?"

I crouch next to her and brush the back of my hand along her chin. "Soon."

"Okay," she mumbles.

Her eyes flutter closed. I never imagined that letting go of something could hurt so much.

Sharp talons are slicing through my chest, trying to tear out my fucking heart. I reach into my pocket and take out the ring I put there earlier. It's one of mine. Just a solid band of plain silver, worth practically nothing at all. I had the jeweler resize it to fit her delicate finger. He tried to convince me that it would be too small, as if I wouldn't know every inch of my wife. Taking her right hand in mine, I slide the band onto her ring finger. Russians traditionally wear wedding rings on the right hand, and I want to honor that custom. The ring is a perfect fit.

"*Farei qualsiasi cosa per te, vespetta,*" I whisper as I lean toward her and kiss her slightly parted lips. "*Perfino lasciarti andare.*"

Vasilisa's lips pull into a slight, sleepy smile before she turns around, tucking her face into the soft cushions of the sofa. I take off my jacket and cover her with it. After one last look, I straighten and rush toward the aircraft exit, feeling like every step is shredding my insides.

The videoconference window pops up on my laptop screen, showing Roman Petrov sitting at the desk inside his office.

"Rafael. It's been a while. To what do I owe the pleasure of your call?"

"My plane will be landing at a private airfield outside

Chicago in ten hours. I'll send you the exact location. You want to be there when it arrives."

"Why is that?"

"Your daughter is on board."

Petrov leaps from his chair, his shocked face drawing close to the camera. "What is my baby girl doing on your plane?!" he snarls.

"She's fine. Don't worry."

"*You* took her." A low growl comes from Roman.

"Yes. I did. Her IT skills are extraordinary. I had her brought to Sicily to complete a job for me. It's all wrapped up, so I've sent her back home."

"If you've touched a single hair on her head, Rafael," he says in a gravelly voice, "I'll level that whole fucking island within twenty-four hours! Don't you ever, fucking ever, dare to look even at her picture, you son of a bitch."

I smirk. "I see where Vasilisa gets her poetic streak from."

"Do. Not. Use my daughter's name, motherfucker!" He grabs the screen, shaking it. "You are a dead man!" he yells.

I watch him lift a gun toward the camera. A split second later, the bang of a gunshot explodes and the video feed goes black. An unmistakable sign our meeting is concluded— Roman shot the laptop, aiming for my head.

Gripping the edge of my desk, I stare at the blank background of my display. It's been less than an hour since I put Vasilisa on that plane, and already I'm feeling as if I'm partially dead inside. What will happen tomorrow, when she's back in Chicago with her family?

Will she forget about me? Will she forget the foolish man who loves her enough to let her go, knowing it will likely kill him? Knowing the chance of her coming back to him is nil?

A raucous roar rips out of my throat. I swipe my arm across the desk, sending my laptop and other shit flying. It doesn't ease the hopelessness and misery that's suffocating me.

How long will it take before she calls me to say she's never coming back?

A week?

A month?

I will fucking die in this goddamned limbo of not knowing.

Grabbing my phone, I send a message to Guido, then, another text with additional instructions to my pilot.

# Vasilisa

The low rumble penetrates my consciousness, ratcheting up the ache in my head. My throat is dry like I've swallowed cotton balls. The smell of leather invades my senses, and there's more. Cypress, with a hint of orange zest.

"Rafael?" I mumble. "What time is it?"

"Almost five in the morning," Guido's voice replies.

I slowly sit up, blinking my eyes open, and take in the interior of the airplane. "What's going on?"

"You should put your seatbelt on. We'll be landing shortly."

"Landing?" I fix my eyes on Guido, who's sitting on the sofa across from me. "Where?"

"Chicago."

Confusion hits me, then morphs into excitement. I'm going to see my family again! Happiness. Relief.

"Where is Rafael?" I ask, looking around.

"He stayed in Sicily."

Pop.

My joy bursts, and I plummet straight into a pit of dread. "Why?"

"You kept asking him to send you home. So he did it. Isn't that what you wanted?" He lays my old backpack on my lap. "Your IDs and other personal stuff are inside. I programmed Rafael's and my numbers into your phone. Now, fasten your seatbelt. We're descending."

My hands shake as I take the backpack and move it to the spot next to me. It feels much heavier than I remember. I stare through the wide elliptical window at the city lights twinkling beautifully and growing bigger with each passing second. Closer to home. Farther away from Rafael.

I'm returning. Alone.

He sent me back.

No explanation. No goodbye. Just dumped me on his plane, like I'm some unwanted package.

I wipe my eyes while a hysterical laugh escapes me. Just months ago I cried like this because he wouldn't let me go home. And now . . . Now I'm crying because he did.

By the time we land, my tears have dried up, but I'm still wrecked inside. I grab my backpack off the seat (it's definitely heavier than it should be) and head down the aisle toward the exit. My feet feel like they're made of lead, each step slower than the previous one.

"Watch your footing, miss," the flight attendant says as I reach the door.

Three people are standing at the edge of the runway, their shapes backlit by the ground lights. I recognize my father's formidable form immediately. My brother, a mere inch shorter, is on the left. And my mom, standing between them. She looks rather funny, flanked by two human mountains nearly plastered to her sides. I dash down the stairs and across the tarmac, falling into their embrace.

"Mom!" I cry out and wrap my arms around her neck, squeezing her to me.

"Vasya, baby." My dad sweeps the hair off my face. "Are you okay? What did that bastard do to you?"

"I'm fine." I release Mom and, a second later, end up wrapped in Dad's bear hug. "I missed you so much."

"Here." Dad sets a tablet in front of me on the kitchen island. The screen displays a map. "Point to the location of that cocksucker's lair."

"Why?"

"Because I said so. Now, Vasilisa."

"Roman." My mom sends him a warning look as she passes me a cup of tea. "Not now."

"That bastard kept our daughter prisoner for two months, malysh! I won't wait another second. Where is he, Vasilisa?"

I press the heels of my hands over my eyes. It shouldn't have happened like this. The plan was for me and Rafael to face my family together. With a happy cover story of how we met. I didn't expect Rafael to tell my father that he kidnapped me. With my father thinking the worst, how can I explain to him that I'm in love with Rafael? Dad would never believe me. And it would just make the whole situation so much worse.

"I told you, I wasn't a prisoner," I say. "We had a deal. I did the work he hired me for, and he sent me back when I finished."

"Really? Just what kind of work did that asshole need you to do?"

"It concerned his company. I can't disclose the details."

"Why did you lie to me then, hmm? And why won't you tell me his location?"

"Because I know you, Dad. Don't you dare send anyone to do something to Rafael."

"Why? Rafael De Santi is a first-rate assassin, Vasilisa."

"I know."

He leans forward, his face drawing level with mine. "Did he touch you? Did that fucker put his dirty paws on my baby girl?" His voice is barely above a whisper. I know that tone. It means he's furious.

I swallow and force myself to hold his gaze. Telling him the truth now is out of the question. I know my father all too well. If he even suspects that there was something between me and Rafael, he'll kill him.

"He was a perfect gentleman." I lay my palms on the countertop. Immediately, my mind is flooded with images of Rafael ravenously eating my pussy on a similar-looking kitchen island.

"Whose jacket are you wearing, Vasilisa?" my brother's voice booms from the other side of the kitchen.

I look over my shoulder and find Alexei leaning against the fridge, his arms crossed over his chest. He's been staying out of this conversation, so I completely forgot he's here. Panic rises in the pit of my stomach. Before he left for college, we were inseparable. But with too-short visits over summer and holiday breaks, not to mention my father's demands on my brother's time when he's here, we've kinda drifted apart. Alexei, however, has always been the most perceptive person I know. And he knows all my tells.

"It's Rafael's," I choke out.

"Mm-hmm." He pushes away from the fridge and approaches me with slow, deliberate steps. "I'll go upstairs and get you a sweater. You can take that off. I'll throw it in the trash."

"No!" I snap and tug the jacket tighter around me. "Don't you dare touch it!"

Alexei's eyes narrow, then he looks at our father. "She's lying."

"I'm not lying! I'm tired and just want to go to sleep. Can we continue this interrogation later, please?"

My father grips the edge of the counter, his fingers flexing on it over and over. Then, he takes a deep breath. And another.

"Sure, baby." He pulls me into him and kisses the top of my head. "Everything is going to be okay. Get some rest."

With a soft stroke on my cheek, he turns around and leaves the kitchen, his cane clicking on the tiled floor. Alexei trails behind him.

"I'll make you something to eat," Mom says as she takes a plate out of the cupboard. "I'll bring it upstairs."

"Thanks," I mumble.

Exiting the kitchen, I notice the light at the far end of the long hallway—my dad's office door has been left slightly ajar. He's speaking with someone in a hushed voice. Whatever he's saying is in Russian, and I don't catch much because of his rapid words. I'm not too great with Dad's language. I do okay, but only in conversations where the speakers don't talk too fast. And right now, my father isn't pacing himself for my benefit.

"I'm going to bed," I say, standing at the threshold of Dad's domain.

He nods, the phone still pressed to his ear. "Okay, baby."

"You're staying up?"

"Might as well. I have some . . . business to discuss with Sergei."

"Tell him I'll drop by soon."

"Sure. Sleep well." His tone of voice when speaking with me is warm, but the instant I turn my back and Dad returns to the conversation with his brother, his words are hard and laced with rage. Uncle Sergei must have fucked up. Again. Real bad this time, by the sounds of it.

On the upper floor, I sneak into Yulia's room and tiptoe to her bedside. After kissing her cheek, I head into my room, which is next door to my sister's, and plop on the edge of the bed. My eyes wander over the familiar walls and furniture, yet everything feels surreal. I glance at the window overlooking the backyard. The early rays of the sun are breaking through the clouds. If I were in Sicily now, I'd be hearing the crickets perfecting their song. And I'd be lying next to Rafael, with my face buried in his neck. I dip my head, pressing my nose to the lapel of his suit jacket. It still smells like him.

Taking my backpack off my shoulder, I drop it on the bed beside me and unzip the main compartment. More than a dozen velvet boxes of various sizes are inside. Tears gather in the corners of my eyes as I pull out the packages, one by one. No wonder the damn backpack was so heavy. Rafael sent me home with several pounds of jewelry. And . . . My hand wraps around a smooth bell-shaped object at the bottom of the bag. A single fig.

I carefully pull it out, but it's beyond saving. Almost fully squashed by all those jewelry boxes he piled on top. My old phone is also beneath the loot, fully charged. I unlock the screen and find Rafael's name in the contacts list. My finger shakes a little as it hovers above the call button. I swipe to the right and press the phone to my ear.

"Vespetta," his husky voice answers immediately. "Is everything alright?"

"Yes. We landed a couple of hours ago."

"I know. Guido told me."

I take a deep breath and lean the back of my head on the wall behind me. "Why weren't you on the plane with me?"

"I never said I would be. You made that assumption on your own," he says. "Do you like the ring?"

My eyes dart to the simple, thick band. Quite a change in aesthetic from his prior presents. "A parting gift?"

"Well, that depends on you." A small pause follows. "It's one of mine," he continues after a breath. "If you don't like it, I'll take it back and buy you something prettier. If you decide to return."

"Just like that? You dumped me on the plane, while I was unconscious! You sent me home without even a goodbye. What if I just decide to stay here? What then? Why did you do it?"

Nothing but silence on the other end of the line.

"Why, Rafael?"

"Because, if I'd have waited for you to wake up, if I held you in my arms even a second longer, I never would have let you leave, Vasilisa! I would have found a way to keep you with me. I would have lied and spewed empty threats against your family! It's the only thing that ever swayed you."

"Did it never occur to you that I may have wanted to stay with you? That you didn't need the fucking threats?" I bury my face in my hand. "Jesus, Rafael."

"Don't you 'Jesus, Rafael' me, Vasilisa. I'm not delusional. Why the fuck would you want to be with someone like me? I hoped that buying you pretty things would somehow help diminish the ugliness you were exposed to while being at my side. To somehow lessen the hideosity of waking up to a fucking beast in your bed every morning. It was the only way I could outmatch all the other perfect men who would take you from me. So yes, you're right. I pressured you to stay because I was afraid that given a choice, you would never choose me."

A loud crash, something big and heavy, sounds through my phone's speaker.

"So I did it. Kept you caged. You—the most precious thing in my world. And it didn't matter a lick that it was all because I'm in love with you. I've hurt you, manipulated everything to make you stay. I'll have to live with that. Will have to keep pushing the air through my lungs while the truth punches me in the gut every day. Because I do love you, whether you believe me or not, and I realized that I would rather let you go than force you to stay with me when it's not what you want."

More crashing sounds come through the line, as if he's demolishing everything in his vicinity.

"You said you want the freedom to make your decision, vespetta. I simply granted that to you. So choose," he growls. "My plane is still at the same airfield where it landed. Waiting for you. You have until seven tomorrow night to make your decision. If you're not on board by then, it will depart without you. And I'll take that as your answer."

He cuts the call.

My vision blurs with unshed tears. I throw the phone on the bed and rush into the bathroom so I don't wake Yulia. Sitting on the closed toilet lid, I press my hand over my mouth to keep the whimpers from escaping. God! I thought all that damn jewelry he's been showering me with was nothing more than his way of flashing his wealth. A tactic to show off how much "better" he is than everyone else. It never occurred to me that he actually viewed himself as somehow lacking. As if he wasn't good enough. How could I have been so blind and didn't realize that?

I swallow the bile that's threatening to choke me, and give in to the ugly tears. They burn like acid down my cheeks while my heart feels like it's being squeezed inside my chest.

He loves me.

He wants me.

Why did I not see his pain?

I never saw him as anything other than drop-dead gorgeous. That's my only justification for being so oblivious to his insecurities. And he hung up on me before I got the chance to tell him that. To tell him that I'm in love with him, too.

And that I am coming back.

"Vasya?" My mom's voice drifts in from inside my bedroom. "Where are you? I thought you—" Her words get cut off as soon as she opens the bathroom door. "What's wrong?"

"Nothing." I wipe my nose on my sleeve, then smile. "I'm returning to Sicily."

My mother goes eerily still. "What?"

"I'm in love with him, Mom. I'm in love with Rafael."

Mom rushes to me and crouches by the toilet, wrapping her arms around me. "Hush. You're just confused, baby. It'll pass."

"I'm not confused, Mom. This is the first time in months I'm thinking clearly." I squeeze her arm. "I'm going back to him."

She rears back and grabs my shoulders. "What? No. I won't allow it."

"I don't need your permission, Mom." I wipe the tears off my cheeks, then meet my mother's frantic gaze. "You of all people should understand that when your heart chooses someone, there's no coming back from that."

"You can't fall in love with someone in two months, Vasilisa!"

"Oh? How long did it take you to fall in love with Dad?"

"That was different."

"Yeah. He blackmailed you into marrying him! Twice, I might add." I snort. "He says you fell for him within a day."

"Absolutely not! It took me at least a month."

A laugh rumbles out of me. "There you go."

My mother's face falls, concern written all over it. "Are you sure you have feelings for that man?"

"Yes."

"How old is he?"

"Thirty-nine. What does that have to do with how I feel?"

"I'm just saying. He's much older. Experienced. I understand how someone like him can make a young woman fall for him. It's just an infatuation, and it *will* pass."

I take her hand and press her palm to the middle of my chest. "There is a hole inside me, right here. It formed the moment I woke up on that plane and realized Rafael wasn't there with me. Just thinking about the possibility of never being with him again makes that hole spread. I feel empty without him. I came back. But my heart remained in Sicily. With him. And no one can live without their heart, Mom."

"But . . . You can't just take off. Your dad is going to lose it, Vasya. He would never allow you to leave."

"I know. So I'd like you to explain to him that I'm no longer a little girl he needs to shield from monsters. That's not what I need from him anymore. I want him to understand that even though I love him and always will, it's time for me to start living my own life."

"You know how maniacally protective your father is about you and Yulia."

"Yes. But I don't need his protection, Mom. I need his support."

"Okay," she chokes out. "You know, there are times when your father still wakes up covered in sweat because of a dream about that explosion at the mall. I have nightmares about that, too. God, I'm so grateful you were so little then that you don't remember it."

"It was ages ago."

"Doesn't matter. Things like that lodge in your mind, and, no matter how much time passes, you can't forget them. You can't even imagine how terrifying it was, Vasilisa." She squeezes my hand and shudders. "So much blood. Roman got to you first and had to basically extricate you from that man who saved you. He was clutching you to his chest—so hard—practically enveloping you with his whole body. Shards of glass were embedded in his hands and arms. And his face ... Jesus Christ. I will remember his shredded face for as long as I live."

His hands ... His face ... The floor falls out from beneath my feet. My mother continues speaking, something about the ambulances arriving, but the words don't penetrate. *Hands and face. Shredded. No, it can't be him.*

My mind zooms to the afternoon we spent together in the bath. Rafael, asking me about the scar on my back. He said something ... Something about kismet.

Destiny.

"What did he look like?" I whisper. "The man who saved me?"

"I ... I don't know. He was covered in blood. I think ... He had dark hair. And he was tall. Broad. I remember thinking— his being so big was likely the reason he was able to shield you from all that glass. Roman tried to locate him. After. He went to Endri Dushku, the leader of the Albanian cartel, because of the tattoo your dad saw on the young man's arm. But Dushku told him that none of their members got hurt that day."

"And . . ." I swallow. "What does the Albanian gang mark look like?"

"Um . . . I'm not sure. I think, it's two daggers with a green snake—"

"Coiled around them," I interrupt, as tears once again threaten to spill from my eyes.

"Yes. How do you know that?"

"I've seen it."

He knew. He knew and didn't say a word. He must have figured it out when we were talking about my scar. But he didn't let on to gain an advantage. No bargains. No deals. No calling in the debt to make me stay.

You're not indebted to him, he said.

I wrap my arm around my mother's back and press a kiss on her cheek. "Yulia will be mad because you guys didn't bring her along to the airport with you."

"She hasn't been feeling well the past few days, so we let her sleep. And we weren't sure what to expect, Vasilisa. We didn't know what state you'd be in. That man kept you for months and . . ."

A sad smile pulls at my lips. "Let me assure you of one thing, Mom. *That man's* arms are the safest place I could ever be."

"What do you mean?"

"Because it was him," I whisper. "The man who saved my life all those years ago. It was Rafael."

CHAPTER eighteen

Rafael

"**Y**OU CANNOT, UNDER ANY CIRCUMSTANCES, LET even a single man pass," I tell the men gathered around me and check the magazine of my semiautomatic rifle. "One stray bullet, and this whole area behind us will blow to shit."

"Boss, I have your brother on the line."

I grab the phone off my man's hand and press it to my ear. "Did you get the flight back?"

"Yeah. Just heading toward the gate. Regular airports fucking suck, and I'm dreading having to take a commercial flight. But I'd rather deal with that than sit on my ass for the next thirty-six hours waiting for your wife to make up her mind. You're my brother, Raff, and I'm no longer a helpless child. I won't hang back, letting you handle this asshole on your own again. What's going on over there? I had to call Onofredo 'cause I couldn't reach you. What's this about you leaving a small team at the estate and taking the rest of our men to Messina?"

"Calogero decided that rather than face me head-on, it

would be a good idea to send his forces to attack my oil refinery. I got word he was planning to make it look like an industrial accident. We've set up an ambush at that gas station west of Messina that's still under construction and are waiting to intercept them."

"Jesus fuck. How did you find out their plans?"

"Nazario Biaggi called me this morning. His father must be impatient to snatch the don's position to have leaked this." I cock my rifle. "How was my little wasp?"

"Happy to see her family. They were waiting for her at the airfield. Looks like they're all really tight. What will you do if she decides she wants to be with you, but insists on living in the States? I mean, I know you'd never do it."

"For her, I would. If she chooses to come back to me and can't handle being separated from her family, I would move us to fucking Chicago."

"But . . . you've fought half your life to be able to return here. You love Sicily."

"I do. But I love her more."

"Fuck, Raff. You're a total goner for that woman."

"Yes, I am. I have to go. My intel says Calogero's guys are just minutes away."

"Biaggi again?"

"Grandma network." I cut the line and take up a position around the corner of the building.

Exactly four minutes later, a convoy of black cars emerges from the curve in the road, heading fast in the direction of the refinery.

"Wait," I instruct a man crouching on my right. He's controlling the remote spike barrier we laid across the road.

The vehicles close in. Half a dozen of them. Fuck. I expected three or four. When the lead car is about thirty yards from the gas station, I tap my man's shoulder. "Now."

The steel blades of the tire killer half-hidden beneath the

dirt rise up almost instantly. A heartbeat later, the unmistakable pop and hiss of the punctured tires erupt. The car begins to swerve left and right. Fishtailing the whole way, the driver tries to maintain control but fails in no time. The next two cars that follow suffer a similar fate. Traveling too close to the lead's tail, the second smashes into the back of the first car, sending both vehicles skidding off the road. The third car over the heavy-duty spike strip continues for a short distance before it ends up in a shallow ditch at the side of the road.

"Tires first, then the drivers!" I bark into the mic. "Can't risk having any of the vehicles get through."

The sound of gunfire fills the broad daylight.

Bullets whoosh overhead as two of my snipers on the roof of the gas station pick off Calogero's goons when they exit the vehicles. All too soon, the noise is joined by the rattle of handguns when our targets return fire. It's getting harder to see and aim with all the dust that's been kicked up into the air. I manage to hit the asshole running in my direction but have to retreat when several bullets pepper the wall right next to my head. By my guess, there were at least twenty men inside those vehicles, yet the number of dead or wounded bodies on the ground is less than half of that. The remainder have holed up behind open car doors and are shooting at my guys. Those vehicles must be armored.

I run to the car that spun out into the ditch. With the dip in the terrain, I know the targets will be out of sight of the sharpshooters' scopes. The driver's door is hanging open, and the man's bloody head is slumped on the steering wheel. Two other guys are crouched by the side of the vehicle, firing at my men who are still using the unfinished gas station building as cover. I round the busted ride, approaching from the rear, and spray them with what's left in my magazine.

Amid the commotion, an engine revs to life. My head snaps up, eyes darting to the trailing cars of the convoy that were able to stop more or less unscathed—aside from the blown-out tires—just after crossing the strip of steel spikes. Calogero's man is behind the wheel and, despite the flat tires and damaged rims, is swerving between the other vehicles and dead bodies, trying to get clear.

I'm out of ammo in my rifle, so I drop it and reach for my gun. The first few shots either ricochet off the windshield or barely make a dent. I keep shooting, aiming at the driver's head while the car slowly advances toward me. The fucking bullet-proof glass finally cracks, and a spiderweb appears along its surface, yet the windshield remains largely intact. My last bullet finally penetrates it, shattering the fibers but missing the driver.

The car is nearly through the obstacles of dead bodies. Any moment now, the bastard will reach the open road. Fuck! I run toward the vehicle, my eyes trained on the dickhead plowing his way through.

The whipped-up dust hangs in the air, as thick as soup. It feels like I'm caught in a damn desert storm. The ringing of gunshots is everywhere. Shouts come from all around. Cries of pain among the deafening noise. All these sounds blend with the crunch and thump of tires scraping over the body of another fallen goon as I leap onto the hood of the moving car.

For a split second, the driver freezes. Punching through the hole in the windshield, I grab a fistful of his hair. Our gazes meet. With an ironclad grip, I yank him forward and slam his face right into the jagged edges of glass jutting up from the windshield frame.

"Boss!" someone yells. "Get the fuck down!"

I roll off the hood just as a bullet whizzes above my head.

The firefight continues to rage between my team and my godfather's remaining force. I peek over the front end of the vehicle and spot Allard down on his ass with his back against another car. His left leg is drenched in blood, but instead of trying to reach cover, he's still shooting. Staying low, I rush toward him.

"Want to bleed to death?" I snarl as I grab the back of his Kevlar and start dragging him toward the gas station building.

"Loved the hood-surfing maneuver you did back there, boss." The maniac laughs while changing his magazine, then resumes shooting. "Does this mean you'll be back on an active team from now on?"

I prop him against the wall and squat to check his leg. The bullet only nicked him, thankfully.

"I'm retired, Allard. That's why I have you—to do all the dirty work." I grab his hand and press it over the wound. "Keep pressure on that."

"Hate to burst your bubble, boss, but you ain't looking so spick-and-span at the moment."

Shaking my head, I pick up his gun and turn toward the road. The gunfire has finally ceased, and the dust is slowly settling on the bodies of Calogero's men. I turn on my phone and call Onofredo.

"I need a cleanup crew. Stat."

"Already on their way," he replies.

"Authorities?"

"Two patrols were sent out when someone reported hearing shots fired. I made a few calls. They won't be bothering you."

"Good."

I disconnect the call and put the phone away. Calogero will have to be dealt with immediately. I don't want any threats hanging over my head in case my vespetta chooses to return.

Vasilisa

"Have you decided what you're going to do?" Yulia asks as she runs the brush through my hair. "Or are you going to spend the entire day just staring at the wall?"

I shrug. "Yes. I'm going back to Sicily."

Three hours ago, Yulia stormed into my room and jumped on my bed while I was dozing, scaring me shitless. We laughed. We cried. Then, she yelled at me for not waking her up when I arrived home. We spent the morning holed up in my room, eating Igor's partially burned cinnamon rolls while I told her all about how I ended up in Sicily.

"What if Mom tells Dad?" she asks as she divides my tresses down the middle and starts weaving the first braid.

"She promised she won't. I think she believes I'm confused and I'll come out of it eventually."

"And are you? Confused?"

"Nope."

"Mm-hmm. Dad's going to be really mad. He's been quite invested in the 'nice accountant' strategy."

"I know. That's why *you* can't say a thing. Not to Mom or Dad. I'll call them and explain everything when I arrive at Rafael's."

"When are you leaving?"

"Tomorrow, at the latest."

"What? But you just got here!" she shrieks, pulling on my hair in the process.

"Ouch! Yes. Rafael has a plane on standby for me. It departs tomorrow evening, and I'm planning to be on it when it does. I just need a small window of time when I can leave the house without anyone noticing."

"You can stay home for a while and take a commercial flight over at a later date, Vasilisa."

"I know. But Rafael expects my answer tomorrow."

"There are devices called phones, in case you forgot."

"I can't say my first 'I love you' to the man I love over the phone," I whisper. "He told me he loves me days ago, but I never said it back. I wasn't sure then. Or maybe I was simply afraid to admit it to him because I was scared that his feelings weren't true."

"I can't fault you for believing that. The man is a master manipulator who threatened to kill us if you didn't stay with him. Who in the world does that to someone they love?"

"Someone who is fearful that love is only skin-deep." I look down at the ring on my finger. "He kept getting me gifts, every new item more outrageously expensive than the last, trying to buy my love. It took him a long time to realize that the most valuable things in life are free."

"You believe he finally understands that? To be honest, in your place, I'm not sure I would. People rarely change. What if, down the line, he finds something else he can use as a bartering chip against you?"

An ache squeezes my heart, but I smile. "He already has one. And he's chosen not to use it."

Chapter

nineteen

Rafael

The following day
Sicily: +7 hours of Chicago
Private property, 20 miles outside of Palermo
Three hours before the scheduled flight departure
from Chicago

B LOOD RUNS ACROSS MY FISTED HAND, THE RIVULETS
dropping to the ground and dissipating over the already
sodden soil under my shoes. Guttural gurgling leaves
the security guard's throat as I rotate the knife I've buried hilt-
deep in his neck. His body twitches a few times, then gradually
goes still. I release the dead man, letting his body fall at my feet,
where it lands with a loud thud. With rain coming down for the
last few hours, most of the guards have taken shelter under the
trees or inside the guardhouse, making the job of killing them
less complicated.

Keeping to the shadows and the cover of foliage, I circle
the house that's been the primary residence of the Sicilian Cosa

Nostra don until I spy another one of his men. The guy is leaning on the corner of the building, tucked under a slight overhang, his rifle casually draped over his back. A length of white cord extends from the phone in his hand to an earbud jammed into his right ear. I shake my head. Moron is listening to music while on guard duty.

The wet grass muffles my steps as I approach him from behind and yank the cord. He startles, turning around, but I already have the earbuds wire wrapped around his neck. When he starts flailing, hands reaching to free his windpipe, I push his face into the wall and tighten my grip on the cord. He manages a few weak whimpers before going to meet his maker.

There are no motion detectors or video surveillance anywhere on the property. Just manpower and a rather basic alarm at the front door. Like all narcissistic, overly self-confident men who have risen to power without much effort, my godfather believes he's untouchable. He will find out very soon how utterly wrong that conviction is.

It takes me a little over half an hour to dispose of the remaining twelve guards. Afterward, I take a casual stroll around the building until I find an unlatched window to serve as my entry point. Infiltrating a target's location is significantly easier when you can first eliminate the security detail. Aside from that double-tap in Germany a couple of months back, the last assassination I handled myself was more than a decade ago, and it took me almost four hours to get inside the guarded house. I had to sneak past twenty of my own men to reach my mark. Not an easy feat, considering I trained them all in the first place. To this day, Allard still occasionally brings up that Boston job, cursing the son of a bitch who managed to circumvent his team and force-feed cyanide to the guy being held in the basement cellar.

By comparison, sneaking into Calogero's home is a fucking cakewalk. It's been a long time since I've been inside this house, but I still remember the layout. I climb the stairs and head toward the master bedroom. When I reach the second to last door on the left side of the hallway, I unscrew the silencer from my gun and tuck it into my pocket. No point in keeping anything quiet since there's no one left alive on the grounds other than me and my cumpari.

The door opens without a sound. The wall-mounted TV in the room is playing a documentary of some kind, its volume muted, but the screen is throwing plenty of light onto the bed where my godfather is snoring. I lean my shoulder on the jamb and cock my gun.

Calogero's eyes snap open.

"Buonasera, Cumpari."

For a few breaths, he just stares at me, then jerks upward. His hand extends toward the nightstand. I aim at the drawer and pull the trigger. Pieces of wood splinter off, and the flimsy stand topples over and crashes to the floor, some of the debris ending up in the corner.

"What do you want?" Calogero rasps while beads of sweat collect on his hairline. "How did you get in here?"

"Through the study window. The one you always forget to lock. And as for what I want . . . I'm sure you know that already."

"Even you can't be so bold. What would your mother say if she could see you now? How can you kill the man who held you up at the altar before God to baptize you? Who helped raise you into the man you are today?"

"Don't you dare speak of her!" I snarl.

"She knew the rules, Rafael. Breaking the code of silence means death! There was nothing I could do. She understood it. And she forgave me. I saw it in her eyes."

I take him in, this man I once revered, waiting for even a speck of regret over what I'm about to do. It never materializes. The man who took me and Guido fishing when we were kids, who showed me how to change the tire on my bike, who gave me advice about girls . . . he is already dead. To me, he died the moment he watched Mancuzo press the gun to my mother's head and pull the trigger, and did nothing. That man who chose Cosa Nostra over the woman he once swore he loved.

"I'm sure she did." I lift my gun. "But I never will."

The gunshot sounds like cannon fire in the silence of the room. Calogero's head snaps back. He falls onto the bed, his eyes wide and glassy, while a swell of crimson surges from the hole in the middle of his brow.

Vasilisa

Chicago
One hour before the scheduled flight departure

I park my car in front of Uncle Sergei's freshly painted two-story house and exit. I wasted three hours hiding in my room while I waited for Dad to finally get bogged down in his office, giving me a chance to sneak out of the house unnoticed. If I want to catch Rafael's plane—and I do—I can't spare more than ten minutes on this visit.

Roaring barks explode on the right as two enormous black dogs round the corner and run toward me. I take a deep breath and brace myself for the impact. A second later, I'm assaulted by paws and warm wet tongues.

"Jesus. I forgot how big you guys are," I groan. "Uncle Sergei! I need help here."

"Well, well, well. Isn't that my favorite troublemaking little cousin?" a male voice says from the porch.

I look up and find Sasha, Uncle Sergei's son, leaning on the doorframe. He's dressed only in gray sweatpants, his partially inked bare chest in full view.

"I'm a year older than you, you schmuck!" I laugh as I try to keep the dogs from turning me over. "Help, please?"

"Bambi! Flora!" he yells. "Down. Now!"

The dogs immediately retreat and plant their butts on the ground, their eyes fixed on Sasha.

"You need to forbid Uncle Sergei from naming your dogs." I laugh and run up the steps and into his arms. "I've missed your ugly mug."

"We missed you, too. Come on in. We've got some leftovers. Mom made her famous chicken and Mexican rice. Besides, if you stay out here, I'll need to get my shotgun to ward off the horde of salivating men that will soon start to gather."

I smile. I'm wearing some of Yulia's pretty clothes that she let me borrow, not my usual baggy jeans and shapeless shirts. Can't wait to see the look on Rafael's face when he sees me descending the stairs off the plane. He'll be surprised. I haven't told him that I'm coming back.

"I can't stay," I say. "I thought you moved out."

"I did. But you know how my mother gets jumpy every time Dad goes out into the field. So I came over to keep her company."

"And get free food?"

"Yeah, that, too." He winks. "Dad is coming back sometime tomorrow. You can drop by then."

"I'm . . . actually leaving right away. I'm on my way to the airport." I throw a look at my watch. "I have less than an hour or the plane will depart without me."

"Leaving? But you just got back. Where are you going now?"

"Sicily." I can't suppress my grin.

"Oh. What a coincidence. Dad's there now."

I stop in my tracks. "Uncle Sergei's in Sicily?"

"Yeah. Roman needed him to off some asshole over there. He took off yesterday."

My legs nearly fold under me. Panic grips me and horror

washes over me from head to toe. I can practically feel the tight squeeze of fate's hand around my neck. Squeezing. Squeezing. I can't breathe.

"Vasya? You okay?"

I spin around and run out of the house, straight to my car. Ignoring Sasha's calls after me, I grab my phone while starting the engine and dial Rafael's number. It rings. And rings. I try twice more, but he doesn't answer.

"Shit!" I merge onto the road leading to the highway that will eventually take me to the private airfield and keep calling Rafael. No answer.

I call Dad's number next. The call goes directly to voicemail.

"Oh God," I choke out, then redial. Voicemail again.

My eyes dart between my phone and the road in front of me. I can't get on that plane unless I manage to contact Rafael and warn him. Or make my dad call off Uncle Sergei. Fuck. Fuck. *Fuck!* I turn the steering wheel sharply to the left, making a U-turn, and floor the gas pedal, heading toward home instead of the waiting airplane.

Minutes pass. Five. Ten. Half an hour. I keep dialing, switching between Rafael's and Dad's numbers. No answer. Voicemail. No answer. Voicemail. I pull up the contacts list and scroll, searching for Guido's, but I can't find it!

"Fuck!" I scream and restart my search from the top of the list. When I finally find his name, I hit dial and turn on the speakerphone.

Please. Please pick up!

"Vasilisa?"

"My father sent a hitman after Rafael!" I cry. "You need to warn him!"

Silence. A second feels like a lifetime. "Who did he send?"

"My uncle. Sergei Belov."

"Shit," Guido whispers.

The line goes dead.

285

"Guido? Fuck." I call Rafael again. Nothing.

I hit my mom's number next. She answers on the first ring.

"He sent Uncle Sergei to kill Rafael!" I scream into the phone.

"What? Who?"

"Dad! I've been calling Rafael but can't reach him. And Dad's line goes directly to voicemail."

"He's in his office. I'm heading down there." I can hear the slam of the door and the hurried footfalls of running feet. "You should have told Roman, Vasilisa. If you'd have told him the truth, he never would have sent Sergei. Your dad believes that man was keeping you against your will and that he hurt you. And since you wouldn't give your father any details, he assumed the worst."

"I didn't want to tell him because I was afraid he'd do exactly this!"

"Call Sergei," she says over her rapid and shallow breaths. "Tell him to stay put."

"You know he won't," I whimper. My uncle takes orders only from the pakhan. I could cry and beg, and he would still follow through on what he was ordered to do. He won't waiver unless my father rescinds the command. "I'm ten minutes away. Please, Mom! Convince Dad to call off Uncle Sergei!"

"I will, baby. Don't worry."

Roman Petrov

"What do you mean, he canceled the shipment?" I snarl into the phone.

"I'm speaking rather clearly, am I not?" Nikolai replies.

It took me years to find someone who could adequately replace Anton as a *brigadier*, overseeing the ranks of our men.

Managing Bratva's foot soldiers is akin to handling the reins on a herd of maniacal hyenas. They won't take orders from just anyone. But even when they do, many often feel at liberty to make their own interpretation as to how the orders should be carried out. To keep everyone in line, and not go apeshit in the process, the man in charge must either possess an extremely calm demeanor and be methodical in exercising his authority, or be someone who is basically nuts himself. Nikolai Levin is the latter kind. Most days, I'm not certain if I should promote the disrespectful fucker or simply snap his neck. The lunatic took a bullet for me two years ago, so I guess I have a soft spot for him.

"Watch your mouth," I bark. "And explain."

"We arrived at the border as planned, only to have one of Ramirez's men relay a message to us that the backstabbing cunt found another buyer. I tried getting a hold of Belov, but he's not answering his phone."

"My brother is dealing with another issue at the moment. Do you still have Ramirez's guy?"

"Yes."

"Break his legs," I spit out. "Make him talk. I want to know who got what's supposed to be mine."

"Already did. It was Artem Voloshyn. He offered Ramirez a forty percent cut."

Fucking Ukranians. I thought I was done having to deal with those assholes two decades ago.

"There's more," Nikolai continues. "One of my guys caught Artem's dealer in West Town last week."

"And you're just telling me this now?"

My office door suddenly bangs open, and my wife barges in, flushed and breathing heavily as if she ran here at break-neck speed.

"What have you done?" she chokes out, eyes distraught and flaring.

"I'll call you back." I throw the phone on my desk and lift

my hands up in defense. "Whatever it is, it wasn't me. I swear, malysh."

I have no idea what could have distressed her so much, but I know it can't be anything I've done. I would rather cut off my own hands. And legs. Slit my own throat. I'll have to consider a proper order, but the sentiment remains the same.

"You sent Sergei to kill Vasya's Sicilian!"

Oh. Well, I guess that *was* me. "That fucknut is not *hers*. De Santi is a hitman who's kidnapped and held our daughter hostage for over two months. You didn't actually expect me to let it go?"

Nina rushes across the room. "Please, Roman. You need to call Sergei and tell him to abort."

"Absolutely not."

"Vasilisa is in love with him, kotik." Grabbing a fistful of my shirt, she practically thrusts her nose against mine. "You're calling Sergei off. Now!"

"What? No, she can't be in love with him."

"She's planning to return to Sicily!" Nina yells into my face while shaking me. "I tried to convince her to tell you the truth, but she was scared *this* is exactly what you would do!"

I stare at my wife while a firestorm rages inside me. My baby girl can't be in love with a goddamned De Santi, can she? I've already arranged dinner, inviting my accountant and telling him to bring his son. The boy works in the records management department of a retirement home. A nice, safe guy. One who's the same age as Vasilisa. Not a fucking assassin-for-hire who lives on another continent.

"Nina, baby, she's just confused."

"She's not fucking confused! She loves him!" My sweet little wife is now roaring so loud that I fear the windows may shatter. "You can't do this! Her father cannot kill the man she loves! It will destroy her, Roman! And it will destroy you!"

"Vasya deserves someone nice. Someone who will keep her safe."

"Don't you understand? She doesn't want nice. She wants him. And he's kept her safe all along. Even when you couldn't."

I furrow my brows. "What are you talking about?"

"The mall. The explosion twenty years ago. Rafael De Santi is the man who saved our daughter's life!"

That's . . . that's not possible. But . . . *Oh fuck.* As much as I want to deny Nina's words, somehow I know it's the truth. Since the moment I met De Santi more than decade ago, I've always wondered what happened to him. I never made the connection.

Vasya.

I leap out of the chair and grab the phone.

Vasilisa

The needle on the speedometer is hovering over the one-hundred-miles-per-hour mark. I press the gas pedal harder, swerving between the other vehicles on the road. It's five minutes after seven. Rafael's plane just took off. Without me. Doesn't matter, I'll take the first commercial flight I can get on, as soon as I know the man I love is safe. There's still time. My uncle prefers to work during the night. I take a calming breath, but the air suddenly gets caught in my lungs, and I almost plow into the car in front of me.

The time difference. I forgot about the goddamned time difference! Sicily is seven hours ahead of Chicago. It's two in the morning there right now. No. No. *No!*

The streetlight in front of me changes to red. I hit the gas harder. A pickup truck approaches from the side road, and I barely miss it as I fly through the intersection. Our neighborhood is just a mile away. I call Rafael again. And again.

No answer.

Slamming on the brakes in our driveway, I'm shaking so

much that I can hardly open the car door. I don't bother shutting it, just take off at a run, taking the stone steps to the front door two at a time.

The door of Dad's office is ajar. I stumble inside and stare at my father. The words are stuck in my closed-up throat. Dad is standing next to his desk, the phone pressed to his ear. Mom is in front of him, clutching his shirt.

"Sergei." My father's deep voice breaks the silence. "Abort."

A choked sound of relief leaves my lips. I lean back on the wall because my legs are threatening to give out. My eyes stare blazingly into my father's. He's still holding the phone to his ear. The muscles of his jaw are tight, and his eyebrows are furrowed.

"*Мне он нужен живым, Сергей. Понимаешь?*" he barks and lowers the phone.

I don't even breathe as I wait for the great Roman Petrov to say something.

"Dad?" I whimper.

My father takes a deep breath, his eyes downcast. Avoiding looking at me.

Rafael

15 minutes earlier

My phone rings as soon as I turn it back on, and just as I'm reaching for the front door. The pilot's name lights up the screen. I take a look at my wristwatch. Five minutes after two.

"We're ready for takeoff, boss."

"Alright." I nod, even though he can't see me, then wait. I can't bring myself to ask for confirmation of what I already know.

"She didn't come. I'm sorry, boss."

Slipping the phone back into my pants, I head to the

kitchen. My steps sound hollow in the huge space, echoing off the walls, the sound eerie in the darkness of the house. I don't bother turning on the lamps as I cross the room. There's enough moonlight illuminating my way to the fridge.

Some people say that it's a sacrilege to drink red wine cold rather than at room temperature. I've always found it tastes rather bland that way. Grabbing a stemmed glass and then a bottle out of the fridge, I walk through the living space and stop at the threshold to the terrace. How many times did I have those workers paint these French doors? Four? Five? The guys certainly made plenty of noise while doing it. Just as I ordered them to. All so my vespetta could feel more at home.

Funny thing, how I spent over twenty years making heaps of money, building my empire. The entire time I was convinced that it would bring me happiness. Too late did I realize that all of it was nothing but dust in the wind. All my wealth couldn't help me attain the one thing I want most. Vasilisa's love. Just like none of the expensive jewelry I gifted her ever garnered a smile on her face, unlike the silly doodles I've sketched for her. And here I am, at the pinnacle of my success, owning so many things . . . Yet possessing nothing of value.

Warm wind blows into my face as I step out onto the terrace and take a seat on the deck chair at the far end. The tiny lights of distant fishing boats are scattered across the dark expanse of the sea, twinkling as they ride the waves. I pour myself a glass of wine and watch them.

"Getting reckless in your old age, De Santi?" a man's voice says from the shadows to my left.

"Seems that way." I lean back and take a sip of my wine. "Been a long time. How's life, Belov?"

"It was quite fine, actually. Until some motherfucker decided to kidnap my niece." He steps out of the darkness and leans his backside on the banister, crossing his arms over his chest. The glow of the moon reflects off the gun he's holding.

"So, the pakhan ordered you to take care of that problem for him, did he?"

"I would have, even if he hadn't," he snaps. "What the fuck, Rafael? We've had dealings for years. Was it some sort of payback? And if so, for what?"

"It wasn't."

"Then what? Did someone hire you to do this? At what price? Shit. If you'd called Roman when you got the contract, he would have paid you double just to send her back right away."

"I was told that not all things have a price tag. I'm now convinced that's true." I nod toward the gun in his hand. "Feel free to do what you came here for."

"What, you just gonna sit there and let me kill you?"

"That's the plan."

"Why?"

"Because the alternative outcome of this meeting is me killing you, Belov. And, unfortunately, I can't do that."

My gaze glides along the route Vasilisa and I traveled when we spent the day on my yacht, feeling the Russian's eyes on me the entire time. He probably thinks I'm bluffing, expects me to pull out my weapon at any second. If it was anyone else in his place, Petrov's avenger would already be dead. But Vasilisa adores her uncle. And I could never kill anyone she loves.

"Are you going to spend the whole night just staring at me?" I ask.

Belov laughs. "You know, I could have sworn you were one of the sane ones."

"Acquired madness is one of the worst kinds, I'm afraid. When you catch it, there's no cure." I meet his gaze and throw back what's left of my wine. "Take good care of her."

He lifts his gun, aiming at my chest. "I will."

A gunshot explodes into the night.

The bullet slices through my flesh; shockwaves radiate throughout my body. Pain shreds my insides, setting every nerve ending on fire. If someone buried a superheated rod through my breastbone, twisting it in the process, I imagine this is how it would feel.

Notes of a familiar song suddenly sound somewhere near. I almost laugh when I recognize "Gangsta's Paradise." The music gets louder when Belov reaches inside his pocket and pulls out his phone, pressing it to his ear. Unperturbed by the interruption, he lifts the gun, aiming at my head.

I can see Belov's lips move as he speaks with whoever is calling him, but all sound gets muted now, only low mumbling remains. It's getting harder to draw a breath. The light of the boats are a lot more blurry. I close my eyes and let the darkness take me. But on the cusp, a fleeting thought invades my mind.

I should have stuffed one of my shirts into her backpack.

CHAPTER
Twenty

Vasilisa

"**D**O NOT TOUCH ME," I choke out and pull my hand from my father's hold.

He's been hovering over me for the entire ten-hour flight. If there were parachutes on board, I would have forced one on him and kicked him out of the damn plane.

"Vasya, baby . . . He's going to pull through." He tries to take my hand again but I slap it away.

"You sent Uncle Sergei to kill the man I love," I snap, barely keeping the tears from spilling over. "In your sick, maniacal need to keep me from harm, you inflicted the worst possible pain on me. I hate you. God, I hate you so much."

"Please, Vasya . . ."

"Roman," my mom says from the seat next to me. "Go sit in the back."

"But . . ."

"Now, kotik," she growls and wraps her arm around me. "What did Rafael's brother say?"

"He's still in surgery. His second one. Surgeons had to go

back in to stop the internal bleeding. That's not even the worst of it." Gulping for breath, I try to get the next words out. "He flatlined on arrival, and they had to resuscitate him." I press the heels of my palms over my eyes.

It's been hours since I've been able to draw a full breath. Quick, shallow intakes of air are all I can manage to get past the knot that's formed in my throat. The survival rate for a gunshot wound to the chest is low, especially from a high-powered weapon and at close range. And knowing my uncle, he probably used one of his big-ass guns.

Mom squeezes my hand. "He's going to be fine, Vasilisa. I promise you. He's going to be fine."

The plane tilts. My ears are ringing but not because we're landing. There's a scream that's been building inside me, pushing on my lungs and mind, ready to burst free. I want to let it out, but I'm afraid if I do, I won't be able to stop.

There is a slight bump when the wheels hit the ground. I'm out of my seat and running for the door even before we stop moving. It took hours to find a jet that could fly us to Sicily on short notice, and I'm not losing another minute to get to my man.

The flight attendant sprints before me, blocking my way to the door. Protests, likely, leave her mouth, but they sound like nothing more than mumbling to me.

"Move!" I snarl and try to get past her, but two strong arms wrap around me from behind.

"Vasilisa . . ." My father's voice next to my ear. "Please."

"Let me go." I try to wriggle free. "Don't ever fucking touch me! I can't even stand the sight of you!"

He keeps speaking, words that are meant to soothe me, but nothing penetrates my brain. All my focus is on the aircraft door a few feet away. The minutes it takes for the plane to taxi over to the tarmac feel like years of my life. When the door finally opens, I rush through it and down the steps.

Uncle Sergei is standing by a parked car, pulled up to the edge of the runway. He's still dressed in his regular tactical outfit, his usual attire when he's hunting someone down for Bratva. I can't bear to look at him, either.

"Take me to him," I say as I pass by my uncle, heading toward the passenger-side door.

"Let's wait for—"

"Take me to him!" I roar. "Now!"

Uncle Sergei throws a look over his shoulder, toward the plane where my mom and dad are just descending the stairs. I don't really expect him to move from his spot since his loyalty is only to the pakhan, but he nods and gets behind the wheel.

The car surges forward. I clasp my hands in my lap, frantically twisting the plain silver ring around my finger.

"I apologize." The nurse at the information desk shakes her head. "But as I've already told you, I can't disclose patient information to anyone other than immediate family members."

"Please," I beg, squeezing the white counter before me. "Just tell me if he's alive."

"I can't. I'm sorry."

I press my hands to my mouth. That scream in my throat is ready to explode, the pressure so great it's pounding in my temples. My lungs must've shrunk because I can't seem to get enough air.

I turn around, looking at the multitude of hallways and closed doors. Rafael is alive. I won't accept any other possibility. He's somewhere out there, and I'm going to find him, even if I have to fight my way past every damn member of the hospital's security personnel.

My eyes fall on the figure of a man in jeans and a bright-yellow T-shirt, sitting hunched over in a chair halfway down the hall to the left. It's Guido. I run toward him at break-neck speed. The bastard didn't take any of my calls for the past hour, and I've called him at least fifty times.

"How is he?" I whisper. "The staff won't tell me anything."

Guido's jaw hardens. "Still in surgery."

A strangled whimper leaves my lips. "How bad?"

"It's bad," he rasps, gaze glued to the floor. "I knew, you know? The moment you told me your father sent Belov, I fucking knew."

"Knew what?"

He looks up, his eyes red. "Rafael has been a mercenary for nearly two decades. How many times do you think my brother has been shot in all those years?"

"I don't know."

"Not once. But here he is, with a team of five surgeons trying to patch him up after a point-blank bullet to the chest." He points a finger at me. "Rafael just sat there and let Belov shoot him. Because of you!"

Guido's raging words hit me like a sledgehammer to the chest. I stagger back, bumping into the hallway wall. "No."

"Yes!" He leaps out of the chair and closes the distance between us. His face is a mask of fury and pain as he leans forward, drawing level with my eyes. "He is so in love with you that he'd rather die than kill someone you care about. I hope now you have your fucking proof of how much he loves you."

My vision is completely obliterated with tears, and I don't notice the papers Guido must have taken out of his pocket until he slams them against my chest. "You'll need this if you want to see him. If he makes it, that is."

I wipe my eyes, then look down at the document in my hand. The first sheet is an official-looking certificate with a stamp at the top. It's dated as of three days ago. The text is in Italian, but I notice Rafael's name. And just below it, mine. My eyes jump back to the header of the document. I may not speak or

297

read Italian, but I recognize the word *matrimonio*, and I know what it means.

Marriage.

"What . . ." The word tumbles from my mouth. "How?"

"My brother might be a love-blinded idiot, but he's still a scheming ass who always finds a way to get what he wants." Guido turns to head down the hallway but then halts. "He left you everything. If he doesn't pull through, you'll get almost seventy million in cash and ten times that amount in investments. It's all yours, Mrs. De Santi."

"I don't want his money!" I scream.

"Well, as I said," he retorts as he walks away, "Rafael always gets what he wants. In the end."

I stare at the two doctors before me. "What do you mean 'he's not waking up'?"

The older one, a short man in his late fifties, sighs and turns to Guido who stands next to me. I have no idea what the surgeon says in Italian, so I focus on his face, trying to gauge something from his expression. There's nothing, besides a stoic look. His much younger coworker, however, is holding a folder to his chest and not saying a word, but gaping at me like a dumbstruck fool.

"Will you please tell me what's going on?" I ask, praying to God the young guy's English is better than the older doc's, because I'm going out of my mind. Panic courses through my veins. I'm just about to lose it.

"Um, well, your husband is . . . Is he really your husband?"

"Yes!"

"Oh . . . I thought I misunderstood. It's just . . ." His eyes scan me from the top of my head, over my short body-hugging dress, all the way to the tips of my heels. "Um . . . he's experiencing delayed emergence, a failure to regain consciousness following general anesthesia. It's been more than thirty minutes but he's still unresponsive. For now, he's breathing on his own. However, if he doesn't wake up in the next half an hour, we may need to consider administering more potent drugs and, potentially—"

"He'll wake up," I interrupt him. "I'll make sure my husband wakes up. Let me see him."

"Ma'am, I don't think you can help."

I grab his sleeve, twisting the fabric in my hand while tears burst from my eyes. "He. Will. Wake. Up."

The young doctor looks at his colleague, and they exchange a few sentences in Italian before glancing back at me.

"Five minutes," he says and sets a brisk pace toward the recovery room.

My whole body trembles as I rush after the doctor down the hallway and across the waiting area where my parents and uncle are seated.

"Vasya." Mom leaps out of her chair as I pass them by. "What's—"

Wiping my eyes, I keep walking without slowing. Several sets of footfalls trail behind me, along with a distinctive click of Dad's cane against the tiled floor. I can't talk to them now. Not before I look upon Rafael and see with my own eyes that he's okay. Guido can fill them in on what's happening.

Another long hallway, and then the doctor stops in front of a sturdy-looking door.

"Ma'am, you need to understand that—"

I grab at the knob and step inside the room.

The constant beep of a heart monitor pierces the absolute silence. I put my hand over my mouth, but a pained whimper still manages to escape my lips. The metal door handle digs into my back as I stand rooted to the floor and just stare at Rafael's unmoving form.

I take a tentative step. Then another. When I finally reach

the bed, I'm a crying mess again. Cupping Rafael's cheek with my hand, I bend so my mouth is just next to his ear.

"I'm going to burn everything," I choke out. "That pretty house you left me. The hotel. Your cars. There will be nothing left of them."

I press my lips to his temple.

"Those two yachts you love so much? I'll scuttle both and watch them sink to the bottom of the sea." I kiss his eyebrow. "Your private security company? You can forget about it, Rafael. I'm going to destroy it so completely that, in a month, no one will even remember it existed."

His skin is so cold and clammy. I move my hand to his neck, setting it over the pulse point. The monitor beside the bed is beeping, but I need more tangible proof that he's alive. Only when I feel the steady beat under my fingers, do I let myself relax a tiny bit.

"The money? I'm going to give it all away. I'll find some stupid charity, A Better Life for Goats or something equally idiotic, and I'll transfer all your millions to them. They can use all that wealth to create a fucking Goatland. A paradise where they can groom the goats, bathe them in donkey milk, and give the animals neck massages all day long."

Why isn't he waking up? I continue peppering his face with kisses, feeling the ridges and valleys of the multitude of scars under my lips. Most of the time, I forget they're even there. I don't see the stretch of badly stitched flesh that healed askew and twists his cheek. Or the one pulling his upper lip, making it misshapen. Or those on his chin that fades into the short stubble across his jaw. I just see him.

Rafael.

Knowing that, because of these scars, he believed he needed to buy my love with jewelry and other presents makes me incredibly angry. And completely devastates me. He got these scars by saving me. And he never intended to reveal that truth.

His face is an expressionless mask, but his lips are slightly parted. I pull his lower one between my teeth and nip.

"I swear, Rafael. If you don't come back to me, I'll make it my life's mission to destroy your whole empire," I whisper into his mouth.

He doesn't stir. Not even a little. There are no sounds other than my sniffing and the rhythmic beeps of the heart rate machine. I press my cheek to his and bury my nose into his neck.

"Please," I choke out, inhaling his scent. "I love you, so much."

Even with all the hospital scents all around, he still smells the same. Like cypress and orange. Briny air and the sea. Leashed danger, but my undeniable safety. Like home.

I can't lose him.

A light touch lands on the back of my head, and then a raspy breath just next to my ear. "You forgot . . . the jet."

A relieved cry makes it past my lips. I squeeze my eyes shut and nuzzle my face deeper into his neck. My throat feels completely raw, and, even with my lids closed, tears still run down my cheeks.

"I haven't." I can barely form the words. "I'll use it to send the goats on an annual vacation somewhere in the Caribbean."

His fingers tunnel through my hair, petting me soothingly. "You came back."

"Of course I came back."

"You weren't on the plane. The pilot called me. Said you didn't come."

Slowly, I lift my head and take him in. His skin is still ghastly pale, and there are dark circles under his eyes.

"I'm sorry. I was preoccupied with trying to find a way to stop the assassin my dad sent to kill you, and I missed it." I stroke his cheek. "I'm afraid your father-in-law isn't your biggest fan."

"So, Guido told you?"

"That you got me wasted and then got us married, leaving me none the wiser?" I press my lips to his. "Yeah, he told me."

"Are you mad at me?"

"I can't be mad at you when you're in a hospital bed with tubes and shit sticking out of your body."

"Those will come out. Eventually." His chest rises with a deep breath. "Maybe you'll contemplate slicing my throat when they do." He takes my hand and moves it to his crotch. "See? Just thinking about it makes me hard."

"Jesus, Rafael." I snort through the tears.

"Please don't cry, vespetta."

"You almost died because of me. Again." I brush my palm down his forearm, right over the daggers and snake tattoo. "Why didn't you tell me it was you?"

Anger flashes across Rafael's face. He grabs my wrist, glaring at me. "Is that why you came back?" His voice is low, the tone infused with menace. "Because if it is, you can leave right now."

I lean down until the tip of my nose touches his. "No. I came back because I'm in love with you."

"Why? How could you be in love with a manipulative son of a bitch like me?"

"You are a manipulative jackass. And I love you despite that quality. Or, maybe, because of it. Because you care. Even when you say you don't. You care deeply about the people in your life. Your men. Your brother. Me. I adore the fierce protectiveness that practically radiates from you, even when you try to mask it as something else. You're willing to wade through a sea of dead bodies to safeguard the people you care about."

I reach out and sweep back a few strands that have fallen over his face. Rafael watches me without blinking, his eyes sharp and assessing.

"The sheer force of your will and unrelenting determination that made you who you are leaves me in awe," I continue. "And your stubbornness . . . It's an entity of its own. I don't think I've ever met a man as bullheaded as you. It's rather sexy, you know?"

Tilting my head, I brush my nose against his. "I'm in love with you because no one else makes me feel the way you do. Cherished. Loved. Special. And it has nothing to do with the lavish trinkets you bestowed on me. Rather, it's the sticky note drawings you left me. The stolen figs. The scratches from the poisonous shrub, all because I asked you to save that stupid cat."

"You were extremely persistent," he says in a raw and raspy voice.

"Yeah, that's the *only* reason you did it." I smile. "You make me feel worthy. And competent. Only when I'm with you, Rafael, I do not need to prove myself. My whole life, I've been hearing how beautiful I am, as if I'm some expensive piece of furniture. Pleasing to the eye, but easily forgotten when the viewers move on to the next room. Only once have you called me beautiful, and yet, you make me *feel* like I am, every single day. Not on the outside, but within."

Rafael takes my chin between his fingers. The corner of his lips tilts into a barely-there smirk. "Are you fishing for compliments now, Vasilisa?"

"Maybe?" I sniff.

"You are so beautiful, that every time I'm with you, I have the urge to pinch myself to prove you're real." He pulls my face closer to his. "And you're pretty on the outside, too."

Something between a laugh and a whimper escapes me. Setting my palms on his cheeks, I slam my mouth to his. "I will never forgive you for letting yourself get shot. And I'll never forgive my father."

"Don't be so hard on him. I would have done the same in Roman's place." He bites my lip. "Does he know we're married?"

"Nope."

"I'm sure he'll be beyond thrilled."

"He'll grumble a bit, but—"

303

NEVA ALTAJ

"WHAT?!" A loud male yell explodes outside the room. "That *сволочь* made my little girl MARRY HIM?"

The door flies open with such force that it slams into the adjacent wall, and my father steps inside. Irate doesn't even come close to describing the look on his face. Unbridled rage. Savage indignation. His breathing is deep and slow. A sound akin to a bull's snort leaves his chest with each exhale. The picture is made more perfect by the way his nostrils flare with each gasp.

"You!" he roars. "You scheming"—inhale—"lying"—inhale—"stealing . . . motherfucker."

"Roman!" My mother's squeal erupts somewhere behind him, and, a second later, she squeezes between my father's body and the doorframe. Then, she presses her palms to his chest. "Leave them alone!"

"I'm going to kill him!" Dad yells while Mom tries to push him out of the room. "I'm going to skin him alive and hang his hide over my office window as a curtain!"

"Don't mind him," my mom chirps, grinning at us over her shoulder. "He's just really excited about the news and can't find words to express his happiness. Aren't you, kotik?"

"I won't be using a knife, oh no," the pakhan keeps roaring while Mom maneuvers him backward. "I'll use a fucking potato peeler. You're going to make amazing burlap drapes, De Santi! And every time your remnants rustle in the breeze, I'll remember your screams of agony!"

"We'll come back later," Mom whispers with a slightly comical, irritated look and slams the door shut in their wake.

I look at Rafael.

He has a very smug grin on his face. "Well . . . I don't think we'll be heading out fishing together anytime soon."

I laugh and kiss him.

epilogue

Rafael

One month later

THE TWO-STORY MODERN WHITE HOUSE LOOMS BEFORE us, bathed in the soft glow of the sunset. My father-in-law's home. I park the car in the empty spot next to the flower bed and turn off the engine.

"Remember what we agreed on," Vasilisa says as she checks her makeup in the sun visor mirror. "You will not rile my dad up. He's still mad at you for 'stealing' *my* wedding day. This will be our first . . . um, normal gathering with my family, so let's keep it civil."

"Sure." I take the mascara tube from her hand and throw it onto the seat behind me.

"Hey! What—"

"I'll behave. But I think I need some incentive." I push my seat back, then wrap my hands around her tiny waist and lift her over the console and onto my lap.

"Rafael, we're not having sex in my father's driveway."

"No?" I unfasten the first button of her silky blouse. "In case you forgot, my doctor said I'm still recovering. No stressful situations whatsoever are allowed. And one part of my anatomy feels rather stressed at the moment." I push the sides of her blouse apart and nip her breast.

"We can work on calming your cock after dinner," Vasilisa murmurs.

My hand trails down her ribcage, then lower, to cup her exposed pussy. Her satin panties were left discarded somewhere on my plane. Guiding my thumb between her slick folds, I find her sweet bud and start circling. A couple of light strokes at first, then I apply slightly more pressure before sliding my finger inside her heat.

"Changed your mind?" I keep teasing her clit with my thumb while listening to her soft little moans of pleasure.

"Yup," Vasilisa chokes out, riding my finger and unzipping my pants.

I'm hard as a fucking rock, to the point of pain. I almost come when she wraps her hand around my cock to pull it out. The degree to which I'm obsessed with my wife is unparalleled. She only needs to touch me—or simply threaten to slice my throat—and I'm a goner.

Slipping my hands under her ass, I position her above my dick and start slowly lowering this incredible woman in my arms. My brain is fried before I'm even halfway inside her.

Two dark eyes bore into mine from between the long black strands covering her face. Piercing. A little feral. Mine.

It's still somewhat unreal that I get to have her as my own.

"I'm not sure I can ever show you how much I love you, Vasilisa."

"You already have, you lunatic," she whispers, taking more of me inside. "Try pulling another stunt like that, and I swear I'll strangle you to death."

My cock twitches violently inside her pussy, and I barely

contain my imminent orgasm. I thrust into her from below, filling her completely, and capture her lips with mine at the same time.

"I love you," her lips say into mine. "So, so much."

My heart swells and expands, feeling as if it's suddenly too large for my chest. I cup Vasilisa's face with my palm, soaking in the view of her, flushed and panting, as she rides me, chasing her pleasure with wild abandon.

This ecstasy is all I need to know the old shadows are gone. Those dark thoughts that used to plague me when I was a much younger man. There were dark moments through the years when I reflected on that moment at the mall. That minute just before the explosion.

I'm ashamed to admit it, even to myself, but more than once I've wondered what would have happened if I hadn't been there. How would my life have turned out? What if I'd left before I saw the girl merrily running down that hall? Or if I did, but chose to remain in that stairwell. Those thoughts made me feel sick to my stomach, disgusted with myself. And still, they would surface on occasion. In moments of weakness. In moments of pain.

Now? Now I'm beating myself up over that scar on Vasilisa's back. One damn shard that managed to get past me. That hurt her. That left a permanent mark. I should have shielded her better. That cut should have ended up on me, as well. Never her.

I've always hated my reflection in the mirror. That is until I realized the girl I saved was Vasilisa. Now, seeing myself, the only feeling I have is of relief. Because it was me who was injured, not her.

Was it destiny that I was there to save her? Was our fate sealed by my choice? Or did the unyielding kismet guide her skillfully to me all these years later?

Vasilisa tugs my hair as she arches her back, coming undone in my arms. I finally let go, filling her with my cum. Our labored breaths echo through the space around us. I gently caress my wife's face. My beauty. In the arms of a beast.

"I think that fairy tales exist, after all, vespetta. And I believe, I owe you a present."

"What are you talking about," she pants. "What present?"

I smile. "A library."

Vasilisa

"We're here!" I announce and, squeezing Rafael's hand in mine, step into the entry hall.

My father approaches us, his face grim, suddenly stopping just an arm's length away. His eyes slide over my visage—and I can't help but wonder if my makeup is smudged—then drop to my blouse. I glance down and cringe. I seem to have missed one of the buttons. And my skirt is askew. Shit. I quickly adjust the hem, but there's nothing I can do about the shirt. I'll just have to play it cool and hope this dinner doesn't end in bloodshed.

"Um . . . Hi, Dad," I chirp, grinning widely.

A strange growling sound erupts from Roman Petrov's throat, and I have no doubt we've just landed in the hot seat. Dad's nostrils flare, and he turns his menacing glare on my husband. "You have a death wish, De Santi?"

I close my eyes and take a calming breath. If they start waving their guns and punching each other, I'm leaving.

"I see you're still as dramatic as ever . . . Dad," Rafael deadpans.

Oh God . . .

The look on my father's face turns homicidal. He takes a step forward, nearly bumping Rafael's chest. "You do not call me 'Dad,' you thieving motherfucker! I swear, I'm going to—"

"Yeah, I know. You're going to kill me in a very unpleasant

way." Rafael moves past my father, tapping him on the shoulder as we pass. "Let's eat. I'm starving."

"You promised you'd behave," I murmur as we head toward the dining room.

"Sorry."

"No, you're not."

Rafael's lips curve into a devilish smirk. "No. Not even a little bit."

"He's still coming to terms with everything. Maybe if you would—Rafael!" I squeak, quickly pushing his hand away. He just squeezed my ass while my dad was watching!

"What?"

"Please, can we all put in a bit of effort, so this evening doesn't unravel into a disaster, and actually have a good time?"

Rafael throws a glance over his shoulder. I follow his gaze and wince. My dad is still standing by the front door, his eyes wide like a maniac's as he glares back at my husband.

"I'm already having a great time." Rafael wraps his arm around my waist and lifts me to his chest. "And it's only going to get better."

His mouth slams against mine with such force that I shriek. Everything else becomes insignificant, as usual, when my husband kisses me. I wrap my legs around his waist and squeeze his neck, kissing him back as if there's no tomorrow. Rafael keeps his hand on my chin, holding my head steady while ravishing my lips with his.

"Oh, there you are, lovebirds," my mom chirps behind me. "The food is getting cold."

I quickly break the kiss and practically slide down Rafael's body.

"Um, hey, Mom. Yeah, we're coming. But you may need to get Dad a tranquilizer." I grab Rafael's hand and drag him into the dining room.

Yulia is already seated at the table, fiddling with her phone. Aunt Angelina is sitting across from her.

"Where's everyone else?" I ask, looking at the empty seats.

"Sergei will come shortly." Angelina smiles. "He had to drop off a change of clothes for Alexei and Sasha. They've been arrested."

"What?!"

"Police caught them street racing last night. They were driving way over the speed limit. Roman decided to leave them stewing in the precinct's holding cells today, so they could learn their lesson. He'll send the lawyer tomorrow to arrange bail."

"Great." I sigh and take a seat next to Yulia while Rafael takes the chair on my right.

Mom dances into the dining room with my dad on her heels. His face is still a mask of rage when he takes the seat at the head of the table.

"Did you hear the news?" Yulia pushes me with her elbow. "Dad agreed to me moving out. I've found an amazing studio in Hyde Park and—"

"Forget that studio," Dad interrupts her. "Start looking for a two-bedroom apartment."

"What?" she shrieks. "But I already put down the deposit. And why would I need two bedrooms?"

"The Ukrainian Mafia is trying to invade our turf. We're going on high alert, so you're getting a bodyguard until further notice."

"Not happening!"

The dining room door flies open, hitting the wall.

"You won't believe what Luca got me," Uncle Sergei bellows as he steps inside the room and lays a huge semiautomatic rifle on the table, just next to the platter of pork chops. "What? No lamb today?"

"Get that thing away from the food!" Mom snaps.

"That *thing* is a KR-101X. A premium, civilian-legal, AK

rifle. It's the newest Kalashnikov, peeps," he exclaims, visibly offended. "An exclusive, limited pre-production release, with side folding synthetic stock, a sixteen-point-five-inch barrel, and it takes magazine-fed chambered seven-six-two by thirty-nine caliber rounds."

"It's a five-five-six NATO," Rafael comments as he reaches for the bowl of mashed potatoes.

"No, it's not." Sergei leans over and grabs the rifle, fumbling with the magazine. "Fuck me. It is."

"Jesus fucking Christ!" My dad slams his palm on the table, making the glasses and cutlery rattle. "Put the blasted thing away, Sergei! We're eating!"

"Always a party pooper." My uncle rolls his eyes. "At least Rafael here can appreciate high-quality firearms. De Santi, did you get a chance to try one out?"

"As a matter of fact, I did."

Oh no. I put my hand on Rafael's thigh under the table and squeeze. "Rafael, don't!"

"A shipment for the Ministry of Defense somehow got misdirected and ended up in the Catania Port last week," Rafael continues. "And magically, my name was on the shipment documents. Something must have gone wrong on their server." He looks down at me, pride written all over his face. "Amazing work, baby."

"You hacked the goddamn Italian Ministry of Defense for him?" Dad snarls, leaping out of his chair.

"Don't you dare raise your voice at my wife, Petrov!" Rafael roars back.

Ugh. I put my elbows on the table and bury my hands in my hair. The yelling match continues with my dad and husband exchanging curses and death threats. Over the noise, I can hear my mom instructing my aunt to remove the knives from the table. Uncle Sergei is on the phone with someone—probably

Grandpa Felix—inquiring about the next arms shipment for the US DOD and the likelihood of having it intercepted.

"Is it always going to be like this?" I mumble.

"Probably." Yulia shrugs, reaching for the salad. "I'm definitely marrying a dentist."

A loud bang comes from the kitchen. Everyone stops shouting, snapping their heads toward the source.

"What was that?" someone asks, but the question gets lost in a cacophony of screams and clamor that explodes beyond the adjacent door.

"Um . . . Igor snuck away from the retirement home." My mom smiles sheepishly while hiding the steak knife behind her back. "He's trying out a bourbon shrimp flambé recipe, kotik."

Smoke and the smell of something burning slowly permeate the room. The upgraded fire alarm that Dad had installed after the microwave incident starts blaring, and, a second later, water surges from the overhead sprinklers, soaking the food and everyone sitting at the table.

I push the wet strands of hair off my face and look at my husband. "Welcome to the family, baby."

The End

THANK YOU FOR READING

Thank you so much for reading Rafael and Vasilisa's story!

I would be eternally grateful if you could take a few minutes of your time to leave a review, letting the other readers know what you thought of *Beautiful Beast*.

Your reviews are always appreciated. **Even if it's just one short sentence, it makes a tremendous difference to the author.** The more reviews a book gathers, the greater its exposure in the online store of your choice. And a few words of your honest feedback can help the next person decide whether to give Rafael and Vasilisa a try.

To leave a review for Beautiful Beast scan the code:

WHAT'S NEXT?

As some of you may already know, this is the first book in the
Mafia Legacy, a spinoff series set in the **Perfectly Imperfect**
world, which will feature the kids of the main couples from
the original books. The next book in Mafia Legacy series will
feature Vasilisa's sister, Yulia. The title is ***Dearest Traitor*** and
as you probably assumed—it's a bodyguard romance :D

However, if this is your introduction to my work, and if you
enjoyed this world, you may want to check out other books
by **Neva Altaj**. Each story in the **Perfectly Imperfect**
series can be read as a standalone.

To discover the Perfectly Imperfect series scan the code:

Acknowledgments

Bringing a book to life is not easy. Even though there is only an author's name on the cover, there are many people behind the front line without whose involvement the final product would not be possible.

First and foremost, I would like to thank you, my readers, for your continued support and the love you keep showing for my books. The key reason this book came to be is because you've been asking for the 2nd generation series. I'm happy beyond measure that you've enjoyed the Perfectly Imperfect Series so much that you've been wanting to read the stories about the kids of the main characters from the original books. I hope you love Rafael and Vasilisa as much as I do.

To the best editor in the whole world—thank you, Andie. Your dedication and professionalism blow my mind with every project. Thank you for your amazing insights and valuable advice that help my books be the best they can possibly be. We've been working together since I started my writing endeavor, and even though we began as business colleagues, I feel like we became fast friends. Love you so much.

A special thanks to Wesley (Andie's hubby) who allowed us to pick his brain for all IT-related things and provided suggestions for improvement of those story elements. And a big thanks also to my friend Pedja, who was so kind as to share his extensive experience within the hacking world that helped make the story find its feet.

And to my PA, Caitlen—thank you for your ongoing support, your fierce determination in handling everything thrown your way, and your amazing proficiency. As I keep saying, I would be absolutely lost without you.

And of course, a big thank you to my beta readers—Anka, Shaima, Milica, Jennifer, Tina, and Teodora—for your feedback and ideas that improved the flow of the story. And my whole-hearted gratitude to Chiara for all your help with Italian words and phrases.

This book would have been impossible to pull off without your support and dedication.

Love you all,
Neva

ABOUT THE
author

Neva Altaj writes steamy contemporary mafia romance about damaged antiheroes and strong heroines who fall for them. She has a soft spot for crazy jealous, possessive alphas who are willing to burn the world to the ground for their woman. Her stories are full of heat and unexpected turns, and a happily ever after is guaranteed every time.

Neva loves to hear from her readers, so
feel free to reach out:

Website: www.neva-altaj.com
Facebook: www.facebook.com/neva.altaj
TikTok: www.tiktok.com/@author_neva_altaj
Instagram: www.instagram.com/neva_altaj
Amazon Author Page: www.amazon.com/Neva-Altaj
Goodreads: www.goodreads.com/Neva_Altaj

Perfectly Imperfect
Reading Order & Tropes

1. ***Painted Scars*** (Nina & Roman)
Tropes: disabled hero, fake marriage, age gap, opposites attract, possessive/jealous hero

2. ***Broken Whispers*** (Bianca & Mikhail)
Tropes: scarred/disabled hero, mute heroine, arranged marriage, age gap, Beauty and the Beast, OTT possessive/jealous hero

3. ***Hidden Truths*** (Angelina & Sergei)
Tropes: age gap, broken hero, only she can calm him down, who did this to you

4. ***Ruined Secrets*** (Isabella & Luca)
Tropes: arranged marriage, age gap, OTT possessive/jealous hero, amnesia

5. ***Stolen Touches*** (Milene & Salvatore)
Tropes: arranged marriage, disabled hero, age gap, emotionless hero, OTT possessive/jealous hero

6. ***Fractured Souls*** (Asya & Pavel)
Tropes: he helps her heal, age gap, who did this to you, possessive/jealous hero, he thinks he's not good enough for her

7. ***Burned Dreams*** (Ravenna & Alessandro)
Tropes: bodyguard, forbidden love, revenge, enemies to lovers, age gap, who did this to you, possessive/jealous hero

8. *Silent Lies* (Sienna & Drago)
Tropes: deaf hero, arranged marriage, age gap, grumpy-sunshine, opposites attract, super OTT possessive/jealous hero

9. *Darkest Sins* (Nera & Kai)
Tropes: grumpy-sunshine, opposites attract, age gap, stalker hero, only she can calm him down, he hates everyone but her, touch her and die

10. *Sweet Prison* (Zahara & Massimo)
Tropes: age gap, forbidden romance, only she can calm him down, opposites attract, he hates everyone but her, touch her and die, OTT possessive/jealous hero

Mafia Legacy Reading Order & Tropes

1. *Beautiful Beast* (Vasilisa & Rafael)
Tropes: Beauty and the Beast retelling, scarred hero, age gap, opposites attract, possessive/jealous hero, kidnapping

2. *Dearest Traitor* (Yulia & Nikolai)
Tropes: bodyguard romance, age gap, OTT possessive/jealous hero, touch her and die

Made in the USA
Las Vegas, NV
27 September 2024